FROM DEEP WATERS:
THE COMPLETE ADVENTURES
OF THE MAJOR, VOLUME 1

FROM DEEP WATERS
The Complete Adventures of the

Major

VOLUME 1

BY

L. PATRICK GREENE

INTRODUCTION BY

ED HULSE

ALTUS
PRESS

BOSTON • 2012

© 2012 Altus Press • First Edition—2012

EDITED AND DESIGNED BY
Matthew Moring

PUBLISHING HISTORY
"Introduction" appears here for the first time. Copyright © 2012 by Ed Hulse. All Rights Reserved.
"No Evidence" originally appeared in the November 1, 1919 issue of *Adventure*.
"Two of a Kind" originally appeared in the November 15, 1920 issue of *Adventure*.
"Lines of Cleavage" originally appeared in the February 1, 1921 issue of *Adventure*.
"Ivory" originally appeared in the March 1, 1921 issue of *Adventure*.
"Amnesia" originally appeared in the April 1, 1921 issue of *Adventure*.
"A Deal in Diamonds" originally appeared in the May 1921 issue of *Short Stories*.
"Tools" originally appeared in the August 1, 1921 issue of *Adventure*.
"Bitter Alum" originally appeared in the August 1921 issue of *Short Stories*.
"The Seventh Plague" originally appeared in the September 10, 1921 issue of *Short Stories*.
"Royal Game" originally appeared in the November 10, 1921 issue of *Short Stories*.
"Kruger's Gold" originally appeared in the October 10, 1922 issue of *Short Stories*.
"From Deep Waters" originally appeared in the November 25, 1922 issue of *Short Stories*.
"The Series Story" originally appeared in the May 1925 issue of *Author & Journalist*.

THANKS TO
Richard Hall, Ed Hulse, Everard P. Digges LaTouch, John Locke, Walker Martin, Will Murray
& Ray Riethmeier

TABLE OF CONTENTS

ED HULSE

THE SHEER volume of pulp fiction published in America during the first six decades of the 20th century—tens of thousands of stories in more than 1,100 separate titles—ensures that no one fan can possibly have read all the yarns worth reading. It is true that a majority of these tales were trash; they were, after all, considered ephemeral entertainment at best, good only for momentary escape from workaday pressures and responsibilities. But with so many stories having been printed in the rough-paper magazines, it stands to reason that some were considerably better than others. In my opinion, that can be said about the adventures of Aubrey St. John Major, the African-based adventurer created by L. Patrick Greene in 1919. "The Major," as he was nicknamed, debuted in the pages of *Adventure* and subsequently migrated to *Short Stories,* where he held forth for nearly two decades in dozens of series entries of varying lengths.

English-born Lewis Patrick "Pat" Greene (1891-1971) craved excitement at an early age. The future fictioneer was barely 18 years old when he decided in 1909 to head for Africa, where he spent the next several years as a mounted policeman in Rhodesia. Greene's career as a public servant ended after he sustained a serious injury in a sunstroke-induced fall from his horse. Hospitalized for several months, he was eventually declared medically unfit for further service and returned to England with an honorable discharge.

Still afflicted with wanderlust, Greene sailed to the United States in 1913. Upon arriving in New York City he tried his hand at a succession of unfulfilling jobs—timekeeper, stockbroker, insurance agent—before turning to fiction writing as a profession. By this time he had married and settled in Boston.

To the best of my knowledge, Greene's first published story was "The Snakes of Zari," which appeared in the February 3, 1918 issue of *Adventure*. It was certainly the first he sold to that legendary pulp magazine, at the time edited by Arthur Sullivant Hoffman. Like most of Greene's works, "Zari" took place in Africa and drew upon the author's personal experiences. Hoffman was partial to writers with first-hand knowledge of the exotic locations about which they wrote, and Pat Greene indisputably knew his Africa. "Dealing almost entirely with natives, I learned to speak their language and came to admire them," he wrote in a brief autobiographical sketch for *Adventure*'s "Camp-Fire" department. "They taught me many things that were good for a youngster to know."

Hoffman obviously saw the former Rhodesian mounted policeman a valuable resource as well as a talented storyteller: Before long, the newly naturalized American citizen had won himself a berth on *Adventure*'s editorial staff. By that time he had already penned the inaugural entry—a 6,500-word short story—in a series that would eventually run to nearly 100 installments.

We first meet the Major in the opening paragraphs of "No Evidence" (*Adventure*, November 3, 1919), which find him before the magistrate of Transvaal's Lydenburg district, accused of I.D.B. (Illicit Diamond Buying) but apparently confident that the charges will not stick. In this first series entry Greene proffers a description that, with only minor variances, he will repeat habitually over the years to come:

> His smooth, round, clean-shaven face wore an almost vacuous look, an impression that was strengthened by the monocle which he wore in his right eye. His eyes, however, were steady, cool, and indicated great reserves of brain and will-power. The smoothly brushed hair and natty attire were those of a dandy, but his carriage was that of a trained athlete.

The magistrate, Johnstone, refers to the Major's less-than-savory reputation. In the character's response Greene for the first time depicts the "silly ass" pose maintained by the Major when trying to lull his opponents into a false sense of security. The suspected criminal blathers like an upper-middle-class twit straight out of a P. G. Wodehouse novel.

> "Well, they have got you at last then, Major," said the commissioner. "You are in the same plight as the pitcher that went to the well too often, and now you are going to be jugged. Yes, I foresee it is going

to be my pleasant duty to send you away for a long rest."

"Oh, I say, old top, that's a ripping joke. Pitcher to the well, and now is to be jugged. I didn't think you had it in you," replied the Major. If he had any other name it was not known in Africa, the land of aliases. "But aren't you, well, putting the cart before the horse? Here you talk about sending me away and you haven't even heard the charge. Let me tell you that it just won't do, you know. Here was I talking quietly with my native servant when these two Johnnies arrested me on some ridiculous charge or other. Imagine it! Arrested me right on the public street. Think of my reputation."

L. Patrick Greene in 1925.

(This foolishness is all an act, of course. The Major enjoys being underestimated and carefully cultivates his image as a fop. In reality, he is the coolest of customers, capable of lightning-quick thought and action when those qualities are needed. His languid manner and jovial banter throw his adversaries off balance; only those who have faced him before realize how dangerous he can be. The Major isn't afraid to use deadly force when necessary, although he prefers to outsmart rather than outshoot his opponents.)

The events described in "No Evidence" actually vindicate the authorities' suspicions. Following his release from the Lydenburg court after the arresting officers fail to produce the stolen diamond supposedly sold to him by a native, the Major learns that a native chieftain named Magato is willing to swap a fortune in diamonds for one machine gun and a large store of ammunition. Accompanied by his Hottentot servant Jim, the Englishman adopts the guise of a trader and proceeds to Magato's territory, where a treacherous Dutch shop-keeper named Myburg betrays him.

Two British policemen trailing the Major catch up with him just as Myburg goads Magato's warriors into attacking the faux trader. The white men barely escape with their lives, but not before the Major tricks the officers into destroying the smuggled machine gun and exploding the stolen ammunition to disperse their attackers. Once again having lost crucial evidence that would send the Major to prison, the British coppers are forced to release him from custody.

The early Major stories revolve around the non-stop efforts of both police and villains to have him arrested for I.D.B. The colonial authorities vigorously investigated this particular form of criminality, even though their efforts were mandated largely by political concerns.

The discovery in the 1860s of rich diamond fields in South Africa made huge fortunes for the various European concerns that exploited them. English-born Cecil Rhodes, who originally settled in Africa as a farmer, obtained financial backing to buy up small fields in Kimberley and in 1888 consolidated his holdings into the De Beers Mining Company. He worked hand in glove with the London Mining Syndicate, which at one time controlled 90 percent of the world diamond supply. Backed by influential politicians and moneyed interests in England, Rhodes and his fellow mining magnates exercised control over a huge swath of sub-Saharan Africa. Their business practices were both monopolistic and exploitative, and in his stories Greene took some pains to emphasize that the Major's I.D.B. activities—which were said to be on the wane even in the earliest series entries—had been undertaken less out of a desire to enrich himself than as a protest against the Syndicate's rapacious behavior.

The police came to grudgingly admire the Major, who often helped them solve far more egregious crimes and foil the schemes of plotters who hoped to undermine colonial authority by fomenting rebellion among the natives. In "Tools" (August 3, 1921) a British Secret Service chief even enlists the Major's aid in disrupting a surreptitious Portuguese effort to form a protectorate on the Transvaal border with the assistance of a malleable native chieftain.

What I find especially interesting about Greene's early yarns is his development of the relationship between the Major and his faithful Hottentot servant. Jim is briefly seen and only sketchily limned in

"No Evidence," but he plays an increasingly large role in the series as it progresses. A member of the Khoikhoi race, he is described by Greene as squat and muscular of build, with long apelike arms. Jim's face is "pleasantly ugly" and his command of the English language leaves a great deal to be desired. But he is unusually capable and unflinchingly loyal, rescuing his *Baas* (boss or master) countless times over the course of the series. His one fault is a tendency to overindulge in the consumption of liquor, which opportunity he seldom gets but always enjoys. The Major occasionally chides Jim but never mistreats him physically, nor will he allow others to do so.

The Major-Jim relationship comes to resemble that of later mixed-race teams: the Lone Ranger and Tonto, the Green Hornet and Kato. It is built on mutual respect and an appreciation for, if not total comprehension of, their cultural differences. Jim is unquestionably a servant, not an equal, but he has an abiding affection for his *Baas* and would lay down his life for the Major. This is demonstrated through-out the series. And the Major, for his part, feels the same way. The two men rescue each other from life-threatening predicaments count-less times.

Although Greene can be vague about the exact locations in which his yarns unfold, the Major's early exploits take place primarily in the Transvaal, South Africa's northeastern province. The Transvaal is bordered on the north by Rhodesia (later Zimbabwe) and on the east by Portuguese East Africa (later Mozambique); the Major and Jim are frequent visitors to those locales as well. The city of Johannesburg, which would become the country's most populous, figures promi-nently in early series installments. The Major stories also include numerous references to "Breakwater," which was a prison established near Cape Town in 1859. Most I.D.B. offenders were incarcerated there, and eventually the prison was segregated to keep the Euro-pean detainees separate from the indigenous convicts.

Greene's first-hand knowledge of South Africa's natives and customs not only imbued his fiction with verisimilitude but enabled him to weave into his stories much subtle commentary on the indignities forced upon the indigenous peoples by their European colonialist masters. In reading the Major tales it is quite obvious that Greene sympathized with the natives, even when he was depicting certain tribes as bloodthirsty savages determined to exterminate white inter-lopers. Tellingly, villainous whites often use the derogatory term "nigger" to describe blacks. The Major never does. (Actually, he *did* in the earliest stories, but Greene quickly excised that word from the character's vocabulary as the Major transitioned from likable rogue to knight-errant.) He is portrayed as having empathy for South Africa's indigenous peoples, and as the saga progresses he is described as being welcome in most native *kraals* he and Jim come across.

Greene left *Adventure* to work full time as a free-lance writer. He brought the Major series to *Short Stories,* the Doubleday-published pulp magazine edited by Harry E. Maule. Launched as a periodical with lofty literary pretensions, *Short Stories* originally reprinted high-class fiction. Abner Doubleday purchased the magazine in 1910 and recast it as a pulp with an emphasis on adventure fiction. By the time Pat Greene arrived in 1921, *Short Stories* was emulating Arthur Sullivant Hoffman's *Adventure;* in addition to luring Hoffman's writers away, Maule eventually appropriated the themes and orientations of *Adventure's* back-of-the-book departments.

The Major became a fixture of *Short Stories.* The magazine's covers routinely bore the bylines of its top contributors, but Greene's name was almost always prefaced with "A Major Story by...." The series hit its stride during the mid Twenties, perhaps reaching its zenith with "Devil's Kloof" (May 25, 1928), a novel-length adventure chronologically predating all other entries and explaining how the Major acquired the less-than-stellar reputation he had prior to the events chronicled in that first story in *Adventure.*

Over the years Greene's fiction also appeared in such pulps as *Action Stories, Argosy All-Story Weekly, Blue Book, Danger Trail, Everybody's Magazine, The Frontier* (and its successor *Frontier Stories*), *Jungle Stories, Man Stories, Munsey's Magazine, The Popular Magazine, Popular Fiction Magazine, Red-Blooded Stories,* and *Star Magazine.* The British periodicals *Hutchinson's* and *20 Story Book* also published his yarns. For *The Frontier* Greene wrote a vaguely autobiographical series featuring Rhodesian mounted policeman "Dynamite" Drury. But it was the Major saga that guaranteed his longevity in the pages of *Short Stories,* even during the Depression years, after Maule relinquished the editorship first to A.H. Bittner and then to his long-time assistant, Dorothy McIlwraith.

It was during the early Thirties that *Short Stories* published my favorite group of linked installments in the series. "Barehanded" (January 10, 1933) begins with a clandestine meeting of eight criminal conspirators—six men and two women—determined to eliminate the Major, with whom they all have tangled before. Their leader, Soapy

Sam, is established as a thoroughgoing rotter when, before the assembled crooks, he thrashes his mistress Nancy. The Englishman and his Hottentot servant, Jim, are captured in short order and brought to the Driftsdorp hotel room where the gang waits expectantly.

Soapy Sam doesn't want to murder the Major in town for fear that the inevitable discovery of his body will launch an investigation that could implicate some or all of the plotters. After imprisoning Jim and beating the Major mercilessly, the men toss their bound, helpless victim into a wagon and drive deep into the desert. Seven days into the excursion they leave their captive, still tied hand and foot, in an especially desolate spot, confident he will neither survive nor be discovered. Wild animals doubtless will attend to disposing of the body, so the satisfied malefactors return to civilization.

The Major manages to free himself and, rather than succumb to despair, begins trudging across the wasteland. Greene's recounting of this arduous journey is pulp fiction at its best. He describes the desert with colorful, evocative language and takes his readers inside the Major's head. Fatalistic enough to believe he will not survive the trek, our hero pushes on anyway, driven by the desire for… revenge.

> That was a new word in the Major's vocabulary. It was a new source of strength: Broken into two syllables it gave him a marching rhythm.
> Re-venge! Left-right! Re-venge!
> His feet seemed to hit constantly against the unevennesses of the desert floor. He fell repeatedly and at last he did not trouble to rise but crawled forward on hands and knees, his face very close to the ground.

Weak from hunger and delirious with fever, the Major imagines his faithful Hottentot is nearby and calls for him. As it happens, Jim has escaped his captors and even now plumbs the desert wastes, searching for his *Baas* even though there is practically no chance that the white man has survived.

Eventually the Major stumbles into an area with enough flora to provide fuel for a fire. During intervals of lucidity, he gathers brush and cacti, piling it as high as his weakened muscles will permit. Staking everything on the hope that someone will see smoke from far away, he strikes a match….

Days later, a Dutch missionary driving on the desert's edge sees a Hottentot wearily stumbling across the rugged countryside, carrying a white man who looks more dead than alive. Against all odds, Jim has found the Major. The missionary takes them in and ministers to the Englishman, who revives after spending nine days in a coma.

> *"Baas!"* [Jim] said hoarsely and gently touched the Major's hand
> The Major opened his eyes.
> "Good old Jim," he said with a faint suspicion of a chuckle. "I called you, Jim."
> "Yah, *Baas*," the Hottentot exclaimed. His eyes shone with joy at the sound of his *Baas'* voice. "And I heard you—and I come."
> "You have never failed me, Jim."
> "Au, *Baas*," Jim muttered happily.
> The Major's eyes closed; he slept peacefully.

During his ordeal the Major had been attacked by hyenas, and when he sleeps now they periodically enter his dreams to torment him. On one such occasion, Jim sits by the Englishman's side, already plotting the revenge he is certain they will pursue once the *Baas* has fully recovered.

> "And then," he muttered, scarcely able to restrain his vindictive hatred of the men who had made his *Baas* suffer such privation, "and then there will be an accounting. Then those evil ones shall be made to pay."
> Perhaps his thoughts were conveyed to the mind of the sleeping man, for the rhythm of the Major's sleep was broken for a moment as he murmured:
> "The hyenas! I hate the stinking skellum. We must kill them all."
> "Truly, *Baas*. Truly," Jim said softly. "That is in my mind too." And with a sigh of satisfaction, he closed his eyes and he, too, slept.

Here "Barehanded" ends. It is a powerful story, one of Greene's very best. And it kicks off what I believe to be the most entertaining sequence in this series' long history. Over the next 13 months, in a half-dozen novelettes, the Major and Jim will run the conspirators to earth, one by one. With considerable ingenuity, Greene contrives situations in which the would-be assassins meet their sorry fates at the hands of others, preventing the Major from killing them himself. In the end ("Account Paid," February 10, 1934), only Soapy Sam and his mistress—whose name has inexplicably changed from Nancy to Bessie somewhere along the line—are alive to face the man they once tried to murder. The Major has located them and a showdown is imminent. By this time, however, Bessie has come to regret her part in the affair, and to expiate her sins she shoots Sam before he can open fire on the Englishman. Before gasping his last, the incredulous and infuriated villain returns the favor.

With all eight plotters finally accounted for, the Major and Jim waste little time getting into more trouble, making enemies of the authorities in Portuguese-controlled territory and spending more than a year outsmarting them. This lengthy story arc, like the others, drew on Greene's personal knowledge of the rivalry between the British and the Portuguese over South Africa.

In the 1930s Greene moved to Cliff Island, Maine, with his wife and two daughters, pouring out adventures of the Major on a regular basis. Near decade's end he took his family to England, and in 1939 he ceased writing fiction to join the war effort as Hitler's Third Reich began its conquest of Europe. Little is known of Pat Greene's activities during this period, but after the Second World War he took up where he had left off. *Short Stories,* which had been the Major's home for more than a quarter century, was still being edited by Dorothy McIlwraith. Greene fired off a brace of new series entries, which she bought and published in 1947. But times were changing and the pulps were dying. The Major's foppish pretensions and Wodehousian exclamations seemed anachronistic; his time had come and gone. Postwar Africa was in the process of a wrenching transformation that would see a steady diminution of European influence and, eventually, for better or worse, the death of colonialism on the continent.

When he died in 1971, Lewis Patrick Greene left behind more than 200 works of fiction—short stories, novelettes, and novels. Nearly three dozen volumes of his works were published between hard covers, 19 of them devoted to the Major's adventures. One might think that such a legacy would have guaranteed him recognition, if not fame. Yet Greene is unknown today, save to the small coterie of pulp-fiction aficionados who collect the magazines in which his yarns first appeared. Thankfully, Altus Press has stepped up to redress this sad situation. The Major and Jim the Hottentot are sorely in need of new readers to enthrall. If you are one of them, settle back and relax: You're in for a real treat.

Ed Hulse
October 2012

NO EVIDENCE

JOHNSTONE, THE native commissioner and magistrate of the Lydenburg District of the Transvaal, was very tired and cross. The day had been unusually hot, and he had tried many cases. Most of them were of a trivial nature: natives traveling without a permit, out after nine o'clock—and such petty misdemeanors. One case was so much like the other, and yet each had to be treated differently, with an understanding and a fatherly regard for the backslider.

At least such was the way in which Johnstone tried the natives who came before him. He was conscientious, almost to a fault, and always made it clear to the native in what way he had broken the laws and tried to convince him that the punishment meted out was a just one.

The entrance of two plain-clothes men, escorting a third white man, caused the commissioner to forget his tired feeling. He looked up expectantly and eyed the prisoner with interest. The latter's appearance was baffling. His smooth, round, clean-shaven face wore an almost vacuous look, an impression that was strengthened by the monocle which he wore in his right eye. His eyes, however, were steady, cool, and indicated great reserves of brain and will-power. The smoothly brushed hair and natty attire were those of a dandy, but his carriage was that of a trained athlete.

"Well, they have got you at last then, Major," said the commissioner. "You are in the same plight as the pitcher that went to the well too often, and now you are going to be jugged. Yes, I foresee it is going to be my pleasant duty to send you away for a long rest."

"Oh, I say, old top, that's a ripping joke. Pitcher to the well, and now is to be jugged. I didn't think you had it in you," replied the Major.

If he had any other name it was not known in Africa, the land of aliases. "But aren't you, well, putting the cart before the horse? Here you talk about sending me away and you haven't even heard the charge. Let me tell you that it just won't do, you know. Here was I talking quietly with my native servant when these two Johnnies arrested me on some ridiculous charge or other. Imagine it! Arrested me right on the public street. Think of my reputation."

"Yes, I'm thinking of just that thing, Major," the commissioner responded dryly. "What is the charge, officer?"

"Just as he says, sir, I.D.B. (Illicit diamond buying.) We saw a native accost the Major just outside Joburg Smith's saloon. They talked for a little while and then the Major gave the nigger some money and the nigger handed over a diamond. We arrested the Major at once and brought him right here. The nigger got away. Not that that matters, for we got the Major."

"Prisoner, what have you to say?"

"I tell you that it's all positively ridiculous. These two dear chaps must be suffering from the sun. You look a little warm yourself, if I may say so. Diamonds! Well, if they're so sure of what they say, why don't they search me and produce the evidence?"

"Yes, that would be a good plan—pardon the omission. Search him, officers."

Carefully and methodically the two detectives went over the Major. As they searched, the joy at having captured such a famous character red-handed faded from their faces, to be superseded by looks of blank amazement. Twice they went over him from head to foot, searching every seam of his clothing, deaf to the Major's caustic offers of assistance.

"Say, old dears, wouldn't you like to give me an emetic? I may have swallowed the bally thing, you know."

Finally the men gave up their search in disgust.

"It's not on him, sir," said the senior detective in a bewildered tone.

"Of course it's not. I told you that you were making a mistake when you arrested me, but you were so bloomin' pig-headed you simply wouldn't listen."

"That will do," said the commissioner curtly. "But don't forget, Major, about the little fable of the pitcher. Case dismissed for lack of evidence."

"Thanks for the little sermon, old top. If I ever am tempted to try

my hand at I.D.B., I'll notify these two gentlemen—"bowing to the detectives—"I'm sure they would keep me in the straight and narrow path. They are so deucedly clever."

When he had left the court room the two detectives heatedly discussed the cause of their failure.

"I don't see how he possibly could have got rid of it. The nigger handed him the diamond; we can swear to that, and we watched every move he made on the way here, besides holding on to his arms. He must have dropped it on the way, or—"

The detective's hand was in his pocket feeling for a match. His fingers closed on something hard. Slowly withdrawing his hand, he held the object up in front of him. It sparkled in the sunlight.

"Well, I'm jiggered, what do you know about that?"

THE MAJOR was resting at Joburg Smith's place, having recently returned from a successful labor-recruiting trip.

He was generous and open handed when in funds, and a down-and-outer could always be sure of a stake from the Major. So, when "Cockney Joe" asked to speak with him alone, he put his hand in his pocket—"How much?"

"Gorblimme, guvnor. You ain't arf quick on the tike up. Wite a jiffey, Hi ain't beggin'. Hit's hinformation I'm selling."

"Really! Do you think you have information that will interest me?"

"Ow, come dahn orf ye —— perch and listen to this."

He whispered fast and furiously, the Major listening first with amusement, then with keen interest.

"Oh, come now," he said when Cockney Joe had finished, "you don't expect me to believe that fairy-story."

"But it's Gawd's trewth, Major."

"Well, let's hear it again, and speak louder; we are all alone. Oh yes, and please try to speak a little more distinctly. Your dialect is so beastly thick I can almost smell London."

"Yus, an' hit's back there Hi wish I was now. I'm sick of this 'ere Gawd's country. 'Owever, you want my story again. Hand it's true, I tell yer, Major. A hold nigger put me hin on the ground floor three years ago. Magato 'as set 'is bleedin' 'eart on gettin' a machine gun. There's a calabash full of diamints waitin' for the bloke what can run a gun through to 'is country. Diamints that 'is young men stole from the mines.

"Has I told yer, Hi 'ad a try at it meself but the cartridges didn't fit the gun, an' Magato nearly 'ad my life. Seems 'e 'ad seen the Portugeese practise with them and 'ad bought twenty goats for them to use as targets. The wily old cove says 'e won't tike a gun unless hit'll kill twenty goats, sime as the Portugeese's done. My, but 'e lost 'is bloomin' rag when my popper wouldn't work. Threatened to flay me; alive—me a white man!

"An' then the old skinner showed me the sparklers, enough to fill a quart measure, just to let me see, 'e says, wot Hi 'ad missed by bein' a liar and a fool. Hordered his blink'n' soldiers to tike me hover the border and promised to kill me on sight hif I entered hit again. That's w'y I'm telling you. If 'e 'adn't said that, yer can bet your sweet life Hi would try it again. Now ain't that worth somethink, Major? A fortune for the asking, so to speak."

"Yes," drawled the Major, "it's all very interesting and very easy, as you say. However, you overlook one or two trivial details. But your story was pretty and nicely told, so here's twenty-five quid. Now hop along, old chap; it wouldn't do for me to be seen with you. Your reputation is—ah—unsavory, and the officials might arrest me on the premise that 'birds of a feather'—eh, what? But, by the way, if I do go and get the diamonds, I'll give you a quarter share."

SIX MONTHS later a small canvas-topped wagon, drawn by four oxen, stopped at the store of John Myburg.

"Outspan down by the trees, Jim," a voice directed the Hottentot driver.

The long whip cracked and the wagon lumbered on, soon to come to rest again in the shadow of the trees. Here the Hottentot outspanned and turned the oxen loose to graze. Then, going to the wagon, he took out and set up a portable wash-stand, which he filled with water, and then hung, near by, a small mirror. Not until then did the owner of the voice show himself and begin to lather his face preparatory to shaving.

"This shaving is a beastly bore, Jim," he said in English, "but one has to do it or lose caste."

"Yah, *Baas*," said Jim as if fully comprehending and, squatting on his haunches, he watched his master shave, as if it were some religious rite.

"The man from the store is coming, *Baas*," he said presently. "He looks like a pig. He is so fat that the grease drips off him."

The man did not answer; he was busy rounding his chin.

"He grunts like a pig as he walks, *Baas*," Jim continued, "and his eyes are evil—there is no truth in them."

The shaving operation was over and the men turned round to face the storekeeper, who was now close at hand.

"Good day, Major," said Myburg in Dutch.

The Major was taken aback for a moment. He had hoped that he would meet none who knew him on this trip. He feigned not to understand, hoping that he would thus be spared the necessity of answering the numerous questions that a man of Myburg's type would be sure to ask.

"So you do not speak the *taal*," said Myburg in English.

"Oh, I didn't mean you to think that. It was that your speech was indistinct. I have the same trouble in understanding my boy Jim at times. He speaks the *taal* with a burr something like yours," drawled the Major.

Myburg turned an angry red under his swarthy skin. The Major's remark hit him hard, for it was rumored that he had Kafir blood in him.

"What are you doing up this way, Major?"

"Oh, I thought that I would try a little trading trip. You fellows seem to make so much money at selling things to the simple nigger that I thought I would try it myself. So far I've had bally bad luck. I wish you would come and look over my stuff. Perhaps I haven't got the right things to trade."

Together the two men went to the wagon. Myburg's shifty eyes took in the contents almost at a glance.

"Well, what do you think of my stock?"

"Alamachtig! If it is to the good Boer *vrouws* you would trade, then have you got stuff that is good. But, man, who told you that a harmonium and a lot of squiffers (concertinas) was good trade with these —— niggers? The niggers up in this man's country ain't got money enough for things of that sort."

"But I was told that musical instruments were very good trades."

"Music, the man says! Yes, a jew's-harp maybe, yes, but harmoniums and concertinas—it is to smile."

"Then I may as well go back, you think?" said the Major mournfully.

"Well now, there is no need for that maybe. You come up to my place. I'll fit you out with the proper stuff."

"That's jolly decent of you, considering I'm poaching on your preserves."

"Oah! I'd just as —— soon sell to you as to the niggers. Come on up now—scoff's ready."

When they had seated themselves at the table in the room at the back of the store, two native women brought in the food and then sat at the table. The Major rose to his feet and looked expectantly at Myburg.

"Voor den donder! What ails you now?" burst out the storekeeper. "Oh, I see," he added with a sneer. "Get out of here, you black sluts, thy presence is an offense to this white man."

After the meal the Major spent much time and money in purchasing articles recommended by Myburg as having good sale among the natives, ignoring the fact that the storekeeper was charging him exorbitant prices. When the bargaining was over he said—

"Now I must get down to the wagon and turn in, for I want to get away before sunup tomorrow."

"Let your Hottentot bring your blankets up here. Stay and split a bottle. A bedmate I will get for you." He leered evilly.

"Jim was right," said the Major. "You are a pig. I suppose you can't help that, but please don't try to run me in with your Utter."

NEXT MORNING the Major, eager to inspan and get on trek, called in vain for Jim.

"He's probably up at the piggery buying some snuff, and Myburg's trying to pump him. I suppose I had better go after him," murmured the Major. As he drew near to the store, he heard Jim speaking—

"I tell thee that I know nothing, *Baas*."

"Dog of a liar, whose mother was a snake! Here I have given thee *maninge puza*—three tots of whiskey have I given thee, and what do you give me? Nothing but lies. Tell me, or I will beat the hide off thee, whither and for what purpose goes thy *Baas*?"

"I have told thee that I know nothing save that we go, perchance, to Magato's land to trade."

"How will ye trade there, for well ye know, and thy *Baas* knows—for all that he plays the fool—that it is death for a white man to enter Magato's land unbidden, unless— Now tell me truly, what will thy *Baas* trade? Guns?"

"Nay, how can that be? He carries none save his own."

"Liar!"

The *sjambok* was raised and came down with a swish on Jim's naked back. The arm rose again, but before it could descend the Major had wrenched the *sjambok* out of Myburg's hand.

"Get back to the wagon, Jim," the Major said, "and inspan. We trek within an hour."

When Jim had left the store, the Major faced the angry but cringing Myburg.

"Now, you cur, I'm going to give you a taste of your own medicine. Of course I could have you arrested for giving liquor to a native, but I'm afraid there's not enough evidence to convict you."

The Major chuckled at a sudden memory.

"Will you stand up and fight? I thought not. You haven't the pluck of a louse. Well, take this, and this, and this!"

At the first stroke of the *sjambok* Myburg whimpered; at the second he howled for mercy, at the third he groveled on the floor. The Major, in disgust at the craven spirit of the man, tossed the *sjambok* to the ground and strode to the door.

"Just a moment, Major. I was a bit hasty with the Hottentot. I ought to have known better than to interfere with another man's nigger. But there's no hard feelings, is there now?"

"Well, what is it?" said the Major curtly.

"Oh, come now, don't be harsh. Perhaps I can help you. One of my women is from Magato's country."

He watched the Major closely.

"Well, what is that to me?" The Major lapsed into a drawl—silkily menacing.

"Oh, I can see through your game. Running guns through to Magato. I don't blame you. The reward's a big one. Oh you're slim, *verdoemte* slim, but you can't put this through without me. I have been there and I know Magato. Och, sis man! I tell you that I have even seen the diamonds. Five years ago I saw them when I took him a gun."

"You took him a gun? Then you have the diamonds. I congratulate you."

"*Stilte!* I took him a gun, yes, but it was no proper one—where would I obtain such a thing? And I did not get the diamonds. The wily old *schelm* wanted to see the gun work, and of course it wouldn't. Now you, you will be killed if you go into Magato's country. But me, I tell you man I can come and go just as I please, and any one who is with me is safe, too."

"Go on—you interest me."

"I thought I would." Myburg was growing confident. "Take me with you, Major, on equal shares."

The Major laughed.

"Yes, you interest me, Myburg. You are such a fool, so full of romantic visions—diamonds and gun-running and sudden death. You have seen my wagon, but did you see any signs of a machine gun? Or perhaps you think I carry the bally thing in my pocket. What distresses me, though, is that you take me for a fool, too. You know the penalty for gun-running—twenty years on the Breakwater at Cape Town. Who's going to risk that for a mess of diamonds? But what annoys me most of all is that you entertain the idea that I would go into a partnership with you."

Turning abruptly on his heel, the Major returned to his wagon. Jim had inspanned and with shouts of "Ah now, *schelm!*" and the cracking of the whip they were once more on trek.

Myburg watched them from the stoop of his store—every now and then shaking his fist in anger at the retreating wagon.

"I must have been wrong," he muttered. "At any rate they are not headed for Magato's country now. That is due north, and they are traveling west. But that swine needs watching. He is tricky. And *alamachtig!* How strong he is!"

LEISURELY THE Major trekked from *kraal* to *kraal,* trading with the natives the articles that he had purchased from Myburg.

On the fourth day, when they were about an hour's trek from a large *kraal,* the Major took an aniline pencil and covered his face, hands, and all the visible parts of his body with spots.

In answer to Jim's look of fear when he saw his *Baas* so strangely marked the Major said:

"Do not be afraid, Jim, it is but a game. When we come to this village, ye will ask the people to bring us much food. Say that thy *Baas* hath the smallpox and would go away from all, that he may not pass on the disease."

At the *kraal* Jim faithfully carried out his instructions, with the result that when they had brought the required provisions the people besought the Major to hasten from their village.

"Go ye from us, white man, lest the great spirits afflict us also."

The Major chuckled as he saw his plans working out as he wished and resumed his trek. But from this time on he traveled due north toward Magato's country.

At Jombo's village, the last on the Transvaal side of Magato's land, the Major met with stern opposition. Jombo, the headman, refused to let him get water.

"The great spirits," he said, "have marked thee for death. Who then am I to give thee water, that ye may cheat the spirits a while longer?"

As the Major had a long, dry trek before him, it was imperative that he should get water, and he finally won over Jombo by presenting him with a rifle. Three days later he set off on the last lap of his journey.

By means of his native spies Myburg was kept well informed of the Major's movements, and his joy knew no bounds when one of them told of the dreaded disease that had attacked his enemy. He poured out a stiff tot of whisky for the messenger.

"Ye say the white man is smitten with the evil spirit that eats away the flesh?"

"Yea."

"Art sure of this?"

"With my own eyes I saw him."

Myburg chuckled.

"The swine! Well am I avenged. He will die the death of hunger and thirst, for the people will refuse to deal with him. Every hand will be against him."

"Ay, that is true, O keeper of the store. He, knowing that, hath purchased much corn—paying heavily for it—intending, he says, to dwell near unto the border of Magato's land. Thither he even now is trekking."

"What say ye?" Myburg asked fiercely. "He treks toward Magato's land, say ye? Fool! Why told ye not that before? He hath tricked ye. No disease hath he, but is cunning even as the Jackal."

"Nay, how can that be? It was no trick. I myself saw his face, and it was all spotted."

"Spotted, say ye? Nay, the spots are in thy eyes, blinding thee to the truth. But it is no great matter. I now hold him in the hollow of my hand. He shall learn that I have indeed no small influence with the people of Magato. Saddle the black horse and hasten, for I ride far.

"*Alamachtig!* Who would have thought the cursed *roinek* with his womanish voice could be so *verdoemte* slim."

"BONA LAPA—SEE, *Baas,* men on horseback follow us!"

The Major looked back over the plain and could discern a cloud of dust which gradually grew larger and nearer. Even as he watched, the cloud developed into two horsemen riding furiously.

"Um!" he mused. "Some one after me. Well, they are too late, whoever they may be. Another hundred yards or so and we'll be in Magato's country. They can't touch me there—not legally anyway."

"Hasten, Jim."

The long whip cracked and in response to it and Jim's shrill cries, the oxen responded gamely, breaking into a slow lumbering trot. When they were well over the line that marked the boundaries of Magato's country, the Major called a halt. He lit his pipe, affixed his eyeglass and waited for the horsemen to overtake him.

"Well," he drawled as they drew near, "if it isn't my good friends, Sergeant Blake and Trooper Barton, of the police."

The horsemen rode up to the wagon, dismounted and advanced, covering the Major with their revolvers.

"This is a pleasant surprize," he said as he rose to greet them. "But why the poppers?"

"Oh, cut out your rottin', Major. We've got you this time. You're under arrest."

"Under arrest? Me? Why what—?"

"Of course you would play the innocent, but you know why—gun-running."

"Oh! You mean because I gave that gun to old Jombo. That's a good one." He laughed boisterously. "Why that—"

"Don't trouble to explain. We know the gun was useless, barrel sawed through, ejector removed and all the rest."

"Then why all this?"

"Listen to him, Barton," said the sergeant. "Isn't he a ducky? You'd never think he had a maxim gun hidden in that wagon, would you? Don't play the injured innocent, Major; we know all about it. You see Cockney Joe was arrested—just drunk and disorderly—and was tried before Johnstone. He told the commissioner how you had given him money for information received and it didn't take the commissioner long to find out what that information was. Since then we've been watching you pretty closely, though I must admit you threw dust in our eyes when you faked smallpox. But we've got you now, all right."

"You chappies weary me," drawled the Major. " 'Pon my soul, but you're as bad as Myburg. Can't a fellow go on a trading trip without your blasted interference? It's perfectly monstrous. I'll write to the papers about it. And anyway, even if all you said was true, you can't touch me here."

"No? We're two to one and we've got you covered. Hey, boy! Swing round the oxen; we're going back. And be quick about it, too!"

Jim looked at the Major for confirmation of the order. The Major nodded absently, but no sooner had the order been obeyed than he called a halt.

"Look here, you fellows, I don't see why I should go back with you. It's a beastly bore coming all this way for nothing and then having to go back—also for nothing. It's just occurred to me that you'd better produce this machine gun that you talk about so glibly. Otherwise I don't budge."

"All right, if you must make trouble. Keep him covered, Barton. I'll soon find the evidence."

The sergeant climbed up into the wagon and searched carefully but fruitlessly.

"It's no good, Barton," he finally called. "We're bilked again. I believe the man is a fool after all. And yet—"

"Oh, come now, sergeant, don't be peevish. I don't blame you. It's all the fault of the commish. The dear, silly man has got it into his head that I'm a bad character and is always seeing evil where it ain't, as Cockney Joe would say. Speaking of Joe, I'd suggest that in the future you discard any evidence given by drunks. How about scoff? I'm deucedly hungry. Will you join me?"

"Might as well. What do you say, Barton?"

"Righto, sergeant. And, seeing how near it is to sundown, can't we camp here for the night? There's water just beyond the bushes yonder, the boy says, but this is the better place because we are freer from mosquitoes here."

Jim outspanned the oxen and drove them down to water, leaving the two horses. When he returned he found that the white men were commencing their meal. The horses he tethered to the pole of the wagon, leaving the oxen to graze until he had had his scoff.

THE MEAL over, Barton peered curiously at the trade stuff which cluttered up the wagon while the other two men sat on the cushioned seat in front—the Major traveled luxuriously—and smoked.

"You seem to specialize in musical instruments, Major."

"Yes—I expect to make a good trade for them with Magato's people."

"You're going on, then?" asked the sergeant.

"Of course, why not?"

"A harmonium, by all that's wonderful," exclaimed Barton. "Haven't played one for years. Mind if I give you a tune?"

"It's out of order, old chap. The bellows won't work. I've been meaning to fix them."

"I'll fix 'em now for you. I always was a dab at fixing things."

"Don't bother—"

A cry from Jim put a stop to further conversation.

"Soldiers of Magato are coming."

The Major, followed by the two policemen, got down from the wagon and awaited developments. Coming at a run toward them was a scouting party of about twenty natives, armed with *assegais* and old-fashioned muzzle-loading guns—the latter likely to be more dangerous to the users than to those in front of them. Eighty paces distant the party halted and held an excited conference. Then one, the leader, advanced alone.

"Let me handle this," said the Major. "I have the language better than either of you.

"Greetings, O man of Magato, by what name shall I know thee?"

"Ye may call me Tapa. But in truth I come not to bandy words with thee. What make ye in Magato's country?"

"I do but come to trade, O man of might."

"Know ye not the order of the king, that no white man may stay in his country?"

"Yet have I the thing he greatly desires. Ye know well of what I speak."

"Ye mean that which speaks with many tongues?"

"Aye, even that."

Then, in response to the looks of the policemen, the Major added in English:

"The dear fool is talking about a Maxim too, I suppose. Well, a harmonium has many voices, too."

"If ye say that, ye lie, white man, and think not that by lies ye can avert the wrath of Magato the King."

"In what way have I erred, O Tapa?"

"Do ye still bandy words? We know well that thou art sent hither by the white men to spy out the land and to afflict the people with the disease that eats away the flesh."

"That is folly. See, with the chalk did I make the spots, so fooling the people in the country beyond. I tell thee also that I spoke not lies but truth concerning the other matter."

Tapa stood as though undecided what move to make; then he turned toward his comrades, seeking inspiration. In answer to his unspoken appeal, a voice cried from among the group of natives:

"Believe him not, O Tapa. I myself have seen his wagon. He hath no gun. Verily, he is the father of all lies."

"That voice sounds familiar," said the Major to the sergeant. Then aloud, "Who is he that says I lie? Come out from the shadow of the warriors, O snake that hisses but dares not strike."

A man stepped out in response to the challenge.

"You shall learn that the snake has fangs, Major," he said in English.

"A white man!" exclaimed Barton.

"No! It's Myburg."

"Yes, Major, it's Myburg. You —— *schelm* of an Englisher, now you shall pay for the lashes you gave me. To the women you shall be given for torture. But first shall you be bound to your wagon wheel and I will thrash you till you howl for mercy."

"You're an amiable sort of chappie, aren't you? But it's not your turn to sing yet, old dear. What say ye, O Tapa? Wilt listen to the croaking of this vulture? Does a soldier of Magato listen to one who is neither white nor black?"

"Yet have ye not shown us, O white man, that his words are lies."

The Major climbed up into the wagon and pushed the harmonium into full view.

"Then look ye here," he called, "and know that a white man does not lie."

"Why do ye mock us?"

"Nay, have patience."

He released several catches; the sides of the harmonium fell away disclosing a machine gun which glinted evilly as the last rays of the setting sun flecked its barrel.

"Well, I'm," cried the sergeant.

"No wonder he told me not to bother about mending the harmonium." This from Barton.

"What now, O keepers of the store, what shall be thy punishment? Verily thou hast lied," said Tapa.

"Am I then a wizard," retorted Myburg, "that ye expect me to see through wood. Yet listen—"

He held a whispered conference with Tapa, while the three white men, their rifles held in readiness, watched their every move.

"Now heed ye, white men," Tapa began. His voice was now menacing. "Ye have entered the land of Magato. The punishment is death. Moreover, the man with the eye of glass hath treated this one, who was ever my friend, evilly. Glass Eye shall die by torture."

"But I bring the gun to Magato. The road is open to such a one."

"That you never shall," muttered the sergeant.

"Let's get out of this mess first," replied the Major.

"That is all one to us," went on Tapa. "We will take the gun to Magato and thus win great honor and riches. The gun and all that thou hast shall be ours. The vultures shall pick thy bones."

"But these others—what of them?"

Tapa hesitated.

"They die too," shouted Myburg. "They also are spies. They came to seek out the strength of Magato's land. Kill them! Their horses, their guns shall be added to the plunder. So shall all be rich and leaders among the people. Kill them all!"

This Myburg said, knowing that if the police were allowed to escape he would never be able to return to his store.

DURING THE parley the rest of the scouting party advanced slowly toward the wagon and grouped themselves around Tapa and Myburg.

"Kill the white men," they cried fiercely, and one of them leveled his gun threateningly.

Barton, seeing the gesture, fired, wounding the man in the thigh. A perfect hail of slug shots from the muzzle-loaders was the reply and the three white men bolted for the slight shelter afforded by the wagon, closely followed by Jim. From the wagon they opened a rapid fire—not aiming to kill but to discourage any attempts to rush them. In this they were successful, for the natives sought shelter among the rocks and contented themselves with returning the white men's fire. Their aim was poor, but, even so, the slugs pattered unpleasantly near.

"Well, you've done it now, Barton. What the —— made you plug the nigger. We had a chance before, but a —— slim one now."

"Oh, don't slang him, sergeant. There was no way out. Myburg would have seen to that. He's playin' for high stakes and hasn't the guts to be a sportsman."

"Well, what are we to do?"

"I haven't thought. Let's see. There's we three and Jim—though to be sure Jim isn't much of a hand with a gun. We've plenty of ammunition. What's to hinder us from inspanning and clearin' out. With the maxim and rifles it would be easy to keep them from closing in on us."

"That's good—let's hurry. Inspan, Jim!"

Jim shook his head.

"The dogs have stampeded the oxen, *Inkosi.*"

"——!" The three white men spoke as one.

"That puts plan number one on the blink, but what's to hinder you chaps from getting away on your mounts? They're safe anyway."

"No you don't, Major. How do we know this ain't a put-up job? No, we stick by you; besides—well, it wouldn't be playing the game."

"You're deucedly suspicious. However, I thank you for the rest."

"Look," said Barton. "They are closing in on us."

"Open up some of those concertinas, and we'll put a music roll in the harmonium."

Barton swiftly obeyed. Each concertina he opened contained a belt of cartridges for the machine gun.

"I take it you don't want to kill all these poor devils off, sergeant? No, I thought not. That might have been the third plan, but it's very messy; besides, Myburg is at the bottom of all this trouble. If it wasn't for him I would have gotten through to Magato, and you—you would have been firmly escorted out of the country."

He fired several rounds just in front of the oncoming natives, sending the dust flying up in their faces. It was enough. They retreated to the rocks once again.

"Ye see, men of Magato, I have in very truth the gun of many tongues. Art still of the same mind?"

"We can wait," called back Tapa. "Time is long, our patience great. But how long, think ye, can ye live without water? Consider, we are betwixt ye and the river."

Myburg echoed Tapa's mocking laugh.

Darkness covered the bush like a thick mantle. The stillness of the African night was upon them, intensified, it seemed, by the occasional shrill cry of the tiny tree hyrax, the mournful note of the bell bird, or the *rat-a-tat-tat* of the Maxim gun.

A twig snapped close by and was answered by a volley of shots from the wagon. A stifled groan told that not all the shots went astray in the darkness.

"Evidently they are not so patient after all," said the sergeant. "If they ever do rush us we're done for."

Again all was silent.

A spear of flame suddenly shot out of the darkness, followed by another, and another. All fell short of the wagon.

"Ah! I wondered how long it would be before they tried to set fire to the wagon. We must discourage that."

Again the Maxim spat fire. Yells and the noise of men running through the bush told of the accuracy of the aim.

Myburg's voice could be heard rallying the men.

"What, are ye all women? Is it thus that ye scorn great riches and honor? The white men are few, nor can they see to aim straight with their guns. What! Will ye wait till this matter comes to the ears of Magato? Desire ye to share the plunder with the *impis* of the king?"

"We must get away," said the Major, "before Myburg induces them to attack us in force. Aren't you chappies assured that this is not a plant now? Won't you get away on your mounts?"

"Nothing doing, Major. All or none."

"Thanks. Now keep up a steady fire while I make a few preparations."

In the center of the wagon he made a pile of its most inflammable contents, drenching it with the oil he carried for his lamp, and then constructed a slow-burning fuse.

"Jim, saddle the horses and lead them slowly to the clearing. We will cover your noise. You will wait there for us."

Joining the two policemen, the three fired with renewed speed, till it seemed the whole bush would awake to the tumult.

"Jim's had time to get to the clearing," said the Major after a while.

"Let's go." He opened a trunk. "Wait a minute, I want to get a few papers. You'd better destroy the gun, Barton, in case the fire doesn't take hold."

Barton smashed the delicate breech mechanism of the gun with an ax.

"I'm ready now," said the Major. "Have you a match, sergeant? Good! Light the fuse. It starts here."

A match glowed in the darkness of the wagon—went out—and in its place a tiny spark that ever moved appeared.

FAR OUT on the plain the Major called a halt.

"It's time the fireworks began; let's watch. The horses can't go any further tonight with a double load. Let's camp. We're safe if we keep a good watch."

They unsaddled and watched in silence.

Suddenly a tongue of flame burst out of the brush.

"It worked, by Godfrey, it worked."

The flames gained headway. They could hear the reports of exploding cartridges and the yells of the balked natives.

"I hope the pig gets singed, *Baas*," muttered Jim.

The flames died out and all was still.

Next morning, as Barton was saddling up, he burst into a roar of laughter.

"Well, what ails you now, Barton," said the sergeant peevishly.

"What will we do with the Major?"

"I hate to say it, but he'll have to go along with us."

"But you can't arrest him. We've no evidence. You destroyed it yourself—you lighted the fuse."

"Yes, and you smashed the Maxim."

The two men looked at the Major, chagrin and admiration struggling for the mastery.

"Did you—" began the sergeant, then stopped.

The Major met their glance coolly, held it for few moments; then his face relaxed. He lost the alert, erect carriage he had borne hitherto. His face became vacuous as he fumbled in his tunic pocket for his monocle.

"Bah Jove!" he said, screwing the glass in his eye. "I never thought of that."

TWO OF A KIND

A **GGIE, THE** presiding goddess of "Kaffir" Smith's bar, looked up languidly from her book as Sergeant Blake of the Mounted Police entered.

"What cheer, 'Porky?'"

The man scowled.

"Give me a whisky and soda."

With an air of boredom Aggie placed the drink before him.

"Because they call you Porky and you look porky, that's no reason why you should act like a pig, old dear."

He grunted inarticulately.

"I think you are a pig," she said lightly.

He emptied his glass and sat down morosely at one of the tables.

Aggie watched him amusedly.

" 'Jong' Dempster's waitin' for you in the parlor."

She jerked her head toward a door leading to an inner room.

Blake rose with a curse.

"Why the —— didn't you tell me that before?"

"Slipped my mind, dearie."

"Any one else in there?"

"Only a sundowner. He rolled in about an hour ago, looking all in. Said he'd been over a year prospecting on the veldt. Said he'd struck gold but it doesn't look to me as if he found anything but a ragin' thirst. You're not a bad hand at hiding away booze, Porky, but the lad in there could drink you under the table before a night was half-over."

"What did you let him in there for?"

"He seemed to know the ropes and looked harmless. Besides he—"

But Porky had passed on to the inner room, slamming the door behind him viciously.

"Wonder what's the matter with Porky this morning," murmured Aggie. Then, dismissing all thoughts of him from her pretty, empty head, she picked up the latest atrocity by the housemaids' favorite author and read avidly.

The inner room, known to its habitués as the "parlor," of Kaffir Smith's saloon was a dark and dismal place totally lacking ventilation. It reeked of stale liquor and tobacco-smoke. It was a mysterious room, a room of many exits cunningly hidden in the paneling, and because of the secrecy whereby one was enabled to enter and leave the room, it was the favorite meeting-place of members of South Africa's underworld.

"A successful raid of Kaffir Smith's inner room," had said one police official, "would bag ninety per cent. of the illicit diamond-buyers, gun-runners and other law-breakers in the country."

"Yes," replied another, "and fifty per cent. of South Africa's public officials."

Of course both of these statements were grossly exaggerated but, because of the element of truth in the latter statement, it was tacitly admitted that Kaffir Smith's place was under protection. The secret exits were seldom used save at such times when a raid—of which the occupants of the inner room had been warned—was made to quiet the demands of certain obnoxious reformers.

A BIG loose-limbed Dutchman greeted Porky boisterously as he entered.

"Alamahtig, but you're late, ma-an."

"The chief was down from Johannesburg. I had to see him off on the northbound train," Porky explained shortly. He sat down at Jong's table and poured out a stiff peg from the bottle of whisky which stood on the table.

Jong watched him curiously.

"You ain't sick, are you? Got fever?"

"No. I'm —— worried. This game's getting dangerous." Jong laughed.

"It would be more dangerous to leave it."

There was a note of menace in his tone, and Porky looked up quickly.

"What's the matter, ma-an?" The Dutchman spoke in a sort of nasal singsong.

"Aggie said that there was a sundowner in here," Porky said, disregarding Jong's question. "Where is he?"

Jong pointed to a table in the darkest corner of the room, where Blake could dimly make out the figure of a man.

Walking over to the table, Porky shook the man, apparently asleep, violently.

"Let's have a look at you," he growled.

The man sleepily opened his eyes.

"Lemme alone," he whined. "I ain't done nothin'."

Porky closely scrutinized the man's face, noted the shaggy, unkempt beard and tangled mass of hair, his bloodshot eyes and tattered clothing.

"What are you doing here?"

"Sleepin' and drinkin'; drinkin' and sleepin'."

"Ach sin! ma-an, let him alone. He's harmless," said Jong.

Porky released his hold on the sundowner, who sprawled across the table and was soon sleeping noisily.

"They say the Major's in town," he said in explanation as he returned to Jong's table, "and I'm not taking any chances of letting him slip through my fingers."

Jong roared with laughter.

"Allemahtig! What's the matter with you —— fools of the police? A ma-an only has to speak of the Major and you all get the wind-up. But what's your worry? I heard he was in Portuguese Territory."

"So he was. But he's back again, the chief said."

"Well why didn't your chief arrest him?"

"There's no evidence against the man, and besides the chief didn't say he saw him; but he did see the Major's nigger, Jim, and they say the Major can't get along without his nigger."

Porky cursed fluently and then lapsed info a moody silence.

"Is it this Major ma-an that's on your mind?"

"No. They're on to our game at Headquarters. Some one's been spilling the beans, and the chief—he's newly appointed—is running straight."

"Do they know anything for sure?"

"I don't know; I don't think so, but—"

Porky hesitated, then burst out in a paroxysm of child-like rage.

"He's a slim one, the new chief. We can't pull wool over his eyes. He did a lot of noseying around and wanted to know how I could support a big racing-stable on a policeman's salary. Blast him!"

Porky's thoughts turned to the parting words of the chief.

"I'm not making any accusations, sergeant," the official had said curtly as he boarded the train, "but there's something going on down here that I don't quite understand. We of the Mounted have a reputation for straight dealing, and I'll show no mercy to the man I discover endangering that reputation. Understand?"

"Blast him!" said Porky again. "I'm going to pull out and run straight, Jong."

"Don't be a *verdoemte* fool, Porky. They can't prove anything on you. You don't take any risk. All you do is to take the sparklers from the natives and hand 'em over to me. You don't hold 'em over twelve hours. Where's the risk? Who's going to search you—Detective Sergeant Blake of the Mounted Police? It 'ud look fishy for me, a diamond-merchant, to be seen in company with natives from the mines, wouldn't it?"

Porky shook his head in indecision.

"You lost pretty heavily at the races yesterday, didn't you?"

"Dropped a cool thousand, and you know I did."

"Well, listen, ma-an. There's a chance for you to get some of that back. The compound manager of the Lonely Mine lost at the races yesterday, too."

Porky straightened up in his chair.

"Ah! I thought that 'ud interest you. We've drawn a blank at the

Lonely Mine—up to now; up to now." Jong looked meaningly at Porky.

"Did you get next to him?"

"I did. He was a bit shy at first, but when he saw the color of my money there was nothing to it. Listen. A bunch of his natives are going home to their *kraals* today. Of course he'll search them—he's an honest man—but he won't think of opening a wound in a black boy's thigh; he's too kind-hearted for that. And there's six of them," Jong continued triumphantly, "six of 'em with big cuts in their thighs, and the wounds are festering. You know why? They call for an operation and you're going to be the doctor."

JUST THEN the man at the corner table began to pound noisily on his table.

"What do you want?" demanded Jong.

"A drink—you. I want a drink," the other replied thickly.

Jong pressed a button near his table, and when Aggie entered pointed to the sundowner.

"He's still thirsty, Aggie."

"What'll it be this time?" she called.

"Gin and bitters, Ducky."

Aggie tossed her head. "My, how that lad can mix them," she said confidentially to Jong.

"Oh, get out of here," Porky grunted impatiently.

"I've no desire to stay," she replied haughtily. "There's a proper gentleman waiting for me out there."

"Yes?" questioned Jong with interest.

"Wears a monocle and says 'bah Jove!'" Aggie's imitation of the drawl was grossly exaggerated. "Oh, he's a regular Bond Street Johnny, all right."

"What's his name?" said Porky with a show of interest.

"He didn't say, and I'm too much of a lady to ask him."

"Bah!"

"Tut-tut! Ain't we quick-tempered this morning. Well, I'll go out of here glad enough. The bloke out there's a gentleman, and that's more than I can say for you."

After the girl had left the room the two men looked at each other significantly.

"That sounds like the Major!"

"Have you ever seen him, Porky?"

"No. But I've heard his description lots of times. Round, clean-shaven face; stands about five-foot-ten, but looks less; wears a monocle and speaks with a drawl."

Jong looked disgusted.

"That's a —— of a description."

"Oh, I don't know. There's not so many men wearing monocles round this *dorp*. I bet it's him all right. Don't forget that his boy was seen in town. Where one goes, the other's not far off."

When Aggie reentered with the sundowner's drink, that man lurched forward to meet her and collapsed heavily on a seat nearer to the two men.

"Keep the change, sweetheart," he hiccuped, throwing a half-sovereign down on the table. "It's all 've got."

"Is the Johnny still out there, Aggie?" questioned Jong.

"Yes. He says he's going to stay here a while. Wanted to know if we had a 'room and bawth!'"

Porky slipped a shilling into the girl's hand.

"Call him the Major, Aggie, and let us know what he says."

A few minutes later Aggie reentered, smiling broadly.

"Business is good this morning," she giggled.

"Well?" questioned the two men.

"Says I, 'It's terrible hot today, ain't it, Major?' An' strike me pink, he was so taken aback you could have knocked him down with a feather."

" 'How did you know,' says he, 'that I was the Major?' Then he takes out his monocle, polishes it and screws it back again. ' 'Pon my soul,' he says, 'but you're a deucedly discerning young lady. But you won't tell any one else, will you?' And he slips me half a quid. He's a gentlemen, he is."

"Well, here's another," said Jong. "Go out there and talk pretty to him for five minutes or so, and then see if you can get him to come in here."

"You blamed fool. What do you want him in here for?" said Porky, rising wrathfully as the girl left the room.

Jong's hand shot out and grasped him firmly by the wrist.

"Sit down and listen, ma-an. Here's a chance for you to make a clean-up and clean your record at headquarters."

Porky sat down unwillingly.

"Well?" he grunted.

"The Major doesn't know you're a policeman—who would for that matter?—does he? No, I thought not. Well, when we get him in here, we'll let on that we've got word of some blacks who've got some diamonds and we haven't got the money to buy them or the chance to negotiate. Better than that, we'll let him in on this game tonight, on equal share. He'll take us up if all I've heard of him's true."

"That's a —— of a scheme," interjected Porky.

"Wait, ma-an. I'm not yet all through. You'll take him with you when you go to meet the niggers tonight, get the diamonds and then arrest him for illicit diamond-buying."

A light of comprehension spread over Porky's face.

He saw that Jong's plan offered him the opportunity to put himself in right all round—to square his losses, to regain the confidence of the chief, thus making it possible for him to act as agent for the I.D.B.s yet longer, and to earn the enormous reward offered by the Diamond Mining Syndicate for the arrest of the leader of a gang of I.D.B.s. It would be easy to fasten the leadership on a man of the Major's reputation.

Turning the plan over in his mind, Porky could see no possible chance for failure.

"But what about the diamonds—are we to hand them all over to the syndicate?"

"Ach sis, no, ma-an. Let the Major have some of the smaller ones. That'll be all that will be necessary to convict him. For the rest—Quiet. Here he comes. Let me handle him."

THE KNOB of the door turned and the door opened slowly, admitting a tall, immaculately dressed man.

"Ta-ta, old dear," he called to the girl in the bar. "As the bally Dutchmen say, 'If I don't see you, so long, hullo!'"

Closing the door, he turned and took in with a shrewd glance the other occupants of the room.

His jaw dropped and his face wore a vacant expression as he fumbled with his eyeglass.

" 'Pon my word, I hope I'm not intrudin'," he said apologetically. "The lovely damsel assured me that there was no one in here. I—er—"

At the sound of his voice the sundowner looked up, grinning inanely.

"Come off yer perch, cocky. Blimme, I thought fer a minute it was a bloomin' girl."

Porky rose to greet the newcomer.

"Don't mind him—he's drunk. You're not intruding, Major. Come and join us in a drink."

"I don't mind if I do," said the other, drawing up a chair. "But I'll give you my word that I find it perfectly astounding that I appear to be so well known here. I came here strictly incognito, if you know what I mean. I didn't think any one knew me in this *dorp.*"

"The Major is well known throughout the colony."

"Really I'm afraid you flatter me. But if that's the case I'd better remove myself to distant spots before some of my friends of the police see me."

Jong laughed.

"We're all in the same boat here, Major. You don't have to worry about the police; you're too slick for them."

"Do you really think so? Then I'll stay. But you gentlemen have the advantage of me. You know my name, while I—pardon me—don't know yours. What?"

"My name's Brown," said Porky, "and this," indicating Jong, "is Smith. We are in the same line of business as yourself—diamond-merchants." Porky winked.

"'Pon my word, gentlemen, but that's perfectly rippin'. I'm charmed to meet you. And what delightfully unusual names. Mine, by the way, is Jones."

He laughed gleefully. "And how's the diamond-business, Messrs. Brown and Smith?"

"I was wondering," said Porky slowly, "if you'd care to enter the firm—"

"Making it Brown, Smith and Jones? Delighted, I'm sure. But why rope in an utter stranger?"

"We've got to have some one we can trust, and the Major's got the reputation of playing square with his pals."

Jones bowed.

"Drop this fooling," growled Jong, "and let's get down to business. Listen, Major—"

"Jones, if you please, Smith."

"All right, Jones then. You've heard of the Lonely Mine?"

"I've heard that it's made the richest finds round here."

"That's the one. Well, we've got next to the compound manager of the Lonely Mine. He's a hard man to tackle, and no one has, up to now, been able to get next to his niggers. But he lost a lot of money on the races yesterday and was only too glad to listen when I made him a present. Well, six of the blacks who are going home today carry with them a hatful of stones as big as walnuts, so the manager said, and we've made arrangements to meet them for a trade."

"Why call in a third party? Can't you swing it alone?"

Jong spat disgustedly.

"—— no. We spent all our capital bribing the manager and haven't enough left to pay the niggers, let alone getting the stones to a good market. That's where you come in. We'll split equal shares. There ought to be a thousand clear profit."

Jones coughed deprecatingly.

"As I see it," he said, "you want me to pay the bloomin' niggers for the stones, take the risk of sellin' them and then to divvy up on equal shares with you two. That's a bally generous proposition—I don't think."

"What do you expect?" exploded Porky heatedly. "We've already taken the risk of getting information and have spent all our capital squaring the compound manager—he wouldn't work on shares—and getting next to the natives. Besides I'll have to go with you to make the deal with the natives; they wouldn't deal with you."

"You mean you don't trust me," said Jones softly.

"Oh, have it any way you like. At any rate we're trusting you to make a fair split of the money you get for the diamonds. I don't see where you stand to loose."

The other was silent.

"Oh, come on," said Jong contemptuously. "He's got no guts. Let's go and raise the money somewhere else."

"Wait a minute, Messrs. Brown and Smith. I'll join your firm. When and where do we meet the niggers?"

"Tonight at an old working I own. I'll call for you here about nine o'clock."

"Top-hole. I'm going down to a place the girl told me of to sleep.

I'll meet you here tonight all right. Until then I'm going to stay doggo. Can't afford to take any risk. Toodle-oo."

He passed gaily out into the bar and they heard him chaffing the barmaid.

Jong looked at Porky contemptuously.

"And that's the ma-an who's been playing merry —— with the police?"

Porky flushed.

"He does seem to be a —— fool, but he's slick just the same. Hadn't you better keep an eye on him, Jong?"

"No. We've nothing to fear from him. What could he do?" Jong rose lazily and stretched his big bulk, chuckling softly.

"It's great, ma-an, I tell you. We get the diamonds for nothing; the reward for capturing an I.D.B., and you'll be able to work for us, free from suspicion, from now on. Who'd think of suspecting Detective Sergeant Blake, the man who captured the Major? I wouldn't be surprized if they gave you a commission!"

Still chuckling, he pressed a hidden spring in the paneling of the room. A door opened and the two men passed through it into a narrow passage leading to two exits at opposite sides of the building.

The door closed silently behind them and the sundowner was left alone.

About ten minutes later he lurched noisily to his feet and stumbled awkwardly through the door leading to the bar.

Aggie looked up in surprize from her book.

"Going so soon?"

"Yes—hic—money's all gone. Mus' go an get some more."

"Have a drink on the house before you leave."

She poured out a generous potion which he swallowed at one gulp. Then he staggered out of the door and down the empty street.

"My, but he's got a nawful thirst," said Aggie as she passed into the parlor to tidy up.

Near the corner table where the sundowner had been sitting was a large flower-pot containing a withered rose-bush.

The earth was moist almost to the point of muddiness. And that was strange, for Aggie had for a long time neglected to water the plant. As has been said, Aggie was empty-headed, but a close ex- amination of the pot explained, even to her, the sundowner's colossal thirst.

"I never knew a rose-bush to thrive on whisky straight," she mused. "I must tell Porky."

Then returning to her book—she was at that exciting part where the hero confronts the villain with proof of his claim to the title—she characteristically forgot all about her discovery.

ON THE edge of the veldt that surrounded the township, and in the shade of a stunted baobab-tree, stood a small bell-topped tent such as is used by prospectors of the fortunate kind.

Near by a grizzled Hottentot was puffing furiously at the red embers of a camp-fire, seeking to bring them to a blaze that the water-billy might be brought quicker to a boil.

Two horses tethered to a light Cape cart were contentedly munching the sweet green grass that was placed before them.

Within the tent was the sound of splashing water and a man's not unmusical voice singing a rollicking ballad.

After a while the splashing ceased and the song was punctuated with grunts as the unseen singer vigorously toweled himself.

"*Baas.*" The Hottentot took the billy from the fire.

The singing stopped.

"Yes, Jim?"

"The shaving-water is ready."

"Good. Bring it here."

The Hottentot took the water into the tent and, emerging, sat down by the half-opened flap of the tent so that he could see the tall, well built figure of his *Baas.*

"The *Baas* lied today."

"Yes, Jim?"

"Yah! The *Baas* said, 'I stay here. You go Jim to the *dorp* and buy scoff.' I went, but the *Baas* did not stay."

"No, Jim?" The white man turned his well-lathered face toward the Hottentot. There was a gleam of amusement in his gray eyes—eyes which could look so bland and child-like.

"Yah!" Jim spat into the fire. "The *Baas* was not wise."

"No, Jim?"

"The *Baas* has work tonight, perchance, and with the man called Blake."

The white man's chin was receiving the gentle caress of his razor, and for a moment he did not speak.

"So that's his name, eh, Jim?"

"Yah. The *Baas* had better not go tonight. The man Blake did not say he was a policeman?"

"No. He called himself—" The white man stopped abruptly and stared at the Hottentot in amazement.

"How did you know all this, you imp of darkness?"

Jim grunted.

"I am not altogether a fool, *Baas*. If one knows how, it is possible for a black one to buy firewater at the place of Kaffir Smith. And—my ears are keen. Many things are known to me."

"I had always suspected as much. But some things are hidden even from thee."

"That is true, *Baas*. Not yet do I understand why thou didst wear the glass in the right eye. Such is not thy custom."

The white man laughed.

"I have said that some things are hidden from thee."

He sluiced his face in a basin of cold water.

"The towel, Jim," he said, spluttering.

" 'T is at thy hand, *Baas*," said the Hottentot. "But thou wilt not go tonight, *Baas*."

"My boots, Jim."

The Hottentot helped the white man pull on a pair of well-polished riding-boots.

"Thou wilt not go, *Baas*?"

"Being forewarned, what harm?"

"That is well an' I go with thee, *Baas*."

"Of a truth, yes, thou shalt go." The white man considered Jim silently; then—

"Do you know the *donga* near the man Blake's old mine, Jim?"

"As I know my hand, *Baas*. At that place I have met white men who had firewater to sell."

"Good. Then take the horses to that place tonight and wait for me there. Go secretly after the setting of the sun and all is dark, so that no man shall see ye."

"But what of the tent and the Cape cart?"

"Leave them here; they will come to no harm. We return here again ere the rising of another sun."

Two hours later, when the sun had set and the veldt was encompassed by a heavy darkness, the white man left the tent.

"I'm going to the *dorp*, Jim," he said, "to see that the appointment is kept. In an hour start for the place—the *donga* near the man Blake's mine."

"Yah, *Baas*."

Whistling gaily, the man strode out toward the town and was soon lost in the blackness of the night.

"THE PLACE is near here, Major."

Porky gasped for breath. The trip from the township to the deserted mines had sorely tried his little-used muscles. Fearing to arouse comment, the two men had made the journey on foot, slinking unobserved through the narrow street that led through the native quarter and out on the veldt.

Soon a long, low object loomed up out of the darkness before them.

"That's the slag-dump," explained Porky. "Come on; the shanty's this way."

Turning abruptly to the right, they soon came to a dilapidated hut. Opening the door, Porky entered, closely followed by the other.

Porky struck a match and lighted a candle, then looked triumphantly at his companion.

"Pretty slick place to make a trade, ain't it, Major?"

The other closely scrutinized the place, noted the heavily barred door and the blanketed windows, which prevented any glimmer of light being seen from the outside.

"Bah Jove, yes," he assented, "it's pretty slick. But where are the blacks?"

Porky looked at his watch.

"It's not quite time. They'll be here any minute now though."

Even as he spoke stealthy footsteps sounded outside the hut, and a hyena screamed once.

"That's them now," Porky said excitedly. "Douse the light while I let them in."

The light was extinguished and Porky cautiously opened the door. Dark, silent forms glided into the hut.

The door was closed again.

"Now the light, Major."

The flickering light of the candle showed six natives huddled to-gether as if for mutual encouragement. They were gaudily dressed in garments bought with the money earned by twelve months' hard labor in the mines.

"Do any of you speak English?"

They looked at each other blankly; then one was pushed forward.

"I speak it, *Baas*."

"What's your name, boy?"

"Sixpence, *Baas*."

"Well, Sixpence, my bucko, fork out your diamonds."

Sixpence turned and conversed volubly with his comrades.

"They saying," he said after a while, "that first you must give the money."

His face now wore a bold, defiant look as he looked at the two white men. He had no fear now, for were they not all on equal footing, partners in crime?

"Don't try that game with me," Porky said threateningly. "How can we give you the money until we've seen the stones?"

Sixpence still hesitated.

"Let me handle him," said the other white man.

"Is it that you don't trust us?" He spoke the native dialect. The faces of the others lighted up. Here was some one with whom they could all deal. Yet were still content for Sixpence to be their spokesman.

"How are we to know, *Baas?* We have been tricked many times by white men."

"And think ye that I would trick thee?"

Sixpence rubbed his head doubtfully.

"Thy pardon, *Baas*, but thou art with this other; him we do not trust."

"How much do ye ask for the stones?"

"Five pounds for each one—big and small. The risk was great."

"It is a fair price. How many have ye?"

"Two each we carry here—" he pointed to his thigh—"and I have these others besides."

In his hand he held a thick-stemmed knob kerrie which he gave to the white man. It was surprizingly light.

"It is hollow?"

"Aye, *Baas.*" Sixpence took back the stick, pried out a plug, and six large diamonds rolled out on the floor.

Porky pounced on them eagerly.

"Lor', what a haul!"

The other held out his hand for them and Porky, as if reluctant to lose sight of them, gave them to him.

"As I make it, Sixpence, the count is sixteen."

"The *Baas* forgets that I have two others here."

The white man whistled softly.

"'Pon my soul you're a glutton," he said.

Taking off his money-belt, he counted out thirty sovereigns.

"Thou see'st, Sixpence, I pay thee now for these I hold in my hand. As the others are given I will pay."

"It is good, *Baas,*" answered Sixpence; pulling up one trouser leg way above the knee and disclosing a long, ugly-looking wound. This he gently opened with a sharp knife, bringing to light two diamonds. These, which were much smaller than the others, Sixpence carefully wiped and gave to the white man.

"Ten more pounds for thee, O Sixpence," said the white man. "Thou wilt be a rich man. Dost desire to become a headman?"

"Nay, but there is a maiden I greatly desire."

The white man laughed.

"It is ever thus."

Meanwhile the other natives were quickly following their leader's example. All had deep wounds in the fleshy part of the thigh, and each took from his wound two diamonds.

Porky nudged the arm of his companion.

"You're a fool to give them that price. Why didn't you beat them down? They'd have accepted a quid apiece and been glad to get it."

Porky begrudged the money which he counted as out of his own pocket; he intended to appropriate all he found on the Major after the arrest.

The other shrugged his shoulders.

"There's enough for all," he said. "And they've earned their share."

Soon the bargaining was finished.

Once again the light was extinguished that the door might be opened to permit the natives to leave.

"Trek hard and stop not on the way to drink firewater," ordered Porky.

"We will hasten that we may catch up with the others of our *kraal* ere sunrise," answered Sixpence. *"Shlaha gaghle, Inkosi."*

"Aye. *Hambagaghle*—may thy path be smooth."

The natives quickly disappeared in the darkness, and as the two white men turned to reenter the hut they were hailed softly.

Porky's hand leaped to his revolver.

"It's only me," said Jong Dempster as he joined them.

"Couldn't trust me, eh?" sneered Porky. "Well, let's go inside. It give me the creeps hanging outside here."

They entered the hut and Porky busied himself with lighting the candle. Suddenly he wheeled round, revolver in hand.

"Throw up your hands, Major. You're under arrest for illicit diamond-buying."

There was a look of amazement on the man's face; then smilingly he raised his hands.

"So that's the game, is it, Porky Blake? I might have known better than to trust you and Jong Dempster."

The two men grinned.

"So you know us, do you? Well, much good that'll do you. Frisk him, Jong."

The Dutchman quickly turned out the captive's pockets.

"The fool hasn't got a gun," Jong grunted.

"Get the stones then. They're in his money-belt."

Jong removed the belt, opened it and pawed lovingly over the stones.

"You've got the reputation for being —— slick, Major, but you've run up against a snag this time."

"Bah Jove, yes. But I'm glad to know you're an honest man, old top. It's a fine thing, honesty—more precious than rubies, and all that sort of thing, don't you know."

Porky glowered.

"Give him his belt back, Jong. Only be sure to leave a couple of stones in it—we can afford to—so that I can find them on him when I search him at headquarters. Give me half his cash—I ought to have it all, by rights."

As they divided the spoils a look of triumph passed over the face of the captive.

"Not so honest after all, are you, old top?"

"Stow your gab."

"You'd better get a move on, Jong, if you're going to catch the mail train south."

"Can you manage the Major alone?"

"Here." Porky threw a pair of handcuffs on the table. "Put these on him. He can't play any tricks then."

AT THAT moment the door opened violently and a tall masked figure appeared in the aperture.

"Hands up, Messrs. Brown and Smith," drawled the intruder, "and you too, my gentle double, keep yours up."

Porky and Jong put up their hands with a curse and glowered viciously at the newcomer.

" 'Pon my word," went on the newcomer, "but I hate to break up a little family party. I hope that I'm not intrudin'."

"Who the —— are you," shouted Porky.

"Tut tut, my dear sergeant. Don't get profane; it's such deucedly bad form."

The man who had elected to call himself Jones watched the newcomer with a smile of baffled amusement.

"You're the Major," he said finally.

"Then who are you?" Jong exploded.

The masked man smiled and bowed.

"Let's postpone the inquiries, gentlemen. I've no time to spare, I'm sorry to say."

Reaching behind him, he tore down the blanket which covered the window. As he did so there was a crash of broken glass and the muzzle of a rifle appeared in the opening.

"Jim."

"Yah, *Baas?*"

"Keep them covered and if any one moves, shoot. Understand?"

A grunt from without signified assent.

"Pardon me, Jong." The Major took the Dutchman's revolver and threw it out the door. Porky's quickly followed.

"I'm surprized," said the Major, running his hand over the man who had impersonated him, "that you are unarmed. It is not the thing, you know, when playing with gentlemen like these two. They are a pretty pair, aren't they?" he went on, serenely eying the baffled men. "Turn out your pockets, old dears. No, not yours, old chappie. I can't imagine that they've left you anything. You will please keep your hands elevated—a little higher. That's splendid, thanks. You're simply perfect."

Turning his attention to the table, he surveyed the contents of Jong's and Porky's pockets. Disregarding the money, he picked up the little chamois bag into which Jong had put the stones.

"This is really too good of you, my dear Jong. I've always heard that if one kept one's ears open when in Kaffir Smith's back room one could learn something to one's advantage. But I never expected anything like this, 'pon my word, I didn't. Diamonds, as I live, and all for me. Of course there may be more but—*tempus* fugits, and I must follow its good example."

He backed toward the door as he spoke.

"I'm going now, but please keep your eye on the rifle in the window. It will keep you covered for another five minutes. I must have a little leeway before allowing a zealous policeman like you—'pon my soul I don't know who's the policeman and who's the thief—give chase to me. And now—" the voice changed and he winked broadly—"to sleep and drink, to drink and sleep."

With a quick leap he was outside the hut and slammed the door behind him.

In wrathful silence the three men watched the unwavering muzzle of the gun in the wilderness. Soon to their ears came the sound of mocking laughter and the rapid drumming of horse's hoofs. The sound quickly died away in the distance, but still they were held up by the threat of the gun.

The minutes flew by quickly. Then Jones wearily let his hands sink to his side and walked over to the window. Taking hold of the gun-muzzle, he pulled into the room the useless barrel of a rifle.

"Held up by that," he said in disgust.

Porky and Jong lowered their hands in amazement.

"It was the sundowner," they exclaimed, remembering the Major's last remark.

"It was the Major," said the man Jones.

"At least he didn't get your diamonds," said Jong, not sensing the full meaning of the other's statement.

"No. He didn't get mine."

"Look here," said Porky belligerently, "if he was the Major who the —— are you?"

"Perhaps Sergeant Blake would know me better if I wore a black mustache and the uniform of the corps he has disgraced," said the other curtly. "I did not make any accusation this morning, Blake, but I do now."

Porky's jaw sagged.

"The game's up, Jong. It's the chief," he said weakly.

"Exactly. I told you this morning that I couldn't understand some of the things that were happening down here. I left the train at the siding, shaved, changed into civilians—with an eyeglass—and came back on a freight to investigate.

"My plans miscarried a little. First, because you couldn't play even a crooked game straight, and secondly, because the Major—the real one—butted in unexpectedly."

Intercepting the desperate look that passed between the two men, he went on:

"No. Murder wouldn't help you. I took another leaf from the Major's book and wrote a letter to my next in command, telling him of my suspicions and plans.

"You'll return to your quarters and report yourself under arrest, Sergeant Blake. As for you, Jong Dempster, I've no evidence that will hold in a court of law against you. But your license as diamond trader expires tomorrow, doesn't it?"

Dempster nodded glumly.

"I thought so. Well, if I were you, I wouldn't apply for a renewal."

With that the chief walked briskly out of the hut and toward the town, leaving the two men to mutual recriminations.

ENTERING THE police office and making himself known to the trooper in charge, the chief entered an inner room and ordered that Juffa, one of the police boys, be brought before him.

"Well, Juffa," he said when they were alone, "did ye obey?"

"Aye inkosi. All this day I kept a close watch over the Hottentot."

"And noted ye what white men he spoke with?"

"He spoke to no white men, *inkosi.*"

"Where went he?"

"To the veldt beyond the town, to the south. There stands a white man's camp, a tent and a Cape cart with two horses. A white man was there, but him I did not see. He was in the tent; him I heard singing."

"It was well done. Go outside and wait. In a little while I will come and thou shalt show me the way to this white man's camp. See that ye keep this secret."

"It is an order, *inkosi.*" Saluting smartly, Juffa withdrew and passing out of the building, waited in the darkness near by.

The chief left the inner room and chatted for a little while with the trooper; then he too left the building.

Outside the door he paused while he lighted a cigar and then moved slowly off down the street.

He was quickly joined by Juffa.

"It is this way," said the police boy softly.

The two broke into an easy run, soon coming to the place where the Major had pitched his camp.

A light was burning in the tent.

"That is all, Juffa," said the chief. "Ye may return to sleep—and forget."

"To hear is to obey."

Juffa melted silently into the blackness of the night, and the chief went forward alone. Just as he was about to pull back the flap of the tent and enter, revolver in hand, a curt voice from within challenged:

"Who's there? Throw up your hands."

"Oh, come now, my dear Major," the chief replied, "that talk doesn't go. You can't see me and I have a good idea where you are."

He was answered by a soft chuckle right at his elbow.

"I've always found it convenient," went on the voice, "to have two exits to my tent. It provides a—draft, shall we say?"

The cold barrel of a revolver was pressed against the chief's temple.

"Enter, if you please, kind sir," the voice mocked.

Concealing his chagrin, the chief went into the tent closely followed by the Major. Seeing by the light of the lamp who his visitor was, the Major made a gesture of apology and threw his revolver down on the cot.

"Please forgive me, old top," he cried. "I had no idea it was you; 'pon my soul, I didn't." He waved to a deck-chair. "Take a seat—or perhaps you'd prefer the cot."

The chief slowly lowered himself into the chair.

"Have a smoke, Major," he said, proffering his cigar-case.

"Thanks, I don't mind if I do."

The Major lighted a match.

"A light, old man?"

"Thanks!"

For a while the two men smoked in silence, each striving to take the other's measure.

"I'm glad you came," drawled the Major finally. "I was rather expecting Porky or Jong—the bally rotters."

"Is this game worth the candle, Major?" said the chief quietly.

The Major looked blank.

"Worth the candle? Oh, yes, I see what you mean. Why, my dear old chap, you have no idea what a bully time I'm having." The Major leaned back on the cot and puffed luxuriously at his cigar.

"We need men like you in the police, Major."

"Thanks for the compliment, old top, but you will pardon me if I reply that I don't need the police. Blake's a policeman, isn't he?"

"He was."

The Major chuckled. "You have the official curtness, old dear. Have a drink?"

"Don't mind if I do."

The Major poured out two drinks.

"A toast, chief."

Both men rose.

"I give you 'the queen,' Major."

Solemnly they drank to the toast.

"Now to fox-hunting, chief," cried the Major gaily.

Again they drank with an almost religious observance of the ceremony. Then they sat and talked for a while of England, of the Hunting Shires; and the argument waxed fast and furious over the respective merits of the Quorn and Cottesmore Hunts.

There came a time when the conversation lapsed and both men sat smoking quietly, meditating on past days.

"Major," began the chief abruptly.

"Yes?"

"—— it all, man, why are you running against the law?"

"That's a bally personal question, don't you think," said the Major a trifle heatedly.

The chief flushed.

"Yes, it is, under the old footing. But we're not. I'm in command of the police and you," he hesitated, "you are what you are."

"And what's that?"

The chief made a gesture of impatience.

"We're not children; don't let's bandy words. Why don't you play straight? A pardon could be arranged and—"

The Major's hand went up in protest.

"Don't say it, old man. Did you know that I'd served a jail-sentence?"

The other made no attempt to conceal his amazement.

"No. When?"

"It was a few years ago. I won't say how many; you might be tempted to look up the records. I bought a diamond from a man—I was innocent then—and that same man arrested me for I.D.B. They sentenced me to two years on the Breakwater, working among the scum of the earth. That diamond was to have been set in a ring and— But I never went back after I was released. How could I?"

"I'm sorry, old man," said the chief with an awkward attempt at sympathy.

The Major straightened up.

" 'Pon my soul, but I'm getting deucedly sentimental."

"Yes," assented the other, "you almost made me forget why I came out here."

"Just why did you come, chief?"

"I want the diamonds you took from Porky and Jong tonight."

"I took diamonds away from a policeman? You flatter me, old top."

"Oh, stop joshing, Major. I know you've got them, and you know that I know you've got 'em."

"Gettin' rather complicated, what? But how do you know I've got them?"

"I saw you take them."

"Yes, so you did. But what then? You can't find them and you can't prove that I took them."

"I think that my word," began the chief gently.

"Would be taken before mine," finished the Major. "Exactly. But what of the rest of the story. How would it go? Porky and Jong and you—the head of the police department—in a deserted hut, at night, out on the veldt. Diamonds galore. Pray what was our good friend the chief doing there? Understand that is not my question, but that of the judge and—oh, you know how the talk goes around."

The chief made a gesture of impatience.

"So some one took the diamonds away," went on the Major airily.

"You took the diamonds."

"Can you prove it? Remember, the light was dim and the man was masked."

"Are you going to give me the diamonds?"

"Really, you are bally persistent. Supposin' I had 'em. Why should I give them back? Who loses? You've got the information you wanted regarding Blake and Jong. You win. You can't say that the Mining Syndicate loses when they close down the mines part of the year for fear of flooding the market. No, I can't see—"

"You forget, Major," interposed the chief, "that I paid five pounds apiece for the stones."

"Bah Jove, did you? That's rich. I wonder if Jim could get a line on the natives you dealt with. It 'ud be rich to bring a charge of I.D.B. against you. What with the natives and Jong, and Porky I'd have a good case."

The chief smiled.

"But I couldn't do that," went on the Major, "though you do see, don't you, old chap, that there's no moral reason why I should give you the stones—always supposin' I had 'em."

"No. I don't see that quite."

"I'm afraid you're a little tired; the old brain's not working at top pressure. But at least you'll admit that you have no case against me?"

"You forget my witnesses, Jong and Blake?"

"No I don't forget them. But they couldn't swear to me. They've never seen me unmasked and, as I said before, the light was very dim. Of course they couldn't possibly swear that the man in the mask, the sundowner and the Major, are one and the same person. Besides I can't imagine that they would relish giving evidence to help you win a case. Really I can't."

"Supposing I offered to forget all about their past misdeeds on condition that they swore to your identity. What then?"

"What then? Why you'd have me bluffed—supposin' I had the diamonds. But you couldn't do that."

"No I couldn't do that."

"So you see," exclaimed the Major triumphantly, "your case falls flat."

"It does," admitted the chief, rising to leave.

"Won't you stay a while longer? It's ages since I had a chat like this. I'd like to be able to persuade you how moral I really am."

"That's what I'm afraid of," said the chief with a smile. "Good night, Major."

"Wait a minute, old chap." The Major opened a small trunk and took out a roll of bank notes. Counting out sixteen five-pound notes, he handed them to the chief.

"It's a reimbursement of the money you paid for the stones," he said in explanation. "We can dispense with a receipt."

"Thanks, Major," said the chief, pocketing the money. "And, Major—"

"Yes, old chap."

"Some day I'm going to send for you and—"

"Perhaps I'll come. Sure you must go? Good night."

"Good night."

LINES OF CLEAVAGE

THE MAJOR let the magazine—it was an English weekly and Open at the Society Notes—fall from his hand and heaved a deep sigh.

Jim, the Hottentot, looked up quickly from his task of putting a final polish on the Major's riding-boots.

"The *Baas* is sick?"

The Major nodded his head wearily.

"Aye, Jim. Sick of all this."

With a wave of his hand he indicated the sun-scorched veldt.

"I'll mix the *Baas* some mouti—whisky and quinin." How Jim did stumble over that word. "It will make the *Baas* feel like a new man."

"It's not a body sickness but a soul sickness that troubles me, Jim."

Jim was puzzled. Never before had his beloved *Baas* talked so strangely.

"A sickness of the soul, *Baas?*" he said wonderingly, and picked up the paper which the Major had dropped. "This then must be evil medicine. I will cast it on the fire and thus shall the evil spirits be driven from thee."

The Major made no effort to prevent Jim from burning the paper though he had read but half of it and English papers were as manna in the wilderness in those days of infrequent mails.

He smiled grimly as a passing breeze spread the ashes of the paper thither and yon about the veldt.

"It is not thus, Jim," he said, "that the evil spirit is destroyed. Hast ever dreamed?"

"Many times, *Baas*," Jim answered promptly. "But last night I dreamed I was a powerful chief. Cattle I had more numerous than the sand of the river-bed; three-score wives dwelt in the shadow of my hut and called me lord. Aye, three score wives brewed beer for me to drink. I was thirsty and I beat upon the drum that beer might be brought me. Then I awoke. The beating of the drum was, in very truth, a peal of thunder, and barely time had I to get within the shelter of the tent ere came the rain. I was thirsty no longer!"

The Major laughed.

"But the dream is still with thee?"

"Aye," assented Jim sorrowfully. "The dream is still with me; the beer is not."

"And so it is with me. The paper which thou hast destroyed brought me dreams; the dreams are still there."

"Is there aught the *Baas* desires, that the *Baas* has not?" Jim asked incredulously.

"Thou hast food enough and drink; all the veldt is open to thee and none shall say to thee 'stay,' when thou desirest to go; and none say 'go' when it is thy will to stay. Can there be anything lacking?"

"There is one thing lacking. What do men call me?"

"White men call thee, 'the Major,' and we black ones, 'the Just One,' 'the Wise One,' or yet again, 'the Man of Single Heart,'" and— thou art my *Baas.*"

"I have yet another name. That ye do not know and shall not know, lest ye remember it at a time it should be forgotten. The name of my father and my father's father I have not heard these many years. There is a desire within me, new-born, to be called by that name. To that end I am going away from this place—back to my own people."

"It is the coming of the season of rain that makes the *Baas* talk thus. Other white men have I heard talk that way; other men have left this country, cursing it from the depths of their heart. But with the end of the rains they returned, loving that for which they professed hatred."

"Nay, but this is different."

The Major lapsed into English and the drawl, absent from his speech when talking the native language, now became strongly evident.

"I'm going back to the Old Country where a chap can meet decent people; can do decent things in a decent way. I've always been honest with myself but from now on I'm going to play square with the bally laws; 'Render unto Caesar,' and all that."

Jim, understanding but little, replied as in duty bound—

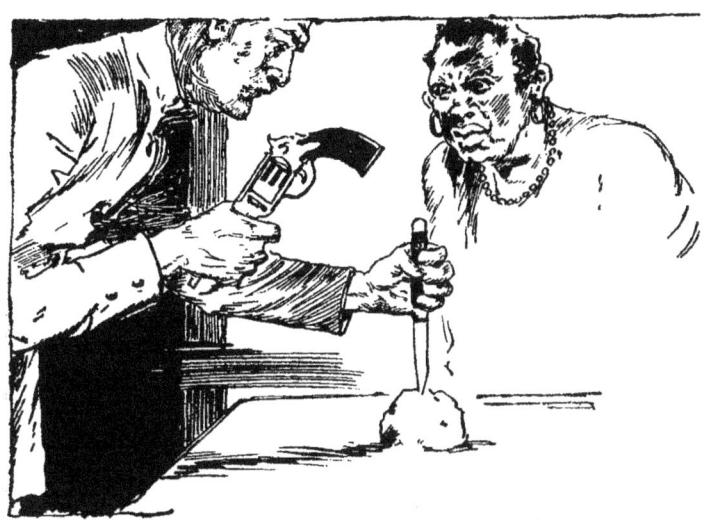

"Yah, *Baas!*"

"Yes, Jim," continued the Major. "I'm going to render the Government its pound of flesh—three-fifths the value of all the diamonds I find. This other game—there's nothing in it. I've made money, lots of it, and lost it all. Yes, Jim, we're going to be honest and we're going home."

"Yah, *Baas,*" agreed Jim.

AT THAT moment an aged negro came into sight. He was beating his way through the thick undergrowth of the bush veldt and heading directly toward the tent.

Jim, on sighting the newcomer, rose quickly to his feet and ran to meet him.

The Major adjusted his monocle and stared in amazement.

"Wonder who the old codger is," he muttered. "Never seen him before to my knowledge, and I've never seen Jim so deucedly polite. Bah Jove! He's kotowing to the old chappie as if he were the Lord High Executioner."

Jim and the newcomer were by this time at the green wood fire—so built that the smoke from it kept the flies away from the horses which were tethered near by—and Jim, first seeing that his companion was comfortably seated and plentifully supplied with tobacco, came forward alone.

"It's Mangwato, *Baas.* Chief Mangwato," he said excitedly.

The Major was instantly on the alert. Fabulous tales are told of the wealth of Mangwato and of his hatred and distrust of the white men. Few white men had attempted to enter Mangwato's land. The Major was one of the few; the adventures that befell him have been chronicled elsewhere.

"And what desires Mangwato?"

"A word with thee, *Baas.*"

"My ears, are open. Tell him to come hither. Nay. Say I will come to him, for he is old, in a little while."

Jim carried the news to the aged chief, who grunted approval and bade Jim sit beside him.

The Major turned his back on the two and, lighting a cigarette, smoked it slowly to the end. Then, and not till then, he walked over to where Mangwato and Jim sat and squatted on his haunches opposite them.

"*Sauka bona*—Greetings to thee, O Mangwato."

Mangwato did not look up and spat into the fire before answering.

"Aye. Greeting to thee, also, white man."

The Major let the monocle fall from his eye. He was too wise in the ways of natives to attempt a conversation while wearing an eyeglass.

"Distrust a man," runs the proverb, "who can not look thee squarely in the eye, and a woman who can."

The eye speaks all languages under the sun, and if the eye says one thing and the tongue another, it is the words of the eye that the native will believe. But how shall the eye speak if it looks through a piece of glass?

In response to a look from his *Baas* Jim rose to his feet, explaining that he must cut fodder for the horses.

"Mangwato, the chief, is far from his *kraal,*" said the Major, softly when Jim had departed.

"Two weeks have passed since I left my place," the other replied briefly, "and I have not tarried on the way."

"And the chief is old. Surely the urge must be great."

Now for the first time Mangwato looked up from the ground and, gazing unblinkingly at the white man, was well satisfied with what he saw.

"Thou hast not seen me before, white man?"

"Nay. Yet once I desired to call upon thee. The gun of many voices I brought with me, intending to give it thee for a present. But thy watch-dogs would have none of me."

A grim smile crossed Mangwato's face.

"Word was brought to me of that. Of a truth thou didst deal hardly with my people that day, but not more hardly than I dealt with them when the news was brought me."

"Was it of that thou wished to talk?"

Once again Mangwato closely scrutinized the white man, then speaking slowly, he said—

"It would ill become such men as we, white man, to bandy words as if we were foolish maidens.

"Thou knowest that it is not my custom to hold any dealings with white men. My country is barred to them and none may take up their residence therein, for I have observed that where enters the white men there also enters evil."

"Yet thou hast come to me."

"Aye, for look you, not all the cattle in the herd are black; not all the white men are evil. Much talk have I heard of thee and am well convinced that thou walkest in a straight path."

"White men hold yet another opinion, chief."

The old man made a gesture of impatience.

"Aye. I have also heard of that, but thy heart is clean. Now heed well what I have to say. It hath been at all times my order that no man from my country should go to labor in the mines of the white men. But, alas, there is little respect for wise counsel in the minds of the young men, and many of them, won by the false promises of the agent of the white men who came seeking to recruit them, have disobeyed my command. Thou knowest how the white men's gold hath power to lure my people from their traditions?"

"That I well know, chief."

"Also thou knowest how they return to live once again among us, wearing strange clothes and swearing by strange gods—ever breeding discontent. But this alone would be as nothing. This I can forgive for in time the disobedient ones return to the customs of their fathers.

"Of late my young men who have worked in the mines return to us broken in spirit and in body. Some—ah me—return not at all, for, as they journey to my country after serving the allotted time at the mines, evil men—white men look ye—have set upon them, beating them sorely and taking from them all that they had earned during those months of labor."

The Major was silent. He knew only too well to what the chief alluded. Certain low, degenerate white men looked upon the native laborers returning to their *kraals* after a year's service at the mines as their legitimate prey. Nor were they content in simply robbing the natives of their hard-earned gold but savagely attacked and mutilated—in some cases, killed—such natives who dared to make a stand to protect their property.

"It is a thing of shame, O Mangwato. With such white men I claim no kin. Yet hath not this very evil much in it to commend itself to thee? Will not the tales of the young men thus abused prevent others from seeking work at the mines?"

"The buck is killed at the water-hole, white man, but others still go there to drink. Further, the time draws nigh when certain of my young men will be released from the mines to return to their *kraals*."

"And is it to greet them that chief Mangwato hath trekked thus far from his own place?" The Major's tone was mildly sarcastic.

"For them I have no care, white man. Yet one among them is my son and for him I fear. What though I declared before the people that I would put him from me dared he to seek service with the white men! What though I ordered that none should speak his name, no, not even in the darkness of the huts! He is my son and I—I am less than the spirits. He is the last of my name. Should he die or come to severe hurt at the hands of these jackals who prey at night, then my name will be forgotten, for there is no other to take my place."

Mangwato's voice broke.

"Why dost thou come to me? Can not the police aid thee?"

"I trust them not. It is whispered that they know of the evil but, shutting their eyes, declare that they see it not."

"Then go to thy son warning him of the perils which beset his path."

"I would not have my son—my disobedient son—know that I am concerned for his welfare. Neither would he relish being treated as a maiden. He is a man; he would go his own way, brooking no interference."

"Then?"

"It is to you I appeal, white man. Save my son from the evil ones. Let him return, unharmed, to the place of his fathers."

"What is thy son's name?"

"Simba is his name, white man. Simba, the lion."

The Major rose to his feet signifying that the interview was at an end.

"What I can do, I will do, O Mangwato. Wilt thou wait here to greet thy son?"

"Nay. He must find me at my own place; my hand must not appear in this."

"It is well. *Hamba gaghle*—May thy path be smooth."

"Good rest be thine," intoned the chief.

"JIM," SAID the Major, when the Hottentot rejoined him after having escorted Mangwato to the trail which ran through the bush veldt some distance beyond the tent, "said Mangwato anything to you of his errand?"

"Aye. But what can the *Baas* do? These evil white men who rob the returning laborers have no fear of the law; they kill in the dark and there is none to bear witness against them."

"Yet I have given my word. Here is money, Jim. Go down to the compounds and keep thy ears open for talk of Simba and of the way in which these white men do their evil work. Without doubt they have spies in the compound who take word to them of the time certain laborers will be released from their mines, the amount of their wealth and the trail they intend to take."

"And what if none speak of these things?"

"Thou hast money. Money will purchase beer, and beer unloosens the tongues of men."

"That is true, *Baas*. I go now. But what of thee?"

"I will go to the place of Kafir Smith. Mayhap I will learn of something there."

IN THE dark alleyway forming one of the many entrances to Kafir Smith's saloon the Major bumped into a thick-set, flashily dressed man who was conversing with a heavily veiled woman.

"—— you! Look where you're going," blustered the man.

"I beg your pardon, really. It's so dark here, you know, coming out of the blaze of Old Sol. What?"

"A bloomin' dude, eh?" sneered the other. "Well get to —— out of here before I kick you out. I'm having a business interview with this lady."

The Major doffed his helmet.

" 'Pon my soul!" he ejaculated, "I didn't see the lady." Seeing that the man was holding the woman firmly by the wrists he went on—

"You will forgive me, madam, I'm sure, if I suggest that this is hardly the place for a charming lady like yourself to hold, er—a business interview with this—er—gentleman."

"Why, you—toad!"

The man released his hold on the girl's wrists and turned threateningly on the Major who, smiling happily, awaited the expected onslaught.

"Please don't." The girl's voice had a sweet note of entreaty.

The Major dropped his hands and bowed.

"Dreadfully boorish of us, I'll admit, and of course, dear old walrus—" the man had a heavy, black mustache—"we can't fight when a lady says 'No.' The Major has never been deaf to the appeals of the well-known weaker sex."

He looked at the girl meaningly as he concluded, hoping that she would understand his offer of help.

She lifted her veil a moment and the Major read her thanks in her clear, gray eyes. She let the veil fall and crouched back against the wall, making room for him to pass by and on into the saloon.

"Mornin', Major," Aggie called gaily as he entered. "What've you done with Porky and Jong? Nobody has seen 'em since they went on that business-trip with you."

"Give you my word, dear old thing," he drawled. "I can't imagine where they've gone."

He looked around the deserted barroom.

"All alone, eh? No one in there?"

He nodded toward the door leading to an inner room.

"No. I'm all alone. The police are getting nosey and asking too many questions. Seems they've got a new chief who means business, so the boys are keeping away."

The Major nodded and turned to leave. No need for him to waste time here. Perhaps, if the police were playing a straight game, it would be better to put the matter of protecting Mangwato's son in their hands. Yet—

He stopped at Aggie's voice.

"Stay a little while, can't yer, Major? If you only knew how sick I am of this place. Not a thing to do except serve drink to drunken beasts who've forgotten they were ever born of woman."

The Major, surprized at such an outburst from one whom he had considered vapid and empty-headed, walked over to her.

"So you're sick of it too?"

She laughed harshly.

"I wish to —— that I'd never come to the place. I had a good situation in London"—she sighed reminiscently—"a mahogany counter with solid-silver taps. Only real gents came there. Gents like you. They used to call me 'Miss Harris.' Here it's 'Aggie this,' and 'Aggie that,' till I fair forgets that I've got any other name."

"It's like that with me, too," murmured the Major. "Why did you leave London?"

"It was the money. I thought I'd be able to save up enough in a year or two to buy a pub of my own somewhere in the country, back home. But what's the use of money when every decent woman turns up her nose at the sight of me?"

She buried her face in her hands and sprawled across the bar, heedless of the suds of beer, the dregs of many glasses, which soiled her much belaced blouse.

"Cheer up, Miss Harris, old thing."

The Major placed a kindly hand on her shoulder.

She suddenly sat erect and passed a heavily scented handkerchief across her eyes.

"I'm a fair cut-up, ain't I?" she sighed. "I had you going for fair. *Whoop la!*"

But underneath the gaiety was the suggestion of utter despair.

"Why don't you go back home? There's nothing to stop you."

"A fat lot you know about that. How can I go home without money?"

"But—er—I thought you made a lot?"

"So I have, but Kafir Smith, my boss, has been keeping it for me. He said it would be dangerous for a woman to have a lot of money about her in this country. And now he won't give it to me."

"Have you any receipt?"

"No. I never thought he would play me such a dirty trick. I thought he was a gentleman."

"What's Kafir Smith look like? I've never met him."

"There's his picture." Aggie pointed to a large portrait in colored chalks which adorned one side of the barroom.

Examining it, the Major recognized it as the picture of the man he had met in the alleyway. Also there was something hauntingly familiar about the man. The Major felt that he had met him before in some other place; at some other time.

"Is he married?"

"No." The girl's tone was bitter. "He made up to me until I gave him my money for safe-keeping. Kafir Smith ain't got no interest in women save for the money he can get out of them. They say he's got a hold on most of the women in this *dorp*."

"A blackmailer, eh?" And the Major's thoughts reverted to the girl he had seen with Smith in the alley.

Aggie nodded.

"Yep. Something like that."

"How does he get his hold over them?"

"He runs a gambling-outfit and a lot of women owe him money. Then some of them were barmaids before they married and turned respectable. They don't want their old profession thrown in their faces."

"I see. How much money has Kafir Smith belonging to you?"

"Five thousand pounds."

The Major whistled.

Aggie flared up angrily.

"It's all honestly earned, too. I may be a barmaid but I've always run straight." Aggie was unconsciously quoting from her favorite author.

The Major was all apologies.

"I never doubted that for a moment, Miss Harris, old top. But if you had the money, would you go home?"

"You've said it," Aggie replied with fervor. "But what's the use of whining? I've made my bed and I must lie in it and I'm so —— tired I can sleep most anywhere."

THE MAJOR found Jim awaiting him when he returned to his tent which was pitched on the edge of the township. The Major preferred sleeping in his tent on the open veldt to the filthy accommodations provided by the town's one hotel—Kafir Smith's saloon.

"I've talked with Simba, *Baas*, and also with the native police at the compound; they, as ye supposed, are in league with the white men."

"What said Simba?"

"Ten men of his *kraal* return to their own place, leaving the compound, before the setting of today's sun."

"So soon? Then Mangwato came just in time."

"Perhaps, though it may well be that Simba will never live to pay homage to his father."

"How then?"

"He hath made much money, won at games of chance. This the white men are determined to get, and they have planned well.

"Simba they have prevailed upon to wait for the rising of the moon, before setting on his journey homeward. He hath a greed for the liquor of the white men and much of this they have promised to give him. One hath already arranged with him the place of meeting.

"After they have taken his money they intend to kill him—they fear the wrath of the white police should he live to bear witness against them—making it appear is if he were killed in a drunken fight with his own people. Aye, the plan is a cunning one and likely to succeed for I could not shake Simba from his purpose of keeping his tryst with the white man."

"And the other men of Mangwato's *kraal* they will not touch?"

"Nay, *Baas,* for they are penniless."

"Thou knowest the meeting-place?"

"Aye. It is not far from this place. One white man will meet Simba and take him to where the others are hidden, fully an hour's trek away, for they dare not do the deed near to the trail for fear of being seen. It is whispered that the eyes of the white police have of late been opened."

SO IT happened that the lewd song which Hawkins, a rat-faced little cockney, was singing to keep up his courage while awaiting the coming of Simba was rudely interrupted.

Without a chance for outcry, failing to catch a glimpse of his captors, he was bound hand and foot, securely gagged and rolled into a thick clump of bushes near by.

A few minutes later Simba, a finely developed native, came to the place.

"Art thou there, white man?" he called softly.

"Aye."

A tall figure stepped forward out of the shadows.

"Then let us hasten to the place ye spoke of, for I have far to go ere I catch up with my brothers."

"I can not take thee." There was fear in the white man's voice. "The white police have taken my friends; they have taken also the beer. Further, word has come to my ears that they are even now seeking thee."

"To what end?"

"Thou hast played the game of chance, winning much money from the men at the compounds. Knowest not that it is against the white man's law thus to gamble?"

"Then I will get from this place ere day comes and finds me."

"How canst escape them? They are mounted. Canst outrun the horse?"

"Nay." Simba's tone was one of despair. "What will they do to me, white man?"

"Send ye back to labor in the mines. But see, I am sorry for thee. I will be thy friend. Hast twenty pounds?"

"That and more would I give rather than return to labor in the mines."

"Give me twenty; it will serve. In return take thou this horse and ride fast. Should any white man call to thee answer not, but ride on."

A moment later the rapid drumming of horse's hoofs told that Simba had followed the counsel of his benefactor.

A second figure came out of the shadows and joined the first.

"That was well done, *Baas*. Mangwato will be well pleased."

"Aye. Also I received a good price for the horse. He was getting old and of no further use to me. Take thou the money, Jim. It is thine."

"Thanks, *Baas*. What shall I do with the jackal back yonder?"

"Untie his hands, Jim. The rest he can see to himself. At any rate he can take the gag from his mouth and cry for aid. Before that comes we shall be safely in the camp, knowing nothing of the happenings of this night."

When they had reached the tent Jim, contrary to his custom, did not go straightway to his blankets by the camp-fire, but followed his *Baas* into the I tent.

"What is it Jim?" the Major asked sharply. He wanted to be alone with his thoughts; to plan the campaign that would reinstate him in the eyes of the law.

Jim fumbled in the cavernous depths of the pocket of one of the Major's discarded great coats which he wore. From it he produced what appeared to be a bundle of filthy rags and held it out toward the Major.

"Mangwato bade me give thee this if thou succeeded in saving his son from the evil ones."

The Major looked at the bundle with mock horror.

"Does the chief wish me to become a thing unclean, that he sends me such a present?"

"When one is thirsty it is not well to consider the outside of the pot, *Baas.*"

"Then break the pot, Jim, and let us see its contents."

Jim slowly unwound the greasy rags, disclosing what at first appeared to be a solid piece of glass, shaped roughly like a paperweight. The Major took it amusedly in his hands and was surprized at the weight of it.

"Nearly three pounds, if I'm any judge. I wonder—"

He held it up to the light of the oil lamp and examined it closely, turning it over and over.

"I must be dreaming," he muttered. Then he almost dropped the stone in his excitement. "But it is; it is! There's no doubt about it! And there's nothing like it under the sun. Jim, old top, there's the price of a kingdom right here in my hand, and it's mine, honestly mine. All the stories told about Mangwato's bushel of diamonds are true; this is one of them. Tomorrow I'll make an application for a diamond-mining permit and when that's granted I'll register the discovery of the biggest diamond the world has ever known. Don't you see what this means?"

"I see nothing but a dirty piece of glass, *Baas,*" Jim replied stolidly.

The Major laughed, a happy, care-free laugh. In his excitement he was a boy once more.

"Hush, *Baas!*" Jim warned. "Some one is coming here, on horseback."

The Major sobered instantly and they both listened.

"The horse is lame, Jim," the Major commented.

"May I come in?"

The Major started at the sound of the voice, recognizing it as belonging to the girl he had seen with Kafir Smith earlier in the day.

He went to the flap of the tent and held it open so that she could enter.

She looked about her, half-blinded by the glare of the lamp, then sitting down in the camp-chair which the Major pushed toward her, buried her face in her hands and began to cry softly.

The Major looked on helplessly.

"Do you think you are wise coming here at this time of night? I have a bad reputation, you know."

She looked up quickly.

"I know you must think dreadful things but I had to take a desperate chance that you could help me. There's no one else I can appeal to, and you did offer your help this morning, didn't you? Besides, I am armed."

She held a toy revolver in her hand.

"And I'm not."

The Major unbuckled his revolver and pushed it toward her.

"Yes, I will help you if I can," he continued gravely. "But don't you think you'd better allow me to escort you home?"

"No. You must listen to me first. I often go for moonlight rides, and tonight my horse went lame. That will be an explanation for my late return."

The Major nodded.

"Suppose you begin at the beginning. It's about Kafir Smith, I suppose."

"Yes. I first met Kafir Smith when I was a barmaid in Johannesburg. Yes," she said vehemently in answer to the Major's look of incredulity, "I was that. When my father died, leaving me penniless, there seemed nothing else I could do. Father had, at one time, owned a large saloon, and—"

"I see," commented the Major.

"Three years ago I met and married Roger Griffin while I was on a holiday at Durban and never told him I'd served behind a bar."

"That was a mistake."

"Yes, I know that now. But Roger's proud and comes of an old family. To have told him would have meant losing him. Well, shortly after we were married Roger was smitten with the diamond fever and came up here. Smith recognized me at once and I wrote to him, begging him to keep my secret. He did not answer and later he accosted Roger when I was with him and told him that he had known me in Johannesburg. That night I wrote another letter to Smith, couching it in even more urgent terms than the first. Ever since then he has kept those letters, threatening to show them to Roger if I refused to do as he ordered."

"But what harm if he did?"

"Can't you see? I didn't say in the letters what my secret was and you can imagine the vile interpretation Smith would make of it. First of all he demanded money as the price of his silence. Then he made me persuade Roger to invest all his capital in some worthless mining property. Roger's trying to sell it now, so that we can raise sufficient money to pay our passage home.

"This morning Smith said that I must go to him tomorrow night. If I don't he says he'll give Roger the letters, and besides he says he's got evidence that Roger has been buying diamonds from the natives. I know that's a lie, for Roger has always scorned the I.D.B.s. He says they are robbing the Government of a legitimate revenue and so set back the development of the colony."

The Major winced.

"So you think that—er—Roger is not guilty of I.D.B.?"

"I know he's not. But that won't prevent Smith from framing a case against him. Smith's got a lot of influence."

She rose wearily to her feet.

"There, now I have told my story. I don't know why, or why I came here. There's nothing that you can do. Tomorrow I'll go to Smith, but I'll go armed."

Then, before the Major could answer her, she ran from the hut, mounted her horse and rode swiftly toward the town, urging her lamed mount to his best speed.

"JIM."

The Hottentot, who had left the tent at the first appearance of the girl, came running to the call.

"Yah, *Baas?*"

"What make you of the white woman?"

"In the light of day it is hard to read a woman's face, *Baas.* At night! Ow! It is a task for the spirits."

"She sounded true to me," the Major mused. "Poor little woman! What have ye heard of the white man, Griffin, Jim?"

The Major knew that the natives at the compounds always talked of their bosses, comparing their merits and their failings, and that if you would know a man's true character go to the natives who work for him.

"The blacks at compound say *Baas* Griffin good man. Treat his men —— well. But he's a fool. He know nothing about mines. He look for diamonds in vain. He has no money and has not paid his boys for long time."

"Yet they still work for him?"

"Aye. They say if their *Baas* thinks there's diamonds in mine they'll keep on working so long as they have food. That will not be long."

The Major paced up and down the tent for a few minutes. At each turn, as he passed the big diamond which lay on the table, he paused and looked at it in meditation.

"It is too big," he said at length. Picking it up, he discovered a flaw running right through the center of it. He put the diamond on the camp-table in the tent and opening a large hunting-knife, held the blade firmly along the flaw—the line of cleavage.

The Major then delivered a tremendous blow on the back of the blade with the butt of his revolver and the diamond parted in two almost equal parts.

On each side of one of the pieces he pasted a snapshot of himself and then put it in his pocket. The other he gave to the wondering Jim.

"Thou knowest the mine of the *Baas* Griffin?"

"Aye, *Baas*."

"And it is unguarded?"

"What need to guard? There is naught of value in it."

"Then come with me; we have much work to do ere the rising of the sun."

SO ENGROSSED was Kafir Smith at his task of reckoning up the day's takings that he did not hear the door of his room open and close, but at the click of a key in the lock he turned round with an oath.

A tall, immaculately dressed man, wearing a monocle, came toward him.

"Who the —— are you and what do you want?"

The other laughed.

"Tut tut! That's no way to treat a visitor. I want to have a little chat with you, and this—" he playfully dangled the key of the door between his fingers—"tells me that we are going to have it free from interference. Isn't that rippin'?"

A sudden light dawned on Smith.

"Oh, you're the English dude they call the Major, are you?" he sneered. "Well, this is the way I talk to you!"

He made a lightning grab for the revolver which hung beside his desk.

"No you don't." The voice was curt and crisp. The monocle had dropped from the Major's eye and with it the inane, almost vacant appearance of the Major's face.

Smith's hand dropped to his side. He was too wise to disobey the commands of a man who held a revolver in his hands and was reputed to be a dead shot.

"Well, what is it you want?"

The Major replaced the monocle and sat down in a chair close to Smith, holding the revolver carelessly on his knees.

"That's better," he said. "Now we can have a comfy chat. Nice place you've got here."

He waved one hand airily, indicating the pictures of nude women which covered the walls. "Nice, that is, for a swine like you."

Smith's face turned purple with wrath, but he made no reply.

"You know," said the Major confidentially, "I've got a feeling that I've seen you before somewhere. Now where could it be?"

"How the —— do I know? I don't remember every fool I meet."

"You don't? I do. Now let me see. You're not Spike Dougan by any chance?"

"My name's Smith, you fool."

"Ah, yes. And of course you couldn't be Spike. He died of D.T.s years ago. How silly of me. Wait, I have it. Hold up your left hand."

Reluctantly Smith obeyed. Three fingers were missing.

The Major put his head back and roared with laughter, but the muzzle of the revolver which he held on his knee did not waver from its aim at the pit of Smith's stomach.

"Oh, this is too rich," chortled the Major. "Really it'll be the death of me. I came here to rob, but instead I'm going to blackmail you."

Smith flushed and moved uneasily.

"What do you mean?"

"Fancy meeting you here of all places, dear old Three-Fingered Sam, wanted for forgery, bigamy, jail-breaking and the Lord knows what besides."

At the sound of his old-time nickname Smith turned pale under his tan.

"Not so loud," he implored. "Some one may hear you. You said you came here on business—came to steal. Well, what do you want?"

"The letters written to you by Mrs. Griffin."

"So you're after her, are you?"

"Don't make me angry, Sam, because anger contracts the muscles and that would be very unpleasant for you. This revolver has a light touch and the slightest contraction of the finger would—well, I would hate to be hanged for killing a swine like you. Get the letters."

Smith opened a drawer of his desk and took out a bulky package of letters. Selecting two, he handed them to the Major. The others he was about to put back but the Major held out his hand for them, and Smith grudgingly handed them over.

"I'll see that they are returned to their proper owners, Sam. You ought to thank me for saving you so much trouble."

"Is there anything else you'd like?" Smith's tone was almost meek.

"Why yes, now you mention it, there is. Five thousand pounds, please."

"You'll ruin me, Major," Smith whined.

"Oh, I don't think so. I'm letting you off bally easy, really. Just think. I'd only have to go to the police and say that Kafir Smith is another name for Three-Fingered Sam and even your pull wouldn't save you."

"I know, I know. I'll give you the money. Will my check do?"

"Yes. I fancy you won't dare go back on it. Make it out to A. Harris."

"Didn't know that was your name." Smith had forgotten, if he ever knew, that Aggie, his barmaid, was named Harris.

"The trouble with you, Smith, is that you don't remember the name of every —— fool you meet."

The Major carefully folded the check and put it in his pocket.

"I think that'll be all, Sam, except that young Griffin is a friend of mine. I don't want to hear of his being arrested for I.D.B."

"You won't squeal, will you, Major?"

"No. You're safe as far as I'm concerned. Ta ta!"

Next morning the Major dropped in at Kafir Smith's place before applying for his mining-permit at the registration office. Aggie was talking to some men at the other end of the bar, but when she saw him, she hurried over.

Her face was wreathed in smiles and she hummed a gay little tune.

"You're happy, Miss Harris?"

"I'm going home, Major, I'm going home. Smith sent me a check this morning by the first mail. I've already booked my passage and I'm leaving for Cape Town on the night train."

"Congratulations, I'm sure, and the best of luck."

"Major." Aggie's voice dropped to a whisper. "You've always treated me as if I were a lady, and I'm going to do a thing for you that I've never done before. I'm going to squeal on the boys. Listen; you know Cockney Hawkins?"

The Major nodded.

"Well it seems that he and his bunch have got it in for you. When you were away from your tent last night, they hid some diamonds in your baggage, and one of them followed you and your boy to Griffin's mine, though what you should want there —— only knows. Hawkins went up to the police office this morning and said that he had seen you and the black go to the mine and afterward bury some diamonds in your tent. He said that he turned queen's evidence because you hadn't split fair with him on some other deal. They captured your boy down at one of the compounds about an hour ago, and two of the police have taken him to your camp."

This news staggered the Major. He knew that it would be hopeless to try to face the thing out. His reputation would not stand for it. But it was hard that the blow should come just at the time when he had determined to run straight with the Government.

"You'd better run for it, old dear," Aggie whispered softly. "Come back to England with me. I've got enough money to buy that pub I was speaking of the other day, and—"

He took her hand and pressed it.

"You're a brick, old dear, but I can't do it, really. I must look after my man. Have you some paper and string? A want to wrap up a little present. Oh, yes, and some writing-paper too."

Aggie brought him the things he asked for and the Major swiftly wrote a short note. Then taking from his pocket the diamond on which he had pasted his photo, he wrapped it up, enclosing with it the letter he had written. The package he addressed to the chief of the police.

"Mail this for me, old dear, will you? I've no time to spare."

"All right. Good-by, and the best of luck."

THE REST is better told by extracts from *The Diamond,* the weekly newspaper of the township.

The first is headed "A Big Find at the Griffin Mine," and runs, in part:

"Mr. Griffin's eye was caught by the gleam of a brilliant object midway up the bank of one of his excavations. Climbing up to it, he discovered it was a brilliant crystal. Digging it out, his first thought was that some practical joker had planted a large chunk of glass there for him to find, for it was so large he knew it could not be a diamond. Determined to test the stone on the spot, Griffin rubbed the dirt from one of its faces and soon convinced himself that it was not a lump of glass but a diamond crystal of exceptional whiteness and purity.

"Taking it to the office of the registrar, where it was properly cleaned, Mr. Griffin found to his happy astonishment that it weighed all of three thousand carats; more than three times that of any other diamond that has been discovered. The diamond is a fragment, probably less than half, of a distorted octahedral crystal. Who will be the fortunate miner to discover the other portion?

"Mr. Griffin has sold his mine to a syndicate headed by Kafir Smith, and will sail with his beautiful wife for England some time this week."

Another extract is headed:

"The Major Misses a Fortune, but Gets Away."

"Word having been brought to a member of our efficient police force that a certain notorious I.D.B., commonly called the Major, was seen leaving with his native servant the Griffin mine, steps were at once taken to apprehend him. Added zest was given to the chase when Hawkins, an old confederate of the Major's, turned queen's evidence and stated that he had watched the Major hide some diamonds in his tent.

"Jim, the Major's Hottentot servant, was arrested at one of the compounds and taken by troopers Blake and Sims to the Major's tent, intending to make him show where his *Baas* hid the diamonds.

"Suddenly, while they were cross-examining the native, the tent collapsed on top of them, entangling them in its folds. When they finally extricated themselves it was to find that their prisoner had vanished, their horses galloping back to town; while in the distance, and in the opposite direction, was a cloud of dust which told only too plainly that the Major had escaped the arm of the law once again.

"Colonel Hammond, the chief of police, who is down here on inspection duty, tells us that on the day of the Major's escape he received through the mail a large glass paper-weight, on the top and bottom of which were pasted portraits of the Major. Enclosed with the paper-weight was the following letter, couched in the Major's well-known style:

> Dear and honored Chief:
> I foresee that I am about to take a long journey. Will you therefore accept the enclosed as a memento of,
> > I have the honor to be,
> > > Sir,
> > > > Your Obedient Servant,
> > > > The Major.
> P.S. Some day I shall come back for the paperweight. I hope you will keep it safe for me.

"Colonel Hammond is highly delighted with his present and thinks that for once the Major has overreached himself.

"'We have always wanted a portrait of the Major,' he said, 'and now I have one that will always be before me when I sit at my desk. You may rest assured that when the Major does call for his paper-weight I will give it to him and,' the colonel added with a sly smile, 'perhaps I'll give him something else—who knows?'"

IVORY

"**SO YOU** think you've got evidence to convict the Major?" Trooper Fenwick of the Transvaal Mounted Police, in charge of an out-station near the Portuguese border, made no attempt to conceal the sarcasm in his voice.

His companion, a plain-clothes man from the Johannesburg headquarters, spat his disgust.

"What do I care about evidence? I've suspicions; that's enough for me. If I can't get evidence it's easy enough to manufacture."

"No wonder they call you 'Dirty' Norton," drawled Fenwick.

"What do you mean?" snarled Norton.

"Oh, nothing in particular. But they do call you that, don't they?"

"From what I heard on the way up here you are too bloomin' thick with the Major. First thing you know I'll have you in irons for aiding and abetting."

"Fat chance," laughed Fenwick. "Why, I'd be tickled to death to be able to get the goods on him and arrest him myself. I tried it once," he added reminiscently.

"Yes, and everybody's been laughing at you since," said Norton with vindictiveness.

"Well, from what I've heard he's made a fool of you once or twice."

"Yes, and he's going to pay for that."

"I suppose it's no good asking you to play a sportin' game with the Major? You wouldn't understand. I'll admit that he's broken more laws probably than any other white man in the country. But I doubt if he has any enemies—save you and a few others like you.

"There's not one of us in the 'Mounted' but would give a year's pay if we could only get the Major. But we play fair—we want to get the goods on him. The Major is royal game and is protected from traps and poison."

"Bah! You're all alike when you talk about the Major. I've got orders to get him. He's made laughing-stock of the police force long enough. The papers are calling him the African Robin Hood. Robin Hood, ——!

"But he's got his nerve with him, I'll say that. He camps up here within a mile of a police out-station and buys diamonds from the natives returning to their *kraals* from the mines. Yes, he's doing that right under your nose."

Norton laughed triumphantly as he noticed the look of blank amazement on Fenwick's face.

"And you've proof of that?"

"Yes. Right here."

Norton slapped his pocket, but he did not tell Fenwick that the proof consisted of several diamonds which he intended to "find" on the Major's person, failing to secure legitimate evidence.

"I'll ride out to his place," went on Norton. "It's too hot to walk."

"You'll have to. My horse is lame. Don't you want me along?"

"No. I'll handle this alone. I'll start in half an hour and be back here before sundown. And the Major will be with me—handcuffed."

Neither man had noticed a grizzled Hottentot gossiping idly with the Native Police boys, and who departed unobtrusively at this juncture.

When Norton arrived at the Major's camp he found it abandoned. Pinned to the door was a note:

> Dear old chap (My boy didn't get your name. Is it Dirty?): I'm sorry I could not be at home to greet you, specially after your hot walk. And I'm so curious to know what your proof was. Diamonds? Tut! Tut! You really must be careful. You're under suspicion yourself. That's why they sent you up here after me—to get you out of the way for a while.
>
> Ta-ta. Jim—he's up a tree watching the trail—says he can see you coming over the rise. It's time for us to depart.

The air resounded with Norton's curses as he made his way slowly back to the out-station. Once he stopped to throw a stone at a hyena whose laughter seemed to mock him.

Fenwick regarded him curiously as he drew near.

"Well, you didn't get him."

It was a statement rather than a question. Norton's answer was a stream of curses.

"Come into the hut," said Fenwick. "There's something I want to say to you."

Fenwick seated himself and played with the revolver on the table before him.

"Well?" snapped Norton.

"The mail-boy came while you were away. There's a warrant for your arrest."

"No you don't," he said sharply as Norton reached for his gun. "I've got you covered. Hold out your hands."

Sullenly Norton held out his hands.

"I don't like doing this to a white man," said Fenwick, snapping on the handcuffs. "But I can't take chances."

"What's the charge?" growled Norton.

"Accepting bribes from a diamond-running syndicate. It simply means you'll be broke, I suppose, and that won't worry a man like you any."

All of which simply explains why the Major thought it necessary to make a prolonged stay in Portuguese territory—knowing only of the fact that the order had gone out for his arrest and of how Norton swore viciously that he would one day get even with the Major, whom, by some queer twist of reasoning, he held responsible for the evil that had befallen him.

"FOR WHAT purpose doth the white man desire to dwell among us?" The old head man's tone was truculent. The warriors behind him nodded their approval.

The Major dismounted, and, adjusting his monocle, said:

"As ye see, great chief and warriors, my horse is lame and can go no farther. Far have we traveled, far and fast, since the going down of the sun on the day that was yesterday, until now it sets again. Also the wagon is broken and I needs must make repairs. I am at thy mercy, great chief."

He pointed to the small wagon, drawn by four mules, in which sat Jim, the Hottentot.

"Aye; I see, I see," replied the old fellow, visibly pleased at the Major's broad flattery. "Yet do I not see why thou didst come like a thief in the night to my country."

"I have heard that the lord of the jungle, the elephant, is wont to spoil thy crops, and thou hast no lead for thy guns."

"It is true; it is true. What then?"

"Methought I could assist thee in the killing of the wicked ones. Also I have much lead. But I see that thou dost not need me."

He made as if he would mount and called to Jim:

"We must trek still farther, Jim. The great chief hath no need of us."

"Stay," called the head man. "It was in my mind to pray thee to dwell for a space among us. Yet have I no hut worthy of thy acceptance. Thou hast lead, thou sayest?"

The Major walked to the wagon and took from it a large lump of lead weighing all of twenty pounds. This he held on outstretched palm toward the head man, who, unsuspecting the true weight of it, took it with one hand. But the weight was too much for him and he let it drop to the ground.

The warriors behind him shook visibly with mirth, but the Major gravely picked it up and gave it back to the head man and then put another on top of it.

"It is for thee, great chief," he said.

The head man turned and ran quickly with the precious gift to his hut.

"Outspan, Jim," commanded the Major. "We are going to stay here for a while."

FOR TWO weeks the Major lived at the village of Ugubu. Every day he explored the country round, sometimes with Jim as his only companion, but more often in company with the young warriors of the *kraal*. Game was plentiful and never before had the people of the *kraal* been so abundantly supplied with fresh meat. Because of his hunting-prowess and his knowledge of medicine and ability to pull teeth the Major became a power in the *kraal* and was regarded by all as a miracle-worker.

The evenings he spent gossiping with the head man and the old men, or watching the dances of the young men and maidens.

It was not until he had been with them two weeks and had fully won the confidence of the old head man that he spoke about the elephant-tusks that were built into the stockade that encircled the hut of Ugubu.

"Whence came the tusks, my father?" he asked.

"They were brought here by my father's father."

"He was a great hunter then—as thou art?"

"Nay, he was no hunter. Moreover the tusks were yellow with age, even as thou seest them now, when he brought them to this place."

"And knowest thou not whence they came?"

"It was whispered among the people, white man, that, having sold his snake to the spirits of evil, he was shown the place to which all bull elephants go when their time has come to die. Of the truth of that I know not.

"In the night-time, so said my father, my father's father was wont to leave the *kraal*, not returning until sunup of the next day. And when he returned he brought with him a tusk. He would not say where he had been, and because he was a head man none durst question him.

"One day he did not return, and warriors went out to look for him. But it had rained heavily in the night-time and they could not find his spoor. Without doubt he was carried off by the evil spirits."

NEXT DAY word was brought that a large herd of elephants was moving toward Ugubu's *kraal,* and the Major with Jim, accompanied by several of Ugubu's picked hunters, went down to the corn-patches. The native hunters were armed with heavy muzzle-loading guns, and among them was Umwese, Ugubu's only son.

It had been the custom for ages past for the hunters to await the elephants close by the corn-patches, but the Major demurred.

"If we wait here," he said, "we accomplish no good purpose, for even should we stampede the elephants some would run amuck through the corn, causing great damage. Let us therefore go farther along the way by which they must come."

The Major knew that could they succeed in killing the "bull," the leader of the herd, the rest would undoubtedly be frightened away from that vicinity. Being a true sportsman, he detested the wanton slaughter of the majestic creatures that so often was excused by the bald statement, "They were destroying the crops."

"Thy words are words of wisdom," assented the hunters.

"Then ye will do as I command?"

"Even so."

"It is my order then that ye shoot not the cows nor the young bulls. At the old bulls only shall ye fire, and the big bull, the leader of the herd, ye shall leave to me."

The party went forward, calling softly to each other at intervals that they would not lose track of one another in the dense jungle growth.

After about an hour's trekking Umwese, who was to the right and a little ahead of the Major, gave a grunt of astonishment. He had nearly walked into a young bull which was standing under a big tree, and as the wind was blowing from him showed no knowledge of the presence of a human being.

In his eagerness to get the first kill Umwese forgot all about the white man's instructions and neglected to give the word of warning.

Resting his gun on a convenient branch, he took steady aim and fired.

There was a terrific explosion. Somehow his barrel had become choked up with sand. The gun flew out of his hands, and he was knocked flat on his back. Quickly recovering, he sprang to his feet and saw the elephant, trumpeting with rage, charging at him. Umwese turned and ran swiftly back and toward the Major.

And now it seemed that the forest was alive with elephants charging madly this way and that. The jungle creatures of the night were awakened from their sleep by the loud cries of the natives, the report of guns and shrill trumpetings of pain as a bullet found its mark.

The big bull, the leader of the herd, seemed to rise out of the ground directly in front of the Major and threshed about in savage indecision with his trunk.

Just as the Major was about to fire Umwese came dashing through the undergrowth, hard chased by the angry bull. The Major pivoted quickly and fired. It was a head shot. As if struck by a mighty pole-ax, the big beast swerved in his tracks and toppled over, dead.

"Quick, *Baas*," said Jim. "The big one is going to charge."

The Major took the rifle Jim put into his hands.

"I'm going to try the 'knee halter'," he drawled in English, then fired.

The bull nearly fell as the bullet struck in the knee-joint; then, trumpeting shrilly with pain, he turned in his tracks and limped slowly away.

"Quick; another shot!" exclaimed Jim.

"It is enough."

"Umwese," he said, addressing that crestfallen but grateful hunter, "bid the others to come here."

A long hail quickly summoned them, elated at the success of the hunt; for no less than five bulls had fallen.

"Thy crops are safe. Is it not so?"

"Aye, white man. Yet the big bull still lives. They will come again."

"Not so. His leg is broken. There is naught for him to do but die. No longer can he run with the herd."

"That is true, white man. Yet he still lives, and his tusks are mighty and his hide of great value to us. Let us therefore follow and kill him."

"Not so. I have said he was my meat. Now go ye back to the *kraal* and tell of thy prowess. Bring all the people hither that they may witness with their own eyes what thou hast done.

"And now," said the Major, speaking in English as he was wont to do when alone with Jim, "we'll find out where the old chappie at the *kraal* got his ivory."

"Yah, *Baas*," assented Jim. "But first kill the big bull."

"You're a rum codger, Jim," mused the Major. "You want me to kill the old fellow because he's got a big pair of tusks. I want him to live long enough to show us where there are hundreds of tusks."

"Yah, *Baas!*"

"Now we will follow him, but slowly," as Jim started off on the spoor at a run, "because I don't want to hurry the old fellow."

Though the elephant had had a good thirty minutes' start it did not take them long to catch up with him, so handicapped was he with his crippled knee. And once the trailers caught up with him it was no difficult matter to keep to his trail.

Though at times he was hidden from their sight, lost—giant of the forest though he was—among the thickly leaved trees and creeping vines, his spoor was plain in the soft ground, and always they could hear the crashing of his huge bulk and the snapping of branches which he tore down in his rage.

For a time he followed the trail taken by the fleeing herd, of which he had once been the prideful leader.

Where the trail crossed a small *spruit* he stopped for a while.

He stopped perchance to give his crippled leg a rest, perchance to send a silent farewell to the herd which had forsaken him. Certain it was that his stopping had nothing of indecision in it.

He trumpeted once; then, slowly turning, followed the course of the small stream.

The trail now was hard, leading as it did up-hill, and was strewn with boulders. Here he had much ado to keep his footing, hampered as he was by the broken leg which he trailed painfully on the ground. At first he essayed to make his way easier by removing with his trunk some of the smaller boulders. But evidently the process was too slow, and he soon gave it up.

At a shallow pool in a hollow of some rocks he filled his trunk with water and squirted it on his wounded leg. This seemed to revive him and he went on for a while at a faster gait, so that the two men had to break into a run in order to keep up with him.

He now left the course of the *spruit,* which skirted—as they now saw—the base of a rocky hill, and picked his way among the big boulders. He headed directly up the gently sloping sides of the hill toward the top, which was fringed with a queer rock formation. Sheer up from the ground stood the reef, some thirty feet in height, forming a solid, impassable barrier.

RESTING OCCASIONALLY—FOR the big fellow was weakening—he made straight for the rock, and when but a hundred yards from it broke into a ludicrous attempt at a charge.

"Well, I'm jiggered," said the Major as he breathlessly seated himself on a boulder. "Have I come all this way just to see the bally blighter commit hara-kiri by dashing his bloomin' brains out on a rock?" He bent down to loosen his legging and was occupied with a balky buckle when a shout of amazement from Jim made him quickly look up.

The elephant had vanished.

"Where did he go, Jim?"

"I don't know, *Baas.* Straight to the rock he went and it opened and swallowed him up. Let us go; this is a place of evil."

"Nonsense, Jim. He must have doubled on his tracks somewhere—or perhaps he's down behind a big boulder."

"Ikona, *Baas!* With my own eyes I saw it. To the rock he went and then I saw him no more. Not once have my eyes left the place he entered."

And indeed Jim's eyes stared fixedly ahead of him, hypnotized by fear of the unknown.

"Deuced funny," quoth the Major. "Come, Jim. Let's go and look at this rock that swallows elephants alive."

Jim refused to budge and the Major, knowing the folly of trying to argue with a superstitious native, walked alone up to the rock.

He followed closely the path taken by the elephant; then at the place where it had spurred up its courage to a game attempt of a charge he stopped short. He walked a little way to the left; back again; then to the right; back again; and stopped.

"Come here, Jim," he shouted gleefully.

"Nay, *Baas*. It is a place of evil."

"Thou speakest folly," he cried in the vernacular. "Come here."

Jim tremblingly obeyed. Great as was his fear of the spirits, his fear of the Major's wrath was even greater. When the Major commanded in that tone Jim, spirits or no spirits, obeyed.

"Look, Jim. What do you see?"

The Major pointed to the rock. Jim looked fearfully as if expecting to see the souls of the Wicked One awaiting him. But seeing to what the Major pointed he grinned foolishly.

"It is an opening in the rock, *Baas.*"

"Yes. It's the opening that swallowed up the elephant, and this is the only place from which it is visible. Come on."

The Major was excited, and as he ran to the opening he shouted like a boy released from school.

On reaching the cleft in the rock he sobered down.

"Bai Jove! It's a decidedly spooky feelin'. Just think, Jim, we're the only living mortals who've been here."

"Yah, *Baas*," agreed Jim.

"It must have been a tight fit for the old fellow," said the Major as he and Jim passed into the cleft.

This they now saw was a deep ravine, as if the rock had been split by an earthquake. Though the entrance to it was, as the Major said, narrow, it at once widened and was all of twelve feet in width. The sides of the ravine, however, converged as they neared the top, and in some places actually touched.

Turning and twisting as the ravine did, they did not come in full view of the elephant—though at times they heard his shrill trumpeting—until half an hour later, when they emerged, as Jim put it, "from the belly of the earth."

Then they saw the bull leaning against a big rock, his breath coming and going in big choking gasps.

But their attention was held elsewhere. Before them, a sheer drop of twenty feet or more, was a small valley enclosed on all sides by the queer rock formation; a valley devoid of vegetation save round the edges where grew luxuriant vines and here and there, like sentinels, giant baobab-trees.

All was deadly calm. No living thing seemed to have its habitation there, and scattered on the ground in endless profusion were the skeletons of elephants—hundreds of them.

"They've been coming here to die," mused the Major, "since the birth of the world. It's majestic."

He doffed his helmet, as one in the presence of honored dead.

"Watch the bull, *Baas*," whispered Jim.

The big fellow was slowly collecting his strength. Gradually he righted his big bulk until finally, disregarding the torture to his wounded leg, he stood on all four feet.

Then began the dance of the elephant, that monotonous lifting of the feet and the swaying of the big body.

Perhaps he saw the ghosts of his ancestors rise before him; heard their trumpeting of welcome; for suddenly he stopped the dance and sounded the shrill call proclaiming the lordship of the elephant. Still trumpeting, he lunged madly forward to the edge of the cliff, then out and down on to the rocks below, where the Major could see him rolling over and over with the impetus of his fall.

The Major took his rifle.

"It seems like sacrilege to do it and I fancy the old chap would rather await his end patiently, as his fathers did before him. But—"

A shot rang out and then all was still.

IT WAS long past sundown when the Major and Jim returned to the *kraal* of Ugubu. Their advent was heralded by glad shouts, and a number of young warriors surrounded the Major and escorted him in triumph to the guest hut.

After he had bathed and changed into a suit of white duck he strolled down to the hut of the chief to partake of the feast that had been prepared in his honor.

Ugubu with ill-concealed impatience waited until the Major had finished his meal before questioning him as to the happenings of the day. For it is not courteous, look you, to hold speech with a guest until he has eaten.

"Thou art a man," he said when the Major could eat no more and contentedly rolled himself a cigarette.

The Major, making no reply, lighted his cigarette with a brand from the fire.

"Aye. Thou art a man and a hunter."

"Thy young men are hunters also."

"But one, my son—it is to my shame I say it—played the part of a fool."

"He is yet young; he will learn. But he is a man."

"How sayest thou?"

"Having done foolishly, yet made he no attempt to hide his folly from thee. Yet none knew of his folly."

"Save thee?"

"Aye. I knew, but would not have told."

"And will not tell?"

"Nay. To what purpose?"

"Then can my son's folly be kept secret, for to none other hath he spoken. I have said thou wast a man. I thank thee." Ugubu spoke with simple dignity.

"It was but a small matter."

"Not so, white man. Thou hast preserved mine honor; that is no light thing. Also thou didst save my son from death."

"Thy son meant much, then, to thee?"

"He is my only son, and as yet no man child calls him father. Had he died this day my name would have passed out of the memory of this people. But say now how I reward thee."

The Major leaned forward.

"Hark thou, Ugubu. Rememberest thou that time thou didst tell me the story of the elephants' place of death?"

Ugubu nodded his assent.

"I have found that place."

"Is this how I can repay thee—by listening to tales of folly?" said Ugubu whimsically.

"It is no folly. I speak a true thing."

"What then?"

It is characteristic of the race that Ugubu showed no signs of undue interest.

"On the morrow I go with Jim to Lourenço Marques, the place of the white men, to make a bargain for the tusks that are at the place of the elephants' death. When I come again, or should I send that black one there—" he pointed to where Jim sat with the other hunters, roasting big chunks of elephant meat—"wilt thou give order to thy young men to do all that I command, that the ivory may be taken to the place of barter? It will mean great wealth for thee—guns, powder and lead in abundance."

"All shall be as thou desirest, white man. It is but a small thing thou askest."

"It is well, Ugubu. Tomorrow I and the black one go, as I have said, to the place of the white men. Ere the passing of another moon I will return."

TEN DAYS later the Major entered the office of Nathan Abraham, "Dealer in Ivory, Loans, etc.," with a bland smile on his round, clean-shaven face.

Dressed in a suit of immaculate white duck, eyeglass firmly in place, he looked just what he pretended to be—the foolish son of a wealthy English family sent to Africa to acquire wisdom.

Abraham looked up at his visitor with no show of interest. Such men did not ordinarily have dealing with him save when their remittance was overdue. Then they came to negotiate a loan, and if the interest was exorbitant—well, as Nathan put it, "business is business."

He motioned the Major to a seat and watched him as he peered aimlessly round the room.

"My name is Aubrey St. John," he pronounced it Sinjun—said the Major by way of introduction.

Nathan bowed his acknowledgement.

"Top-hole place you have here, old chappie," continued the Major.

"Quite up to the minute, what? Typewriter and all that bally rot."

Nathan nodded patiently. They were all alike at the first visit. Talked about anything rather than the loan for which they had come.

"Say, old chappie, I'm in a deuce of a fix."

Nathan beamed. His visitor was running true to type.

"I've got a chance to make a bally lot of money, but I don't quite know how to go about it."

"There are a lot of us like that," assented Nathan. "I suppose you want me to loan you some money until you find out 'how to go about it.' Well, if your securities are all right I'll——"

"Oh, no. Really now, old top. Nothing like that," interposed the Major with a show of confusion. "No, really. I want some advice on a real business deal."

"Business deal? You?" Nathan laughed.

The Major looked peeved.

"That's always the way. People always laugh at me when I talk about business. They must take me for a bally fool."

"Well—" Nathan made no attempt to conceal his mirth—"I'd hardly say that. But what's your scheme?"

"Scheme? Oh, yes; you mean, how I mean to make a lot of money. I knew you'd help me. They told me at the hotel you were the best business man in town. Of course I might have gone to some of the other dealers, but I don't speak Portuguese."

The Major tiptoed to the door, opened it cautiously; then, shutting it, came back and drawing his chair up closer to Nathan, said in a whisper—

"You're a dealer in ivory, aren't you?"

"Yes; what of it?"

"Hush! Not so loud. I know where I can get lots of it."

"If you think you are going out to shoot a lot of elephants like they did in the old days, you are on the wrong track. Elephants are protected game nowadays."

"Oh, I'm not going to shoot them. I wouldn't know how. Always was frightened at guns ever since my brother lit a firework under me one Guy Fawkes Day."

"Then what are you going to do? Hypnotize them while you saw off their tusks?"

"Oh, now you're spoofin'," expostulated the Major. "I'll tell you what I'm going to do. Have you ever heard that when elephants are getting old they all go to the same place to die? A sort of old elephants' home?"

Nathan nodded wearily. He had heard the legend many times. What African ivory-trader has not?

"Well, I'm going to find it."

"Yes? And what do you want me to do? Advance you money to outfit your expedition? Because I won't."

"There you go again, talking about loans. I've already got my outfit ready."

"Then what *do* you want?"

"I want you to buy the ivory, old chap. What good will it do me unless I can sell it?"

"Well, I'll buy all you find."

"Do you really mean it? How much will you give me for each tusk?"

"We don't buy ivory that way," Nathan chuckled, "but by the pound."

"Really! Then how much a pound?"

Nathan reached for the local paper and made a pretense of looking up the latest ivory quotations.

"Ten shillings a pound," he said.

"Good," said the Major. "It's a bargain."

He rose to go, hesitated, and slowly reseated himself.

"Well?" said Nathan impatiently.

He wanted to get rid of his visitor and tell the story to his boon companions at a near-by saloon. The joke was too good to keep.

"Well?"

"I hope you won't misunderstand me, old chap, but I do want to be business-like. Won't you put that offer in writing?"

Nathan crossed to the typewriter, and, picking out the letters with one finger, wrote for a few minutes.

Taking the paper from the machine, he handed it to the Major, who, screwing his eyeglass more firmly into place, read:

> I, Nathan Abraham, contract to buy from bearer at ten shillings a pound all the ivory that may come into his possession.
>
> (Signed) NATHAN ABRAHAM.

"Thanks, old top," drawled the Major. "This is going to make me rich."

AS THE door closed on his visitor Nathan threw himself back in his chair and laughed long and loudly. He was still chuckling when a few minutes later Dirty Norton burst into the room.

Since being cashiered from the police force as Fenwick had predicted, Norton had deemed it wise to leave the Transvaal before other charges could be brought against him. Now more than ever did his appearance and conduct warrant the nickname Dirty, so unkempt was his dress, his mode of living so questionable. Possessed of a certain low cunning, he had been useful to Nathan in many unsavory episodes—fraudulent schemes for separating newcomers to the colony from their money.

"What was the Major doing in here?" he asked abruptly.

"The Major? Oh, you mean that fool who just went out. He—he's—" Nathan spluttered in his mirth—"got a scheme for getting rich quick."

"Yes, he would have. What is it?"

"He's going to find where all the good elephants die, and I've given him a contract to buy all the ivory he finds. Ten shillings a pound I offered him. Oh, these fool Englishmen will be the death of me."

"You gave him a contract, did you, and at ten shillings?" exploded Dirty. "Then he's fooled you as he's fooled all of us, —— him!"

"What do you mean?"

"Why, he's the slimmest thing in pants that you ever ran up against. If he talked ivory you can gamble your soul that he's got it. He's no fool for all his soft ways, his cursed drawl and his pink, manicured nails. He's wise, I tell you; he's wise."

Nathan looked anxious, then, remembering his late visitor's appearance, quickly recovered with a chuckle.

"What are you trying to frighten me for, Dirty? He's just a monocled Johnny."

"Yes, and he's the same monocled Johnny that's played merry —— with every police force in this country. I've been up against him before, and I know. He's got the goods all right."

"And I contracted to buy ivory from him at ten shillings a pound and the highest it's ever gone is ten shillings and sixpence. I'm a ruined man," wailed Nathan.

"What did you want to give him that price for?"

"How did I know who he was? He looked and acted like a —— fool. I thought I was safe and only did it for a joke."

"Well, the joke's on you,"

"I'll repudiate the contract."

"Fat chance you'd have. He'd go to court and you don't want to get your face known there. You've fleeced too many of the officials. There's a better way. I've got an old grudge to settle against the ——, and now I'm going to settle up with him. Have you got anybody you can trust, and knows his way about the country a bit?"

"How about Smithy?"

"No. The Major knows him."

Nathan thought deeply.

"Hawkins then? I've got him under my thumb. He tried to raise one of my checks."

"Fine. Send him with a note to the Major. Write it now; I'll tell you what to say."

Slowly Nathan typed at Norton's dictation:

> Dear Sir:
> In order to protect my interests and as evidence—should the Portuguese authorities raise any question—that you did not shoot the elephants, I must ask you to take the bearer, Thomas Hawkins, along with you on your trip.
> I have the honor to be, sir,
> Your obedient servant,
Nathan Abraham.

"What then?" questioned Nathan.

"Hawkins will find out where the ivory is, or whatever the Major's little game happens to be. As soon as he finds out he'll invent some excuse for leaving the Major and report to me. I'll be a day or two's trek behind them. I'll take care of the Major afterward. White men die violently in this —— of a country and no questions are asked."

WELL PLEASED with himself—having extracted from Nathan a promise to pay a higher rate than he had dared hope for the ivory—the Major walked jauntily to the hotel.

Outside the building that served as a hotel Jim accosted him.

"*Baas,* the man from whom we ran is here."

"You mean the policeman, Norton?"

"Yah, *Baas.* Nigger boys down at the compound say he no more a policeman."

"Well, well," said the Major thoughtfully.

"You'll be careful, *Baas?*"

"Yes, I'll be careful, Jim. Bring the horses round early tomorrow. We'll be on our way to Ugubu's *kraal* before sunup."

In the hotel lobby a man stepped up to the Major. His clothes were faultless, but he wore them with the air of one who finds himself clad in unaccustomed raiment.

In marked contrast to his white linen were the marks of moral filth which gleamed in his eyes. He looked like an unrepentant prodigal who after years of living with the swine had suddenly acquired wealth.

"Are you Mr. St. John?"

The Major nodded.

"Mr. Abraham asked me to give you this."

The Major read the proffered note.

"Bah Jove, I'm glad to know you, Mr. Hawkins. And you're going with me? That's top hole. I was just thinking how deuced lonely the trip 'u'd be. Have you had tiffin yet? No? Then let's go and eat."

After dinner they went out on to the wide porch to enjoy the cool breeze. A bottle of whisky stood on the low table between their chairs, and from it the Major poured out for himself a stiff drink.

By the time the bottle was empty the plant at the Major's right hand, and away from Hawkins, was plentifully "watered."

"It's a 'str'ordi'ary thing," he hiccuped presently, "but I've forgot the name of the shappie who sent you."

"Nort—Nathan Abraham," answered Hawkins, whose senses were momentarily dulled.

The slip was a slight one, but the Major noted it with satisfaction.

"Oh, yes. Stupid of me."

He began to laugh softly.

"Pardon me for seemin' rude, but the fact is I worked old Nathan splendidly."

The Major leaned forward confidentially.

"You know I got him to sign a contract to buy some ivory. And he signed it because he thought I'd never get any, and the joke of it is I know where it is all the time. We'll start tomorrow."

When the Major retired a little later Hawkins lost no time in carrying the news to Norton and Nathan.

"What did I tell you?" Norton said triumphantly.

"Watch him closely, Hawkins," begged Nathan. "I'm a ruined man if you let him get away from you."

Norton went over the details of the plan with Hawkins; then, first drinking to the Major's confusion, Hawkins went back to the hotel that he might be ready to leave with the Major in the morning.

He had not thought it necessary to tell Norton of the slip he had made.

Early-riser though the Major was, he found Jim and Hawkins awaiting him. Waving a gay good morning, he mounted his horse and cantered slowly up the street with Hawkins but a pace behind him. Jim, also mounted, brought up the rear with the pack-mules at a more sober pace.

As they passed the building which Abraham used as an office, a window-shade was pushed slightly to one side and Nathan and Norton peered out at them.

"Well, things are going our way," said Nathan, rubbing his hands.

"Yes, —— him. I'll get him this time."

ONCE WELL out of the town, the Major pulled up his horse and waited for Hawkins to catch up with him.

"So you've really found the elephants' dying-ground?" Hawkins questioned.

"How did you know that? Have you been talking with my boy?" said the Major angrily.

"Why, no. Don't you remember telling me so last night, and what a joke it was on Nathan?"

"Did I tell you that? Then I must have been drunk. But it doesn't matter; I've got old Nathan's contract. He can't go back on that."

"Yes, I've found it. The only drawback is that it is also the burial-place of a native chief who was a big pot in his day. We'll have to go slow for fear of offending the niggers."

"Is it near here?"

"We ought to make it in eight or nine days."

"It's strange it hasn't been discovered before."

"Oh, it's off the beaten track a ways. Very few of the natives know of it, and they're sworn to secrecy on pain of death and all that. I stumbled upon it by accident. It's a gruesome place." The Major shivered.

At the first opportunity Hawkins questioned Jim.

"Is it true that your *Baas* has found where the elephants go to die?"

"Yah. I have seen the place. It is a place of evil. The spirit of a dead chief watches over it."

"And there are many tusks there?"

"Yah. Many tusks. The ground is strewn with them like the sand on the river-bed."

On the seventh day the Major sent Jim on ahead.

"The place is near here," he explained to Hawkins. "I have sent Jim to get the porters I engaged for the job on my last trip. We will wait here until he returns with them."

That day passed very slowly, and the next morning Hawkins could no longer conceal his impatience.

"Let us go to the place," he suggested. "We could locate the best tusks and save that much time when the porters arrive."

"That's a good idea," said the Major, pulling on a pair of rubber hip-boots. "Too bad you haven't a pair of these. You'll need them."

The Major led the way directly into the heart of the jungle. The going was hard and Hawkins, ill-conditioned as he was, had a hard task to keep up with the swift pace set by him. Striking a small *spruit,* the Major followed its course for about half an hour when suddenly the jungle opened out into a swampy clearing and directly in front of them lay a large tract of heavily wooded jungle—a sort of island in a swampy sea.

"Come on," said the Major. "That's the place over there."

Then, seeing that Hawkins hesitated as the mire came over his ankles:

"Don't he afraid, old chap. That's as deep as it gets anywhere save for one or two holes that I'll try to avoid."

With no liking for the thing Hawkins gingerly followed closely in the Major's footsteps.

"This swamp goes all round the island—the Isle of the Dead I call it, but perhaps you don't know the picture—like a moat. This is the narrowest place across."

Once across the narrow swamp Hawkins was anxious to take the lead.

"Where now?"

"Straight ahead through those two big trees; they—"

Hawkins did not wait to hear further, but darted eagerly forward, the Major following at a slower pace.

Suddenly Hawkins gave a yell of fear, and turning, ran back as fast as he could. Behind him, yelling fiercely, raced a party of savages brandishing ugly-looking spears. Some had guns which they fired as they ran.

The Major turned and ran, but the big boots impeded his progress and Hawkins swiftly caught up with him.

"I'm hit," gasped the Major. "Help me, Hawkins."

Hawkins gave one look at his blood-soaked shirt, then sped on with increased speed.

The Major stumbled after him a few paces, then fell to the ground, his big shoulders heaving convulsively.

Paying him no heed the warriors swept on after the fleeing Hawkins, crying:

"Death to the defilers of the grave of a chief. Kill, kill!"

At the edge of the swamp the warriors stopped and contented themselves with shaking their spears at Hawkins, who with never a backward glance was soon lost to sight in the thickness of the jungle beyond.

IT WAS a weary and frightened Hawkins who crept into Norton's camp several days later and told his story.

"You are sure the —— is dead?" Norton asked.

"If he wasn't killed then they finished him off afterward. The devils meant business, I tell you."

"Well, he's out of the way. That makes it easier for us. You're sure you can find the place again?"

"Yes. But you are not going there now, are you?" Hawkins' voice was panic-stricken.

"No, you —— fool. I'm going back to get a crowd together that will know how to handle the niggers. It'll mean a smaller share for us, but at that there ought to be a fortune in it. Thousands of tusks, the nigger said, didn't he? Think of it, man, and brace up."

THREE WEEKS later Norton and Hawkins, accompanied by ten men of their kidney, all heavily armed, crossed over the swampy moat to the "Isle of the Dead." Getting their footing on the "island," they scouted carefully about, rifles at the ready.

Nothing stirred, and save for the droning of mosquitoes and the harsh scream of a "go-away" bird nothing broke the unnatural silence. The island seemed devoid of life.

"Come on," shouted Norton. "There's nothing here to be afraid of."

But the others still hung back.

"Bah! I'll show you," sneered Norton, and he went forward alone while the others watched, their rifles ready.

He made for an opening in the thick jungle growth and saw right in his path a small piece of flannel tied on a stick. At the foot of the stick was a small canvas bag.

With a feeling of foreboding he stooped and opened the bag. In it was a note. It read:

> Dear Dirty:
> (I think you're at the bottom of this, though I may be mistaken.) There's no fun spoofin' you, you are such a gullible idiot. As for Hawkins, oh he's impossible and has a yellow streak too. You should have seen him run when Jim—you ought to know Jim—led the savages to the attack. It was simply priceless! But don't be too hard on him. I was bleedin' frightfully—a few crystals of permanganate of potash and a wet handkerchief make an awful lot of blood.
> Soon—perhaps while you are reading this—I shall be collecting on my first delivery of ivory to our mutual friend Nathan. Won't he be surprized to see me! And he won't dare to refuse payment, for I shall take the Commissioner of Police with me. He's a friend of mine, and has no liking for Nathan.
> I can't tell you how sorry I am not to be able to see you. Really.
> I have the honor to be, sir,
> (Do you recognize the style?)
> Your obedient servant,
THE MAJOR.

In the bush nearby a tiny tree-hyrax screamed in derision.

AMNESIA

THE MAJOR whistled gaily as he strode down one of the less frequented streets of Lourenço Marques, that sleeping seaport of East Africa. Undoubtedly things were going well with him; he had just collected on a second delivery of elephants' tusks to Nathan Abraham a sum that made that avaricious individual whine for sympathy.

"Let me off, won't you?" Nathan had begged. "Giving you this high price for ivory will ruin me. Lower the price a shilling a pound and I'll come out even. That contract is not a fair one. You tricked me into giving it to you."

"Oh, be a sport," the Major had answered. "You would have tricked me if you had been able to. And don't forget that you planned with 'Dirty' Norton to kill me— Oh, don't try to deny it; there's a good fellow. It was not his fault that he failed. You must pay for your pleasures, old top, and attempted murder comes high. A check for the full amount, please."

And Nathan had no option but to comply.

Yes, the Major had good reason to be happy. He had already cleared about fifty thousand dollars on his lucky discovery of the "Place of the Elephants' Death." He chuckled gleefully as he thought of how he had outwitted Dirty Norton, a disgraced police official from the Transvaal, who had endeavored to discover his secret, planning to kill the Major afterward to square an imagined wrong.

The fifty thousand and the money he would receive from a deal he had just concluded with the Portuguese officials made it possible for him to—

He became conscious of a voice—a woman's voice—calling him to stop.

He turned round and waited for the owner of the voice to catch up with him.

She was young and attractively yet simply dressed. Her figure was slim, almost boyish.

The Major swept off his sun helmet and made her a profound bow.

"Oh, please forgive me," she gasped breathlessly, "for hailing you, but—you're the Major, aren't you?"

The Major screwed his eyeglass firmly into place, and his round, smooth-shaven face wore an almost vacuous expression.

"I'm afraid you're mistaken, madam. My name is Aubrey St. John, but upon my word if this Major chappie is a friend of yours I'd like to change places with the lucky beggar."

She made a little gesture of dissent.

"Please!" she said supplicatingly. "I know you are the Major—they pointed you out to me and said you'd help me. And I do so need help."

"Madam," said the Major, "when a charming lady like you is in need of assistance I'll be the Major or whosoever you please."

She clasped her hands tightly together.

"Then they were right? You will help me?"

"I'm yours to command, my dear lady. But who told you that I could help you?"

"The Major's reputation for chivalry is admitted by every one," she said shyly, then went on hurriedly:

"It's about my brother. He's been gambling and drinking a great deal; he's breaking mother's heart."

There was the sound of tears in her voice.

"He's gotten in with a bad crowd, and a horrible beast of a man named Norton seems to have a hold over him."

"What is your brother's name!"

"Hawkins—Jim Hawkins. I am Nan Hawkins."

The Mayor gave a little grunt of astonishment.

"And he's your brother?" he said incredulously.

The Major was thinking of the time Hawkins had left him, wounded, to the mercy of a band of savage warriors. At least Hawkins had thought him wounded, and the warriors savage!

"Do you know him?" the girl cried.

"Well, I've met him and—er—yes, I think I may say I know him."

"Don't condemn him too quickly," she pleaded, "He's always been

spoiled—and I know he's selfish. But he's good at the bottom and if we could only get him away from this man Norton's influence he would be all right, I'm sure."

The Major looked closely at the girl; noted her sweet face and the big gray eyes welling with tears.

"Where is your brother now?" he asked curtly.

"At Norton's place back of the hotel. I've just been down there trying to persuade him to come home. But he was drunk. They were all drunk, and Norton—he—"

She started to cry quietly.

"Don't try."

The Major patted her hand awkwardly.

"I'll get him for you and take him to my room to sober up. Afterward we can talk the thing over quietly together."

"Oh, thank you, thank you. I knew you would find a way."

She raised his hand to her lips.

"That's all right," he said with a show of embarrassment.

"Now dry your pretty eyes and run along home. It's getting late, and little girls shouldn't be out alone down this quarter of the town."

He watched her until she disappeared around a corner and then hastened down the street that ran at the rear of the hotel.

Outside the door of a rough wooden shack he paused and listened. Snatches of drunken brawling and obscene songs sounded clearly on the night air. Peering through a chink in the door, he could see Norton, Hawkins and one other whom he did not know sprawled in drunken postures around a rickety table on which stood several whisky-bottles. Even as he watched Hawkins drank greedily from one of the bottles.

That decided it. Whatever doubts the Major may have had of the truth of the girl's story vanished. Shifting his revolver from the holster that swung at his hip to his coat pocket, he knocked at the door.

There was no response save a louder outburst of song and the voice of Hawkins vociferously clamoring for another drink.

He knocked again.

"Come in, blast you," a voice thick with liquor shouted. "Come in and shut the —— door behind you."

The Major opened the door and entered.

THE MAJOR was floating on a cloud of pearly pink; visions of light flashed swiftly by him; ages passed. Then the cloud suddenly dissolved from under him and he fell down, down into a dark and troubled sea.

"He's coming to," a voice said; and it sounded strangely distant. "Give him another douse."

A wave broke over him. He spluttered and gasped as if fighting hard for breath, then slowly opened his eyes and gazed vacantly about him.

His head throbbed violently. Something warm trickled down his face. He put his hand up and when he took it down it was red and sticky with blood.

He looked wonderingly at the men who stood before him.

"I say, what happened? Was there an accident, or what? How did I come here? I don't seem to remember."

His face wore a troubled look.

One of the men laughed.

"Listen to the ducky, Dirty. 'E don't know where 'e are. Tell 'im."

"Here, take a drink of this."

Norton poured out a stiff peg of whisky and handed it to the Major.

He drank and with the drinking gained strength.

He essayed to rise to his feet, to discover that he was bound securely to a heavy chair, only his hands being free.

"Why am I tied like this?" he asked indignantly. "You can't do this sort of thing, you know. It isn't done."

The men were convulsed with merriment.

"Isn't 'e the love, though?"

Norton scowled.

"You think you're —— clever, don't you, Major? But I've got ahead of you this time. You never suspected the girl at all, did you? Why should you? She was all open and aboveboard.

"She told you the true story—she's a deep one, Nan is. Hawkins is her brother, and he's drunk—the fool always is—and I've got a hold over him. She told you that and you walked into the trap with your eyes open.

"Only you didn't see Joe here—" he indicated the scrubby little cockney—"get behind the door with a billy, ready to knock you out as you entered. He's pretty strong, Joe is, for all he's so small. We thought for a while he had knocked you out for good."

The Major did not answer, but gazed fixedly before him.

"Well, why don't you say something? You are fond enough of writing letters."

"I don't know what you are talking about."

The words came slowly, as if he were not sure of himself.

"Why do you keep me here? Let me go."

Norton sneered.

"Oh! So you don't know what I'm talking about. You'll be saying next that you don't know me, Major."

"I don't know you. Never saw you before in my life. And why do you call me Major? My name is—"

He stopped and looked around appealingly.

"What is my name?"

"Don't try to be funny. I know who you are, and you know me. What's more, before you leave here you're going to tell me where the ivory is. See?"

"I don't know what you are talking about."

Norton hit him viciously in the face with his clenched fist and laughed in derision as the Major flinched.

"Bring in the nigger," he said.

Two of them went into an inner room and a moment later came out dragging a prostrate form.

It was Jim, the Major's Hottentot servant—his comrade on many a wild venture.

"Take that gag out of his mouth so the black can speak."

"I suppose you don't know who this is," scoffed Norton.

"I've never seen him before in my life," said the Major blankly, "and

I'm quite sure he doesn't know me."

Norton looked nonplussed for a moment. He had been watching the Major closely since Jim's entrance, but had failed to see anything in the Major's behavior that would indicate in acquaintance with the native.

He laughed shortly.

"Well, I guess we can soon find a way to open your mouth," he said. "You're supposed to be sort of fond of this nigger. Well, we'll see. Get the *sjambok*, Joe."

Joe took down from the wall a vicious-looking whip.

"Where does your *Baas* get the ivory?"

"I don't know."

The rawhide whip came down on Jim's naked back with a sickening thud.

"Where does your *Baas* get the ivory?"

Jim maintained a dogged silence.

Again the whip fell.

"What do you think of it, Major?" sneered Norton. "We are going to keep this up until you or him tells. We don't care which.

"Afterward— Well, there, won't be any afterward for you. I've been waiting a long time to even up scores with you, and I've got you this time. No questions are asked in this town if a man happens to be found with his throat cut."

Again came the torture of the question and the whip, and Jim moaned with pain.

A light of anger shone in the Major's eyes.

"Stop it, you beasts."

"Ah! I thought this 'ud bring you to your senses. Well, will you tell us where the ivory is?"

"I tell you I can't know."

"Did you hear that, nigger? Your *Baas* 'ud rather see you beaten than tell where the ivory is. You won't get anything from him. Tell us and we'll let you go and give you plenty of whisky besides."

"I know nothing, *Baas*," replied Jim.

"Give him a few lashes to go on with, Joe," ordered Norton.

BEFORE THE order could be obeyed the door was suddenly opened and the girl Nan rushed breathlessly into the room.

All looked at her for some explanation.

"You'll have to get out of here, Norton," she cried.

They crowded around her.

"What for, Nan? What's the game?"

"The police officials are after you."

Norton made a gesture of contempt.

"That's not all," went on Nan. "You might get away from the Portuguese police, but there's a man here from the Transvaal. He's got an extradition warrant for your arrest."

Norton cursed.

"I wouldn't lose any time, if I were you."

"Yus. She's right, Dirty. Better light hout w'ile the goin's good. We'll take care of the Major fer yer."

"Yes. You can trust us," supplemented Hawkins.

Norton turned on them with a snarl.

"Like —— I can. If I go, you go with me. Inspan the mules, Cockney; and you, Hawkins, get some grub together."

"Where are you going, Dirty?"

"To Cenambo's *kraal*—over the border."

Hawkins looked horrified.

"Cenambo's!" he cried. "Why—"

"Oh, there's nothing to be afraid of. Cenambo's an old friend of mine. Now get busy; we ought to be on trek in half an hour."

The two men hastened to do his bidding. "What are you going to do with the Major?" Nan asked.

Norton pulled out his revolver and looked at it suggestively.

"Don't be a fool, Dirty. If you kill him here they'd get you sure as fate. As it is they are not liable to chase after you. Besides, you would lose all chance of getting the ivory, for if you killed the Major you'd have to kill the Hottentot too. Take them both with you. You ought to find a way of opening their mouths when you get to Cenambo's."

"You're right, Nan. I'll do that. Are you coming with us?"

"Not me. The wild and woolly doesn't appeal to me. Ta-ta!"

With a flounce of her skirt Nan ran from the shack.

EIGHT DAYS later a trek wagon drawn by eight mules pulled up near by the *kraal* of Cenambo.

It was at once surrounded by a horde of savage-looking warriors armed with large, business-like spears.

"What make ye here, white men?" asked one who seemed to be in authority.

"Thou art not Cenambo," said Norton.

"I am Cenambo's mouthpiece."

"Then run and bid Cenambo to come hither. Say that I come bearing gifts."

"Other men have brought gifts to the chief, yet went they humbly on foot to him—not he to them."

Norton turned to Hawkins and Cockney Joe, who were listening with ill-concealed fear to the conversation.

"I am going up to the chief's hut," he said. "You stay here and—"

There was a movement among the warriors as they made way for a newcomer.

"It is the chief. Hail to thee, Cenambo," they cried.

A fat, gross man approached the wagon. He waddled in his gait like a duck, yet his carriage had somewhat of a kingly dignity—or rather that of an autocrat who would brook no denial. His evil, vicious eyes peered constantly from side to side, and the man upon whom they momentarily rested shrank back as if he would efface himself from their basilisk glare.

"What make ye here?" His voice was harsh.

"It is I," called out Norton. "Thy friend, Uglubu."

"Oh, 'tis thou, O pig. Come ye to another feasting? Or desire ye to be a sacrifice?"

"The chief jests," said Norton somewhat hurriedly. "Yet listen. I have brought thee many presents—guns and powder. Also— But first say, O mighty one, is this how thou greetest thy friends? Is it by thine order that this one should threaten me with death?"

Norton pointed to the big warrior.

Cenambo looked fiercely at the now shrinking man.

"Art eager for death?" he said mildly. "If so there are many hungry bellies yonder."

He made a gesture toward the river which flowed at the foot of the hill.

The warrior fell to his knees and patted the feet of the chief.

"Nay, O great one! How was I to know that this one was thy friend?"

"Then get from my sight ere I forget that I am merciful."

Cenambo turned once again to Norton.

"Thou wilt stay with us for a while? Good. The guest hut is waiting for thee, and for these others so be they are thy friends."

Quickly the wagon was unloaded of its contents, which were carried by natives to the guest hut, save certain gifts of guns and powder which Norton gave to the chief.

Only once did Cenambo show any interest in the proceedings. That was when the Major and Jim, both tightly bound, were lowered from the wagon.

"These are not friends of thine?" he said hopefully.

"Nay, O chief. Let them be closely guarded, I pray thee."

"Death is a good guardian."

"Aye. But it is also a stopper-up of tongues. First I would hear them speak certain things; then—"

Norton shrugged his shoulders.

"That is well."

Cenambo rubbed his hands gleefully.

"I have discovered many ways whereby a man can be made to speak the truth. But not yet have I tried any on a white man. It will afford good sport."

"Tomorrow is another day, great chief, and we are hungry."

"Ah, sayest thou? Then go ye to the guest hut—thou knowest the way. Food will be brought you, and when ye have eaten I will talk again with thee. These black ones—" he indicated certain of the warriors with a contemptuous wave of his hand—"will do thy bidding in all things."

With that Cenambo, escorted by his body-guard, departed to his hut.

Norton turned gleefully to Hawkins and Cockney Joe, who were looking at him with a certain new-born admiration.

"What did I tell you?" he cried triumphantly.

"You've got 'im sittin' 'up on 'is legs and beggin' like a bloomin' dorg," chortled Cockney Joe.

"Y-e-s!" assented Hawkins. "But I'm afraid of him."

"You would be," Norton sneered.

"Hi! You!" he continued, addressing the warriors. "Take this dog—" he kicked the prostrate Major—"to one of the huts and there guard him well. Ye may loosen his bonds and give him food and drink, but see ye that he comes not near to this other dog."

He spat on Jim.

"The black one, also, shall ye guard closely."

"It is an order, white man."

The warriors picked up the two men and carried them away.

Shortly afterward they threw the Major violently down in a filthy, vermin-infested hut. There they released him from the ropes which were cutting into his flesh.

"In a little while food will be brought to thee," said the warrior. "In the mean time see that thou dost not seek to leave this place. Death awaits thee outside."

LEFT TO himself, the Major gazed around the hut with lack-luster eyes. He was weary, body and soul, and the slightest move was torture to his cramped limbs. He had been tightly bound during the whole trip from Lourenço Marques; only at the brief mid-halts had they given him a chance to exercise a little.

Blows had been frequent, for he persisted in his statements that he did not know Norton or what was meant by the talk of ivory. This attitude had puzzled Norton and the other two, leading to much altercation between them, Norton accusing Cockney Joe of having "knocked all the sense out of the blighter" and then having great difficulty in restraining the cockney from giving the Major another "bat hon the bleedin''ead to knock the sense back again."

He was still somewhat dazed from the heavy blow Cockney Joe had dealt him, yet under normal circumstances it was a blow he should have quickly recovered from.

But to be fed only the minimum of food required to keep in life; to be deprived of water; refused the chance to exercise; and to be trussed up like a fowl for days together—riding on the floor of a springless wagon driven at full speed over the rough veldt land—are not conducive to a quick recovery.

The white duck suit which he wore at the time of his abduction was spattered with blood and filth. His face was drawn and haggard-looking; his eyes were bloodshot and staring.

There was nothing in his appearance to suggest that he was Aubrey St. John, the dandy, and still less to indicate that he was the Major—a man whose wit, gallantry and clever evasions of the law were the talk of the Dark Continent. He looked instead like a man brutally debased;

a man from whom all power of reason and intelligence had fled.

Norton had carefully seen to it that he had held no conversation with Jim the Hottentot, to whom they had allowed a certain amount of liberty—his services being valuable at such times they made camp. But this precaution was unnecessary, for at such times that Jim had artfully contrived to get near to the Major the latter had turned a deaf ear to his speech and showed no signs of recognition—a fact which worried the loyal native exceedingly.

Now the Major ate greedily of the food that a native shortly brought him and then slept soundly; nor did he awaken until long after sunup tie following day.

FEELING A little stronger in body, the Major looked up indignantly when Hawkins entered the hut accompanied by four natives armed with *assegais*.

"You're to come with us, Major."

He raised his eyebrows.

"Really? How interesting. And to what purpose?"

Hawkins shifted uneasily.

"Look here, Major," he said. "Why don't you cut out this fooling? Norton's bound to find out where you got the ivory from. Why don't you tell him and let us get away from this rotten hole? I don't half like it."

He gazed round apprehensively at the four warriors.

"I tell you I don't know what you are talking about" said the Major dully.

"Don't be a fool, Major," pleaded Hawkins. "That black devil Cenambo has been telling us of some of his favorite modes of torture. It made me sick. You can't expect me to stand by and watch a white man tortured by a nigger. Besides—"

The Major made no response.

"Well, you can't blame me. I've warned you. Come on or they'll be sending after us."

Hawkins gave a brief order to the natives, who picked up the Major and carried him bodily to the hut of the chief.

"He is a proper man," said Cenambo to Norton, rubbing his hands gleefully. "It would well please me to deal with him according to my will, yet because ye are my guests things shall be as ye order."

"We thank thee, O powerful one," answered Norton. "We seek not to take from thee thy pleasure. Only do we seek to question him, and if he will not speak we look to thee to open his mouth."

"Ah! That is well said."

"Well, Major? Are you going to tell us where you found the ivory?" asked Norton.

"I tell you I don't know anything about it. How many times must I say that?" answered the Major wearily. "By Jove, you chappies really try me too far. I shall report this matter to the—"

"Stow ye gab," growled Cockney. "What's the good o' torkin' to 'im lady-like, Dirty? Let the chief 'ere 'ave a go at the blighter."

"All right. Remember, Major, you've only got yourself to thank for what happens.

"His mouth is closed, O chief. Use thy wisdom."

"That's good."

Cenambo almost purred his approval. He leaned forward on his stool and placed his hands on his fat thighs.

"Heed well, white man, enemy of my friend. It is a thing abhorrent to me that I should cause pain to such a man as thou art. Yet what wouldst thou? Certain things must be told and thou art silent."

He sighed heavily as one contemplating a hated task.

"There have been other men who refused to speak when I, the chief, commanded them to open their mouths. An evil spirit bade them keep silent even as one commands thee so to do. What then? The evil one must be banished.

"One man, I well remember, was possessed of a stubborn spirit, and it was only by tearing off the nails from his fingers—seven we removed—that we released the evil one. A red-hot spear slowly, very slowly lest we cause pain, run through the fat of the belly has oft opened a closed mouth. Yet with thee methinks that would not do, for thou art not fat—as I am. Or again the cutting off of a man's eyelids hath ofttimes let light into a darkened mind, so that the in-flicted one could see where before he was blind.

"Ah, there are many ways, and I would try them all, for it is well greatly to honor a white man. But first we will try yet another way—see how merciful I am! A fire shall be lighted on thy belly. Only a little fire and of damp wood so that the pain will be small. Water we will keep close by to quench the fire at such time the wicked spirit leaves thee.

"Fasten him down, my children," Cenambo ordered, and the natives quickly carried out his bidding, tying the Major to stakes driven into the ground.

Cenambo closely examined the ropes.

"Are they too tight for thee?" he asked solicitously. "My children are perhaps overzealous.

"Loose these a little, ye black ones. It is better that he should be able to move a little. It is my chief delight," he went on as if in explanation, "to see into what contortions the evil one will cause the body of a man to twist as the fire bites.

"Now the wood, my children. Place it carefully and see that the pieces are small; we would not make the fire too hot—at first."

"Dirty!" gasped Hawkins. "You won't let the —— do that? ——, man—you can't."

His face was white with terror.

"Don't be a fool," said Norton angrily. "Do you want to be treated the same way? Watch out; the chief's looking at you."

Hawkins gave a little jump of dismay as Cenambo came up behind him and placed a hand on his shoulder.

"All is ready, O white man, friend of my friend—if that thou art. Thou shalt light the fire. See how I honor thee."

He put the burning brand in Hawkins' hand.

Hawkins looked appealingly at Norton.

"I can't do it, Dirty. Tell him I can't do it."

"He says he can't do it," Norton explained to Cenambo. "His stomach turns to water at the thought. Give the brand to me; he is a chicken-heart."

Norton spat contemptuously.

"Nay. I will do it myself."

CENAMBO WALKED to where the Major was fastened, and, stooping with difficulty because of his fatness, applied the lighted brand to the twigs.

A thin wreath of smoke floated upward and Cenambo, gazing at the white man's face, gloated as the Major flinched at the bite of the fire; the next moment Cenambo dashed the water from one of the guards on the fire, quenching it.

Norton looked at Cockney Joe in amazement, and Hawkins, heaving a sigh of relief, wiped the beads of perspiration from his face.

"This is a mighty man," said Cenambo in explanation. "Not thus shall we cause the evil spirits that bind his tongue to depart from him.

"Bring in the black dog. First we will deal with him, letting this one see somewhat of the pain of things."

In response to his order men brought Jim the Hottentot to the enclosure. He struggled in sullen silence with his guards as they staked him out on the ground. Despair was in his eyes, yet he made no plea for mercy.

"Untie the white man," said Cenambo, "that he may gaze upon his servant's happiness."

Again the order was quickly obeyed and the Major was held between two of the guards so that he could clearly see what was taking place.

Soon all was ready, the wood properly placed on Jim's heaving chest. Cenambo approached him with the lighted brand.

At that moment the Major caught Jim's glance. It held a mute appeal for mercy, a look of terror, and a lively knowledge of the torture before him.

The sweat rolled down the Major's face and a thick haze floated before his eyes. Something seemed to snap in his head.

"Wait!" he cried.

Cenambo looked at him disgustedly.

"Thou art made of poorer stuff than I first thought," he said.

"Well, Major," exulted Norton, "do you remember now?"

"Yes. I remember everything now, Dirty."

He passed his hand wonderingly across his brow.

"Then tell us where you got the ivory."

"If I tell you"—the words came slowly as if he were not sure of himself—"what do I gain? Will you let us go?"

Norton grinned.

"At least you won't be tortured."

"You can promise that?"

"I'll give you my word of honor."

"Thanks," drawled the Major, "but I don't care to take it. What sayest thou, O Cenambo? If I tell these white men are we spared the torture—I and this black one?"

"Aye. I have other things in store for thee. Yet am I grieved that thou didst speak so quickly."

"Jim!" the Major called out. "You have my leave to speak fully concerning the Place of the Elephants' Death."

"Yah, *Baas*," responded Jim. "Yet would I not have spoken."

"Take him away from here," said Norton.

"You and Hawkins go with him, Cockney, and get his story. I'll question the Major here; afterward we can compare notes. If they have lied—well, we can try the fire again."

After they had left with Jim, Norton turned to the Major.

"Now, you, draw a map of the place."

By means of diagrams the Major quickly gave Norton the directions to reach the Place of the Elephants' Death—that mysterious valley where the bull elephants go to die.

"It is but a four-hour trek from the village of Ugubu, you say?"

"That is all."

Again and again Norton made the Major go over the directions, noting carefully that the accounts always tallied. Finally he was satisfied, and at that time Hawkins and Cockney Joe returned with Jim.

Norton compared the directions the Major had given him with those of Jim. They were the same save for one or two minor differences.

Norton slapped Cockney Joe on the back in triumph.

"We've got it," he shouted exultantly. "We can get out of here today."

"But how about the Major and the nigger?" asked Hawkins.

"Leave 'em here for the chief, of course."

"'Arf a mo', Dirty," said Cockney. "Suppose when we get to this place we find the —— have lied to hus, we'd be in a —— of a mess, with the Major and the nigger dead. Let's ask the chief to keep 'em for hus until we find out whether they've given us the straight goods."

"You're right, Cockney. Now, O chief, it may be that these men have lied. We start today for the place whereof they have told us that we may learn whether they have said a true thing or no. Wilt thou then keep them safe until our return?"

"Ye try my patience sorely," grumbled Cenambo. "The spirits of the river are hungry."

"It will be but for a little while," pleaded Norton. "It is but a four-day trek to the place whereof they told us. In nine days—but nine days—we will return."

"In nine days it will be the full of the moon, a proper time for the sacrifice," mused the chief. "Yet it grieves me to wait that long."

"More powder and guns, will we bring thee," urged Norton.

"Aye; but perchance ye will not return. What then?"

Norton conversed hurriedly with Hawkins and Cockney; then, overriding Hawkins' expostulations, he said—

"This one"—indicating Hawkins—"will stay here with thee as a surety of our return."

"All then shall be as ye desire, white men. This man shall be my guest—my honored guest—until the full of the moon."

Two hours later Norton and Cockney Joe drove hastily away from the *kraal* of Cenambo.

"Hare yer comin' back fer that blighter, 'Awkins?" asked Cockney as they quickly left the village behind them.

"——, no," said Norton shortly. "We'll divide his share between us. Who cares what happens to him?"

THE FOLLOWING morning an old woman brought the Major his food. Old in sorrow, not in years. Her face was sadly scarred; in her eyes shone a fire of hate that years of suffering had failed to quench.

She watched the Major curiously as he ate.

"Thou art hungry, white man?"

"As thou seest, O maiden of incomparable beauty."

She laughed sardonically.

"Thou art blind, belike?"

"Perchance. Thy beauty hath dazzled me."

She rocked back and forth in her mirth.

"And this is the village of Cenambo?"

"Thou hast said."

"That same one who is Lord of the Crocodiles?"

"Even he. Thou hast heard of him?"

Again she laughed.

He pushed the empty platter away from him wearily.

"Who hath not heard of that dread lord of life and death? Thou art a slave of his?"

Her answer surprized him.

"Nay. No slave am I. Once was I his head wife, but now am I less than his dog. Yet still am I his wife."

Her voice was pregnant with hate; her eyes blazed fiercely. Then, the mood changing, she began to laugh again.

"But what is that, to thee?" she chuckled. "Thou art fated to be a sacrifice to the spirits of the river. Sleep well—eat well; so shalt thou become proper food for the cold, crawling ones of the river."

With that she left the hut, nor did the Major see any one until she returned after sundown with his evening meal.

"Thou art indeed hungry," she said in amazement as the fowl she had brought him quickly disappeared.

"Aye. This past seven days food has been all but a forgotten thing with me. And at no time have I eaten a chicken like unto this one. Thou didst cook it?"

"Even so," she replied, apparently well pleased.

"With such an one as thou to prepare the food, it is small wonder that Cenambo the chief is fat."

"If I cooked for him the fat would roll away from him like the mist before the rising sun; his belly would tie itself into knots in protest."

"Sayest thou so? Then must the lord of life and death be a hard man to please."

"'Tis not that he fears the food I prepared for him would be ill cooked; rather that he fears the sauce with which I might garnish it."

The Major drank deeply of the gourd of beer she had brought him before answering.

"Cenambo fears thee, and thou art alive!"

"Aye. I am alive, for it is fated that his death shall follow mine in but a little space."

"Strange are the ways of the spirits," the Major commented. "Yet this does not explain why thou, O woman of honey sweetness, who was once the head wife of the dread lord, should now be less than his dog. There is a tale to be told?"

"Aye, there is a tale to be told. But what art thou? Methought a man, but thy tongue wags like an old wife's."

She spoke with a show of impatience.

"A man I am in very truth, but the wonder of thy beauty hath gone to my head like old beer. Can I then control my tongue?"

She rose with dignity.

"Time was, white man, when thy words would not have been words of jesting. Many men in other days looked on me—Inyoni—and found me favorable in their eyes."

"I am well chidden, mother," the Major said gently. "Yet I spake not altogether in jest. Sweetness is not in the form alone. Consider the wild orange—a thing of no beauty, yet is its meat of a sweetness beyond compare."

Inyoni chuckled gleefully.

"Words are thy soldiers, white man, and thou dost lead them skillfully to the attack. But not thus canst thou charm the spirits of the river. Their ears will be deaf to thy pleas; their teeth will cut short thy arguments. Nay"—she placed her claw-like hand soothingly on the Major's arm—"be not overly distressed in spirit. The death is an easy one if thou strugglest not."

And with such scant words of cheer she left him.

DURING THE succeeding days the Major was given a certain freedom. He was permitted to take exercise—always with a strong guard in attendance—and gradually his strength came back to his cramped muscles.

Jim he rarely saw, and then only at a distance that made speech impossible. Still he tried to convey to the faithful Hottentot that all would yet be well, though he himself was far from feeling that assurance.

His efforts to inveigle his guards into conversation were unavailing. Apparently they had been forbidden to hold speech with him.

Only once did one of them speak to him.

It was on the sixth day, and they had walked down to the river. It was near sundown and all the people of the *kraal* were lined up on the bank. Just as the sun's last rays struck the smoothly flowing waters Cenambo appeared, carrying a small goat in his hands. He stood for a moment motionless as if offering up a prayer, then heaved the struggling animal far out into the water. A giant crocodile which had been lying inert on a sand-bank made a rush for its prey and then vanished into the depths of the pool.

"Seest thou?" said the Major's guard. "The big one of the pool is hungry. In but a little while he will be well fed—thou art somewhat larger than the goat."

That same night Cenambo visited the Major.

"Are my people taking good care of thee, O white man? It would grieve me sorely if ye lacked anything."

"I am well content save for one thing. The woman, Inyoni, where is she? I have not seen her for these four days. Of a truth none can prepare the meat of a chicken like unto her."

Cenambo scowled.

"She hath gone on a journey. With tomorrow's sun she will return."

"Then am I well pleased. Yet say, O chief, art thou altogether wise in thy dealings with me? Hast no fear of the vengeance of the white man?"

"Why should I fear, O white man? Who is there to say that thou didst come to this place? Who to tell of the manner of thy death? Nay, I have no fear; and as thou didst see this day the spirit of the river is hungry."

He rose to go, but at the door of the hut he halted a moment and said—

"Yet can I find it in my heart to wish that other—he who is called Hawkins—were in thy place and thou in his."

One other visitor the Major had that night. It was Hawkins. He entered stealthily soon after the chief's departure.

The Major looked at him curiously. He had not seen the man since the day of the torture, and was surprised to note his haggard appearance. Hawkins' eyes were bloodshot and his hair was unkempt, and he continually looked behind him with a half-furtive look.

"Come to gloat, Hawkins?" asked the Major.

"No; not that, Major." He laid his hand on the Major's arm.

"But I'm afraid."

"You've good cause to be," said the Major curtly.

"Why, what do you mean? Do you know anything?"

"I told the truth about the ivory. They'll find it all right; but do you think they'll come back for you? Hardly."

"That's just what I've been thinking," said Hawkins despairingly. "And if they don't come back, what's going to happen to me?"

"Well, you know what's going to happen to me."

Hawkins nodded.

"I know. Cenambo keeps telling me what a nice meal you'll be for the crocs. Then he looks to me and grins—you know how he does."

The Major nodded his comprehension.

"Yes. I'm afraid you're booked for the same fate as Jim and myself unless— Why don't you clear out?"

"Where would I go?"

"They don't watch you, do they?"

"No. But I'm afraid to go alone. I don't know this country."

The Major looked at him with contemptuous pity.

"Afraid to go and afraid to stay, eh?"

"Why don't you try to make a break for it, Major?"

"Don't be a fool, Hawkins. How many guards are there around this hut? An even dozen. Fat chance I've got, haven't I?"

Hawkins rose despondently to his feet.

"Ta-ta, old man, if you must go," said the Major. "Call around tomorrow."

Next morning, to the Major's joy, it was the woman Inyoni who brought his food.

"Greetings, O Inyoni," he said. "What said the witch-doctor to thee?"

She looked at him in amazement.

He laughed.

"Nay, think not that I am in league with the evil ones. Thou hast been away on a long journey; today thou didst return; and thou wearest a new charm."

"Truly thine eyes are sharp, thy wit keen. Dost know anything else?"

"Mayhap," he said carelessly, "Cenambo was here last night."

"So?"

"Of a truth. Methinks he was greatly angered with thee."

"I felt the weight of his anger this morning. Behold."

She slipped the goatskin off her shoulders. Big angry stripes showed where a *sjambok* had bitten deeply.

"Au-a." The Major was all pity.

"It is nothing," she said, and replaced the goatskin. "The pain is nothing when I think of the vengeance to come. Mine uncle the witch-doctor even now makes ready for it. It was to that end I went on my journey, bringing him back to this *kraal* and to his hut."

"Thou meanest the hut that is next to Cenambo's?"

"Nay, foolish one, but to the left of the fence as thou enterest the *kraal*."

"When comes the time for thy vengeance?"

"After thou—together with the other white man and the black one, thy dog—have been sacrificed to the spirit of the pool is the time appointed. It irketh me that ye will not be alive to see the greatness of my vengeance."

"May the spirits bring thee comfort."

He yawned lazily.

"The time passeth slowly, O most worthy of women. Hast not a tale to tell?"

She hesitated a moment.

"Aye. I will tell thee a tale. Thou mayest have wondered—as many men have wondered—how Cenambo came to be chief of this *kraal*, for his father was but a common man, a tender of herds, and at no time was Cenambo a mighty warrior or a cunning hunter.

"Thus befell it:

"One day the young men were watering the cattle at the river—aye, and maidens were there too, for it was ever the meeting-place of lovers—when suddenly there was a swirl in the waters, and a crocodile rushed forth and toward the young men. Some fell before him in their eagerness to flee; these the crocodile heeded not, but made straight for Cenambo, who stood as if he were a carven stone. Him the crocodile seized and took back with him to the pool, and when we looked again he was no more seen, and we fled in terror from the place.

"The next morning as the men-folk went down to the pool, intending to kill the evil one, suddenly the form of Cenambo was seen as if rising out of the belly of the earth. The people trembled in fear, thinking him an evil spirit. Cenambo opened his mouth and spoke to us.

" 'Look well upon me, O ye people,' he cried, 'and give praise to the spirit of the river. As ye see I am alive and unhurt, yet did ye see me taken but yesterday by the crocodile. But he was no crocodile but a form of the Spirit of the Great Great. Ah! Many things did he whisper to me.

" 'I say unto thee,' Cenambo cried, 'that I am thy chief. So was it ordained by the Spirit.'

"And so after much cunning talk, white man, Cenambo became chief—for how should the people refuse one who had spoken with the Spirit of the Great Great? My father, my brothers—aye, all of the kin of the old chief, my father—he caused to be thrown to the crocodiles. Only Marko my uncle did he spare, for Marko was—aye, and still is—a mighty witch-doctor, and Cenambo feared him. Me, he married, first killing my betrothed before me.

"So the story is told, white man. It is a pity thou canst not see the end."

"Aye. I grieve for that, too. But thou hast not told all. Think'st thou that thou canst have a vengeance on one who is so regarded by the spirits that they deliver him from the jaws of a crocodile? 'Tis not a good deed to spoil the tale."

The woman laughed softly.

"Thou art like a child crying for more. Listen and I will tell thee."

She leaned forward and whispered in the Major's ear.

"It is a story well told," the Major said when she had finished. "Now wilt thou bid the other white man to come hither?"

"Thou wilt not tell him what I have told thee?"

"Nay. And will not speak of it until after the night of the full moon."

She cackled with laughter.

"Thou art a great jester, white man. Thou wilt say nothing after the night of the full moon."

"HAWKINS," SAID the Major, "I'm going to make a break for it tonight. I'm sick of this bally hole."

"How?"

The Major looked at him keenly.

"I'm not going to tell you that, old dear. That's my little secret. You'll pardon me if I say that I don't quite trust you?"

Hawkins flushed.

"I haven't given you much cause to, have I? But why tell me any-thing?"

"Oh, it isn't that I don't trust you; you're in the same boat as I am," said the Major airily. "Besides, no one can stop me if they don't know how I'm going to do it. But how about you? Are you going to stay, and be food for the crocs?"

Hawkins was panic-stricken.

"Of course you won't," continued the Major. "Pack all the am-munition you can about you and announce you're going out shooting. Don't take any food—it might make 'em suspicious. You'll have your gun and revolver, of course. Think you can make your way to the last camp we made on the way up here? It was near a large baobab tree, I think."

Hawkins nodded.

"Well, stick close by that. If I don't get there before sunup you'd better go on, or come back here. That'll be up to you. The camp's only about six hours from here. You ought to make it easy before sundown."

"But won't they follow?"

"Maybe. But I think not; they'll have other things to think of. Tomorrow's the night of the full moon, you know. Give me that knife."

The Major pointed to a large hunting-knife which hung at Hawkins' belt. "Thanks. Have you got a spare revolver? Good. Then see if you can get it to Jim. Tell him he's to do nothing, no matter what he hears about me. Now good-by, and good luck."

It was not until late in the afternoon that the Major asked his guard for permission to take exercise.

"I would go down to the pool," he said, "for a cooling wind always blows there."

When they came to the bank of the river he sat on a rock watching the men-folk watering cattle and the maidens getting the water for the evening meal at a part of the river which had been fenced off and was thus secure from the attacks of crocodiles.

Beyond, on the sand-bar in the center of the river, were several crocodiles, but the big one was not among them.

"Where is the father of crocodiles?" the Major asked. The guards laughed and one answered:

"He is a crafty one. See where he watches close by the fence that guards the watering-place?"

The Major, following the pointing finger, saw the monster floating idly on the surface of the water, watching with unblinking eyes the noisy scene before him.

"Why does he wait there?"

"One time a young heifer rushed headlong into the poles, knocking them down and so out into the open river. The big one was on the sand-bar, and though he was swift the heifer was turned safely shoreward and he was beaten off. That was many moons ago, but the big one always watches where he is now at the time of the watering."

The Major was silent for a while and surveyed the scene before him. Then as if I continuing a conversation, he said—

"And so thou wast present when Cenambo, the dread lord of life and death, was taken by the Spirit of the Pool?"

"Aye. I saw it all, white man."

"And again when he returned?"

"Aye."

"The place where he first appeared to the people is near here, thou sayest?"

"But a spear's throw."

He pointed to a thick clump of bushes about twenty yards from where they were sitting and about ten feet back from the water.

"Is it permitted to go to that place?"

"Nay. None have gone near it since that time. It is a place sacred to the spirits, and death is the portion of any who venture near. The chief hath so ordered."

The Major rose and paced nervously up and down the bank of the river. One of the guard rose as if to accompany him but was pulled back by the others.

"Let be, let be," they said. "What harm can he do?"

And so they watched him, sleepily, for the sun was hot and they had drunk much beer.

Up and down the Major paced, each time lengthening the distance just a little before turning. Gradually he drew nearer to the clump of bushes, and when but a few yards from them he halted and began to sing loudly, thus drawing the attention of all the people to him. With angry curses the guards rushed at him with spears uplifted, for he had approached too closely to the forbidden place.

The Major ceased his song and stood gazing for an instant at the onrushing warriors. Then with a cry of fear he ran swiftly to the river-bank. On the very brink he stumbled and fell headlong into the river.

At the sound of the splash the crocodiles on the sandbank slipped noiselessly into the water and made toward him.

He called despairingly for help, then suddenly vanished under the water and was seen no more.

THAT NIGHT two silent forms came to the hut where Jim the Hottentot was held prisoner.

Their heads were completely hidden by the hideous masks worn by the witch-doctors at the time of "wonder-working," and their bodies painted with weird designs.

"Who are ye? What make ye here?"

The guard's voice held a note of fear.

"Hast a desire to look upon the face of Marko and see death?" said the smaller of the twain.

"Nay, O mighty one. Yet forgive me. I do but obey the chief's command."

"And I obey the command of the Great Spirit. I go to prepare the black one for tomorrow's sacrifice, lest he too be taken before the appointed time. Perchance thou wouldst like me to go hence. Have ye forgotten the punishment of those foolish ones who permitted the white man to escape from them?"

"Nay, O Marko. Enter and make thy magic. The cries of those others are still ringing in my ears. Of a truth the chief was greatly angered."

The guard lowered his spear.

"But this other. Him I know not."

"He is a stranger to thee, but a mighty man, one well thought of by the spirits. He will tread in my path when I have gone to the Land of the Great Great. Now must I dally further with thee?"

"Nay, O mighty one."

The two masked figures entered the hut.

But a short time elapsed ere they emerged again.

The guard came toward them wonderingly.

"Have ye so soon made your preparations, great ones?"

"Aye. Now listen well," answered the taller of the twain. "It is our order that none enter this hut until the appointed time for the sacrifice. If any desire to become jackals that howl in the night, let them disobey. See; I place this as a sign to all that this hut is a forbidden place."

He took from his neck a necklace of snakes' fangs and human teeth.

"When the last rays of tomorrow's sun strike this—and not till then—may ye enter."

With that the two figures vanished into the shadows of the night.

"It is a strange thing," mused the guard, "that Marko held no speech with me after the wonder-working, and it seemed to me that he was somewhat smaller. Without doubt something went from him as he was communing with the spirits. Who shall question the ways of the great ones?"

WHEN HAWKINS, at the camp by the baobab tree, awoke the next morning it was to find Jim the Hottentot sitting by the fire cooking some food.

He rubbed his eyes wonderingly and was about to spring excitedly to his feet, but Jim motioned him to keep quiet and pointed to where the Major was sleeping peacefully.

"Let the *Baas* sleep a while," Jim whispered. "He hath need of rest."

Hawkins rose silently and came over to the fire, for the air was chill.

"How came ye here?"

Jim laughed softly.

"The whole story I do not know, white man. The *Baas* will tell you in his own time. This only do I know. But yesterday, before the setting of the sun, the *Baas* leaped into the river and was taken by the crocodiles."

"Then how—"

Jim made a gesture of impatience.

"It happened as I am telling you. He leaped into the river and was seen no more. Of a surety he was taken. Yet listen to the wonder of it. Last night I was awakened by the voice of my *Baas* calling softly to me as in a dream. Opening my eyes, I saw him standing beside me, and he wore the dress of a witch-doctor. Another was with him—even Marko; the witch-doctor of Cenambo's *kraal*.

"On my head they placed the mask of Marko. Then my *Baas* said—

" 'Now suffer us to bind thee, O Marko, that none may accuse thee of aiding us.'

" 'It is well said,' answered Marko. 'Stop up my mouth also.'

"So we bound him and put a gag in his mouth. Then we twain, the *Baas* and I, left the hut and came to this place. None questioned us; for was I not Marko the witch-doctor, and the *Baas* my disciple?

"But see, the *Baas* wakes."

"Mornin', Hawkins. Scoff ready, Jim?"

"In a little while, *Baas*."

"How did you do it, Major?" asked Hawkins. "Jim's been telling me what little he knows. Did you really jump into the river?"

"Aye, tell us, *Baas,*" pleaded Jim.

The Major sat down on a log by the fire.

"Yes," he drawled. "I did exactly that. You've heard the story of how Cenambo became chief?"

Hawkins nodded.

"Well, Inyoni, the woman who brought me my food, used to be his head wife, and she got his secret from him a long time ago when he was drunk.

"It seems that after the croc seized him it carried him under the water and half-drowned him. When the blighter returned to consciousness he found himself in a cavern under the bank but just above the water-line. Leading from the cavern, back from the river, was a sort of tunnel.

"He wormed his way along this until he came to a place where the light filtered through, made an opening large enough for him to crawl through, and so appeared to the people as if he were rising out of the ground. The hole was hidden by a clump of bushes, and no one has been allowed to go near there from that day to this.

"Well, I decided to try the same stunt. It was a long chance, for the cavern might have closed up, or the crocs might have got me before I found it. Still I had a good idea where it was, and if I failed—well, I was only anticipatin' the end by one day.

"Luck was with me. I found the entrance to the cavern the first time I dived, entered it and wormed my way up the tunnel just as the big croc came. *Faugh!* How the beast did stink.

"The rest was easy. I waited there until long after sunset, and then made my way to the hut of Marko. Thanks to the suddenness of my approach—and your hunting-knife, Hawkins—I had no difficulty in persuading him to help me get Jim. Besides he's got a grudge against the chief that he's going to pay off tonight. I gave him a few suggestions for that. And that's all."

"Scoff's ready, *Baas.*"

The Major commenced eating leisurely.

"But what are we going to do now?" said Hawkins. "We've got no food and—"

"You're eating now, man, aren't you?"

"Yes. But we've got a three days' trek before us before we get out of Cenambo's country."

The Major turned to Jim.

"Where did you get this food, Jim?"

"I hid it when we camped here on the way up, *Baas*—at every camp I hid some."

The Major looked at Jim in admiration.

"Jim," he cried, "you're simply priceless! Eh, Hawkins?"

"Yes. But how about you, Major? Supposin' Norton and Cockney Joe do come back. Aren't they liable to get you?"

The Major sobered for a moment, then burst out laughing.

" 'Pon my word, I'm the most forgetful chappie! I forgot to tell them that I had sold my claim to the ivory to the Portuguese authorities. I completed the deal the very day Cockney knocked me on the head. They won't come back."

He fumbled in his breast pocket.

"Confound it," he said in tones of annoyance, "I've broken my bally eyeglass."

A DEAL IN DIAMONDS

WANTED FOR I.D.B.

FIVE THOUSAND POUNDS REWARD for information leading to the arrest of the man generally known as "the Major." Has many aliases. Last seen heading toward Portuguese Territory by way of Barberton.

On the posted reward notice there followed a brief but succinct description of the Major: "well-built man, about six feet in height, and weighing close to two hundred pounds. Fair complexion; light hair; gray eyes. Always immaculately dressed; wears a monocle, and speaks with a pronounced drawl."

Tales of the Major's activities in his chosen field were legion. As far as the reward went, even the police were prone to remark "first catch your Major." There was the time, for instance, when one police officer had attempted to trap him into buying a diamond. The Major had bought the diamond and got away, but the police officer had himself been arrested for illegally offering a diamond for sale! Yet the police themselves regarded him with some compassion as a good sport and a political offender rather than a criminal—the diamond monopoly laws were pretty stiff. Not but what it wouldn't be a feather in the cap of any trooper who brought in so notorious a character.

SO, JIM, the Hottentot, waited, and watched unceasingly.

Hungry, shivering with the ague of fever born of exposure to the torrential rains, still he ignored the obvious way of alleviating his sufferings.

He had but to cross the river and seek service with the white men who had farms bordering along the river. That he would be successful in obtaining work goes without saying. There were few natives who understood cattle better than he; mules and Jim seemed to speak a common language, and the most waspish of those obstreperous animals would become as gentle as a lamb before the magic of Jim's voice.

And Jim was not a fugitive from justice; there was no price on his head. He could cross the river and enter British territory at any time, immune from arrest, though undoubtedly the police would like him to open his mouth and tell what he knew of the machinations of his *Baas*. And they would pay well for the information, as witness their reward notice.

Yet, Jim chose to be an exile.

The Portuguese side of the river was destitute of inhabitants, black or white, and the only indication that man had passed that way was the winding, dusty road which led to the port, hundreds of miles away.

Even so, Jim took no chances.

In the daytime he kept well back from the bank of the river. He lighted no fire, fearing that it would attract unwelcome attention; would result in a close watch being kept over the ford, thus making it harder for his *Baas* to cross in safety.

His food consisted of wild honey, berries, and herbs—barely enough to keep in life. Biltong—the dried buck meat—of which he had a slender supply, he did not touch. His *Baas* would be hungry when he did arrive.

Jim had selected for his camp a small circular clearing in the thick bush not far from the edge of the precipitous bank of the river. At no time was he out of sight and hearing of the ford, some two hundred yards below his hiding place.

Sometimes in the darkness of the night he would awake from sleep disturbed by a splashing in the river, the beating of hoofs on the road—only to find that a "river horse," a hippopotamus, was disporting himself, or a lone buck was galloping down to the river hoping to find shelter from the pursuing wild dogs.

Jim was in constant fear that his *Baas* would cross the ford and go on his way unobserved by him; for once in his life Jim had disobeyed orders.

Fifteen days had elapsed since the Hottentot had last seen his *Baas*. It was just outside Barberton, seven days' trek from the border, with the police hot on their trail, that they had parted company.

"It is best, Jim," his *Baas* had said, "that we go our separate ways. Two spoors are harder to follow than one and this is the end. Take

thou the wagon, with all that it contains, and one horse. It is my gift to thee, for thou hast ever been faithful."

"For that there is no need of reward," Jim grunted. "Let me go with thee, *Baas.*"

"Nay. Go to thy own people."

"I have no people, *Baas.* That thou knowest. I will come with thee."

Then his *Baas* had been very angry.

"Dog! Thou wilt obey my order. Alone, I can go swiftly. Thou art but a stumbling block in my way."

Jim had made a gesture of resignation.

"At least, *Baas,* tell me whither you go."

"I know not; hither and yon as blows the wind."

"That is not the *Baas's* custom. Is it that the *Baas* fears my tongue will wag too freely that the truth is withheld?"

"You're an old fraud, Jim," his *Baas* had said affectionately. "I am going to make for the ford near the Martin Homestead. Few white men dwell thereabouts and there are no police. But, and remember this well, I do not wish to see thee again. Thou hast wandered afar too long. It is time for thee to dwell among the people of the *kraals.*"

"My ears are open, *Baas,*" Jim had said dully.

And after his *Baas* had ridden away, not an hour after, two troopers of the mounted police caught up with Jim.

"Where is thy *Baas?*" they had demanded.

"I have no *Baas,*" he replied mournfully. "He hath ridden swiftly away, owing me for many years' service. This horse and this wagon he gave me, but that is poor pay for the years spent in labor."

"He lies; let's search the wagon."

"When did thy *Baas* go?" asked one of the troopers after an examination of the wagon had failed to reveal anything incriminating.

"Within the hour."

"And in what direction?"

Jim hesitated.

"That way he went." Jim pointed in the direction his *Baas* had taken. "If ye catch him will ye make him pay me what he owes?"

"He'll pay all right," had laughed one of the troopers.

They mounted their horses and made ready to go but, turning swiftly on Jim, saw that he was grinning widely.

"Didn't I tell you he was a liar? The 'Major' wouldn't treat his servant that way. Let's thrash the truth but of him."

"Oh, come on; we'd only be wasting time. We can get hold of the Hottentot any time. He can't get away. Come on, the 'Major' can't be far off."

And the two had wheeled and galloped away in the opposite direction from that taken by the Major.

That same night Jim had been joined by a native, in whose upright carriage and general bearing he had no difficulty in recognizing a man used to wearing the uniform of the native police.

Later, this man had reported to his superiors.

"Without doubt the Hottentot spoke truth. He hath sold the wagon and horse. He returns to his own people, vowing he will never again seek service with the white men. Even now he seeks a maiden in marriage.

"This he told me about the man who was his *Baas;* and this—"

Then followed sundry tales regarding the white man, Jim's *Baas,* all lending color to the Hottentot's claim of unjust treatment.

Yet when the spy returned to the *kraal,* in which Jim had sworn he would spend the rest of his life, the Hottentot had vanished and none had seen him go!

"But he will come again soon," assured the Headman, "for already he hath paid me a large marriage gift—that he may marry my daughter."

THE STORY of Jim's journey to the ford is an epic, and one rather regrets that this is not Jim's story; that it is not possible to tell of his adventures—they were many and hazardous—with men and beasts.

Let it suffice that he did reach the ford after seven days weary trekking on foot.

Occasionally through stray voyagers of his race word had come to him of his *Baas*. Of how he had, again and again, been forced to double and redouble on his tracks; and of how each redoubling had brought him nearer to his objective, the ford where he hoped to meet this *Baas*.

On the very morning that Jim had crossed the river he learned that his *Baas* was but a two days' trek away, and with a calm assurance that, in the fullness of time, he would see his *Baas* again, Jim patiently composed himself to patiently await his coming.

Such a devotion as that shown by Jim for his *Baas* gives some clue to the character of the Major. It was a dog-like devotion, but with this difference.

The lowest scum of the earth may boast of the allegiance, sole allegiance, and worship of a dog; but the man to whom a native gives his unwavering allegiance must first of all, be a man. A man among men, just, and without fear.

Eight days Jim had waited at the ford.

Each morning he had said, "Today he will come. If not, I will go back to my own people."

Each evening he assured himself that the morrow would surely bring his *Baas;* and this was the end of the eighth day.

Faintly the drumming of horse's hoofs came to his ears.

He sat suddenly erect, every nerve on edge.

Louder and louder sounded the beating hoofs. His eyes filled with the light of exultation. There could be no doubt this time. Who but his *Baas* would be riding at this hour of the night, in this direction, and at such a speed?

He quickly lighted a fire—he had had the wood all ready against the day—and put on a billy half full of water into which he dropped chunks of biltong. It would make soup of a sort and his *Baas* might be hungry.

Near to the fire he rolled out the blankets, which he had carried with him on his long trek, from their waterproof cover.

Then, running swiftly, he came to the ford just in time to see a horseman ride, out from the bush on the other side.

"*Baas,*" cried Jim. "*Baas!*"

"Jim you old scoundrel," came back the well-loved voice, "what the deuce are you doing here?"

"Eight days have I waited, *Baas*. It is good to know that the time of waiting is over."

Jim's homely countenance was lighted up by a smile of joy.

"I was delayed on the way, Jim."

The Major had crossed the ford, dismounted and placed his hands on the Hottentot's shoulders.

"Didn't I tell you to go to your own people? That my way and thy way no longer ran together?"

"Yah, *Baas*."

"And you disobeyed."

"Yah, *Baas*."

"For that there must be punishment."

"Without doubt," joyfully agreed Jim. "The *Baas* is always just. But first the *Baas* should eat and sleep—he has traveled far. Come."

Jim led the way to where he had lighted the fire.

"Sit down and rest, *Baas*. In a little while the food will be ready."

He unsaddled the horse and tied him to a nearby tree.

The Major watched him, and laughed as the big black stallion playfully nibbled at the naked body of the Hottentot.

"Already he is thy friend, Jim. What d'ye think of him?"

"He is a man's horse and one well worthy of thee, *Baas*."

Jim came over to the fire.

From the "billy" came the odor, faint 'tis true, of buck soup.

"Will the *Baas* eat now?"

"Nay. I have eaten well this day; so now for thy punishment." He looked keenly at the Hottentot.

"Where is the wagon and the horse I gave thee?"

Jim took out a bag and gave it to the Major.

"I sold them, *Baas*. The money is there. Had I not parted with them—the horse and the wagon—men would have followed my spoor to this place."

"Then you journeyed to this place, on foot, carrying my blankets besides stuff of thy own?"

"Yah, *Baas.*"

"And rejoiced because thou were disobedient?"

"As thou sayest."

"Truly the punishment must be great! What hast thou eaten these past days—tell a true thing."

"A plenty, *Baas.* Honey and berries. What can man need more?"

"Somewhat thinner art thou than of old."

"It may well be. Easy living, big belly, slow trekking. It is good to be thin. But the punishment, *Baas.* Delay not further."

Jim trembled slightly.

The joy at seeing his *Baas* again had been great, but now the reaction was setting in. He had been living on his reserve strength which now seemed to flow from him, leaving him quite weak.

"The punishment?" queried the Major. "Sit down, you old fraud, and eat the food you have prepared for me. Nay," he continued as Jim murmured a protest, "No further speech from thee until the food has all gone. It is my order."

Without further word Jim, with the eagerness of a half-starved man, sat down and gulped, noisily the steaming broth; and the Major, puffing contentedly at a cigarette, watched him through half-closed eyes, a wistful, half-wondering smile on his face.

"Fatness has much to commend it," said Jim with a happy chuckle when he had finished. "And now say, *Baas,* whither we go on the morrow."

The Major aroused himself with a start.

"By Jove," he said, speaking in English, "I'm hanged if I know. We can't go back, and if we go forward, farther into Portuguese Territory, we are likely to run into Dirty Morton and his crowd. And I don't want to meet them in my present state of unpreparedness. I can't go to the east— Cenambo may still be chief and claim me as food for his bally crocodiles. To the west there is—Jim?"

"Yah, *Baas?*"

"We will go to Mangwato's country."

"That is good, *Baas.* It is but a short trek from here. Three days, perhaps four, but no more. He will receive thee well, for thou didst save his son."

AFRICAN ADVENTURERS have always looked upon Mangwato's country as a land flowing with milk and honey, an El Dorado. Traders, prospectors, and labor recruiting agents—white men possessed with the highest motives, as well as those possessed of the lowest—the exploitation of the natives for their own selfish motives—have for many years cast covetous eyes toward that rich, but forbidden country.

Chiefly, perhaps, were men interested in the store of diamonds, "the large calabash full of diamonds," treasured by the old chief. At one time they were to be had in exchange for a machine gun, and not a few men had hopefully outfitted small expeditions to take to Mangwato his heart's desire. But of all who had attempted this means of winning wealth, not one had succeeded.

Some had been arrested by the white police of the territory from which they started, on charges of attempted gun running; others though succeeding in reaching Mangwato, had discovered that they could not palm off on him the obsolete, unworkable gun which they had fondly imagined would gain for them the diamonds.

Missionaries and traders, seeing in the land a large field for their endeavors, were refused admission, for Mangwato held that the only way of preserving the entity of his people was to bar the white men from taking up their residence among them. And who shall say he was not right?

The two white powers controlling territory adjacent to Mangwato's preoccupied in establishing their rule in those territories, were content, as long as he refrained from raiding their people, to leave Mangwato alone. It was mutually understood that any white men who entered Mangwato's country should do so at their own risk; that no punitive expeditions (that first step toward annexation), should be sent against Mangwato should he kill any white men in his territory. And, as the two powers jealously watched each other guarding against an infringement of this agreement, Mangwato went on his way with equanimity.

Time was when the wily old chief boasted it was the strength of his fighting men, his cunning leadership, that kept his land unbruised by the shod feet of white men. That time had passed.

He realized now, in his old age, that it was but a matter of a few years before his country would come under the rule of one of the powers, and it was with some bitterness of spirit that he admitted that he was powerless to prevent it.

His young men were getting restless under his rule. Some had left the country to work in the mines of the white men and, returning; had brought word of the wonders in the world beyond the borders. A movement had once been on foot to compel the chief to throw open his country to the white men. This movement Mangwato had stamped out, characteristically, by a wholesale killing of the leaders of the movement.

Once Mangwato had made a visit to the Portuguese fort not far from his borders. He had been royally treated; vast promises had been made to him, in the hope that he would beg them to assume a protectorate. But with eyes that suffered nothing to escape them, Mangwato noted how these white men treated the natives already under their rule; and he was not content.

A visit to British territory left him also dissatisfied. He was treated too much like a child that has to be pampered.

On one side was harshness and lack of understanding; on the other, a too great leniency, and lack of understanding.

So Mangwato refused to choose; refused to seek the protection of either power; resolving to wait for the matter to be settled, as in good time it assuredly would be, between them. It was his only hope that the day would not arrive in his lifetime.

Meanwhile he resolved to walk warily, lest he give offence to the powers and so hasten the dreaded day.

CONSIDERING ALL this, the plan of "Dirty" Norton and Cockney Joe to divorce Mangwato from his diamonds, was, to say the least, opportune.

The two men dressed in the gaudy uniforms of Portuguese government officials, together with native carriers—most of them wearing stolen uniforms—were encamped at a water hole not a day's march from the borders of Mangwato's land.

The little Cockney groaned, and wiped his perspiring face with the back of a not too clean hand.

"Lumme, Dirty, do we 'ave to wear these blinkin' 'h'uniforms 'h'all the time?"

"Of course, you fool. Mangwato's as cunning as the devil. There's no telling where he has spies. If any of 'em see us, they've got to see Portuguese officials. See?"

Cockney Joe grunted.

"I wish that blighter Myburg 'ud come." Norton, who was scanning the veldt ahead through field glasses, took hold suddenly of his companion's arm.

"Look. He's coming now."

Cockney took the glasses and, focusing them, saw a man on horseback rapidly approaching.

" 'H'it's 'im all right. An' abart time, 'e's two days late. I can't see any calabash of diaments, though."

Norton laughed derisively.

"You didn't expect he'd be able to get them alone, did you? He wouldn't be working with us if he could."

"But 'h'I thought 'e was Mangwato's right 'and man? 'H'it ought her be dead easy for 'im to bag 'em. Wot did you want to tork abart it for 'h'if yer knew it was no good?"

"Well, there was a chance, Joe, but a damned slim one."

"Then 'ow abart this other way? 'H'are yer sure of that?"

Norton chuckled.

"Why, it'll be like taking pie from a kid, Joe, it'll be so damned easy. It'll remind you of the days you used to steal money from the kids on the way to the corner pub, to buy their old man's pint of beer.

"You see," he went on patiently and slowly, as though this was the first time he had explained the matter to Cockney Joe instead of the hundredth; it required that much effort to get a thing into Joe's brain. "Mangwato's in mortal fear that he'll be deposed and his country taken under the protection of one of the powers. He'd do most anything rather than have that happen.

"Myburg whispers in his ears that the Portuguese are looking his way greedily, only waiting for an excuse to come in. That makes the old chap a little uneasy, so, when two officials of the Portuguese Government demand a word with him, why he very politely invites them in."

"And we're the two blinkin' Portuguese," said Cockney with a show of intelligence, "an' we tell 'im that we 'as proof that some blokes from 'is tribe 'ave raided our 'unting party and killed seven or 'h'eight of 'h'our bearers."

"That's it." Norton took up the tale once more. "Only we must make it clear that the killing was done on Portuguese soil. Of course that will rile the old duffer and he'll be sure to ask what we are going to do."

"Then we tork abart something else, 'n' and say 'ow 'ard our lot is, an' 'ow we 'n' admire Mangwato an' 'ud 'ate to see 'im lose 'is country. But, 'n'of course, we'll 'ave to report the raid and the killings to the Government. We might get rewarded—and we are very poor."

Cockney Joe entered into the spirit of his story and there were tears in his eyes as he rehearsed his part.

"But do yer fink 'e'll bite?"

"No fear of that. As soon as we talk about the reward we'll get for telling, he's bound to think of offering us a reward not to tell. If he doesn't we can hint broadly; if the hint doesn't work, why we'll threaten. Either he gives us the diamonds or we'll report the raid and killings, and that'll mean, we will make plain, the end of him."

"Won't 'e deny the killings?"

"Suppose he does. He'll see that his word wouldn't go for anything against two high officials like us."

The two men rose at this juncture to greet Myburg who had by this time reached the camp.

Myburg, an unhealthily fat man, with pig like eyes, claimed to be a Dutchman; but it was evident from his sallow, greasy complexion, his crinkled hair, the yellow tinge to the whites of his eyes, and the pinkness of the palms of his hands, that a goodly measure of native blood flowed in his veins.

Once he had been a trader, running a store in British territory, but an unsavory episode, terminating in his inducing some of Mangwato's soldiers to attack two Mounted Police, made it essential that he remain in Mangwato country. Having married a daughter of the old chief, he became a person of some consequence, and was, for a long while, Mangwato's chief adviser. (Not that Mangwato ever heeded the advice if it was contrary to his own judgment.)

"You're late, Myburg," said Norton. "What kept you? We expected you two days ago."

Myburg looked at the two men wrathfully.

"*Alamachtig!*" he ejaculated. "It is a wonder that I come to you at all. Your part is easy—you wait here in comfort, while I—"

"Comfort," snarled Cockney Joe. "Wot d'yer mean? Do ye fink it's comfortable sitting 'ere in the bleedin' sun, dressed like this?"

"Be quiet, Joe. Myburg's not finished."

"No. I'm not finished, but the rest is. There is no way of going on. You must give up the diamonds; I've risked a lot in order to get here to warn you."

"What do you mean, Myburg?"

"Why that man," he almost exploded with wrath, "you call the 'Major' is with Mangwato."

" 'The Major'!" shouted Norton incredulously.

" 'The Major'," Cockney Joe echoed feebly.

"Hell, yes, man. That's what I was telling you."

"But he's dead. I tell you that Cenambo threw him to the crocodiles long ago."

"He got away. You have been in prison—you did not know."

Norton shook his head in amazement.

"What's he doing with Mangwato? Is he after the diamonds?"

Myburg shrugged his shoulders.

"Who knows? He talks of many things, but of diamonds, never. But he is a slick one. Mangwato has made him an Induna; he is a big power in the land, second only to the chief. He holds court in the cursed English fashion—he calls himself, in jest, the Chief Native Commissioner. He has even threatened to drive me out of the country, me, the son-in-law of the chief. And Mangwato looks on and smiles."

A brooding silence settled over the three men, broken only by an occasional oath which told too plainly the depths of despair into which the conspirators were plunged. This plan of theirs had been a long time formulating, and it had seemed sound; now, at the moment of triumph, when all their scheming was to net the reward, it was all to be discarded because of the presence of the Major.

SINCE HIS arrival in Mangwato's country, six months previously, the Major had been enjoying himself hugely.

Sure of the old chief's gratitude, it was an easy thing for the Major to win his esteem and confidence. That done, he had, as Myburg said, practically ruled the country.

For the first time in many years his keen wit, and uncommon understanding of native psychology, had found a lawful outlet. He had succeeded, to Mangwato's great joy, in silencing the malcontents who had clamored that their country should be thrown open for exploitation by white men. He had succeeded in welding the old and new solidly together in a loyal whole.

His inborn genius for organization, his executive abilities had been proved by the way in which he had, even in so short a time, enforced certain laws of sanitation in the *kraals*, and had promoted a deeper interest in agricultural pursuits.

Indeed the Major had, in his easy good-natured way, accomplished the impossible, he had taught the natives the advantages of hard work.

Nor had he neglected the lighter side.

It was a sight well worth seeing to behold the Major refereeing a football match between two teams of wildly yelling, naked savages. And, though the ball was only the bladder of a wild pig, the enthusiasm of the players left nothing to be desired.

At first riots, hand to hand combats with *assegais,* had been an attending feature of the game, resulting in the Major ordering that all *assegais* should be left behind in the huts on match days. They could bring only their knob kerries—that much he was forced to allow.

Gradually they came to the point where the game was played as a game, and, as the players strictly obeyed the rules, so did the people at large, obey the new laws affecting their lives which were promulgated by the white man; the White Induna as they came to call him.

"THERE'S ONLY one thing to do," said Norton suddenly, "and that's to get the Major out of the way."

"That's wot," agreed Cockney Joe.

"But how? Man, I tell you it would be easier to kill the chief."

"I said nothing about killing, Myburg. When the Major's to be killed I want to do it myself. He's blocked my plans too many times."

"I, too, have a grudge to square. He thrashed me with a *sjambor* once."

"Is his servant, Jim, with him?"

"Yah. He's his *Baas's* shadow."

"Well if we can't get at the Major, what's to hinder us getting at the servant?"

"What do you mean?"

"Listen. If we can make it appear that the Major is after diamonds, won't Mangwato kick him out of the country, one time?"

"Yah. But who's going to fool the Major?"

"No one. But the Hottentot? That's another matter. It ought to be easy for a man like you, Myburg, to think up some way of getting the Hottentot in trouble. And, once you've got him in trouble, then you've got the Major."

Myburg's eyes gleamed maliciously.

"Man," he squealed, slapping his fat thighs in his mirth, "you've said a damn true thing. I've got a plan that'll pay off my grudge against the Major and his servant and will, besides, get the Major in wrong with Mangwato. Oh, it's rich. Man, I tell you it's rich."

Once again he gave himself over to merriment at his suddenly conceived plan.

"Well! Wot's it h'all abart?" Cockney Joe asked sullenly.

Joe was always suspicious of laughter, thinking himself the cause of it.

Myburg controlled his laughter with an effort.

"You know," he gasped, "that Mangwato always has someone guarding the hut where he keeps his diamonds—day and night?"

Norton nodded.

"Well then, this is my plan...."

THE MAJOR, his monocle—his "truth seeing eye"—firmly in place, was holding court. Seated at his right hand was the chief, Mangwato.

The Council Place was packed with men folk from the *kraals;* some were principals in the cases to be tried that day, but the greater majority were interested spectators.

The pomp and ceremony of English court procedure to which the Major had introduced them, intrigued their fancy, and they delighted in the whole proceedings, from the "Clerk of the Court's" stentorian shout of "Order in Court" to "The Court is adjourned."

They were somewhat puzzled by the fact that an evidently guilty man should be treated as innocent until found guilty. But this, and other things—the laws of evidence, the jury (whose findings, in the beginning, were often in direct opposition to the Judge's direction, they having decided on a verdict before hearing the evidence) they accepted as necessary to the proper playing of the game.

For the most part the Major dealt with the cases through an interpreter—appointing a man who had spent many years at the mines to that important position—but when, as often happened, a witness proved balky, or a point obscure, he cross-examined in the dialect of the country, and men wondered at his fluency of speech, and his knowledge of their customs.

"Next case."

The Major had just disposed of the twentieth case of petty thieving and he hoped that the end was in sight, for the day was insufferably hot.

There was a commotion among the spectators and two warriors, belonging to the newly formed "Police Force," came forward, dragging Jim, the Hottentot, between them.

A gasp of astonishment ran through the spectators. The White Induna's servant was accused. Now they would see whether the white man, by his dealing with his servant, was truly just.

Mangwato, arousing himself from the state of semi-coma induced by the hot sun and a heavy meal, looked quizzically at the Major.

"What hath this man done?" asked the Major.

"He hath killed a man, Lord."

The news was the signal for a babble of excited voices which ceased suddenly at the sound of the Major's voice.

"Whom hath he killed?"

"Jaika, Lord. He who was to have guarded the Chief's treasure last night."

"Let me hear what proof you have that this man is guilty."

"Umba speaks first, Lord."

Umba, a rat-eyed, crafty looking native, took his stand at the place reserved for witnesses.

At this point the Major turned to Mangwato.

"It would be better, Chief," he said softly, "if you heard, and gave judgment in this matter. This man is my servant and my friend. It will be hard for me to deal justly with him."

"Somewhat I had thought of that, white man. Yet I would have thee see this thing through."

"It is well." The Major turned to the waiting witness.

"Say what thou hast to say, Umba."

"Last night, Lord," said Umba glibly, "Jaika and the Hottentot came to my hut, for my wives had brewed much beer.

"We drank a little and played a game of chance that the Hottentot taught us. Some talk there was, as I remember, of the treasure of the Chief and the Hottentot boasted that it would one day belong to thee, his *Baas*.

"After a little while Jaika rose to leave us saying that he was appointed to guard the Chief's Treasure that night. The Hottentot offered him much wealth if Jaika would allow him to take his place. But Jaika would have none of it and left the hut. With him went the Hottentot.

"Later, Lord, the Hottentot returned to my hut. He was breathing hard and seemed distressed in spirit, but I forebore to question him, for he is a wrathful man and I, I am no fighter. All night he stayed with me sleeping a little and drinking much beer. That is all, Lord, save—" Umba hesitated.

"Tell all," commanded the Major, "fearing nothing."

"There was this," Umba continued with a new courage. "Once, nay twice, in his drunkenness, thy servant said, 'My *Baas* will be angry for I have failed to carry out his commands.'"

The Chief made an impatient movement and seemed about to speak, then relaxing, waited with half closed eyes to hear the rest of the evidence.

"And that is all, Umba?" the Major asked in level tones.

"Aye."

"Then stand on one side."

Mpakwe, a stalwart warrior, was called next.

"Last night, Lord," he testified, "I was guarding the Chief's Treasure. When the time came for another to take my place, I suddenly caught the sound of one approaching."

" 'Is that thou, Jaika?'" I called.

" 'Aye. Art weary of waiting?'" a voice called from the darkness.

"Now, Lord, a doubt arose in my mind for it was *not* the voice of Jaika which answered me. Nevertheless I remained silent, waiting for the man to come nearer to me.

" 'Thou canst go now, Mpakwe,'" said the stranger, and the voice was not the voice of Jaika.

" 'But thou art not Jaika,'" I cried and rushed on him in the darkness, thinking that someone was playing a joke on me. I grappled with him, and for a moment we struggled silently, then, with a curse, he broke from my grip and ran away.

"All that night I watched the Chief's Treasure and no one came near me until the morning. This," Mpakwe handed me a gaudy bead necklace to the Major, "I found at my feet."

The Major took the necklace and looked at it wonderingly. It was broken and looked as though it had been snatched from the neck of the wearer by force.

The necklace was Jim's!

The next witness told of the finding of the body of Jaika. A knife was found driven through his heart—and the knife was Jim's!

The last witness told of the taking of Jim in the hut of Umba.

That was all. The evidence seemed to prove, beyond shadow of doubt, that Jim was the murderer.

The Major felt suddenly old. Had Jim, in an excess of zeal, really done this thing in order to win the approval of his *Baas?* Jim had been so much to him and now the Major would be forced to utter the words that would be the Hottentot's death sentence.

TWICE MANGWATO spoke his name before he shook off the feeling of despondency which had taken hold of him.

"You spoke, Chief?" he said wearily.

"Aye." The chief spoke in a low voice so that only the Major could hear. "Why hast thou done this thing, white man? Was it solely in order to obtain the diamonds that thou hast posed as our friend? Is there no truth in white men? Are ye all liars and evil schemers?"

"But if I say that I know naught of this?"

"That I cannot, will not, believe. The slave is but the hand of the master. The head orders, the hand obeys. If my head tells my hand to do wrong shall we cut off my hand and say that the evil hath been wiped out? I say not so. On thee lies the blame, and on thee only. The Hottentot's life is forfeit to me. That is so according to the laws thou hast taught us. Thy life also is mine by the laws we knew before thy coming. Yet thy life I will give thee, remembering certain services thou hast done me, only let me see thy face no more."

At that moment the Major's eyes roving idly around the assembled spectators, caught sight, for one brief moment, of the leering, evil face of Myburg. On it was a smile of triumph.

The Major shook off the feeling of indecision and, leaning forward, spoke quickly and earnestly to Mangwato.

"I say to thee, Chief," he said, "that I know nothing of this matter. Also it is my belief that the Hottentot is falsely accused."

"Art mad? The thing is plain. Jest not further."

"But heed me. Not yet have we heard the tale he has to tell."

"There is no need. Mpakwe I know well. His words were true. The knife and the necklace belong to thy servant. What need to hear more?"

"Grant me this one thing," pleaded the Major. "Until I have seen this thing through, until the setting of the sun, deal with me as though I were still thy friend and one worthy of honor. It is a small thing I ask, and—did I not save thy son from death?"

"Remembering that, white man, I grant thy request, yet marvel at my folly."

"That is good," said the Major in relieved tones. "See! The people are watching us. Laugh heartily as though I have told thee a story inducing merriment."

And Mangwato, playing his part with good will, put back his head and peals of laughter came from his lips.

THE MAJOR sought out the face of Myburg and noted, with a feeling of satisfaction, that a scowl had taken the place of the leer of triumph.

"What hast thou to say, O wicked one?" he demanded, turning sharply to Jim. "Didst thou kill the man, Jaika?"

"Nay, *Baas.*"

"Then what hast thou to say concerning these things which have been told against thee?"

"It is true, *Baas,* that I went to the hut of Umba, and that Jaika went with me. It is true that we spake of the Chief's Treasure and I may have said that it would some day be thine. I had been drinking heavily, and my tongue was loose.

"Suddenly, it was after Jaika had left, a heavy sleep came over me and I remember nothing more; awakening in wonder this morning, that I should still be in the hut of Umba."

"And that is all? Thou didst not leave the hut of Umba with Jaika?"

"Nay, *Baas.*"

"But the knife and the necklace are thine?"

"Yah, *Baas.* But how they came in the places they were found is beyond my knowledge."

"What thinkest thou?" the Major asked Mangwato. "Which tale is true?"

"Umba lies," said Mangwato. "But what then? The other men did not lie. The knife was the Hottentot's, and the necklace. That alone is enough to damn him. But go thy way; time is still left to thee."

The Major whispered a lengthy order to one of his "Native Police" who passed an order to others, and one quietly took his stand a little behind Umba.

"Umba," said the Major sorrowfully, "this day I lose a faithful servant; I must wipe the memory of him from my mind. But what a case am I in. I have no servant unless—wilt thou be that one."

Umba looked round proudly at the assemblage. Of a surety, the White Induna recognized truth and a willing worker!

"Aye, Lord," he replied.

"Twenty shillings a month will I give thee and here is money to bind the bargain."

"It is good, Lord. What then shall be my task?"

The Major took a large, flat stone from the ground and handed it to Umba.

"Hold that forth at arm's length on the palm of thy hand, and hold it thus until this hearing is over."

"And that is all, Lord?"

"Aye. That is all. But see to it that thou dost not move thy hand—higher or lower—for it is part of a great magic I am about to perform."

Umba grinned at the simplicity of his task, having no eyes for the native who had taken up his stand behind, and a little to the right of him.

The Major turned his attention to the other witnesses, whom he recalled, apparently forgetting Umba.

The stone on the man's outstretched palm seemed to gain in weight with every breath. His arm ached and he shifted uneasily on his feet.

"Are thy words concerning this thing true, Umba?"

The question came with lightning swiftness.

"Yes, Lord. All true."

At that moment the hand holding the stone wavered and was the signal for the "Native Policeman" to deal Umba a shrewd blow with the side of his hand.

"Lord," cried Umba, "is it thy order that this man should beat me? It is the truth I speak."

"I doubt not your word, Umba. The blow was struck because thou didst lower the hand containing the stone, thus spoiling my magic. Said I not that the hand must not be lowered until this hearing be ended?"

The hand was quickly brought to a level.

Again and again the question was put; and the same answer given. Again and again the hand was lowered only to be followed by the numbing blow.

"Lord," pleaded Umba at length amid the jeers of the people. "It is my desire to leave thy service."

"Thou canst not leave my service. The money was paid thee binding the bargain. I have many witnesses."

"We are all witnesses to that," shouted the people gleefully. This was a matter dear to their hearts.

"Is it then permitted that I lower my hand, Lord?"

"When the hearing is finished, but not till then lest my wonder working became a thing of no moment.

"Are thy words concerning this thing true?"

Umba let his hand drop helpless to his side and running forward fell on his knees before the Major.

"I lied, Lord. The Hottentot spoke only a true thing. Of a truth thy magic is a mighty magic. Say now, is the hearing over, or, if it is not, at least suffer that I may hold the stone in my other hand."

At this moment there was a commotion at the distant end of the clearing. Myburg, fearing that the moment of exposure was at hand, had tried to get away. His progress was blocked by a party of warriors who dragged him before the Major.

The Major looked at him contemptuously then, turning to Umba, said, "Now answer me truly lest great evil befall thee. Who bade thee testify falsely?"

Umba looked fearfully at Myburg.

"That one, Lord," he said pointing at the scowling Dutchman.

"Say on," the Major ordered curtly.

"He gave me some of the sleep medicine to put into the Hottentot's beer. This I did, but I would not do the other things he demanded I do. So he—he had been hidden all this while in my hut—took the Hottentot's knife and also his necklace. The rest I do not know."

"But I do."

The Major turned swiftly on Myburg.

"By Jove," he drawled in English. "It was a neat plan, old top, and nearly succeeded. But why did you do it? Someone at the back of you, eh?"

Myburg shifted uneasily.

"If I tell you the whole truth, will you influence Mangwato to let me go free?"

"That all depends on what you have to tell, old chap. But I'll give you my word that if I think it's worth while I'll do as you ask."

And with that assurance Myburg had to be content. There was a chance, after all, that he might be able to save his neck, and so he told the whole story.

FOUR DAYS later Dirty Norton and Cockney Joe saw Myburg coming toward them.

He was on foot and, as he came nearer, they saw that he was apparently carrying a huge calabash in his hands. It was undoubtedly heavy for he was laboring in his gait.

" 'E's got the diamints," the little Cockney shrieked. "Good 'h'old Myburg."

"Look!" said Norton, with sudden alarm, "the calabash is hung around his neck, and his hands are tied behind him!"

When Myburg came up to them he collapsed suddenly, falling prostrate on the ground, and the two men saw, through a rent in his shirt, that his back was marked with the lash of a *sjambok.*

Callously they turned him over.

The gourd was full of pebbles, some of which had spilled out on to the ground.

At the bottom of the calabash was a note.

"The cursed Major again," said Norton wrathfully, but curiosity made him open the note.

> Dear Dirty and Cockney:
> I do always have to write to you about such amusing things, don't I?
> That was a jolly smart plan of yours; really it aroused my professional interest. But, alas, it had its weak points and it failed.
> I am sending some "stones" to you by Myburg. I'm afraid that they're the only kind you are likely to get, unless, and here's a happy thought, you go in for raising toads. I hope you catch the connection. "Which

like the toad, ugly and venomous, wears yet a precious jewel in its head." I don't really expect you to recognize the quotation, Dirty. I'll explain it to you some time, old top, for of course we four will meet again. I'm sure I hope so.

Yours truly,

THE MAJOR.

TOOLS

GEORGETOWN BOASTED of one hotel, the Imperial, and it differed in no degree from the tin-roofed, mud-walled building which holds a prominent place in any typical South African mining settlement.

The Imperial did not cater to transients, and its guests were more or less permanent. For the most part they were miners, their wives and families.

The men can be described offhand as "diamonds in the rough," and if they owned clothing other than the khaki slacks, gray flannel shirts, and high boots of their calling, they never gave evidence of such possession. They worked hard under trying conditions, but the wages were high, and with the optimism of the Eternal Boy which is in every man they were able to look forward to the time when they could go home and live like "fighting cocks" on their savings.

As for the women, some few struggled to preserve their femininity in this little world of men, and eagerly purchased any new toilet preparation guaranteed to preserve the bloom of youth or to protect "the most delicate complexion from the fierce rays of the African sun." Most of them, however, had long since given up the apparently hopeless struggle and slumped physically and mentally.

The evening meal, "dinner," was the one event of the day at the Imperial. Indeed it was the social event of Georgetown.

All the hotel guests came together for that one meal; and the number was augmented by such tradesmen as the town supported, and occasionally officials from the Portuguese territory across the river.

The meal was served in a large barn-like room, known as the Banqueting-Hall. Save for one long deal table, covered with oilcloth

of a once gorgeous pattern, some nondescript chairs, and a few small, round-topped tables, the room was devoid of furniture.

Evil-smelling oil lamps provided the illumination and added their iota to the oppressive heat. Flies buzzed lazily about the room, and above their low drone came the sharper, vicious "ping" of mosquitoes.

A dreary place was this banqueting-hall of the Imperial Hotel; and, it must be said, the diners made no effort to rise above their environment.

Tonight was no exception.

The men folk were weary; and the women, prostrated by the intense heat of the day, spoke rarely. It would have been better perhaps if they had kept altogether silent, for when they did speak there was a bitter rasp in their voices that set all nerves on edge and precipitated more than one domestic quarrel.

Native waiters in once white uniforms moved languidly about, serving the first course—hot, greasy soup in thick, chipped plates.

And then, conjuring up memories of another clime and different surroundings, a vision projected itself into the room.

At the sight of it what idle gossip was being indulged in stopped; domestic squalls were suddenly calmed. Women whose expression had hitherto been listless looked in admiration with perhaps a flicker of regret that they had not taken more pains with their toilet. With fluttering, patting hands, they furtively essayed to smooth into a semblance of order, hair which had been disarranged during the long afternoon *siesta*.

The first effect of the vision upon the men was one of silent amazement; but that was quickly followed by a contemptuous amusement.

Some even gave vent to loud hoots of derision—quickly silenced, to be sure, by the indignant looks of the women.

As for the cause of all this, he hesitated a moment in the entrance. But his hesitation was not one of indecision, rather it was as if he waited for—well, a head waiter to lead him to the table.

Yes. Even so.

At the Ritz Carlton a man in evening dress is, to say the least, inconspicuous unless his attire be faulty. But at the Imperial Hotel in Georgetown, South Africa, such a one is a freak, a monstrosity, a darn fool, or a delectable vision. Have it any way you please.

Add to the very correct attire a man well accustomed to wearing it—and a monocle—and you will understand why these women, so long divorced from the finer refinements of social amenities, called the stranger a vision.

One of the natives finally escorted the stranger to one of the small tables; the next course was brought in, and the meal resumed.

An observer would have been interested to note the sudden change in the conversation and in the general deportment of the diners; and many a man looked at his wife with blank amazement as if he were witnessing a reincarnation, or had suddenly discovered his wife to be some one else.

LATER THAT evening the stranger came to the bar where the men had adjourned. His appearance was hailed by rude shouts of laughter, and ruder jeers.

"Here comes the dude. Watch him, boys."

"My! Ain't he the darlingest pet?"

The man paused, and with nonchalant air gazed dispassionately around the room.

"Pardon me, old chaps," he drawled, and screwed his monocle into place, "but do you see anything funny about me?"

As by a prearranged plan each miner put a make-believe monocle up to his eye. In some cases it was a watch-crystal; others had curtain rings, while the rest made shift with large silver coins.

A broad grin spread over the stranger's face; and, taking his monocle from his eye, he threw it into the air. He caught it on his cheek as it descended, and with a swift jerk of the head once more firmly fixed it in place.

"Now, old dears," he said with a chuckle, "let me see you do that."

A loud shout of laughter greeted this feat, but this time the laugh was with the stranger, not against him.

"That's much better," he continued. "Now we're a nice, jolly little party. Really, don't you know, I was feeling quite embarrassed. Won't you drink with me?"

"We like to know the name of the man we drink with," said one of the men.

He was the owner of one of the mines.

"Ah! Yes, of course. Pardon the omission. But what's in a name? Suppose you call me the Major?"

"The Major?"

They all crowded around him.

They had heard—who had not?—much of this man who had made a laughing-stock of the South African Police; whose tricks and clever evasions of the arm of the law were the talk of the Dark Continent. None doubted that he was indeed the Major. Who else had that debonair carriage, that look—to a casual observer—of helpless inanity and an almost vacuous expression which only served as a mask to hide the keen wit of the man? Who but the Major would have had the nerve to appear at such a place and in such an attire?

The miners knew of the Major by repute. Knew that beneath the clothing of a fop was a red-blooded man; a man whose strength was always on the side of the under dog no matter how great the odds might be against him. They knew that he was, in the eyes of the law, a notorious criminal; but they also understood that his crime—that of illicit diamond-buying—was his protest against certain unjust laws protecting the diamond-mining monopoly. And their sympathies were all with him.

"But aren't you off your beat up here, Major?" asked one of the men. "We're gold-miners. You haven't got a grudge against us, have you? The Lord knows I hope not."

"You flatter me. Really. No, gold doesn't interest me. Some day perhaps I'll— But it's so beastly heavy to cart around. No. This is just my recuperating point, so to speak, before taking a trip into Mang-wato's country."

At this time two Portuguese officials who were sitting at a table in a far corner of the bar looked at each other meaningly, and one of them rose quietly and left the room unobserved.

The Major turned to the barmaid, ordered drinks for the crowd and a moment later they were noisily drinking his health.

One round was quickly followed by another; and the Major entertained the miners by the story, not told boastfully, of his latest escapade.

In the midst of the laughter which marked the conclusion of the tale a young trooper of the Transvaal Mounted Police entered the bar.

The miners looked at him coldly, for Gilkerson was not popular. He was very young and full of self-importance—was apt to take a high-handed attitude.

He carried a police circular in his hand and glanced from it to the Major, then back to the paper again.

"You're the Major, I believe," he said at length.

"Quite right, old dear. Charmed to meet you."

The policeman ignored the Major's outstretched hand.

"I'd like to speak to you outside."

The Major raised his eyebrows.

"But it's so beastly dark, old chap, and there are mosquitoes, stink-flies and what not."

"It is a matter of business, Major."

His hand, the Major noted, rested on the butt of his revolver.

"My word! You mystify me."

The Major turned to the others.

"You'll pardon me, won't you?" he said.

"The law insists—and who am I to go against the law?—that I offer up my bloated carcass as a feast for the mosquitoes."

"NOW WHAT is it?" the Major continued as he followed Gilkerson outside.

"I arrest you," he said in pompous tones, and stopped.

"Go on, old fellow; don't mind me. Complete the sentence. You know. Warn me that what I may say may be used as evidence against me, and all that."

Gilkerson hastily completed the formula.

"It's no laughing matter, Major," he added.

"I agree with you, old thing. Deuced serious, I should say—for you. I've been arrested so many times; and—well, I think I shall write a letter to your commanding officer commending you for the gentlemanly way in which you effected the arrest. Most considerate of you,

I must say.

"But of course I shall have to bring a suit against the Government for false arrest. Yes. I must do that to protect my good name, don't you know."

The Major was enjoying himself immensely. He carried nothing incriminating upon him. As a matter of fact he had not made a deal in diamonds for some considerable time; and he knew that though they might arrest him on suspicion there was no case against him that would hold in court.

"Aren't you interested in knowing what the charge is, Major?"

"Not a bit, dear boy. Probably you have heard that I'm a nefarious highwayman or something of that sort, when as a matter of fact I'm the most law-abiding man in the colony. Really now, I mean that. Still, if it will ease your mind, what is the charge?"

"Murder."

"What!"

In his astonishment the Major allowed his eyeglass to fall from his eye, and it dropped to the ground. With an expression of alarm the Major went down on his hands and knees and groped around for his monocle. But all the time he was conscious that the muzzle of Gilkerson's revolver was not six inches from his head.

"I've found it," he said finally in relieved tones; "and, thank Heavens, unbroken.

"You know," he continued, rising to his feet and adjusting his monocle, "I'd be simply blind without this. Some chappies say that it is an affectation, but 'pon my soul it's not. It helps me to see things as they are. If you know what I mean.

"Well, what do you intend to do with me? And, I say, if it's not too much trouble I wish you would put away that beastly revolver. I'm quite harmless, you know, and revolvers make me deucedly nervous."

"Oh, come along," said Gilkerson impatiently. "You're as long-winded as an old woman."

"But where, dear boy?"

"To the police camp of course. I won't feel safe until I've got you under lock and key."

"But surely you don't expect me to go dressed like this? Let me change first."

"Is it likely? No. You'll do just as you are."

"At least let me talk to my native servant Jim."

"No. Now get a move on; and if you have any thought in your mind of trying to escape, just remember that my revolver is loaded and will be aimed right at your head. And I'm not a bad shot," he added complacently.

The Major shrugged his shoulders and walked down the dimly lighted street, closely followed by Gilkerson.

Five minutes later the heavy door of the tiny cell swung to with a bang, and the Major was imprisoned without hope of escape.

Next day the Major's arrest was the one topic of conversation in Georgetown.

The two Portuguese officials hastened to the police camp; and, having been assured by Gilkerson that the Major was really under arrest, charged with a serious crime, they hastily composed a message addressed to the Commandant of Portuguese territory.

One passage in that message is worthy of notice.

It read:

> Disregard news sent by special runner last night. The Major has been arrested for murder, and there is no reason to believe that he can in any way interfere with our plans.

For three days Gilkerson kept the Major under close confinement by virtue of—so he said—orders from headquarters.

Further enlightenment he would not, could not, give; and, knowing the Major's reputation, he would not allow his prisoner to leave his cell under any pretext whatsoever. Neither would he allow Jim, the Major's Hottentot servant, to see his *Baas,* threatening that loyal native with arrest should he continue to loiter in the vicinity of the jail.

He refused even to send to the hotel for the prisoner's baggage, so the Major was still wearing the evening dress he wore at the time of his arrest.

"You'll be more conspicuous, Major," explained Gilkerson with a laugh, "should you happen to break out of here. Not that I think that's likely. Still I prefer not to take chances; and it would be easy to trace a man wearing a dress suit."

"You think of everything; don't you, old top?" the Major had replied sarcastically.

Early on the morning of the fourth day following his arrest the

Major was awakened by voices outside the door of his cell.

"That's all right," a familiar voice was saying. "You have acted wisely. Can't afford to take chances with this fellow. Now you had better be off to the mines. You understand what you are to do."

"Yes, sir," the voice of Gilkerson replied. "I'm to be on the lookout for a native answering this description: medium build, round-shouldered, and has a crescent-shaped scar on his right shoulder."

"That's right. If you get him the case against the Major will be complete. And, Gilkerson, I'm up here unofficially, you understand. I don't want any one to know that I'm here."

"Very good, sir."

A few minutes later a key grated in the lock, and the door of the cell swung slowly open, admitting a man so like the Major in appearance that the two men might have been taken for brothers.

They looked at each other for a moment in silence, and then the newcomer burst into laughter.

"You do me too great an honor, Major. Really there was no need for you to have dressed for the occasion."

"You must thank your officious trooper for that, chief. I'll give you my word that I will never want to wear a dress suit again. But what's all this about? You are not playing the game, you know."

"Having you arrested for murder, you mean?"

"Yes. What else?"

The Major was slightly peeved.

"That's just what I am doing," retorted the "chief." "I'm playing the game."

"Oh, bosh. You have me arrested on a ridiculous charge and call that playing the game. Try again, old chap."

The other—he was the chief of police—sobered instantly.

"It was very important, Major," he said, "that I should see you— secretly if possible—and I've been trying to get in touch with you for some time; but you are as slippery as an eel. Consequently when I heard that you were making for Georgetown I telegraphed to Gilkerson that you were suspected of murder, ordering him to hold you until further notice."

"But why make the charge one of murder? You have given me some uneasy moments, I can tell you."

"I knew you would stay and face out such a serious charge, whereas you might have been tempted to make a bolt for it had the charge been a trivial one—I.D.B., for instance."

"Fat chance I've had of getting away. Gilkerson has been treating me as though I were a second Jack the Ripper or some other beastly cutthroat, and I'm not used to it. Other Johnnies who've arrested me have always treated me like a gentleman."

"Oh, you mustn't be too hard on Gilkerson. You are his first arrest, and the responsibility sets rather hard on him."

The Major shrugged his shoulders.

"Of course I shall sue you for false arrest."

"No, I don't think you will, Major. We need your help and I hope you will give it."

The chief's voice suddenly lowered; his face became serious; and the Major, realizing that there was something of importance afoot, dropped his pose of injured innocence and prepared to listen.

IT WAS late that night when Gilkerson returned from his errand at the mines. He was very weary and not a little dispirited, for his search had been fruitless. Though he had examined every native working at the various mines he had failed to discover the one he was after, and had come to the conclusion that his commanding officer had been misinformed.

As he came to his hut, which was in close proximity to the cell where the Major was incarcerated, he was surprised to find it in darkness.

Thinking it strange that his chief should have gone away leaving the prisoner unattended, he quickened his steps.

Entering his hut, he lighted a lamp and found on the table a letter addressed to him. He read:

> Dear Gilkerson:
> I am very sorry that I shall not be able to say good-by to you, so I am taking this opportunity of thanking you for the kindness you have shown me, and all that. I trust that you will return early and release the chief at once. The old boy seems to be very peeved. I know he would swear if he could, but I flatter myself that I have gagged him very effectually.
> And isn't it lucky that we are so alike in appearance, and about the same build?
> You will understand, and why, when you see the chief.
> Ta-ta, old man.
> > Yours,

THE MAJOR.

Lamp in hand, Gilkerson rushed out to the cell. The key was in the lock, and, turning it, he flung open the door.

The light of the lamp shone on a man lying prostrate on the floor. For a moment Gilkerson thought the letter he had just read must have been a figment of his imagination. The man upon the floor was surely the Major! He wore the Major's clothes, and—

Then he saw that this man was gagged and was bound hand and foot by all the handcuffs and leg-irons with which Gilkerson was wont to adorn the walls of his hut.

With hands clumsy because of their eagerness Gilkerson took the gag out of his chief's mouth, and the anger that had been so long imprisoned at last found utterance.

"You —— fool!" he exploded.

"But how did he do it, sir?" stammered Gilkerson.

"Don't you search your prisoners, man? Didn't you know he carried a revolver?"

"I searched him, and I'll swear he had no revolver when I arrested him, sir."

"Well, he had one," growled the chief. "He held me up with it. For Heaven's sake don't stand there like a blinking idiot. Get me out of these handcuffs."

"Yes, sir. At once, sir."

But it was a long time before he could succeed in finding the keys to unlock them, and it was fully an hour before he had finally released his wrathful superior.

"I've a good mind to put you under arrest for neglect of duty," snarled that indignant man. "You're a fine specimen of a policeman! Fancy letting a desperate criminal like the Major retain a revolver!"

Gilkerson was silent.

He had hoped that his prompt capture of the Major would earn him a promotion. Instead it seemed that he was to be disgraced.

"Well! What have you got to say for yourself?"

"There's nothing I can say, sir, save to ask permission to go after him."

The chief snorted.

"What good would that do, you darned fool? The blighter is no doubt safe in Portuguese territory by this time, and thumbing his nose at us."

There was an ominous silence.

"Look here, Gilkerson," said the chief at length. "You don't show up very well in this affair, do you? For that matter neither do I. If this story gets out we'll be the laughing-stock of the country."

"That's true, sir," Gilkerson assented mournfully.

"And if it does get out I'll see that your chance of promotion is ruined forever. Do you understand what I mean?"

"I think so, sir."

"Very well, then. The train leaves for the south in an hour, doesn't it?"

"Yes, sir."

"Good. You will, as soon as you have made the necessary preparations, escort me, the Major, to the station, announcing to any one who may see fit to question you that you are taking me to Johannesburg for trial.

"Have you a suit of mufti? You have? Good. Then bring it along with you. I can change as soon as we are on the train. As long as we can fool the people here into thinking that I'm actually the Major, and that you are taking me to headquarters for trial, I can manage the rest. Do you understand what I'm driving at?"

Gilkerson was busy packing his suit-case.

"Yes, sir," he said with a salute. "All ready now, sir."

The chief's voice changed to a drawl strangely reminiscent of the Major.

"That's fine, old dear," he said with a wink, and fumbled in the pocket of his coat. "Where is my bally monocle? Ah! Here it is. Now, I can see to follow you. Lead on, Macduff."

"No. After you, Major."

Gilkerson said it with a bow.

WHILE THEY were waiting at the station for the arrival of the southbound train a man approached the pseudo-Major and, speaking with a foreign accent, asked him for a match.

"I'm sorry, and all that," the other replied, "but you see how it is."

He held up his hands so that the light of the station lamp fell upon his manacled wrists.

The stranger turned to Gilkerson and repeated his request.

"You have a dangerous criminal there; is it not so?" he asked as he lighted a cigarette.

"Yes. He's a murderer," replied Gilkerson. "I'm taking him to Johannesburg for trial."

"So? That makes me nervous."

He moved away, a little smile of triumph on his face.

About this time the Major was riding rapidly toward a camp-fire which twinkled in the darkness of the bush. It was across the river from Georgetown, and way off the beaten track.

As he neared the fire a dusky figure sprang to meet him.

"Scoff is ready, *Baas*," joyfully announced Jim, the Hottentot.

"That's good. I'm deuced hungry, Jim."

He dismounted, washed, and a moment later was eating roast buck with the appetite of a man who has not a care in the world.

"It was well planned, Jim," he said in the vernacular to the Hottentot as he carved himself another slice of the sweet white meat.

"Without doubt, *Baas*. Trekking will be easy for us two. A horse I have, and the wherewithal to get food."

"You mean ammunition, Jim?"

"Aye. That and gold, *Baas*. There is much gold."

"So?"

"Yah, *Baas*. But whither do we go?"

"Truly that is a matter to be thought on, Jim. Was nothing said to you?"

"Nothing, save that I should await you at this place."

"What if we go to Mangwato's country, Jim?"

"It would be wise. Mangwato would without doubt treat you with great honor. Did you not at one time preserve the life of a son that is dear to him? Aye, let us go there and dwell in peace for a time. I am growing old and like not this continual running from place to place."

"You are always free to return to your own people, Jim."

"Nay. The *Baas* knows it was not that I meant. Some little I thought that some day perchance my *Baas* would be caught in a net from which there is no escaping."

"You're a hoary old reprobate," the Major said affectionately in English. "But your words are wise. I too would know peace for a little while, so tomorrow we go to Mangwato's country."

SENHOR JOSÉ ALVARO, a portly little man, dressed in the gay and much bemedaled uniform of a high official in the Portuguese Colonial Service, looked up severely from his papers as a prison guard ushered two men into his office.

"Take off those handcuffs," he ordered, "and then leave the room. You may remain on guard."

In a soft voice, which somehow had a catlike purr in it, Senhor Alvaro requested the two men to be seated.

They exchanged wondering glances as they silently seated themselves.

"I have here," resumed the commandant, rustling some papers on the desk before him, "a complete, and very interesting, record of your respective careers."

"You, Senhor 'Dirty' Norton—" he turned to the taller of the two men—"were at one time, a sergeant in the Transvaal Police, but owing to certain unmentionable activities you were obliged to flee from the Transvaal and seek refuge in this territory. Since coming here you have lived up to your reputation. You are a card-sharper, a confidence man, a thief; and to complete your list of crimes you have committed a particularly cowardly and brutal murder. For that you were sentenced to be shot.

"Pray correct me if I am wrong, Senhor 'Dirty' Norton."

The big man was silent.

The commandant turned to the other, a scrubby little man known as "Cockney Joe."

"Of you we know even more. But what need to enumerate your many and varied crimes? Let it be sufficient to state that you are wanted very badly in England; that the police of the Transvaal offer a big reward for your arrest; and finally that you aided Senhor Dirty Norton in committing the previously mentioned murder. And you too were given the death penalty."

The two men moved uneasily in their chairs.

"The gracious governor of this colony," continued the purring voice, "has seen fit to show you clemency. But of course there are conditions."

"H'i'll promise ter be'ave, gov'nor," whined Cockney Joe. "H'i would never 'ave done nufink h'if h'it 'adn't been for Dirty 'ere."

The other man was silent. He was watching the fat, apparently good-humored face of the commandant.

"That's very nice of you—" the commandant waved his hands

airily—"but perhaps you had better let me do the talking for a little while. Yes, Senhor Norton and myself will converse for a little while."

Cockney Joe lapsed into a frightened silence.

"What do you know of Mangwato's country?"

Senhor Alvaro looked intently at Norton.

"I know that he's reputed to have a big hoard of diamonds."

The commandant looked disappointed.

"Yes. You would know that," he said testily. "But is that all?"

"That's all."

"Then listen."

The commandant turned to a map which hung on the wall behind him.

"Here—" he placed a pudgy forefinger on the map, thereby obliterating some few score square miles of territory—"here is Mangwato's country. You will notice—" removing his finger—"that it is tinted blue on the map, indicating that it is an independent state.

"It is bounded on the east by a patch of yellow and on the west, north and south by patches of red. Is it not so?"

Norton nodded assent, and Cockney Joe grunted something about "a blinkin' geography lesson."

"It is our desire to see that patch of blue—" again the commandant's finger obliterated a big section of Mangwato's country—"marked yellow on the map."

He paused impressively.

"Well, why don't you take it, senhor?" asked Norton. "It isn't likely that a native would put up any fight."

"Ah! That's where you come in, my friends," returned the commandant.

"You see," he continued in confidential tones, "the two powers have always adapted a hands-off policy as far as Mangwato is concerned. We have mutually agreed that any white man entering Mangwato's country should do so at his own risk; that no punitive expedition—the first step, you understand, toward annexation—should be sent against Mangwato should he kill any white men on his territory.

"Of course, if he crossed the border on a raiding party, that would be another matter. But he's too wily for that. He knows of this agreement and has made the most of it.

"His country is the only tract in South Africa as yet undeveloped by white men. And it is a rich country; rich in minerals, in farming-land and in labor. He has absolutely forbidden any white man to enter his country, hoping thereby to preserve the entity of his people. Not only that, but he has forbidden any of his people to seek work with the white men."

The commandant paused to light a black cigar before continuing.

"But that's soon coming to an end. Mangwato's getting old. He realizes now that it is not—as he used to boast—the strength and numbers of his fighting men that keep his country free from white men. He knows that sooner or later his country will come under the rule of the powers."

The commandant flicked the ash from his cigar and looked at Norton expectantly.

"What is it that you want us to do, senhor?" Norton asked.

"Ah! You are direct, my friend," said the commandant. "You would see the end of this wandering dissertation of mine. What you are to do is this. You are to induce Mangwato to appeal to us for protection. How you will accomplish this I don't quite know."

"But why send us? Why not send a representative of your Government?"

Norton was plainly puzzled.

"Don't you see that to do so would bring us in conflict with the British lion? It would be the breaking of our gentlemen's agreement, and we can't afford that.

"But if you two, having escaped from prison, elect to impersonate Portuguese officials that would be another matter. That you should go on hunting expedition along the frontiers of Mangwato's country might if known cause some apprehension; still, if the British happened to make pointed inquiries concerning you, we can disclaim all official connection with you, and, once given knowledge of your whereabouts, would speedily rearrest you.

"On the other hand, should you be successful in persuading Mangwato to come under our flag and without apparent official coercion on our part, well and good. The British lion could snarl as much as he pleased. With clean hands we could plead our cause before the Hague Tribunal, assured of a favorable verdict.

"Yet again. Should Mangwato kill you, ostensibly Portuguese officials on an innocent hunting expedition and on our soil, we would have good cause for sending a punitive expedition against him. And please believe that you would be well avenged."

"But what do we get out of this, senhor?"

"If you succeed and live, freedom and a large reward. If you fail—Let us not talk about failure, my friends. It is an unpleasant subject."

"But suppose we refuse?"

"In that case," said the commandant sorrowfully, "we shall be compelled, regretfully compelled, to carry out the order of the court. In other words, you will be shot." Norton and Cockney Joe held a whispered consultation.

"We'll do it, senhor," said Norton at length.

"Allow me to congratulate you on your good sense. But please do not think that we are giving you an opportunity to escape. We shall not for one moment lose sight of you.

"When you leave here we shall at once notify the British authorities that you have escaped from prison and were last seen heading for the Transvaal border. So, you see, we will be well protected, especially as the natives who accompany you will be instructed by me concerning their duties. Now I would like to make a few suggestions which you may follow or not, as you see fit."

TIME IS no object in Africa, the "Land of Tomorrow," and fully six months had elapsed before Dirty Norton and Cockney Joe had formed a plan which would, they hoped, gain them the promised reward and freedom.

They had, as suggested by the commandant, pitched camp close to the borders of Mangwato's country, using it as headquarters from which they made hunting forays. Dressed with bright uniforms, accompanied by a large number of native carriers—also in uniform—they looked just what they purported to be; officials of the Portuguese Government on a shooting expedition.

They made no attempt to cross the border and enter the forbidden land, but had been content with the fact that their actions were being spied upon by Mangwato's warriors. That was well. It was establishing their identity.

For long months they had shirked facing the problem that was before them, unable indeed to see how they could carry the thing through. Then only the night before Fate had put the means of success into their hands.

Certain of their bearers had crossed the boundary line and had raided the crops of a near-by village. The marauders had been observed and chased back to the camp by angry warriors. One of the bearers was wounded in the thigh by an *assegai.*

The warriors all retreated, however, at the sight of the white men. All, that is, save one, and he proved to be very truculent, insisting that the raiders be given over to him for punishment.

"I am Shimba," he said proudly, "the only son of Mangwato the chief. It is not a light matter for men to raid my crops."

On hearing that he was the chief's son, Norton made many overtures of friendship, and finally appeased the warrior's wrath by offering him a drink of whisky.

A second and third drink quickly followed the first, and in a short time the man called Shimba was overcome by the stupor of drunkenness.

Norton quickly bound and gagged the drink-sodden native.

"Wot's that for, you blasted fool?" queried Cockney Joe.

Norton laughed.

"Why, Toe, that makes everything A I at Lloyds for us."

"H'i don't see 'ow."

"No, you wouldn't. Well, here's the lay. Tomorrow one of us with an escort goes to interview Mangwato. There'll be no trouble getting to see the old blighter when he knows we've got his son prisoner."

"Wot do you do then?"

"Tell him that if he doesn't request the Portuguese Government to form a protectorate we'll take his son to Lourenço Marques and have him shot, and will also send an expedition to punish Mangwato because he has allowed his warriors to kill our bearers."

"But suppose 'e claims that the killin' was done on 'is territory?"

"Is it likely? He knows his word won't go for anything against ours. We're two high officials of the Government, remember. Besides, there's his son. That's a big hold. He'll do anything for his son, so they say."

"Sounds h'all right," admitted Cockney Joe cautiously. "But oo's going? H'it ought ter be you. You speak the lingo; H'i don't."

"I'll go all right. Now let's sleep. I want to make an early start in the morning."

AS HE awoke the next day, another idea had come to Dirty.

"See here, Joe," he said. "I don't expect we'll get much of a reward even if we work the thing all right. What do you say if we lift old Mangwato's diamonds?"

"Lumme! You think of h'everyfink, don't yer? But 'ow?"

"It's so easy, Joe, that it's like taking candy from a baby. It'll remind you of the days you used to steal money from the kids on their way to the corner pub to buy their old man a pint of beer.

"You see," he explained slowly, so that Cockney Joe's lower intelligence might fully grasp the idea, "I'll tell Mangwato that we will be bound to shoot his son; that's the law. Then I'll let on that I hate to do it, but that I'm a poor man and the reward I get will be great.

"He's bound to think of offering me a reward not to take his son in to be shot. If he doesn't I'll hint. If the hint's no good I'll tell him plainly that he either hands ever the diamonds or his son dies. See?"

"Lumme!" exclaimed Cockney Joe admiringly. "Yer does fink of h'everyfink."

"Well, I'm off now. Keep a good watch on Shimba. If he makes a getaway the game's all U-P."

Norton turned to mount his horse, but paused at an exclamation from Cockney.

"Look."

Following the direction of the pointing finger, Norton saw a horseman riding swiftly toward them.

"It's a white man," muttered Dirty. "A trooper of the Transvaal Mounted."

"Wot the ——'s 'e doin' 'ere?"

"I'm going to stay and find out," Norton replied grimly. "Have your revolvers ready, Joe, in case he tries any funny business. And if he talks to you let on that you don't understand the lingo. See? You're Portuguese. You don't speak English."

"BAI JOVE, it's Gilkerson. What the deuce is he doing here?"

These words, almost echoing the exclamation of Cockney Joe, came from the lips of the Major.

That ubiquitous man was hidden from view in a thick clump of bush not a quarter of a mile from the camp of the two conspirators. His eyes were glued to a pair of powerful field-glasses.

"What is it, *Baas?*"

The grizzled Hottentot sensed a note of annoyance in the Major's voice.

"I don't quite know yet, Jim."

Still watching through the glasses, the Major followed the movements of the approaching horseman.

"He's at their camp now," he muttered, "and he seems to be spinning them some yarn. Norton looks rather fed up about something. Gilkerson must have let the cat out of the bag, confound him.

"Ah! He dismounted. Evidently he's going to have scoff with them before coming on. Yes. There goes a native leading away Gilkerson's and Norton's mounts. Well, that gives me some little time to think."

He sat in silent meditation for a while.

"Yes. That will be the best plan," he said to himself. "I'll try it anyway."

Then aloud—

"Jim!"

"Yah, *Baas*."

"Go back quickly to the village and tell the warriors that I have need of them. There is need for haste."

"Yah, *Baas*."

Jim vanished silently into the shadows of the bush, and the Major resumed his watch.

Since his arrival in Mangwato's country six months previously the Major had accomplished many things. He was the only white man who had succeeded in winning the esteem of the old chief, and there was no honor too great for Mangwato to pay to the man who had been instrumental in saving his son from death.

Possessed then of Mangwato's gratitude, it had not been a difficult matter for a man of the Major's caliber to earn his esteem and confidence. As a result the Major was given a high place in the chief's councils, Mangwato deferring indeed to the Major in all things relating to the government of his people.

The Major concentrated his keen wit, his uncommon understanding of native psychology into presenting acceptably the English form of colonial government to the natives, and because he was well versed in native lore and rarely made an unjust decision the natives openly, and Mangwato secretly, acknowledged that the English way was a good way.

Several times Mangwato had sought to learn the reason why the Major should take such an interest in his people.

"It is the way of the English, Mangwato. We are all meddlers."

"Such meddling has much of merit in it," the chief had replied sagaciously. "Tell me, are all men of your race like you?"

"Some better, some worse. Are all the cattle in your herds of like quality?"

"It is well answered. But I can weed out the weaklings from my herds; such a thing I could not do should your people overrun my land.

"Now," Mangwato had continued, "it shall be as the Great Spirits will it. No move will I make toward bringing the white men in. I will not go to your people, nor will I go to the Portuguese. I fear to choose."

"The choice may be forced upon you. It is for no idle reason that two of their people should stay for so long, and so near, your borders."

"I have given thought to that. I think they are but hunters. If it be otherwise I pray that death will come to me ere my people are betrayed."

THERE WAS a slight rustle in the bushes, and the voice of Jim interrupted the Major's reveries. "The warriors are here, *Baas*."

"That is good, Jim."

The Major raised his voice slightly.

"Can you hear me, O warriors of Mangwato?"

"Aye, lord."

The reply came from many men, not one of whom was visible, so cunningly had they secreted themselves.

"Then listen well. There is a game to be played."

"NOW IF you are ready, senhor," said Norton, "we will go to pay our respects on Mangwato. You to seek the—ah—Major, and I to demand punishment of the warriors who killed my bearers."

"All right," Gilkerson replied curtly.

He was not entirely prepossessed by these officials of the Portuguese Government. The one who called himself Senhor Miguel Castello seemed all right, but the other, the one who professed to have no knowledge of English, seemed vaguely familiar; and surely he had heard him curse in very fluent English when a native spilled some hot coffee on his hands!

At that moment rifle-shots and the bloodcurdling cries of natives on the war-path came from the thick patch of bush which marked the boundary of Mangwato's country, and a moment later a horseman emerged, and rode at a furious pace toward the camp.

A second horseman followed, and hard at his heels a party of warriors armed with *assegais.*

The watchers saw the warriors pull the second horseman from his saddle. Spears flashed in the sunlight; and the warriors, first brandishing their weapons at the fast retreating form of the first horseman, picked up their victim and carried him in triumph back into the bush, followed, as a dog will follow its master, by the riderless horse.

The shouts of the warriors died away. Only the thud of the oncoming horse broke the stillness.

"What's it all about?" Gilkerson said wonderingly.

"Can't you see?" Norton—alias Senhor Miguel Castello—cried triumphantly as the rider drew nearer. "It's the Major, the man you're after. He's been after Mangwato's diamonds, and they got wise to him and chased him out. Now he's heading this way, hoping to find protection."

"You're right, senhor," Gilkerson said excitedly. "I'm going to get under cover. If he sees me he might make a bolt for it."

Gilkerson entered the tent and waited in a fever of impatience for the Major's arrival.

"Well!" he heard his quarry exclaim a few minutes later. "This is a delightful surprize. I never thought I should meet you two old friends here."

Gilkerson did not catch the surly reply.

"Just my luck."

The Major was speaking again.

"Another day and I would have gotten the old duffer's diamonds. As it is I had to run to save my bloomin' skin. Poor old Jim! I'm afraid they got him.

"But what are you doing here? After the diamonds too? Let's join forces. I've got a bully play."

Again Gilkerson missed the muttered reply. Still he had heard enough to realize that his first impressions regarding these so-called Portuguese officials were correct. But that was not his business. He was after the Major—that was all he cared about.

"Will you chappies give me some provisions and ammunition and I'll try to make my way to the coast? No? Then I'll have to try my luck at the *kraals* on the way."

Through a rent in the tent Gilkerson saw that the Major was preparing to mount; and, leaving his tent, he said curtly:

"Hands up, Major."

The Major's hands shot above his head, a look of blank incredulity on his face.

"Gilkerson, by all that's holy!" he exclaimed. "What are you doing here?"

"Pretty evident, isn't it, Major?" replied Gilkerson as he walked up to the Major to relieve him of his rifle and ammunition.

"Now hold out your hands."

He snapped on the handcuffs.

"That's right. You can mount now, and we'll be on our way."

"But you can't arrest me here, old dear," the Major expostulated. "This is Portuguese territory. You have no authority here."

"I'll take a chance on that."

Gilkerson turned truculently on the two pseudo-Portuguese.

Norton shrugged his shoulders. It was not likely that he would interfere in the arrest of a man who many times had frustrated his carefully thought-out plans.

"Come on," Gilkerson continued impatiently, "Mount!"

With an ill grace the Major obeyed the command; and Gilkerson, holding the reins of his prisoner's horse, led the way in the direction of Georgetown.

Dirty Norton and Cockney Joe watched them until they were hidden from sight in the thick bush veldt.

"Well, that's all right," said Norton with a sigh of relief. "I tell you, Joe, we can't go wrong now. Lord, what an escape I've had! Suppose the policeman hadn't turned up. I'd have been in a pretty pickle, wouldn't I? Me going to Mangwato and pretending to be a Portuguese; and all the time would have been the Major to give my game away."

"H'i thought the blighter was in clink. whoh'ever would 'ave thought h'of 'im bein' h'up 'ere!"

"Didn't you hear Gilkerson say he escaped? Well, I'm off now. Don't forget what I said about keeping a good watch on Shimba."

ONCE OUT of sight of the camp the Major's horse became suddenly lame.

"I say," said the Major apologetically, "I do wish you'd let me have a look at my horse's foot. I'm afraid he's picked up a stone or run a thorn in his frog or something."

"I'll look at it myself," grunted Gilkerson. "You needn't dismount."

Swinging from his saddle, Gilkerson bent down to examine the lame foot. As he did so the Major leaped upon him, and the two men rolled over and over on the ground.

The Major, being handcuffed, was at a disadvantage, and in a very little while Gilkerson was sitting triumphantly on his prisoner's chest.

"Pretty smart, Major," he panted exultantly, "but not quite smart enough."

"No?" drawled the Major quietly. "But if you'll take the trouble to look around you you will see that you're in the deuce of a mess."

Without releasing his hold Gilkerson looked cautiously behind him, and was amazed to find that a party of warriors had crept unobserved from the bushes and were closing in on him. With another start he recognized that Jim the Hottentot was their leader.

He sprang to his feet and drew his revolver.

"Don't be a fool, Gilkerson," came the curt voice of the Major. "Haven't you any imagination? You thought Jim was killed, and now you see him leading these warriors. Doesn't that convey anything to your feeble brain?

"You thought that these warriors were after my blood. Ask them who I am. You speak the lingo, don't you?"

"Who is this man?" Gilkerson demanded.

"Our lord, the White Induna," replied the warriors.

"What does it all mean?"

Gilkerson turned wonderingly to the Major.

"That's better. Take off these bally wrist-ornaments and we will talk a little while."

"First tell me," the Major continued a moment later, "why you're after me. Not officially, I'll swear."

"No. I've felt such a fool since you escaped that when I was given two weeks' leave I made up my mind to spend it looking for you. I thought I'd square myself with the chief. Instead I seem to have made an even bigger fool of myself."

"There was no need surely for you to worry. You took a prisoner to Johannesburg, didn't you? And every one thought it was me?"

"How did you know that?"

"I planned it, dear boy. Tell me, didn't you ever question the chief's explanation of my escape?"

"Yes. I couldn't understand how you managed to have a revolver, and— Tell me all about it, Major! That murder charge was a fake, wasn't it?"

The Major nodded.

"That was your chief's amusing way—he will have his little joke, bless his heart—of securing an interview with me. But I got even with him for that. He didn't want to be gagged and trussed up as you found him, but once I got one pair of handcuffs on him I had matters my own sweet way. And how the dear man did swear!"

The Major chuckled softly.

"You know that Mangwato's country is an independent state?" he asked suddenly. Gilkerson nodded.

"All right, then. The Secret Service Johnnies discovered that the Portuguese were conspiring to force Mangwato to ask them to form a protectorate, and your chief appealed to me to forestall them. He knew, you see, that Mangwato was friendly with me, and what could be more natural than for me to seek safety from arrest in Mangwato's country!

"The fake escape was necessary because I had told the chappies at Georgetown that I was going to Mangwato's country. Two Portuguese officials heard me, and we knew that they would be bound to be afraid that I would interfere with their plans—pardon me if I flatter myself— though as a matter of fact at that time I was ignorant that international politics were seeking to bottle up Mangwato."

"One of them told me that you were at the hotel," interrupted Gilkerson. "And in order to make sure I'd arrest you he said you were wanted for I.D.B. This, when I had a warrant against you for murder."

"Did he? Oh, that's rich! Well, to cut a long story short, I've been up here nearly six months and have succeeded, I'll flatter myself, in showing Mangwato that the British way of doing things isn't half bad. At the same time I've been keeping my eye on the antics of those two Johnnies back yonder."

"They're not really Portuguese, are they, Major?"

"Great Scott, no! One, Norton, used to be in the Transvaal Police and was kicked out. He's a real mucker. I have several scores to settle with him. Cockney Joe, the other man, has fully as many crimes to his credit as Norton."

"Norton and Cockney Joe! Why, they're both wanted! I can see that I shall have two prisoners to take back. That's something anyway."

The Major smiled at Gilkerson's outburst.

"But what are they doing here, Major?"

"Oh, they're the agents for the Portuguese Government. I imagine they were to be given a free pardon on condition they carried this thing through. I'm not quite sure how they mean to do it. But last night they managed to capture Shimba, Mangwato's son, and I think they mean to use him somehow.

"Norton was just leaving camp to play his hand when you appeared on the scene and told them that I'm on the job. And that put the whole business on the blink again."

"I seem to have played the fool all around," said Gilkerson bitterly.

"Oh, cheer up, old man. It's not your fault. I told the chief to let you in on the secret."

"Why didn't he? Didn't he trust me?"

"It wasn't that he didn't trust you. He only thought that you might not be able to act well enough. Well, there's no harm done. They think I'm safely out of harm's way this time, and unless I'm very much mistaken Norton's on his way to see the chief now."

"What are you going to do? Tell Mangwato he's an impostor?"

"No. That might settle this attempt; but how about the next? Suppose the Portuguese tried again? No. I want to discredit the Portuguese in Mangwato's eyes, not two men masquerading as Portuguese.

"Personally I don't care a tinker's curse whether the British get Mangwato's country or not; I'd rather see the old dear run it himself. But if it's to be a choice between British and Portuguese rule then I'm going to do all I can to help Mangwato choose right.

"Will you put yourself under my orders, old fellow?"

"Do you really mean that I can help?" Gilkerson asked.

"Yes. I take it that you will? Splendid! Then I want you to stay here until dark—say an hour after sundown—and then make your way back to the camp. Take Cockney Joe prisoner—never mind about the bearers; they're harmless—and bring him to Mangwato's *kraal*. I'm going to leave Jim and these warriors with you. I don't fancy there'll be any fighting—Cockney Joe's too much of a cur for that—still you'd better be prepared for anything. Oh, yes. And be sure to bring Shimba along with you. Cockney Joe's holding him prisoner, you know."

"Very good, Major," Gilkerson said with a salute.

"Fine!"

The Major's hand went up in acknowledgment of the salute; and, mounting his horse, he rode swiftly away.

"His horse isn't lame now," Gilkerson mused aloud. "I wonder if I've done the right thing, or—"

"AND WHAT if I give an order to my warriors to slay you?"

Dirty Norton looked around apprehensively at the grim-faced, huge-muscled warriors who lined the large enclosure. Each one held a broad-bladed stabbing-*assegai* in his hand, and it seemed to Norton that they threatened him.

He shuddered involuntarily, and, turning, faced Mangwato again.

He saw that the old chief despite his fierce words was greatly troubled; he seemed to have aged suddenly; his portly form slumped and there was an air of utter dejection about the man.

So, assuming a bold front, Norton replied:

"What would you gain if you killed me, Mangwato? My death would not save your son; and—rest assured of this—the vengeance of my people would be great. All your young men they would put to death, and your women folk they would sell as slaves."

Mangwato was silent; but from the warriors came the ominous cry of:

"Death to the white man! Let us kill him, O Mangwato!"

Mangwato raised his hands and the cries ceased.

"It may not be, my children," he said, "lest we bring down a greater evil upon us. I have for long years known that sooner or later this choice would be forced upon me."

Turning to Norton, he asked—

"What are your conditions for the release of my son?"

"First, O Mangwato," replied Norton with a new courage, "that you give me the diamonds. So shall your son be freed from arrest and the surety of death. Secondly you must send a messenger to the *kraal* of the white men, my people, at Lourenço Marques, praying them to come into your country and aid you to rule it."

"If I do these things will you promise to release my son and to deal gently with my people?"

"Aye. That I promise."

"You will swear it?"

"Aye. I swear it."

Norton's tone was exultant. He had hardly believed that victory would be so easily won.

Again he turned to look at Mangwato's warriors.

At that moment the moon emerged from a cloud and flooded the council-place with her soft light. The broad blades of the *assegais* reflected the light, and it seemed then to Norton that they were so many scintillating diamonds.

"White man," said Mangwato slowly, "this is a deep matter; not one to be settled in the winking of an eye. I would think over it for a little while."

"Are not all things clear? If you do not do thus and so, all things will happen as I have said. Yet to show you that I am just in all things I will grant you until the moon shines directly overhead. That much time, and no more, will I allow."

"That is but a short hour, white man, and I would hold speech with the White Induna—the rod upon whom I lean."

"Who is this white Induna? Much talk this night have I heard of him."

"Do you not know him? He is a white man even as you are, yet not as you are. He has an eye which he can take out and hold in the palm of his hand. When he talks it is as if sleep were still upon him; yet it is in my mind that that man never sleeps. Ah, he is a man among men, and wise in all things."

"He must mean the blasted Major," thought Norton. "If so, what was the Major running away for? Was that a fake? It would be just like him."

Norton was panic-stricken. It seemed that he had after all walked into a trap.

Then came the comforting remembrance of the Major, handcuffed, being escorted back to Georgetown by Gilkerson. He was sure that there was no fake about that arrest. Gilkerson was quite evidently in earnest.

"Your wait will be in vain, Mangwato," he said confidently. "That one will never come here again."

But even as he spoke he was conscious of a stir among the warriors behind him. Turning, he saw that they had opened up their ranks, leaving a narrow passageway leading from an opening in the stockade.

Down this passage, dressed in a suit of immaculate white duck, swinging his monocle nonchalantly by a silken cord, came the Major.

Now and again he would pause before a warrior, and, putting the monocle up to his eye, scrutinize him carefully from head to foot.

It was for all the world like an inspection of a regiment by the commanding officer.

Norton, speechless with amazement, could only watch with mouth agape.

Nor until he had completed his inspection and had come out into the clearing beyond the warriors, did the Major affect to notice Norton.

"Ah! There you are again, dear old chap," he said in tones of well-simulated surprize. " 'Pon my soul, we do meet in queer places. Where did you leave Cockney Joe? And where, where did you get that opéra bouffe uniform? It is simply priceless!"

Norton scowled.

"But you don't understand English, do you? Of course not. How stupid of me! French? No? Well, we'll use Mangwato's language. Who knows? We may set the fashion, and it may be the diplomatic language of the world."

The Major turned to the chief.

"Word came that you had need of me, Mangwato."

"Aye. A deep need, O friend of my people.

"This one—" he indicated Norton—"says that certain of my people, led by Shimba, my son, have killed his servants. My son he holds prisoner and says he will have him put to death unless I give him the diamonds, and send a message to his people asking them to come in and help me to rule."

"And what do you say?"

"I am minded to obey his commands, for my son is dear to me. Further, he hath sworn that with my consent or not his people will come to govern over me."

"But what if I tell you he lies? What if I tell you that your warriors did not kill his people?

"Heed well, and listen to the true story. Certain of his warriors raided the crops of your son and, he, hearing of it, drove them off. Then your son, even Shimba, went to the camp of these white men demanding that the thieves be punished. That is all, save that Shimba they kept a prisoner, holding him by trickery."

Mangwato rose slowly to his feet. His right hand held a toy *assegai*, the symbol of his rank.

The warriors watched him intently. The dropping of the *assegai* would be the signal for Norton's death.

"Is this a true word?" the chief asked Norton.

"It is a lie. But even so, even if it be a true word, what then? Your son's life I hold in the hollow of my hand. Have a care then what you do with me."

"That is true, that is true. I had forgotten that."

Mangwato slowly resumed his seat.

"There is no way out," he said mournfully to the Major. "If I would spare my son's life I must obey this liar, this trickster in all things. Aye, I call him evil names, for I am well convinced that the tale you tell me is a true one. Ah, wo is me that I must give my people over to the rule of men who achieve their ends by evil cunning!"

"Your son is a crafty warrior, Mangwato," said the Major. "It may well be that he has escaped. Listen! Once before this night I have heard the beating of the signal-drums. Now I hear it again. Listen, warriors, and proclaim its meaning."

A deep hush spread over the assemblage.

To their ears came the high, staccato notes of the signal-drum— Africa's primitive wireless.

"IT IS from Shimba's *kraal!*" cried one of the warriors.

"Aye, but the message?"

"Shimba journeys to the *kraal* of Mangwato. Two strangers—white men—are with him."

The Major turned smilingly to Norton.

"Gilkerson is bringing our mutual friend, Cockney Joe, here under arrest. Funny, isn't it?"

With a snarl of rage Norton leaped at the Major and hit him full on the jaw.

The Major reeled before the blow; but before Norton could follow up the blow he was seized and held securely by two massive warriors.

"I didn't think you had it in you, Dirty," said the Major, "and I'm beastly sorry and all that that I can't oblige you with a mill. But it isn't done, you know. We must preserve the dignity of the well-known superior race. Some other time when we're alone I'll be glad to oblige you."

Norton's response was a string of vile curses as he struggled furiously to break away from his guards.

"Be quiet, you fool."

The Major's voice cut like a whip.

"Don't you see that Mangwato's toying with his *assegai*. In another minute he'll give the signal that will mean your death. As it is I'll have the dickens of a job to save your life. Don't make it any harder."

Norton's struggles ceased instantly; and the Major turned to face Mangwato, who had been watching the two white men intently.

The shouts of joy which had hailed the news from the *kraal* of Shimba died away, and all awaited in silence for word from the chief. As they waited, the signal-drum from a near-by *kraal* beat out the news that Shimba and his party were but a short trek from the *kraal* of the chief, and when its notes had died away Mangwato addressed the Major.

"Again I have to thank you, O my friend, and friend of all my people. Again you have saved my son."

"Some little part I played, Mangwato. But not alone did I accomplish this. Another white man, a man of my race, a man high in the council of my people, wearing the dress of a chief, merits your thanks. He saved your son."

"He shall not be forgotten in the time of rejoicing. But what shall I do with this other one?"

Mangwato looked darkly at Norton.

"Death by the spear would be showing him too great an honor. First he must know pain."

"Give me his life, Mangwato. It is but a little thing to ask."

"And is it all you ask?"

"All. And it is but a little thing."

"True. Then I give him to you. Let him be taken away and guarded closely until you have made known your wishes concerning him."

As the warriors were about to lead Norton away Mangwato ordered them to wait.

"It is well," he said, "that one should see this."

"Hear me, O, my people," he cried. "Long have I known that the time would come when I must make a choice between two tribes of white men who sought to rule this land of mine, and but a little while ago it seemed that an evil choice was thrust upon me. And it would have been evil to have made our rulers a people who won that honor through lying and treachery. You know well who kept the evil from us, who restored my son to me. Long has he dwelt among us, and he has been at all times the rod upon which I leaned. He has taught me many things, and through the knowledge you have gotten from him you have made the crops to flourish, the herds to put on fatness.

"Nor is this all. He has ever been at my right hand when I sat in judgment. When I would have pronounced a sentence of death upon one of you he has counseled a more merciful way; aye, a better way. It was he—

"But what need for more words concerning him? He is well known to you all. What say you?"

"Aye, chief. He is a man of single heart; there is no evil in him."

"And you find no fault with his dealing with you?"

"None, lord."

The answer came with a mighty shout.

"After you, he is first in our hearts."

"Then I go to the English, for his way is their way, begging them to come and rule over us as they see fit. What say you now?"

"Your words sound good to our ears, O Mangwato. We are well content."

"It is well. Now I go to meet my son."

A FEW days later Mangwato, escorted by a party of picked warriors, set out on his mission to the British authorities.

Gilkerson accompanied him as far as Georgetown. He had two prisoners—Norton and Cockney Joe, both of whom preferred to face the Transvaal courts rather than the wrath of the soft-voiced, smiling Senhor José Alvaro.

BITTER ALUM

THE MAJOR was bored and the expression on his face, as he looked around his room at the Diamond Town's principal hotel, was one of supreme disgust.

He had shaved; he had bathed; he had manicured his nails; his eyeglass was polished to the highest point of perfection. There was nothing left for him to do!

Three weeks ago he had come into Johannesburg from the veldt looking forward to a long sojourn in that town, surrounded by the luxuries and comforts of civilization. He had dined and wined; wined and dined, to his heart's content. More—he was surfeited. Civilization began to pall on him and he longed to be out on the veldt where a man can breathe.

A little encounter with a would-be blackmailer had afforded a break in the monotony. In order to bring that affair to a successful conclusion the Major had been obliged to move to the Diamond Town and now, having been instrumental in sending the blackmailer to serve five years on the Cape Town breakwater, he was loath to return to Johannesburg and waited with ill concealed impatience for the return of his native servant—Jim, the Hottentot.

Always the Major, most famous of I.D.B.s, experienced this change of heart. Time and time again, after a successful deal in illicitly purchased diamonds, he assured himself that he was through with the vagrant life, and would settle down and become a peaceful, law-abiding subject of the Crown.

But always the call of the veldt was too much for him. The lure of the game had too great a hold on him, and the desire to match his wits against the wits of the detectives made him forget all about his self-made vows. A week, two weeks, a month at the most would see him engaged in the machinations necessary to obtain more diamonds and then, as surely as night follows day, he would be compelled to shake the dust of civilization from his feet and seek sanctuary in some distant part of the bush veldt—usually in a region teeming with big game.

Incidentally, when the Major did make such a move the dust which he shook from his feet invariably blinded the detectives who were eager to arrest him with illicitly purchased diamonds in his possession.

The Major rose slowly from his chair and strolled over to the window which looked out upon the dusty street. It was almost deserted. A few ricksha boys lolled listlessly on the hot pavement waiting for their patrons. A coolie fruit seller wandered idly by, calling out his wares in a nasal singsong. The ubiquitous Chinese laundryman shuffled down the centre of the dusty street indifferent to the taunts and jeers of the ricksha boys. Not a white man was in sight, for it was nearly high noon and the heat waves danced above the yellow roadway. It was the hour when white men seek the comparative coolness of their rooms.

The Major drummed a light tattoo on the window pane, shrugged his shoulders, and was about to turn away when two native policemen, escorting a shackled prisoner, came into his field of vision.

A look of annoyance crossed the Major's face as he recognized in the squat, ungainly figure of the prisoner, Jim, the Hottentot, Jim, his faithful servant.

"I wonder what the deuce the silly blighter's been up to now?" he mused. "This means I'll have to stay in this hole until he's served his time. Confound it."

He opened the window meaning to hail the escort and their prisoner, but as he did so they turned down a side street, and the opportunity was lost.

The Major turned from the window, put on a large sun helmet, adjusted his monocle, and sauntered slowly down the stairs leading to the crowded hotel bar room.

One of the plain-clothes detectives occupied a corner table and the Major walked toward him, his eyes filled with a light of pleased recognition.

"Ha there, Cushing," he drawled, "haven't seen you for ages, old top."

Cushing looked up with a smile which quickly gave place to a frown, and after a moment's hesitation he rose to his feet and left the bar room with a curt, "Good day, Major."

"Deuced astonishing!" ejaculated the Major as he looked blankly after the retreating figure of the detective. "I wonder what's on the old chap's mind?"

Still wondering, the Major passed out into the street and, climbing into a ricksha, ordered the native to take him to the police station.

Twice he saw, and hailed, acquaintances in the uniform of the police and each time was ignored. With these experiences in mind he was not over surprised at the greeting which awaited him at the police station.

There, instead of being received with the customary banter and the rough horseplay of good fellowship, the Major was asked curtly:

"What do you want? Any complaint to make?"

No. The Major was not altogether surprised but he was deeply hurt.

Hitherto the police, with one or two exceptions, had been on the best of terms with the Major. They were good sports and recognized that he also was a good sport. Though they never relaxed in their efforts to effect his arrest, it was an unwritten law of the Force that that arrest should be accomplished in a legitimate manner. The Major appreciated this and had never sought to trade on this friendship; neither, for that matter, had the police, save the exceptions above noted, abused the friendship by trying to trap the Major. Everything between them was open and above board. There was a constant matching of wits and when, as invariably happened, the Major came off trumps, the police were the first to chuckle at the way they had been outwitted. Again, when the Major's plans were successfully balked, the congratulations of the Major himself were none the less sincere.

"Well, what is it?" the sergeant at the desk repeated roughly. "Can't wait here all day for you to make up your mind."

The Major looked in bewilderment, first at the stern-faced sergeant, at the trooper sitting near the door, then back to the sergeant again.

Yes. The Major was bewildered and hurt. He felt like a small child, who, running to his mother, receives a harsh blow instead of the loving caress he expected, and had the right to expect.

"What is it all about, Sergeant, old top?"

The sergeant flushed a little and answered in still gruffer tones,

"That's what I'm here to find out. Have you any complaint? If not, get out of here."

"Oh, my word, yes. Of course I have a complaint, Serg, old dear. I want to know why you Johnnies are so suddenly dignified, and all that. Why, 'pon my soul, you are just like real policemen. I really believe you'd arrest me on suspicion were it not for the fact that I'm above suspicion. Oh, absolutely above suspicion."

Did the sergeant's mouth twitch under his walruslike moustache? The Major thought so, but the policeman's voice was still gruff as he replied, "We're all right. If that's your complaint you'd better *hamba*. I'm busy."

He bent to his papers.

"Oh, but I have another complaint, Mr. Sergeant, sir."

"Out with it then." The sergeant did hot raise his head.

"Well, you see, here am I waiting for my servant Jim—he's a Hottentot, you know—and what do you think? To-day I saw him with two native police boys. He was handcuffed; my servant handcuffed! Do you think, Mr. Sergeant, sir, that he's arrested by any chance?"

"It looks that way, doesn't it?" commented the sergeant sarcastically.

"Really? Do you think so? Then I'm sure it's all a beastly mistake. Jim wouldn't break the law any more than I would."

The sergeant smiled openly at this, then frowned.

"I don't know anything about it," he said.

"Now you're just fooling me," expostulated the Major. "All arrests are reported here, aren't they? Of course they are and—you see I was about to leave on a—er—hunting expedition and Jim's absolutely indispensable, quite."

"I don't know anything about it."

The Major turned to the trooper by the door.

"How about you, old top?"

The trooper shrugged his shoulders but made no reply.

"It's a conspiracy," cried the Major indignantly, "that's what it is. I shall write to the papers. It's monstrous; it's infamous; it's—"

Words failed him.

"You'll read all about it in the paper tonight, Major. That's all I can say," said the sergeant.

The Major looked at him closely and was about to ask a question, but the sergeant's attitude was that of a man who fears that he has already said too much, so with a whimsical gesture of dismay the Major turned to leave.

JUST OUTSIDE the door he came face to face with an elderly man whose twinkling gray eyes were just now clouded by sorrow.

"Hullo, Chief," exclaimed the Major.

"Happy days, Major," said the other with a faint smile and would have passed on had not the Major barred his way.

"Look here, dear old top, you've got to tell me what all this means. Here I go around with a smile on my face, hail-fellow-well-met, and all that sort of thing, and what do I get in reply? The back of the hand and the frozen face—if you know what I mean."

"Yes, I know what you mean, Major," the other answered wearily.

"And you're infected with the same microbe, Chief?"

"Not exactly, Major. But don't call me Chief. I'm all through. In the future I'll be just plain Mister Grayson."

"What do you mean?" The Major was sorely puzzled. "Surely, friend of my youth, you're not going to leave the police?"

"I've already left. I handed in my resignation yesterday—by special request. You'll have to walk softly now, my boy. If you don't, the new chief will have you cooling your heels down at the Breakwater, as I ought to have done—long ago."

"It isn't your fault I'm not now there, Chief," the Major said with a wry smile. "But do you really mean that you are no longer head of the Force?"

"Just that, and I feel twenty years younger already. It's a great relief to be rid of the responsibility of watching rogues like you."

Grayson tried to speak lightly, but his voice shook slightly.

"I see," the Major murmured. He was beginning to see a great deal. "So you're glad, are you? Come and have a drink to celebrate?"

"No, thanks. I've no time. Good-day, Major, and good-bye."

"I'm dashed if I'll say 'Good-bye.' This is all a part of one of your cunning plots and in a few days you'll be trying to put some bracelets on my wrists. Confess now, isn't that your little game?"

But Grayson shook his head sadly and passed on.

"That explains a lot," mused the Major as he climbed into his ricksha. "No wonder, the fellows are grumpy to-day, knowing that dear old 'Daddy' Grayson has left the Force. What, I wonder, can the evening paper have to say that will help me to locate Jim?"

AS THE Major passed through the hotel office on the way to his room, the clerk at the desk handed him a small package.

He took it with a word of thanks. It had come through the mail, he noticed, and the postmark was Johannesburg. Now the Major was not expecting any parcel through the mail, and as it was a fairly common trick for an "informer" to send a parcel containing diamonds to a man and then give evidence to the police that would cause that man's arrest for I.D.B., the Major did not open the parcel until he had reached the privacy of his room. Even then he carefully locked the door, and peered under the bed and in the clothes closet to make sure that there was no one to spy upon him.

The parcel contained, however, nothing incriminating but a large—slightly over-large—cigar case made of gold. The workmanship of it was wonderful and on one side the letter M was outlined with rubies.

Opening it he discovered a little note, which read:

> Dear Major:
> I hope you will accept this little gift from a very grateful woman. My son is to be married next month and, now that I have no more to fear from that horrible blackmailer—thanks to you!—I am a very happy woman.
> If you will examine the case closely you will discover something that may be useful to you. A private safety vault, I suggest, for your valuables.
> > Faithfully yours,
> > ANNE FORRESTER.

"The blessed old dear," murmured the Major, Mrs. Forrester being the chief reason for his presence in the Diamond Town. "Of course she doesn't know that cigars make me most frightfully sick! I wonder what she means by the 'safety vault' arrangement?"

He turned the cigar case over and over between his slender but powerful hands, estimating its weight and endeavoring to discover the secret.

He had about given up when it suddenly occurred to him that the case was much longer than was necessary, and a close inspection of the interior brought to light the fact that there was a space between the gold cover and the bottom of the holder—a false bottom in other words. It was a fairly simple step from that to the discovery that the case was really composed of two thin shells telescoped together, and that by exercising a firm, steady pull the inner shell could be removed. The space between the two shells at the bottom of the case being, of course, the "private safety vault." It was large enough to hold a number of good sized diamonds.

Yet, so well was the case made, it would have defied the Major's detection had not his attention been directly called to the fact that the case was not all that it seemed. His delight in it was that of a small boy with a new toy.

"Yes, by Jove," he chuckled, "I must certainly use this, even if it means that I must smoke cigars. My private safety vault—that's too rich."

Just then there was a knock at the door and, putting the case in his pocket—the note he had destroyed after the first reading—the Major called, "Who's there?"

"I've brought up the paper, Major," replied the voice of the hotel clerk. "There's something in it I thought you ought to read."

"Deuced good of you, old chap."

The Major unlocked the door and a few minutes later was eagerly scanning the paper—still wet from the press—for the item that would explain the arrest of Jim.

Nor had he far to look, for on the first page he read:

"New Chief of Detectives promises to have all the I.D.B.s under arrest before the end of the month."

The Major whistled softly, and read on,

It has for a long time been a matter of common knowledge that the Diamond Mining Syndicate has been dissatisfied with the Detective Force as at present constituted. As a result of the political pressure exercised by the Syndicate the City Fathers have urged Mr. ——, late of Scotland Yard, to take over the task of reconstruction.

Mr. —— (we are not at liberty to give his name at this time or to reproduce his portrait) officially took up his duties this morning, though he has been some few weeks in our midst, incognito, getting a line on local conditions and problems.

Mr. ——, in an interview, stated that he wished to keep his identity a secret a little while longer—even from the members of the Force.

Hitherto, he said, there had been a great deal too much fraternizing between the police and the criminals.

"I do not wish to suggest," said the New Chief, "that members of the Force are dishonest, or that they are confederates of the I.D.B.s. Still, a man is known by the company he keeps, and to-day my first official action was to send out a bulletin to members of the force, announcing that any one discovered in the company of an I.D.B.— except in the line of duty—would be discharged. Why, just imagine. I am given to understand that my predecessor was in the habit of consorting in public—in public, mind you—with this fellow they call the Major. What an example for a chief of detectives to set his men! As a matter of fact, however, it is my private opinion that this Major is nothing but a fool—a dude fool. Oh, I know that he's reputed to have pulled off some very clever schemes, but you don't want to believe all you hear. They're just tales to cover up the inefficiency—or worse— of the Force. I've already had a few words with this Major chap—of course he didn't know with whom he was talking—and it's my impression that if he is an I.D.B., and I very much doubt it, he acts solely on the instructions received from brainier men higher up. Now if he were clever like Paine, the counterfeiter, I might have some slight trouble in dealing with him. As it is—bah! I'll have the goods on him inside a week, if he's crooked. I've already made my first move. The finger-prints and photograph of Jim—the Major's servant—were taken as a result of my orders, and if Jim shows himself at any of the mine compounds in future, he'll quickly find himself on the way to the Breakwater. I believe in the old saying, 'Prevention is better than cure,' and if I can prevent the Major from getting stones through his nigger, I've accomplished a good deal.

"Yes, I can flatter myself that you may safely tell your readers that I'll have this town clean of criminals inside a month."

The Major threw down the paper with a snort of disgust.

"Of all the self-sufficient, conceited animals, commend me to the new chief," he exclaimed. "And he has the nerve to insinuate that Daddy Grayson played a double game. The bounder! That interview will just about break Daddy Grayson's heart. Every one knows that he did more to clean up this country than any other man. As for this Mister Bloomin' Detective Blank— By Jove, if I were only clever like that what's his name counterfeiter, I'd give Mr. Blank a fine run for his money.

"Evidently Jim's arrest was only a temporary affair, so I ought to be hearing from the rascal before long."

As if in answer to the Major's thought there sounded a pattering of footsteps in the corridor outside his room and a guttural voice called softly,

"*Baas.*"

"Come in, Jim, you old heathen."

The door opened slowly and the grinning face of Jim, the Hottentot, appeared in the aperture. He looked at his *Baas* as though striving to read his thoughts, then, sensing that the Major was not displeased with him, he entered the room, and squatted on his haunches by the door.

"The *Baas* sent for me, and I am here," he commented.

"You should have been here yesterday."

Jim nodded.

"Truly, *Baas.* But the road from my *kraal* is hard and strewn with thorns."

"The police were the thorns?"

"The *Baas* knows that then?"

"What is not known to me?" murmured the Major.

"Then the *Baas* doubtless knows that I had committed no fault?"

"Yes. I know that too, Jim. It was but a game."

"A strange game, *Baas,*" the Hottentot muttered. "First they must have the print of my hand, and then my *fot-graf.* Also they took me to the compounds of all the mines and made me known to the Compound Police. Tchat! What folly! Who does not know Jim—the servant of the *Mahjaw?*"

"It was an act of folly, undoubtedly," agreed the Major.

"But what how, *Baas?* Do we play the game again? Of a truth I am over-tired of living in the *kraals.* The beer brewed by the women grows stale, and mellie meal—three times a day, look you—is no proper food for a man."

"And so you have the wanderlust still, have you, you old vagabond? Strange how it gets in the blood."

Jim had a fair understanding of the English language but could only speak a few words—if one excepts a large vocabulary of curses—which he used indiscriminately whenever his *Baas* spoke to him in English.

"Yaas, sir," said Jim.

"Yes, Jim," continued the Major, "we'll go ahunting, my boy. To-morrow I'll get a license and then, heigh ho! for the high veldt. Can't afford to stay around here, you know. That very clever Detective Johnny might try to trap a poor innocent chap like me, and send me to the

Breakwater. And, really, I'm not strong enough to do manual labor."

Jim, thinking some comment was necessary, said stolidly, "No. Go' dam me, yes."

"No—yes, that's the question, you blear-eyed old reprobate," chuckled the Major. "But I think yes. Oh, certainly, yes."

"Yes," Jim assented. "If I don't see you, so long, hullo."

"Jim."

The Hottentot rose to his feet.

"Yah, *Baas?*"

"The wagon and mules? Where are they?"

"I made camp on the veldt beyond the town as the *Baas* ordered."

"Good. Tomorrow I will send out food for a long trek."

Jim's face lighted with joy.

"Does the *Baas* play the game?"

The Major shook his head.

"No. We go at will, and at our own pace. There will be no one seeking us."

"But listen, *Baas*. While I was in the *trunk* (jail) a boy from one of the compounds was also there. He told me that he had hidden six 'stones.' They were big stones he said; so big," Jim traced a circle on the floor about the size of a pea. "He was a fool, *Baas*. He said that he would sell them to me for a tikkey each."

"And what did you say?" the Major's voice was curt.

Jim grinned.

"What do I know about stones, *Baas*. What good would they be to me? I told that very big fool that it was against the white man's law to buy and sell the white stones. But," Jim lowered his voice to a whisper—"I know where that boy works, *Baas*, and if it is your will I can bring him to you so that you may buy the stones."

"But he is in *trunk*, Jim."

"Nay. He was in *trunk*, yes. But as I was coming to this place I saw him on the street. He was returning, he said, to his compound."

The Major smiled. Evidently the new chief had sprung his first trap, a very poor one.

"You know all the white police, Jim?" he asked suddenly.

"Yah, *Baas*."

"Did you see a new one at the trunk?"

"Nay, *Baas*, but I heard one."

"What do you mean?"

"It was when they were taking the print of my hand. There was a man in another room who gave out orders to other men. The door was open and so I heard."

"And what was the manner of his voice?"

"It was the voice of a man, *Baas*, who has small respect for other men. A fat man he was, I should judge, for he grunted when he had completed an order, and he breathed noisily through his nose."

"Is that all, Jim?"

"Yah, *Baas*."

"It is good. You have my leave to go."

Jim paused, his hand on the knob of the door.

"Is there any need to keep thy intentions secret, should any ask, *Baas*?"

"Nay. Speak loudly, for all to hear, that on the morrow, or the next day, we go a-hunting."

THAT NIGHT the Major, dressed with more than ordinary care, sat at a corner table in the hotel dining room.

Since his conversation with Jim he had been busily engaged in purchasing supplies for his trip, and bidding good-bye to his numerous acquaintances. In his wallet was a government license entitling him to shoot all species of game in Class B. Altogether he was well pleased with his accomplishments which would, he hoped, be brought to the attention of the new chief of police.

"If he does get wind of my departure, he will probably boast that fear of him drove me away. And that's partly true, by Jove. I wouldn't mind being arrested—decently, that is—but to be trapped!" the Major shuddered. "On the other hand," he continued, resuming his original thought, "he may be tempted to endeavor to trap me. It would be rather a feather in his cap, I flatter myself, if he were able to commence his reign over the dear detectives by arresting the 'notorious Major.'"

The Major lighted a cigarette and, lolling back in his chair, amused himself by blowing intricate smoke rings. Apparently he was concentrating his whole attention on this innocent diversion. In reality he was watching, very closely, a stout, red faced man, with coarse black hair, who was noisily consuming his food at a nearby table.

Soon the man pushed away his plate with a grunt of satisfaction and, producing a long, black cigar, felt in his pockets for a match. His search proving a vain one he looked around the almost deserted dining room with that helpless expression on his face peculiar to men who are in need of a match, until he encountered the Major's eye. Then he rose and walked over to the Major's table, seated himself, and asked gruffly,

"Got a match?"

"Have a handful, old dear."

"Thanks. One 'ull do." He lit his cigar and blew a cloud of smoke in the Major's face.

"My smoke too strong for you?" he grunted as the Major began to cough.

"By Jove, yes. Do put that beastly thing away, and have one of mine." The Major proffered his case to the fat man, who took out a cigar and smelled it critically.

"Um! Looks like a good smoke. I'll try it—later. A nice case this."

"Glad you think so. It was a present from an old friend of mine. But, I say, I wish you'd put that beastly thing away—no offense meant—and smoke one of mine. Take the lot, if that'll bribe you."

The man grinned.

"Oh, I'll take the lot if it'll please you," he said, and suited the action to the words, handing back an empty case to the Major, "but I can't afford to throw this one away."

"In that case, old top, you'll have to excuse me."

The other put out a restraining hand.

"No. Sit down, Major." His voice dropped to a hoarse whisper, "I've got a little business deal on hand that I'd like to talk over with you."

"Me? Business? Oh, my dear man, I'm perfectly hopeless where figures are concerned."

"But how about stones?"

The fat man winked.

"Stones?"

"Hush! Not so loud. Sit down. I tell you."

The Major obeyed as though impelled by a stronger will.

"But really," he stammered, "Mr.—er— Why you see how ridiculous it would be for me to talk business of any sort with you. I don't even know your name."

"Call me Townley. It's a good enough name for me. Look here; tell me what you think of these."

He held out a pudgy fist toward the Major, opened it, and exposed to view six good sized diamonds.

The Major was frankly envious.

"Wonderful," he exclaimed, "if they are diamonds. Of course one can't always tell, can one?"

"They're diamonds, all right. Handle 'em if you doubt it. Go on; we're safe. No one can see what we are doing."

Gingerly the Major examined them one by one. It seemed a very casual inspection, yet the Major could have described each stone minutely and could have given the approximate weight and value.

"You're deuced lucky," he said. "They seem to be—er—perfect. They represent quite a jolly little sum, don't they?"

"You've said it. But I'm new to this game; I don't know how to get rid of them. There's too many sharp nosed detectives in this place. Give me five pounds apiece and they're yours. What do you say?"

"You must be joking, old chap. They're worth considerably more than that."

"Of course," assented the other; "but I don't want to run the risk of offering them for sale. Now you've got the reputation of being able to handle that end of the business. You take the stones at my price, and you get the profit."

"I don't quite follow you, but I can quite see where it would be possible to make a lot of money. Your proposition is tempting, very tempting, I can assure you. I suppose they're actually worth double the price you're asking?"

"Double? A hundred times as much would be nearer the mark."

The Major's eyes were opened wide in innocent astonishment.

"No—really?" he asked in an awed voice.

"At least that," Townley replied complacently. "Well, are you going to take them? If not, I know a man who will."

The Major hesitated.

"Of course," he said slowly, "I'd like to make a little easy money. Every Johnny does, but, well the fact is I haven't got that much money on me. But, I say, will you hold them for me until to-morrow night?"

"It's a bargain," said the other heartily.

"Oh, and there's one other thing. Do you mind bringing them up to my room? I'm rather afraid to make a deal like that in such a public place."

"Haven't got the heart of a chicken, have you?" scoffed the other. "All right. If it'll make you feel any better, I'll come up to your room. What time?"

"Nine o'clock, old chap, will suit me."

"I'll be there. Good-night."

Townley rose slowly to his feet and with much puffing and grunting, made his way down the dining room out into the bar beyond.

A few minutes later the Major also made his way to the bar room. Townley was nowhere to be seen.

Returning to the dining room the Major stopped to exchange some good-natured banter with one of the waitresses.

"Why so gloomy, Mary, old dear?"

"I'm looking at you, Major; ain't that sufficient?"

"Oh come now, dear miss, tell me the real reason. Is our charming and mutual friend Detective Blake a little cross to-day?"

The girl looked at him in astonishment.

"How did you know Dick had the blues?"

"My superior intellect. What's more, I know a cure for his particular complaint."

"Wish to heaven I did."

The Major slipped a gold coin in her hand.

"Just a little farewell present, Mary old dear. And—er—I hate to ask favors of a lady but, er—"

"Out with it, Major. You know very well that any one of us would jump through a hoop if you asked us."

The Major blushed.

"Don't make fun of my gray hairs, miss. But seriously, do you think you could induce friend Blake to visit my room, very secretly you understand, about six o'clock to-morrow night?"

"I'll try, Major. But what's the game?"

"That's my—er—little secret."

PUNCTUALLY AT nine o'clock the following night the Major admitted the man Townley to his room.

"Well, I'm here, you see, Major," Townley blustered, "Let's get to business."

"You'll pardon me if I lock the door, old man. You see there are no end of sneak thieves and what not, in this town."

"Oh, I don't mind. Bolt it, too, if you like."

Townley was wandering around the room noting, with a sarcastic smile, the formidable array of toilet articles which always formed a part of the Major's equipment.

"Going to start a barber's shop?" he asked, indicating with a wave of his hand the row of bottles.

"What? Oh no. I suffer a great deal from sunburn, you know, and I have to treat my skin very carefully, very carefully indeed, I can assure you. But now, as you so neatly put it, let's get to business."

Townley took out a little chamois bag.

"The stones are here, but where's your thirty pounds?"

"Right here, old top." The Major slapped his hip pocket. "But do you mind if I examine the stones again? I'm not a very good judge you know, and I didn't have time to really examine them last night."

Townley opened the little bag and allowed the stones to roll out on to the table. As he did so there was a knock at the door and in his eagerness to cover up the diamonds, the Major almost overturned the lamp. Indeed it would have fallen to the ground had not Townley rushed to the rescue.

"Who's there?" the Major called in a quavering voice.

"I've brought the can of hot water, sar." It was one of the hotel servants.

"Confound it," exclaimed the Major in tones of confused annoyance, "I'd forgotten all about asking them to send me up some shaving water." His voice was very weak, and Townley noticed that he was deathly white.

"By Jove, old chap," continued the Major, "I can't go on with this business deal to-night. Really, you know, this sudden shock has upset my nerves. I'm subject to these attacks—a bad heart, you know, and I have to be very careful. You don't mind, do you. Honestly, I can't go on with this to-night."

He had taken out his cigar case and was toying with it nervously. Townley thought he was about to faint.

"Don't be a woman, Major. All you have to do is give me thirty quid and I give you the stones."

The Major waved his hands weakly in denial.

"I can't do it to-night," he gasped.

Townley looked at him for a few minutes in deep disgust, then replacing the stones in the bag, strode from the room in a furious temper.

AS THE man Townley walked slowly down the corridor leading from the Major's room, he was suddenly accosted by two uniformed policemen, who, acting on the instructions of a third man in civilian clothes, handcuffed him despite his threats and furious struggles.

"What do you mean by this outrage?" he bellowed.

"You're under arrest, suspected I.D.B., and this," the plain-clothes man produced the chamois bag from Townley's pocket, "contains the evidence."

"You damned fools," howled Townley. "I'll break you for this. Don't you know I'm the new chief of police?"

"That's a hell of a yarn. Tell it to the marines," said one of the men, with a guffaw. "Come on, and the quieter you are the easier it will be."

Having nothing on his person by which he could prove his identity, Townley gave in with an ill grace, though he ventured a protest when the policemen forced him to pass through the crowded bar room.

At the police station he again endeavored to convince his captors and the sergeant in charge, that he was their new chief. But his protests were in vain; neither would the sergeant permit him to communicate with the men who, he claimed, could identify him.

"Time enough for that foolishness in the morning," said the sergeant.

"Better put the evidence in the safe, Sergeant," said the detective as the troopers led away the cursing Townley to a cell. "It's too valuable to leave on your desk. There's six stones in that bag. I'm going to turn in now. I'll be around in the morning to take care of this case."

IT WAS not until eleven the next day that the sergeant agreed to send for a certain influential member of the Diamond Mining Syndicate. But when that potentate did arrive Townley's release was a matter of a few minutes.

His first act was to threaten the detective who had arrested him with discharge, and the sergeant with demotion.

"Oh come," interposed the potentate mildly, "that would be hardly fair, chief. The men didn't know you were the chief, and they were only performing their duty, after all."

The chief essayed to hide his wrath, but the silent threats flashed by his eyes as he scowled first at the detective and then at the sergeant, made those two individuals shuffle their feet uneasily.

"And how did you make out with the Major?" asked the potentate. "I take that you did not succeed in trapping him?"

"No, sir. It's just as I thought. He hasn't the guts to be an I.D.B. He's just a pink rabbit."

"I see," mused the potentate. "I wish I could believe that he's as harmless as you seem to think, Chief. However, that's your affair. If you'll let me have the stones—I take it that you have no further use for them—I'll run along."

The chief turned to the sergeant with a snarl.

"Get the stones."

"Yes, sir, very good, sir."

"Here they are, sir," said Townley. "Six of them."

The potentate opened the bag to verify the count; then, acting on a sudden impulse, let them roll out on to the palm of his hand.

"What does this mean, Chief?" he asked in an angry tone. "Are you trying to play a game with me?"

"What do you mean, sir." stammered Townley.

"These are not the stones I entrusted to you."

"Oh, but they are, sir," Townley replied earnestly. "They haven't been out of my possession until they were taken from me by the detective here."

Yet, as he spoke, Townley remembered, with a feeling of alarm, the incident of the falling lamp in the Major's room.

"Nonsense, man. These things are nothing but alum, sucked to resemble the diamonds. They are very like the real diamonds in shape, size, and color. But they're alum just the same. Look."

He threw one of the supposed diamonds on the ground. It shattered into a thousand pieces.

"It's my opinion, Chief," said the potentate slowly, "that you're a damned fool. I can't imagine Grayson getting in a hole like this. I shall expect you to return my stones, or—"

The end of the sentence was lost in the banging of the door as he passed out into the street.

ABOUT THIS time the Major was watching Jim prepare the food at the first halt of their trek to the big game country.

The Major wore a contented smile, for his plans had been carried through without a hitch. In the false bottom of his cigar case, each wrapped in cotton wool to prevent it from clinking against the sides, reposed six diamonds. And—

The aroma of coffee was carried to him by a vagrant breeze.

"Jim," the Major called.

"Yah, *Baas?*"

"Make the coffee strong." He moistened his lips with his tongue and added in a melancholy voice, "I'll never get the flavor of that alum out of my mouth."

THE SEVENTH PLAGUE

THE LITTLE tin shack which served as an office for the owners of the Star Mine was insufferably hot, but not hotter than the tempers of its two occupants—"Lanky" Johnson and "Squint" Turner.

Lanky's face, usually wearing a meek, mock pious expression, was distorted with rage. He rose suddenly to his feet and with a wild sweep of his hand knocked the whisky bottle from the table.

"That's all you're fit for," he screamed in a high pitched voice. "That's all you do: sit and guzzle whisky all day at a quid a bottle."

"What's that to you?" growled the other. His eyes, bloodshot and rheumy, glared balefully from a jungle of bushy eyebrows, and unkempt beard. "It comes out of my share of the takings, don't it?"

Lanky, with an effort, gained control of his temper, and resumed his seat.

"What's the use of quarrelling?" he asked in a mild oily voice. "We're partners, ain't we Squint?"

"Of course we are," assented the other.

"Then let's get down to business and see if we can't settle this. I'm right, ain't I, when I say we've got to have niggers to work the mine, or else close down?"

Squint nodded.

"Well! Ain't it your job to see we get niggers? That was the agreement. Me to look after the mining; you to boss the niggers."

"Whose fault is it we ain't got no niggers, I'd like to know? Tell me that."

"Yourn, Squint. You treat 'em worse nor dogs, and of course they won't stay."

"How do you want me to treat 'em? Make love to 'em?" Squint laughed, showing a row of uneven, yellow teeth.

"At any rate," continued Lanky, "you might use 'em a bit better at the compound. I don't hold with pampering niggers myself and kick every one who comes in my way; do it on general principles. But that's all right. They don't mind a kick now and then—they'd think something was wrong if they didn't get it. What they do mind, though, is the way you treat them at the compound and the rotten food you dish out to 'em."

"I had a hundred for yer at the beginning of the month, didn't I? It ain't my fault that the most of 'em deserted, is it? If you'd let me report it to the police, the way I wanted, we'd have had 'em all back by this time."

Lanky snorted.

"Use your brains, Squint. We don't want nothing to do with the police one way or the other; can't afford to have them poking their noses into our affairs. The thing for you to do, Squint, is to make a trip to one of the *kraals* and see if you can't pick up a few niggers. Take plenty of whisky with you; that'll fetch 'em in. And when you get 'em see that they don't get a chance to desert. Set a guard on the compound and rope them together when they go to and from the mine."

"Bit risky feeding them with whisky, Lanky. The police might hear of it and then there 'ud be hell to pay."

Again Lanky snorted.

"Police! What can they know about it? Once a month they make a trip through the District. One's due here today or tomorrow and when he's gone we won't be troubled by the law for a month. Where's the risk?"

"I suppose it 'ud be all right," agreed Squint. "I'll try it anyway when the police patrol's been and gone."

"That's the way to talk, Squint. You can do it. Well, so long. I'm going down to the store."

As Lanky left the hut Squint picked up the whisky bottle from the floor and seeing that the contents of it had not entirely been spilled, put it up to his lips and drank noisily.

Then he, too, left the hut.

Just as he emerged from the doorway he collided with a stout elderly native. It mattered little to Squint that the fault was all his;

the native had insulted him by knocking against him and the native must pay. Squint had his own theory of dealing with the native question, and it was a theory he did not hesitate to put into execution.

"Take that, you black dog; and that, and that," he cried in an almost insane rage.

The native reeled before the blows, not daring to fight back, and finally fell to the ground as one of Squint's blows caught him full on the jaw.

At that moment a white man rode up, dismounted quickly, and ran over to where Squint stood over the prostrate form of his luckless victim.

Squint looked up as the stranger approached, and an ugly sneer crossed his face as he noticed the newcomer's immaculate attire, the highly polished polo boots, the glittering spurs, the well fitting riding breeches and the silk shirt, with turned down collar, open at the neck.

"What are you doing?"

The question was put mildly.

"And what's that to you, darling?"

The other fumbled in the breast pocket of his shirt and produced a gold rimmed monocle which he fixed in his eye.

" 'Pon my word, you are beastly rude," he drawled. "I asked a civil question and," he returned the monocle to his pocket. As though a mask had been withdrawn, the vacuous, almost inane expression vanished from his face. "And," he continued, "I expect a civil answer."

"Do you now?" scoffed Squint, with a labored imitation of the other's drawl. "I'm surprised, really."

Squint, was no student of human nature but, even so, had he been looking now at this stranger he would have seen that he was no man to be trifled with. The curve of the man's chin, the line of the mouth and, above all, the steely gray eyes, betokened one in whose presence it were well to walk softly.

But Squint's eyes were fixed on the native who sprawled motionless on the ground before him.

Squint drew back his foot.

"I wouldn't do that if I were you."

"No?" Squint looked up with a laugh. "No?" he repeated, but the mirth had gone from his voice. "Why not?"

"I should feel compelled to—er—chastise you."

"You? Chastise me?" The mirth returned to Squint's voice. He forgot his momentary fear of the stranger. He remembered the monocle and the soft toned drawl. "This is for the nigger," he said truculently, "and then I'll attend to you—sweetheart."

He launched a vicious kick at the native's ribs and the next instant—he never could explain how it happened—he was sprawling on the ground on the broad of his back.

The stranger shouted a curt order to the group of natives who were watching, open-mouthed, this conflict between two white men, and before Squint, uttering vile threats, had regained his feet the natives had all disappeared.

"Now, you hog," smiled the stranger as he lightly evaded Squint's furious rush, "I can deal with you."

Squint grunted as he swung his right for the stranger's jaw.

"That was a powerful blow," taunted the other, "but so wide of the mark. You're a bad judge of distance, really. Let me show you."

He stepped in quickly and shook Squint from head to foot with a right jolt, and before Squint could counter was back out of range once more.

"Fight, damn you, don't dance," snarled the miner.

"In a moment. Don't be so bloomin' impetuous; you nearly hit me that time. Besides, I want to apologize."

Squint laughed.

"Apologize? That can wait until I'm through with you. I'm going to spoil that pretty face of yours; you won't save it by apologizing."

"Oh! You entirely misunderstand me," cooed—yes, cooed is the correct word—the other. "I simply want to apologize for being forced to trip you in the presence of your natives. Of course you can always explain that you—er—stumbled over something. No need to tell them that it was my foot, eh? Have a bad effect on them, you know, if they thought two white men were fighting. But," he threw a hasty glance over his shoulder, "they're all gone now, save the poor old boy here and he can't see much, and we can have a glorious mill."

All the time he had been speaking the stranger shifted his ground continually, evading Squint's bull-like rushes. But now—

"Come on," he said.

Again Squint rushed, and this time the stranger did not sidestep but cleverly blocked the blow, and the two men, standing toe to toe, slugged at each other. There was no attempt at scientific boxing.

In build the two men were evenly matched and for a time it seemed that victory would go to the first man who succeeded in getting in a knockout blow.

But gradually Squint was forced to give ground. Years of evil living had undermined his stamina. His blows lost a little of their sting, and his breath came in big choking gasps.

The stranger, on the other hand, was hardly breathed, and his blows were delivered with regularity and precision. It was idle for Squint to endeavor to guard his vulnerable points. As well try to arrest the motion of a gigantic piston.

The stranger shifted his attack to Squint's face and the miner wearily raised his guard. He was at the end of his rope.

"I don't want to be vindictive, but it is necessary."

The stranger punctuated his words with blows.

"You must remember, really, to treat your niggers decently. It's scum like you who make it hard for the rest of us."

"A nigger lover, eh?" Squint couldn't repress the sneer.

"Exactly. How well you put it. Of course I could knock you out at any moment—you're in beastly bad condition. Where will you have it? On the jaw?"

Automatically Squint raised his guard again. He was making no effort now to fight back. His sole object was to gain respite from the merciless rain of blows.

"Ah. That time I fooled you," laughed the stranger.

It was enough—too much—for Squint, and he dropped to the ground, totally exhausted, whining that he had had enough.

"Get up," said the stranger in tones of disgust. "You haven't been punished half as badly as the nigger here. And I'll bet he didn't whine."

Then, seeing that Squint made no effort to rise, the stranger dragged him by the heels into the hut, and there left him.

As the stranger came out of the hut again a Cape wagon drawn by two mules came to a halt opposite the door.

"You're late, Jim," the stranger called to the thick-set Hottentot driver.

"Aye, *Baas*. The evil spirits have followed me today. First Mafouta," he pointed to one of the mules, "broke her bridle, and then—"

"Thou art ever ready with excuses, Jim," said the white man. "But come now and help me with this one."

The white man bent down and examined the victim of Squint's brutality with a practised eye. His ribs were sorely bruised and blood streamed from an ugly gash over his eye, but apparently there were no bones broken.

"How came he by his hurt, *Baas?*" asked the Hottentot.

"It is no matter. Help me to carry him to the wagon." Silently the Hottentot obeyed and when they had made the unconscious man as comfortable as possible on a pile of sacks which they placed on the floor of the wagon, the white man tenderly bathed his wounds and forced some brandy down his throat.

With much spluttering the native regained consciousness and looked around the wagon with an expression of fear in his eyes. As his gaze fell upon the white man, however, the fear left his eyes and he endeavored, with an attempt at dignity, to sit erect.

"Tomasi, the headman, thanks you, white man," he said.

"There is no need of thanks, Headman," replied the white man.

"I am of another mind. I saw something of the strife between you and that other one before the great darkness came upon me."

"It is best to forget that, Headman. It would not be well to talk in the *kraal* of what happened here this day."

"I understand, white man, and my lips are sealed. Nevertheless, thou art my friend. The *kraal* of Tomasi is open to thee; his cattle are thy cattle, his young men shall spring to thy command, his maidens—"

"Tomasi would do well to remember," the stranger interrupted hastily, "that he is speaking to a white man. Where is thy *kraal?*"

"A long day's trek from here on two legs; a short forenoon's trek on four legs" (he meant on horseback). "In the direction of the setting of the sun from here you must travel."

"And thou art going there, now?"

"Aye. I came hither to hold speech with that—other white man. But the desire is no longer with me. I will go back to my *kraal* and try to forget this shame. Will thou come, too? My young hunters will show thee good sport. A lion hath been troubling us of late."

The white man was silent for a few moments, then asked, "Is there a store in this place, Jim?"

"Aye, *Baas*," answered the Hottentot. "I passed one half a mile or more down the road yonder. Methinks that there is little there to the black dogs who live hereabouts."

The white man nodded.

"Go on with Tomasi, Jim. I will catch up with you in a little while. I will stay at your *kraal*, Headman, and go ahunting with your young men."

He climbed down from the wagon and catching his horse leaped lightly into the saddle.

"Ohé, *Baas!*"

He turned questioningly to the Hottentot.

"Yes, Jim?"

"I was telling you why I was late."

"You told me, Jim. You said the bridle broke—or was it that the heat of the day made sleep very desirable?"

"It was the bridle, *Baas*. I speak true word. Besides, soon after you left me a *Nonquai*, a mounted policeman, stopped me and asked many questions concerning you!"

"All of which you answered?"

"Without doubt, *Baas*," replied the Hottentot gravely. "He spoke also of diamonds, and searched through the wagon, hoping, he said, to find some hidden there."

"Did he find any?"

The Hottentot grinned.

"No, *Baas*."

The white man smiled, took up the reins in his hand and a moment later he was galloping down the dusty trail.

"I'll be with you at sundown, Jim," he called back over his shoulder.

The Hottentot gazed after the fast retreating figure of his *Baas*, a tender, whimsical smile on his squat, homely face.

"What a man!" he ejaculated.

"A man indeed," agreed the headman who had climbed on to the driver's seat beside the Hottentot.

"Thou are not altogether a fool, Headman," agreed Jim. "He is a man among men, and I—I am his servant."

Then with a loud cracking of the whip and much shouting Jim

started his mules off at a swift pace down the dusty road in the opposite direction to that taken by his *Baas*.

AS JIM'S *Baas* came within a few hundred yards of the mud-walled, thatch-roofed huts which comprised the store and the storekeeper's living quarters, he pulled up his horse to a walk and leisurely surveyed the country around.

It was typical African bush veldt country and as such little worthy of special note to the horseman. Behind him, half a mile or more away, the tin-roofed building of the mine reflected the rays of the sun and the heavy thud, thud of the stamps came to the ears of the watcher. Near the mine he could see a large collection of huts, encircled, he knew, by a strong stockade. It was the compound where the native laborers of the mine were housed and carefully guarded.

There is much to be said, for and against, the compound system. True, it protects the mines from desertions and thievery, and also protects the natives from falling victims to the snares set for them by degenerate white men. It all depends upon the compound manager. His power is absolute. He can make the laborer contented and happy, or reduce him to a state little better, often worse, than slavery. For, it must be understood, once a native has entered into contract to work at a mine there is no escape for him until his time has expired, or unless his employer (personified by the compound manager), permits him to leave. He may, occasionally, desert, but without the necessary pass which all natives must carry—and that is held by the compound manager—his arrest is only a matter of time and he will be returned to the mine. But desertions are rare, for the weight of the law also falls upon the headman of the deserter's *kraal*, and it is better to serve the white man, enduring cruel treatment, than to face the wrath of a tribal leader.

An angry scowl crossed the face of the white man as he thought of the man Squint and the hard lot of the natives who were so unfortunate as to be in his charge.

He noticed now, for the first time, that a horse was tied outside one of the storekeeper's huts. Riding up to it he dismounted and hesitated a moment—undecided which hut to enter.

Then from one of the huts came the sound of voices—angry voices.

Entering, he saw a girl, a dark haired, roguish eyed girl, (but just now her eyes flashed with anger). A *sjambok*—whip of rhinoceros hide—was in her hand, with which she was threatening a tall, thin man of smug, hypocritical aspect.

"Don't you think you had better go? You're not wanted, I fancy."

Lanky turned around to face the intruder, his hand falling to the butt of his revolver. For a moment the two men faced each other in silence; then—he was a better judge of human nature than Squint—Lanky hurried from the hut.

"Really, it's too funny," laughed the other man. "I feel like a bally knight errant, or something of that sort, I suppose that the tall gentleman who has just left is Lanky, partner of my friend Squint?"

The girl, who had been watching him closely, nodded.

"Yes. That was Lanky. But if you're a friend of Squint's you must be a friend of Lanky, and if that's so I don't quite see why—"

"No, really, you misunderstand me; Squint is not really a friend of mine. Just an acquaintance, so to speak. I had an occasion to speak severely to him; oh, quite severely—a little while back."

The girl came over to him with an impetuous rush.

"I'm a fool," she said reproachfully as she held out her hand, "but please believe that I'm grateful for your—"

"Not a word. You were holding up your end rippingly. No need for me at all. You had the whip hand, in a manner of speaking." He chuckled softly.

The girl smiled.

"My name is Helene. Helene Paul."

"Rippin' name, absolutely.

"And I should like to know yours."

"Mine? Oh yes, of course. Call me Major. What?"

"Major Watt?"

He looked blankly at her.

"What? Oh, no. You misunderstand me, Miss Helene. Just Major."

"Then please, Major, may I have my hand?"

He released it in confusion, fumbled in his pocket for his monocle and it was not until he had it firmly in place that he could meet the girl's candid glance. Then the hut echoed to shouts of laughter—the laughter of youth, for the girl was barely out of her teens and the Major, though his hair was streaked with gray, was only a big over-grown boy.

"But seriously," he said sobering suddenly, "is there anything I can do to help you? I think I'll go after Lanky. I'd like to have a few words with him."

"No, don't, please," she begged. "It would only make matters worse."

"Worse?" said the Major. "Why are you here all alone anyway?"

"You see," she answered with a sudden burst of confidence—the Major was that sort of man—"my father once owned the Star Mine but he used to gamble, and drink, too, a great deal. He lost a lot of money to Squint and Lanky and he signed over his claim to them in payment of his gambling debts. He has always claimed since that he didn't, but they have his signature to the transfer. Daddy has lived on here ever since. He says that sooner or later the two will fall out and then he'll be able to get the mine back. Daddy doesn't believe in honor between thieves. Lanky was very good to us at first; at least I thought so then. He loaned us money to stock this store and promised us all the mine trade; you know, I mean that he would buy all his provisions through us and let us have a chance to sell to the natives. But he never kept his promise. And now he demands the repayment of his loan or, failing that, wants me to marry him. We can't pay back the money, and I won't marry him, though I did let him think I would in order to gain time. Alan will be here today or tomorrow and then everything will be all right."

"And who's this lucky fellow Alan?"

"Trooper Alan Wade of the police," the girl said proudly.

"And very pleased to make your acquaintance, Major."

The two turned with a start to face a well built, sun browned young trooper, and with a glad cry of "Alan!" the girl ran to greet him. She stopped short, however, and raised her hands above her head in mock horror at the sight of the revolver he held in his hand.

"Mercy, kind sir," she begged.

"Just a minute, Helene. I've a little business matter I want to talk over with the Major."

"My dear chap," said the Major impatiently, "won't you fellows ever let me have any peace? Here I've come on an innocent little hunting expedition and you cheerful idiots camp upon my trail. What is it this time? Do you want to see my hunting license, or my vaccination marks?"

"What *is* the trouble, Alan?" asked the girl. And before he had time to answer she continued, "And whatever the trouble is, Alan Wade, I want you to understand that you're not going to arrest the Major here. He's just stopped Lanky from insulting me and you are going to stay here and talk with me, here in this hut, for fifteen minutes. That will give the Major a fair start."

"I can't do that, Helene," Wade replied slowly. "Of course I'm grateful to the Major, but—"

He stopped, tongue-tied, before the scornful glance of the girl.

"Really, Miss Helene," expostulated the Major, "you can't interfere with an officer of the law in performance of his duty. It isn't done, you know. But what is the trouble, Wade? I think I ought to know what it is all about; 'pon my soul I do."

"Two weeks ago," said Wade, watching the Major's face closely, "one of the detectives attached to the mines at Diamondville, tried to trap a notorious I.D.B. His plan was to get this man—call him the Captain—to buy some diamonds from him and afterward arrest the Captain with the diamonds in his possession. Knowing that the captain was an expert appraiser of diamonds in the rough the detective borrowed from one of the mines a number of good quality stones. He showed them to the Captain who appeared very interested but said he had no money with him, and asked the detective to call at the hotel the following night. When the detective appeared to keep his appointment the Captain again examined the stones, haggled about the price, and finally refused to buy them."

Wade paused for breath.

"Interestin', very," murmured the Major. "But I don't quite see—"

Wade held up his hand.

"There's more," he said. "Next morning, when the detective returned the stones to the mine, he discovered that the Captain had, somehow, substituted imitations for the real stones. Returning to the hotel he discovered that the Captain had departed!"

As Wade concluded his story Helene exclaimed indignantly.

"And it served Mr. Detective right. I hope he gets arrested for I.D.B. Of all the rotten tricks, trying to trap a man that way is the rottenest."

The Major made a fluttering, helpless gesture with his hands.

"But I don't see what this had to do with me, my dear Wade. Of course I understand that I am supposed to be the Captain of your story—you did mean that, didn't you? But granting that, you don't think I'd be such an ass as to carry the diamonds about with me. Why, I should have got rid of them ages ago."

"Perhaps you have. But it seemed rather suspicious to us when we happened to hear that you were heading this way on a hunting trip. But that alone might not have meant anything, only at the same time we heard that a certain Portuguese trader of rather a questionable character was also heading this way."

The Major laughed.

"Really you fellows of the police are getting to be regular sleuths. It's positively delicious the way you put two and two together—and make five."

"I've examined your native, Jim, and searched your wagon," Wade said stolidly, "and now I'm going to search you."

"No, Alan."

"But yes, Miss Helene," remonstrated the Major. "These I.D.B.s, are terrible people, you know, and if dear old Wade here thinks he's on the track of one, who are we to stand in the way of the law?"

"Look here, Major," said Wade uneasily, "if you'll give me your word that you are not carrying the stones I'll—"

"Give you my word? Now what good is the word of a suspected I.D.B? No! I'm afraid you must search me. Will you leave us, Miss Helene? You might like to make the acquaintance of my horse."

HALF AN hour later the Major came briskly from the hut and walked over to where Helene was feeding carrots to his horse. Wade, rather dejected looking, followed closely behind him.

The young policeman was not a little bewildered as the result of the half hour he had spent *tête-à-tête* with the Major.

Thoroughly and painstakingly he had searched the I.D.B. suspect, and everything that was his, without discovering the diamonds.

And the Major had been very helpful, insisting that he examine the heels of his shoes, his revolver cartridges and the chambers of his revolver.

And once Wade thought he was on the right track. The hip pocket of the Major's riding breeches contained an unusually large and well filled cigar case. It was of gold, and a large letter M was picked out with cunningly set rubies.

"I thought you smoked cigarettes, Major?" Wade had asked suddenly.

"Smoke nothing else, old chap."

"Then why the cigars?" He held out the case.

The Major had seemed embarrassed.

"The case was a present and I—er—filled it with cigars because—Well, it would look deuced funny to carry around an empty case, wouldn't it?"

"It would be still funnier if I found the diamonds in it."

"Oh, now you're spoofin'." The Major held out this hand for the case, but Wade, ignoring him, emptied out the cigars and crumpled them one by one between his fingers, conscious all the time of the Major's mocking grin.

"What a waste of good cigars," said the Major as Wade disconsolately let the remains of the last cigar fall from his fingers.

"No luck, Alan?" Helene asked as the two men neared her.

"No. And I'm really rather glad," Wade added. "You're a good sport, Major.

The Major bowed.

"Thanks, old man. But the drinks are on you, aren't they? And that reminds me. I really came down here to get in a supply of cigarette papers and tobacco."

"I'll get them for you, Major." Helene hurried in to the storehouse.

"And bring a box of your best cigars," the Major shouted. "Wade will pay for them."

A few minutes later the girl rejoined them.

"I haven't brought your smokes, Major," she said, "because I want you to stay for scoff. You must meet daddy. I hope you write a good hand, though, for he's so deaf we have to write all our conversation to him and it makes him as mad as a hatter if the writing is unintelligible."

JIM, THE Hottentot, was in a bad temper and sulked beside the camp-fire. Jim thought he had good reason to be angry for his *Baas* had gone off on a hunting expedition with Tomasi, the headman, and a party of warriors from the *kraal*.

"You will stay to watch over the camp Jim," the Major had ordered.

"But who will tend to thee, *Baas*?" Jim had expostulated. "Who will hand thee the gun at the right moment? As for camp, the people hereabouts are thy friends. There is no need for a guard."

But the order had been given and Jim was forced to stay.

Now if Jim had a weakness it was an inordinate craving—rarely gratified, the Major saw to that—for the poisonous concoctions put up by criminal white men and sold to the natives as whisky. Consequently, when a native came to him with the news—it was the second night after the Major's departure—that a white man was down at the *kraal* giving away *puza,* Jim did not lose any time following his informer.

At the *kraal* he found a few young warriors—the rest were with the Major—and all the old men, gathered around a white man who was inviting them to help themselves to the bottles he put on the ground before him.

Jim thrust his way to the front and eagerly grabbed for one of the bottles, but the white man knocked his hand away.

"This is not for you, dog."

"But the *Baas* said—"

"Hold thy tongue. It is not for you, I say. For these others, my friends, yes."

Disgruntled, Jim drew back and watched the luckier natives returning to their places with the coveted black bottles.

A native near him, in a sudden access of generosity, offered to share his bottle with Jim, but again the white man interfered.

"Neither this dog, nor his *Baas,* are my friends," said the one-eyed man. "Shall I then give *puza* to my enemies?"

And the native, fearing to offend this generous white man, snatched the bottle out of the Hottentot's hands. Not, however, before Jim had managed to swallow a mouthful and, by so doing, fed fuel to his desire.

"Won't the *Baas* please give me *puza?*" he begged.

The white man did not answer.

"Please, *Baas!*"

"I will sell you a bottle for five pounds."

Jim turned sadly away. The white man might as well have asked two hundred. Then a happy thought struck him and he ran swiftly through the darkness, back to the camp his *Baas* had pitched on a slight rise overlooking the *kraal.*

Entering the small bell tent he groped among the Major's equipment, finally locating the gold cigar case. Surely that was worth five pounds, perhaps more, and his *Baas* never used it, and would not, therefore, miss it. If he did, Jim would confess. He would be punished, of course, but a future *sjamboking* weighed lightly on his mind compared to the prospect of present *puza.* So, wrapping the cigar case in a piece of paper, he hastened back to the *kraal,* and sidling up to the white man showed him the cigar case.

"I will give you this for some *puza.*"

"Where did you get it?"

"It is mine. My *Baas* lost it, and I found it."

The white man hesitated a moment, then pocketed the case and handed Jim a bottle.

The liquor, Jim and the rest of the natives discovered, was singularly impotent, in a little while they clamored around the white man for more.

"I have no more here," he told them, "but there is plenty in my wagon at the ford."

"Then let us go there, white man," they cried.

"It is well. But there is not enough for you all. These among ye may come."

He pointed out the stronger and more sturdily built of the young men and, with an evil leer, finally included Jim in the number.

Thirty, all told, accompanied the white man to the ford where there was a large wagon drawn by sixteen mules. Two brawny natives of another tribe brought bottles from the wagon in response to the white man's bidding.

The liquor the white man had given them at the *kraal* was greatly diluted, but this stuff was a raw spirit based on refuse of sugar cane, German potato spirit and further doctored by a high percentage of "Blue stone" (sulphate of copper)!

It is no wonder, then, that in a very short time the ground around the wagon was strewn with natives in various stages of intoxication.

With many a rough jest and vicious blows two natives, servants of the white man, piled their drink-soddened brothers into the wagon. The mules were inspanned, and a few minutes later were splashing through the waters of the ford, en route for the Star Mine.

And Squint, puffing at a cigar extracted from the Major's case, felt well content with his labor recruiting expedition.

ONE MORNING, a week or so later, the Major dismount-ed from his horse outside the entrance to the compound the Star Mine and was about to enter, when the two owners—Squint and Lanky—appeared from behind the stockade, revolvers in their hands.

The Major looked at them with an expression of surprise.

"Why all the artillery? Are you expecting a rebellion?"

"Think you're damned funny, don't you?" said Squint with a sneer, "but we knew you'd be coming and know what you are after. So we've been on the lookout for you."

"Really? My word, but you're clever. Just what have I come for?"

"Get out of here before this goes off." Squint's fingers toyed with the trigger of his revolver. "We've got no time to waste with you."

The Major turned to Lanky.

"What has got into the old chap's bean? Is it an attack of the sun, do you think?"

"Let me handle him," Lanky said soothingly to the infuriated Squint.

"You see, Major," he continued, "we've heard of you since you were here last and know that you have the reputation of getting niggers to hand you just what you want. Down in the Transvaal they hand you diamonds; here you might be asking them to steal a little gold from the mine. But we're on to you, and I give you warning that if you're seen hanging around here, you'll be shot on sight."

"But you've got the wrong idea, entirely. I only came to see about my servant, Jim. I hear that he's working at the mine, and really, that's not the thing, you know. Stealing a fellow's servant isn't playin' the game."

"What's your nigger's name?"

"Jim. He's a Hottentot. Rather stockily built and—oh! he's just priceless, I can't possibly get along without him. You see how hard this hits me?"

The Major smiled winningly.

Lanky turned to Squint.

"Do you know anything about his nigger?"

"Why, yes," Squint replied, after feigning to consult a much soiled note book, "we've got a Hottentot named Jim working here. But he's signed on all in proper order. The Major ain't got no claim to him. He didn't have a pass, but I've fixed that up all right."

Lanky turned once again to the Major with an oily smile.

"You see, if this nigger, Jim, is the one you mean—"

"Oh, I'm sure of that. They told me all about it at the *kraal*."

"Well, you have no legal claim to him. You never signed him on, did you?"

"No. It never entered my head."

"Well, we did, and here he stays. If you think you've any complaint, the police camp is only four days away, make it there. But I don't think you will."

"No. I wouldn't do that. No need to call in the police about a little matter like this. I imagine I'll be able to find another servant, though I'll miss Jim frightfully. He's been with me years. You'll take good care of him, won't you? I am rather attached to the old scoundrel."

"I'll take care of him all right," said Squint with a leer.

"Thanks! I was sure you would."

The Major mounted his horse and rode off. He had only gone about twenty yards, however, when he wheeled and returned to the two men.

"Oh, by the way," he said. "You didn't happen to notice whether Jim had my cigar case with him? It was a present and I rather value it."

"No. He had nothing like that."

"Thanks! I thought perhaps he might have borrowed it to buy some *puza*. He does that sort of thing once in a while and I have to speak quite sharply to him, I assure you."

"If I see him with it I'll get it for you."

"You're most accommodating. And you're sure you can't see your way clear to let Jim go?"

"No!" shouted the two men in chorus.

"Very well. I imagine it will teach Jim a lesson. Good day, gentlemen."

LATER THAT same day a number of natives presented themselves to Squint. They had heard, they said, that he had given lots of *puza* to their friends. They had been away on a hunt at the time; hunting with a white man who wore a glass eye. A very fool of a white man, who talked like a woman. And they were thirsty. They, too, would work at the mine if only they had some *puza*.

And so Squint was able to report to Lanky that he had secured ten more laborers and that one of them had been assigned to work in the kitchen.

Had Squint known that the natives reported to him in response to instructions received from the Major it is quite certain that he would not have engaged them so quickly.

NEITHER LANKY nor Squint slept that night, for their sleeping huts were infested by mosquitoes and flying insects of all sorts and sizes. Big red spiders ran up and down the walls, and all the scorpions and centipedes in Africa seemed to have chosen the huts for their rendezvous.

And the strange part about it was that neither Lanky nor Squint could find any hole in the walls or roof of their respective huts, and the mosquito netting seemed to be intact. Yet the insects were there and sleep impossible.

They were in no mood, therefore, to exchange banter with the Major when he rode up to the mine the following morning.

"Good mornin', boys," he hailed them gaily. "You don't seem to be very chipper this morning. Didn't you have a good night? You mustn't lose your tempers. Bad for the blood in this hot climate. Really. But what I came to see you about, putting all joking aside, is, if you won't reconsider your decision. Won't you let my servant, Jim, go? You won't? Then good-by. Hope you sleep better tonight."

And that night Squint found a swarm of frogs in his bed, under his bed, and in the roof over his bed. He did not find them all at one time. The last one insinuated itself between his blankets a few minutes before sunrise.

Lanky's experiences were similar.

And once again the two men were deprived of sleep. And once again the Major appeared, commiserated with them, made his request and, being refused, galloped off down the road.

That same day the water—brought from a hill spring every morning, used for preparing the white men's food and for their refreshment—was undrinkable, having suddenly turned, so it seemed, into blood. An examination of the water would undoubtedly have shown that some permanganate of potash had been dissolved in it. However, simultaneously with the discovery that the day's supply of drinking water was undrinkable the Major appeared.

"By Jove!" he exclaimed, when they told him of this latest development. "It's just like the Bible story, don't you know. Isn't there some old Pharaoh who wouldn't let some people go and was plagued just as you are. Now really, please don't accuse me of witchcraft or anything like. I'm no magician. Oh, by the way, won't you please let Jim off. I'm absolutely helpless without him."

The Major wheeled his horse just in time to avoid being slashed in the face by the infuriated Squint.

"They're weakening," he chuckled to himself as he rode away. "I believe if I pressed the matter I could get Jim now. But it'ull do him good to stay a few days longer. He deserves to be punished and the Lord knows I'd never have the heart to punish him myself. Besides, I want to try a few more plagues on those two."

THE MAJOR was returning to the *kraal* of Tomasi from his sixth visit to the mine. Six times he had asked for the return of his servant Jim, and six times his request had been refused.

Aided by the natives, who, acting on his orders, had volunteered to work at the mine, he had almost broken the spirits of the two men, Lanky and Squint.

As the constant drip of water will wear away a stone, so by many petty annoyances he had completely shattered the nerves of the two miners.

What, for instance, could afford greater annoyance than, when tormented by the heat of Africa, to seek a cooling drink, previously prepared, and find it, and all other water on the place, strongly flavored with salt?

"Tomorrow," the Major told himself, "they'll pay me to take Jim away."

"Major, wait for me!"

He reined in his horse at the cry, and turning in his saddle saw the girl, Helene, riding toward him.

Since his first meeting with the girl the Major had not been near the store; partly because he was never fully at ease in the presence of women, but chiefly because he wanted to be sure that by no possible chance could the girl be accused of complicity in his dealings with the two mine owners.

"What is it, Miss Helene?" he asked as she caught up with him.

She laughed nervously.

"It's almost funny—but not quite. Father knocked down the native messenger yesterday and robbed him of the amalgam he was taking from the mine to the settlement."

"Good old sport, your father."

"Please don't joke, Major. You see daddy has always claimed that he was cheated out of the mine, and he's been dwelling on it a great deal lately—he's getting old, you know. And yesterday he ambushed the messenger, and took the gold. I can't make him see that he's done a foolish thing. He says it is his mine and therefore his gold. And he says he's going to do it again."

"Phew!"

"But that's not all. The messenger made his way back to the mine and told Lanky all about it—you see he recognized father. And as soon as Squint heard about it he sent a native runner to the police camp asking them to come up and investigate. I think Squint suspects you, for Lanky didn't tell him that father took the money and he told the boy—the messenger, you know—not to say anything about it."

"Pretty considerate of Lanky. But why?"

"He says he'll let the matter drop if I'll marry him. If I don't father will be arrested and—"

She hid her face in her hands.

"What did you intend doing?" the Major asked gently.

"I was going to ride to meet the policeman who comes to investigate. It will be Alan. I've stolen the amalgam from daddy's hiding place and I was going to see if Alan wouldn't return it to Lanky and swear that he had found it hidden somewhere along the way. I know it sounds rather a scatter-brained plan, but I couldn't think of anything else."

"It isn't much of a plan, Miss Helene. You see, your Alan is such a frightfully conscientious policeman, isn't he?"

"I'm afraid he is. Oh, dear, I mean, I'm glad he is."

The Major smiled.

"Look here, Miss Helene, do you trust me?"

"Absolutely, Major."

"Then give me the amalgam. I'll fix up everything."

With a hopeful smile she took a small but heavy package from her saddle bag and handed it to the Major.

"What's next?" she asked.

"Why ride home and dream sweet dreams of—er—Alan."

SQUINT POURED himself out a generous measure of whisky and tossed it off in one big gulp. He meant it to be a night-cap, his last drink before turning in. But one drink led to another; to another and yet another.

After all, he reasoned, a man had to have some pleasure in this cursed hole of a country called Africa. If Lanky were only a good sport he'd have some company and wouldn't be forced to drink alone. But as it was! Well, he was just as well pleased, after all, that Lanky kept to his own quarters. He didn't like him; never did, and never would.

He was too sly, too oily. You can never trust a man like that. He, Squint, would watch Lanky carefully; he had to if he wanted his proper share in the earnings of the mine.

Squint's hand groped again for the bottle. He didn't want another drink, really. But a fellow had to take a few drinks in order to ward off fever. Funny lot of things had been happening. He bet that the Major was at the bottom of it all. His hand fondled his revolver. He was going to wear it to bed with him and—

Suddenly his candle went out and the hut was plunged into an abysmal darkness, the darkness of a starless African night.

Dreading to move, not even to light a match, he roared loudly for a light.

Across the way he heard Lanky's high-pitched voice screaming a similar order.

Strange rustlings sounded in the hut. There was a soft pattering of naked feet, and then a native appeared bearing a lighted candle.

Its feeble rays seemed to flood the hut with light, so marked was the contrast to the darkness.

Propped up against the whisky bottle on the table was a piece of paper.

Squint picked it up cautiously.

On it was printed in plain letters.

> Don't trust Lanky too much. He knows who stole the gold. Ask him. And then look in his trunk.
>
>   A FRIEND.

Squint did not stop to consider the origin of the paper but with an angry curse reeled out of the hut and stumbled through the darkness to the hut occupied by Lanky.

A native, with a candle, preceded him into the hut.

"Hullo, Squint?" Lanky said in surprise. He had nothing in common with Squint and the two usually confined their intercourse to the affairs of the mine.

"I've been thinking," Squint said abruptly when the native had departed, "that you know more about that robbery than you say."

"What do you mean?"

"Why, I think you know who stole the amalgam."

"Don't be a damned fool. I know no more about it than you do." But Lanky's protest did not sound sincere to Squint's ears, and without further words he made a sudden rush to Lanky's chest, opened the lid and began to rummage among its contents.

"Leave that stuff alone," snapped Lanky.

Squint turned on him with a snarl of rage and threw down on the table before Lanky, a heavy package—the one which had been stolen from the messenger—

"Yes. I'll leave it alone, you rat. So you'd try to cheat me, would you?"

"What are you talking about, Squint? I'm your partner." Lanky's face was white with fear. "I don't know anything about this; it's a put up job. You ought to know that I won't cheat."

"Won't! You did. A pretty story that about the robbery, wasn't it? You ought to be able to tell it well; you planned it."

"You're a fool to talk like that, Squint."

"I'm a fool, am I?" howled Squint. "I was a fool when I went into partnership with you. You'll be trying to cheat me out of my share in the mine, same as you cheated old Paul.

Lanky's hand leaped to his revolver, but Squint was quicker. A report pierced the stillness of the night and Lanky pitched forward on his face to the ground.

Before the last echoes of the shot had died away two policemen—Sergeant Blunt, and Trooper Wade—and the Major rushed into the hut.

Squint made no attempt to resist them but voluntarily gave up his revolver and submitted to be handcuffed. He muttered continually.

"He had it coming to him."

The men knelt down beside the body of Lanky and examined him closely. They whispered together for a few moments.

"He's dead," said the sergeant. "Have you anything to say, Squint, about the mine? If you make a confession we'll try to make it light for you."

Squint sobered quickly.

"Yes. I'll tell everything. It was all Lanky's plan in the beginning. He—"

With many invectives he told of how they got the old man Paul drunk and then tried to get him to put his signature to the deed transferring his claim to them. The attempt had failed. Drunk though he was, Paul was too cunning, set too high a value on his claim, to be caught that way. Then Lanky had conceived the bold plan of tracing Paul's signature on the deed from an old receipt he had in his pocket.

The story was soon told.

"Sign here," said the sergeant, who had taken down the confession on a page torn from his note book.

Squint eagerly obeyed.

"You'll say I killed him in self-defense, won't you, Sergeant?"

Blunt nodded and after he and Wade had witnessed Squint's signature, the Major threw a bucketful of water into the face of the "dead" man.

Gasping and spluttering Lanky weakly sat up and gazed vacantly about him.

"He is only stunned, Squint, old dear," said the Major with a grin. "Really, you're a deuced bad shot."

Squint made no reply but looked with despairing eyes at the piece of paper which the sergeant folded carefully and handed to Wade.

"You take it to Helene, Major," said the young trooper. "It's all the result of your planning."

"Not for the world, old top. I must be off. Tomasi has a little hunting party arranged for me tomorrow, and I must get to bed. But I wish you'd fish my cigar case out of Squint's hip pocket. Thanks. I've been quite miserable without it. Oh, by the way, Messrs. Squint and Lanky, may my servant, Jim, go?"

Squint's answer was a string of curses. Lanky only looked at the Major with wondering eyes. He did not yet know the meaning of it all.

The door of the hut opened and the Major vanished into the blackness of the night. A few minutes later he came to the mine compound and there found the natives from Tomasi's *kraal* grouped about his Cape cart.

"The game is finished," he told them. "On the morrow ye may return to the *kraal*."

"It is well, lord," they answered softly.

The Major climbed up into the Cape cart and was about to drive away when one of the men sprang forward.

"And what of me, *Baas?*" he asked in pleading tones.

"As for you, Jim, a heavy punishment awaits you. Come up here and drive me to the *kraal* of Tomasi. On the way I will think of a suitable punishment for a drunkard and a thief!"

"There has been evil enough," muttered Jim as he climbed up into the driver's seat.

The Major did not answer him; he had gone to the rear of the cart and was examining by the light of a hurricane lamp his cigar case. He opened it and a few minutes later, was examining some diamonds which he had taken from the false bottom of the case.

Leaning back, still holding the diamonds in his hands, he chuckled softly and Jim, hearing him, sent his mules on at a faster rate through the darkness. He felt assured that his punishment would be light indeed.

ROYAL GAME

SENHOR JOSÉ had not pitched his camp in the best possible site; indeed, he would have had to search far to find a worse one. But then the senhor was not used to life on the veldt; he had no liking for it and was totally ignorant of all things pertaining to camp craft. Also, he was not the sort of man to win the confidence and esteem of his native camp followers; on the contrary, they hated him for his brutality toward them, and despised his petty meannesses. Consequently, as far as they dared—and a white man, even such a contemptible white man as was the senhor, is not to be treated with open disrespect; he represents, in himself, a superior race—they opposed him, and did everything that would tend to detract from his comfort.

And so the senhor groaned and sweated through the heat of the day; nor did he find relief in sleep at night. Mosquitoes pestered him continually; his face and hands were covered with angry red blotches, evidence of the raids of vicious tsetse flies.

No, the senhor was not accustomed to veldt life, else he might have found cause for comment in the fact that the natives did not sleep anywhere near his tent.

They volunteered the information that they slept at a great distance from him as a mark of deep respect; yet not one of them gave him the title which natives give to white men whom they honor. But the senhor was content with the explanation, little dreaming that his "boys" had made their camp in a spot comparatively free from mosquitoes and tsetse flies.

On his own ground, in the slums of the busy port of Portuguese East Africa, the senhor was an entirely different personage. There he was accorded a servile homage by the criminals, greater and lesser, who sought refuge in that place from certain extradition warrants. The senhor had the ear of the police and could make things easy for his "protégés." In Lorenco Marquez the senhor's word was law, and he waxed rich even as he waxed fat.

Of late he had ventured into a new field, an almost virgin field, driven to it by the knowledge that he was losing favor with the Portuguese officials.

The thing that appealed to the senhor most about his new course of endeavor was that it was honest, nearly so, at any rate. Holiest as far as the laws of his territory were concerned, but a most damnable crime in the eyes of certain gentlemen who controled the diamond output of the mines at Kimberly. Yes, the senhor had become an illicit diamond buyer, commonly called an I.D.B. That is to say, he made a business of purchasing "stones" from men who could show no diamond mining permit, or who were not licensed traders; from natives who, by some one or other of the many heroic methods, had succeeded in smuggling diamonds from the mine in which they had been employed.

Such stones were, of a necessity, small ones; many were imperfect, but the profit from the transaction was large, and the senhor was constantly bewailing the fact that his "trades" were few and far between.

It was then that he received a letter from the Major, a man famed throughout the length and breadth of South Africa as the most expert of I.D.B.s; a man whose craft was equaled by the audacity of his exploits.

The letter was very characteristic of the Major. It read:

> Dear Senhor:
> Six perfectly priceless diamonds have, by some extraordinary means, come into my possession. I want to get rid of them as soon as possible as I understand that, should these stones be found in my possession, I am liable to be sent to prison; and I'm sure prison life would not agree with me. I can't sell the bally things here because all the dealers are watched, and I daren't send 'em through the mail because the police—they're frightfully inquisitive Johnnies—are liable to open any package I send. Then, too, I don't know you personally, though I have heard a great deal about you.
> Of course, I don't suggest, for one moment, that you wouldn't pay me a fair price—still; well, you see what I mean?

I leave today on a hunting trip and shall drift to Tomasi's *kraal* near the border. Suppose you amble along in that direction, too (making your camp on Portuguese territory, and so be free of the interference of the Police) and I will meet you there in a month's time.

See you by and by, Josie, old dear.

THE MAJOR.

This letter had piqued the senhor's curiosity and he had made certain guarded inquiries concerning the character of the Major. The information he received was vast and varied.

The Major was just a lucky fool; he was the cleverest I.D.B. in the country. He was effeminate; he was all the things a "he man should be." But the senhor discarded all except the one thing upon which all his informants were agreed. The Major was a man of his word; if he had "something" to sell, well, he had "something," and that was all there was to it.

And that was all Senhor José cared about. He could trust to his own business sense to drive a hard bargain. The Major would take anything he offered, and be glad to get it. The senhor had had too many experiences with I.D.B.s not to know that.

Keeping all this well in mind Senhor José had made the seven days' trip to the appointed place, had seen the Major and—

But that was three weeks ago and the diamonds were not yet in his possession. This was due solely to the Major's objection to seeing a native maltreated. Senhor José's servant had accidentally stumbled against his *Baas's* foot. A terrific *sjamboking* of the luckless native had followed, José beating the cringing native with a very berserk fury.

The Major, taking the *sjambok* away from the infuriated man, dismissed the native and, after threatening José with a thrashing, calmly doubled the price he had at first asked for the diamonds.

It was in vain that Senhor José pleaded and expostulated; the Major was impervious to both.

"If the native made a formal complaint against you, senhor," he said, "for abusive treatment, you would be compelled to pay a heavy fine, I assure you. But he won't complain; the poor devils never do, and, as there's no magistrate here, I've appointed myself to that office. You really must learn to curb your temper. This little fine may help you."

And, as the Major had refused to take a check, the senhor had been compelled to send a messenger into Lorenco Marquez for further funds. The messenger had returned this morning and, before nightfall, the diamonds would be in José's possession.

The senhor chuckled to himself at that thought. Even though he was being forced to pay five hundred pounds, considerably more than he expected, that price left him a big margin of profit; the stones were worth a king's ransom, twenty thousand pounds, anyway.

Buoyed up by the thought of the clever deal he was about to swing, the senhor applied himself with vigor to the unappetizing meal his native servant placed before him. Only a few more days, he told himself, and he would be on board ship, en route for more civilized realms.

HIS GAY visions were suddenly interrupted by an abrupt command. "Put up your hands!"

The senhor dropped the bone he was gnawing and, struggling to his feet, looked at the interloper with bewilderment, anger, and fear struggling for the mastery.

"What does this mean?" he asked querulously. "By what right does the senhor force himself, uninvited, into my tent?"

The other, a stockily built man dressed in the uniform of the Mounted Police, laughed.

"Gave you a scare, didn't I? Sit down and go on with your meal. I can talk just as well while you are eating; if you don't make too much noise, that is."

The policeman, whose stripes showed him to be a sergeant, lazily filled his pipe, lighted it and squatting native fashion on his haunches, smoked contentedly, regarding the senhor through half closed eyes.

Senhor José fidgeted under the scrutiny.

"Just what is it you want, senhor?" he stammered at length.

"You don't know much about life on the veldt, do you?" the other answered.

"No! And don't want to. It's a dog's life. Another few days of this and it'll see me no more."

"So?" The sergeant's tone was mildly sarcastic.

"And I judge," he continued, "that you are not over-popular with your natives. They wouldn't mind a bit, I mean, if you died suddenly or—oh, well, a lot of things might happen to you. If I took it in my head to arrest you, there would be no one to prevent me."

Senhor José laughed forcedly.

"I see you are joking. You English are very funny; you will have your joke. Supposing that I had done wrong, you have no power to arrest me. I am on Portuguese territory and you—"

"Oh, I wouldn't let a little thing like that bother me," interposed the sergeant. "The border is only a few score yards away. It would be easy for me to carry you over, though you are rather fat, and arrest you there. And, anyway, I don't think your government would trouble itself on your account even if I did make an arrest here. You're not exactly in their good books, Senhor José."

"Then you know me?"

"Hell, yes, man. Know all about you, and nothing to your credit. Know why you are up here now."

The senhor was silent. There was, indeed, nothing for him to say.

"Now look here, Senhor," continued the sergeant. There seemed to be an added force to his words. "We may as well get down to brass tacks. I'm not going to let you get away with the diamonds you are planning to buy from the Major."

"Diamonds? The Major?" murmured the other.

"Yes. Diamonds and the Major. The two always go together. Don't try to play the innocent; it won't do you any good. We know the Major has some stones which he wants to sell to you. He couldn't find any other dealer; we are watching them too closely. We know that you've come here for the purpose of meeting him. Very well. You are going through with the arrangements you have made with him, but I shall be on hand to arrest him as he hands over the diamonds."

"But why go to all this trouble, senhor. If you are sure that this Major has illicitly-procured diamonds in his possession?"

"Stolen diamonds," the sergeant interrupted. "Stolen from a detective who used them as a bait to trap him."

"Stolen diamonds, then," the senhor amended. "Why don't you arrest him without trying to drag me into the affair?"

The sergeant snorted in disgust.

"Arrest him, you say. We've done that more times than there are hairs on your head. But what good does that do us? We've never been able to catch him with the diamonds in his possession, and unless we do that we've got no case."

"Perhaps you didn't search him properly."

"We searched him so closely that had he been going to have smallpox ten years from now, we would have detected the symptoms."

Senhor José looked relieved and twirled the waxed ends of his mustache jauntily upward.

"Then isn't it plain," he said, "that you have come on a false trail? I'm here on a hunting expedition, and it is just a coincidence that the Major happens to be in this locality. That's all."

"YOU HUNT!" there was a world of scorn in the sergeant's voice, "Coincidence! Bah! No; you don't seem to understand." The sergeant suddenly stood up. As by some feat of legerdemain a revolver appeared in his right hand; it was leveled at the senhor's stomach. In the sergeant's left hand a pair of handcuffs dangled suggestively.

"You'll do as I say," he continued in an even voice, "or I'll arrest you now and take you back with me. We'll have no difficulty in sending you to the Breakwater for a few years, and do it legitimately too. There was that little gun running affair you engineered, for instance; there are one or two charges of attempted murder against you, and I've no doubt that I could prevail upon your niggers to swear that you shot royal game on our territory. That alone would be sufficient for a thousand pound fine or a year's imprisonment, or both. In your case I think it would be both."

"But you wouldn't do that, surely, senhor. It would be monstrous; it would be illegal."

"It would be all that, and more. But you can make your choice. Either you do as I say or—"

"What of the money this trip has cost me," wailed the other. "Am I to lose everything? And how do I know that you won't arrest me as an accomplice of the Major's?"

"All we want is the Major and the stones. There's a reward of five hundred pounds for the return of the diamonds; you can have that; it'll more than cover your expenses. All I want is the Major. I'll give you my word that you can go free."

Senhor José hesitated no longer. After all he didn't stand to lose anything, and he'd be able to even up his little score with the Major.

"All right," he said. "I'll do as you say."

The sergeant sighed with relief. His bluff had worked after all!

"There was nothing else you could do," he said curtly. "Understand this; you are not doing me a favor, you are only saving your own skin. Now tell me: when does the Major come to hand over the diamonds?"

"Tonight. I sent a message telling him to come tonight. I'd have had the diamonds and been well away from here if the cursed fool hadn't been so squeamish about the way I treated my niggers."

The sergeant looked interested.

"I wondered why you were hanging around here so long."

"I was thrashing one of my boys—the black deserved it—when the Major interfered and made me pay double the price he first asked. I must pay a fine, he said. The damned fool! And so I had to send for more money. That is why you find me here now."

The sergeant nodded absently.

He had objected strenuously to the idea of trapping a man like the Major. This particular instance of his interfering between a brutal white man and a native victim was typical of the man's whole life; typical of his constant warfare on behalf of the underdog. But the order had come from headquarters and the sergeant was too well disciplined to dream of disobeying.

Had this last escapade of the Major's been on a line with his others, the sergeant would have been even more reluctant to perform the duty. All other affairs in which the Major had been implicated had been illegal, without doubt, but were more in the line of political offenses. There were many men who held the opinion that it was grossly unjust for one syndicate to have the diamond mining rights of all South Africa; they believed that should they find a diamond on the open veldt it belonged to them, and not to the De Beers Syndicate; if they purchased a diamond, in good faith, they believed they ought not to be arrested and sentenced to imprisonment for illegal possession.

Such men looked upon the Major as their champion and, while he confined himself to dealings along such channels, he had the good wishes of all, including the police. Though, it must be said, the latter never relaxed in their attempts to catch him with the goods.

But this last affair made one stop and think. It was a plain case of theft and as such so contrary to the Major's usual way of doing things that men wondered if their previous estimation of his character had been the correct one.

"I will stay here then until he comes. I can hide under that roll of bedding yonder. Understand now, if you try to play any tricks, you will go to the Breakwater and not the Major."

"I'll play no tricks, senhor, rest assured of that. Had I known the diamonds were stolen I would never have thought of dealing with the Major. But when will you arrest him—here in the tent, or when he goes away from here?"

"Just as he's about to hand them over to you, of course. Have you seen them?"

"Yes. And it leaves me desolate to think that I shall not have the handling of them. They are stones of the first water, or I'm no judge. The Major does well to value his cigar case so highly."

"Cigar case? What do you mean?"

"Why, his gold cigar case, the one he keeps the diamonds in. Didn't you know it had a little secret compartment?"

The sergeant made an expression of chagrin.

"And to think," he muttered, "that I had that case in my hands not so long ago, and admired the workmanship of it. I might go ahead and arrest the Major without this rotter's aid. But, no. I'd better see it through according to orders. Otherwise I might slip up and then there'd be hell to pay."

GREAT EXCITEMENT was in the air at Tomasi's *kraal,* for on the morrow the White Lord, the man with the glass eye, would lead the warriors on a kudu hunt. The young men were busily engaged in preparing for the rigors of the chase and the old men recounted, to all who would listen, the wonders they had performed in their day.

Seated on a camp stool in the shade of a tree not far from the *kraal* sat the Major, busily engaged in overhauling his gun in preparation for the morrow's sport.

Jim, his faithful Hottentot servant, was seated on the ground nearby, watching his *Baas's* every movement with a look of almost adoration on his face. Whenever the Major looked up from his task Jim would industriously oil the mechanism of his old-fashioned muzzle-loader which the Major allowed him to carry, but not to use, whenever they went hunting together. It was always loaded, however, at such times, as a concession to Jim's vanity. Jim never had fired it, though he was always going to; as a matter of fact he was gun-shy.

He remembered too vividly, perhaps, the time when he had fired off, surreptitiously, one of the Major's elephant guns. Jim's jaw was almost dislocated, and his shoulder was bruised and sore for weeks afterward. Still, he would not have given up the prestige which came to him as a possessor of a real firearm for the world; no matter what load he was called upon to carry on these hunting expeditions, he never relinquished hold of his gun, totally indifferent to the extra burden he was giving himself.

Natives from the *kraal* were continually passing by the white man and all greeted him with affectionate respect. Even in the short time he had been in their midst, this people, shrewd judges of character as they were, had seen the true worth of the man.

Once a small, naked urchin sidled shyly up to the Major's side and was allowed to handle the white man's gun, was patted on the head, called a warrior, and sent away vastly enriched by the present of an empty cartridge case.

The Major gazed after the boy—a whimsical half sad smile on his face.

He wondered, as he had often wondered of late, if he was playing the part of a man. This constant matching of wits with the police was well enough in its way, yet what benefit did he gain from it? The law was the law. It was futile for him to set himself up against it. Then he thought of the last trick he had played upon the police, and he frowned deeply.

"I can't go through with it," he said aloud. "It's not playing the game. They'll have me billed as a sneak-thief if I'm not careful. A sneak-thief, just that. Do you understand, Jim?"

And Jim, whose knowledge of English was of the vaguest, answered: "Yah. Sneak-thief, *Baas*. A dam good thing, too, by golly."

The Major smiled wearily.

"A fat lot of good talking to an old heathen like you," he continued. "But one thing's sure; I've got to tell friend Senhor José that I can't go through with the deal, and then I've got to return the diamonds to the Chief of Detectives at Kimberly. And that'll be a job, a deuce of a job."

"Yah, *Baas*. A deuce of a job," echoed Jim.

The Major lapsed into a moody silence.

After a while a greasy, unkempt appearing native beckoned Jim to come and join him, and the Hottentot rose slowly to his feet and strolled leisurely over to the stranger.

A glint of amusement shone in the Major's eyes. He detected in Jim's swagger an imitation of his own walk.

"Well, old top, golly, O dam," he heard Jim greet the stranger. Jim always delighted to show off his knowledge of English.

But now, the Major noted, Jim quickly dropped his pose of authority as he conversed with the native in low undertones.

"Wonder what's afoot," murmured the Major. "Seems to me that I've seen that native before. If he's come to invite Jim to a beer drink, I'll have to say a few words."

Just then the two men, who had been squatting on their haunches as natives will when carrying on a conversation, rose to their feet.

"Here's a present for you," the Major heard Jim say. "You have rendered me and my *Baas* a great service. Now get you gone to your own place, lest you give my *Baas* cause for offense; his nose is very keen. And see that you tell no one that you have had word with us. Now, go. If I don't see you, s'long, hullo!"

Jim returned to his place by the Major and resumed his seat in silence. His brow was wrinkled with thought, and he had the air of carrying all the troubles of the world upon his broad shoulders.

"Well, Jim?" said the Major at length, realizing that Jim had something of great importance on his mind and wished to be asked concerning it.

"It is not well," Jim replied darkly. "It comes to me, *Baas*, that it would be folly for you to go to the tent of the white man who looks like a pig."

"So?"

"Yah! The *Baas* would be wise not to sell him the stones."

"I had already decided not to do so."

"That is good, *Baas*."

"But I shall go to see the man tonight."

"No!" Jim exploded. "That, the *Baas* must not do. The Great Spirits have whispered in my ears that great evil will come of it."

"Was that one of the Great Spirits you talked with a while ago?"

"It may be, *Baas.* The Great Spirits speak through various mouths. Yet listen, *Baas.*" Jim dropped his prophetic rôle and continued, "*Baas,* you saw that dam fool nigger. He is the servant of the man who looks like a pig. He is the man you saved from the *sjamboking.* He's dirty, alrite, O my, but he is your man. Aye; he says, and I think truly, that his ears are your ears; his eyes are your eyes. Good; dam bad. He speaks English even as he speaks his mother's tongue, but not as well as I speak it. Ver' well. Heed then, *Baas,* to what he saw; to what he heard.

"A white man came to the tent of his *Baas;* a white man dressed as dress the men of the *Nonquai,* the Mounted Police. They talk together for one dam long time. By and by, his *Baas* tells the *Nonquai* of the stones you carry in that case of gold. They whisper together for a while; they make plans. Tonight, when you go to sell the diamonds, the *Nonquai* will be hiding there and then—ah, woe is me. I will be without a *Baas.* I don't think."

As Jim unfolded the story the gloom gradually left the Major's face, and when Jim came to his breathless, but triumphant conclusion, the Major echoed his last words with a hearty chuckle.

"I don't think! You've said it, Jim, old top."

Jim grinned.

"Then the *Baas* will not go?"

"The *Baas* will go. You seek to know too much, Jim. Now get you down to the *kraal* and bid Tomasi to come hither. I would discuss the morrow's hunting. No. Leave your gun. I will load it for you in case you should desire to exhibit your prowess before the men of the *kraal.*"

When he had passed out of sight, the Major took a gold cigar case from his pocket, opened it and, from a cleverly concealed false bottom, rolled six whitish stones about the size of peas on to the palm of his hand. They were uninteresting looking objects; merely bits of dull glass to the eye of the uninitiated. Only an expert could have appraised them at their true value.

The Major wrapped each one, separately, in a small piece of fine chamois leather. Then, recalling his promise to Jim, he took up the old-fashioned gun and commenced to load it.

IT WAS long after sundown when the Major crossed the border on his way to the tented camp of the Senhor José.

The moon was at the full and a quiet peace hovered over the veldt. From the distant *kraal* came a faint lowing of cattle, and the murmuring voices of the men who were singing the chant of good hunting.

It was one of the Major's idiosyncrasies, when engaged in some scheme which called for all his wits, to affect an almost senile expression, accentuated by the monocle he wore, and to talk in a labored drawl which all Americans, who have attended variety shows to any extent, recognize as being typical of "the silly ass Englishman."

Never slovenly in his personal appearance, the Major was somewhat of a dandy when engaged in business. His hair, jet black streaked with gray and thinning at the temples, was slicked back from his high forehead; the skin of his smoothly shaved face was soft and clear. His white flannels were immaculately clean, and the crease of his trousers was of a knife edge sharpness. Jim was a wonder of a valet! The Major's hands were well shaped, and rather delicate appearing. Certainly they gave no suggestion of the terrible grip which they were capable of exerting.

Altogether he was not the sort of person one would expect to see strolling across the African veldt. Had you seen him lazily "punting" on the back reaches of Cambridge's historical river, or mixing with the gay crowd at a Henley Regatta, you would have paid him no particular attention, he would have fitted so well into the picture.

Here, however, beyond the farthest reaches of civilization, where clothes are worn simply as a protection from the burning rays of the sun, and the attacks of predatory insects, the Major's appearance was, to say the least, incongruous.

Something like this passed through the mind of Senhor José as he ushered his guest into his evil smelling tent, and he laughed as he noted the Major's expression of disgust.

"Sit down, Major," he said with an oily smirk, "and let's have a drink before we talk business."

"Thanks, no. I find the stuff they call whisky in this country is beastly bad for me. Phew! Can't we go outside. It's so much, er, cooler there, and I'm sure the moonlight is bright enough for me to count the money you are going to give me."

"May be. But it's not light enough for me to examine the stones properly. How do I know you'd not try to substitute something else for the real thing? I've heard of alum being passed off as diamonds before now," sniggered the senhor.

"No. Really? You surprise me. However, let's get this little affair over. I've got to go on a hunt tomorrow. It's a frightful bore; such a messy business. But I've got to go, and I must get some sleep. Have you all the money?"

"Yes."

The senhor took a package of five-pound notes from his pocket and, before the Major's careful scrutiny, counted out one hundred of them.

"There," he grunted. "Five hundred pounds in all, and a nice price you are making me pay. I'll be lucky if I come out even."

"Oh, come, now. I don't want to be hard on a chappie. I'm willing to call the deal off, you know."

José shook his head.

"I'm a man of my word; I'll go through with it."

"That's good. Now let me see; I've got to hand over something to you, haven't I?"

He reached into his hip pocket and brought out the gold cigar case.

"This," he continued with a chuckle, "is my pocket safety—"

"Hands up, Major," ordered a harsh voice. "I've got you covered."

It was the voice of the sergeant, and in response to the command the Major's hands shot above his head.

"We've got you this time, Major," the sergeant continued, rising and throwing from him the blanket under which he had secreted himself.

"I don't quite understand," stammered the Major. "You've got me? What do you mean, dear old chap?"

"You are arrested. A little matter of stolen diamonds, and I.D.B. I'll tell you the details if you like."

The Major sighed.

"Please spare me, old chap. I don't know what is the matter with you police Johnnies. Wherever I go, I'm sure to find one of you blighters close on my trail. You seem to have I.D.B. on the brain. A form of insanity, I call it, and deucedly annoying."

"I reckon you're right, Major. But when you're on the way to the Breakwater at Cape Town, we'll all show signs of improvement. Your sentence—ten years hard, I should say—will relieve our minds of a great deal of pressure."

The Major looked bewildered.

"How you do babble, and I suppose it sounds most convincin' to you. Of course you chappies have a lot to put up with from these I.D.B.s, and I may have been guilty of one or two little things myself in the past. In the past, mind you. I'm on the level now, absolutely, from this time forth, world without end, and all that, you know. I've arrived at years of discretion, you see."

"You arrived a little too late, Major. As for the present; how are you going to explain this little business deal you were contemplating with Senhor José here?"

"He has told you things, has he? My dear Sergeant, you really are too gullible for words. Of course this—er—gentleman would tell you all sorts of lies. He has to deal in romances in order to make up for a very dirty, and extraordinarily commonplace, career. And then, you see, I'm afraid he has no real love for me. I had to threaten him with a thrashing not so long ago."

The sergeant laughed.

"Suppose you tell me your side of the story. It'll be amusing I know, and I'm in no particular hurry."

"Amusing? No. I hardly think so. Not exactly what you would call amusing. Just a little business deal. The senhor, here, saw my cigar case and coveted it. Now I set a high value in that case; it was given me by a very dear old lady. Still the senhor was willing to pay my price and—well," the Major concluded lamely, "that's all there is to it."

"Quite enough, I should say. Unfortunately I've put in a claim for that case and I'm going to take it."

"Really, old man, you are carrying things too far. I am on Portuguese territory and you have no authority here."

"This is all the authority I need." The sergeant tapped his revolver significantly.

The Major shrugged his shoulders.

"Of course, if you're going to resort to that, I've no more to say. But please may I take down my hands? I'm quite unarmed."

The sergeant nodded assent.

"But no monkey tricks, mind. I've got you covered and I'm counted a first-class shot."

"Thanks." The Major sighed in relief. "Here's the bally case. I hope you are satisfied now." He threw it down on the rickety table.

"Open it, José," ordered the sergeant. "You know how to get at the secret pocket, don't you?"

José nodded. His eyes gleamed furtively as he weighed the chances of making a dash for the veldt and getting away with the stones.

Suddenly he saw an opportunity and as suddenly seized it. As he reached over to pick up the case he stumbled, clutched at the tent pole to save himself and pulled it down about their heads.

WHEN THE cursing sergeant and the hilarious Major finally extricated themselves from the smothering folds of canvas, José had made good his escape.

Intent only on capturing the fugitive, the sergeant made for his horse, followed closely by the Major. As the policeman was about to mount, the Major put out a detaining hand.

"Let him go, Sergeant," he said.

"Is it likely? Let go. I'll deal with you later."

But the Major did not relax his grip.

"Let him go," he repeated calmly. "You know you can't touch him in Portuguese territory, even if you caught him; and that I doubt. He's got a good horse, while yours—"

"I'll catch him; don't you worry. I know the veldt; he doesn't. I'll take my chance on the rest."

"But I give you my word of honor, Sergeant, that José has nothing you want."

"He has the cigar case."

"Yes. But there's nothing in it."

The sergeant was undecided. He knew the Major to be a man of his word.

"But José told me that you kept the diamonds in it."

"Diamonds! There you go again. I tell you that there were no diamonds in that case."

"You mean to tell me that José made off with it thinking that he was getting away with the diamonds? And all the time it's empty?"

"Exactly."

And now the humor of the thing struck the sergeant.

"I'd give a month's pay," he exclaimed amidst peals of gargantuan laughter, "to see José's face when he opens that case and finds it empty. He loses all around." Then, sobering quickly, he continued, "I'm going to search you, Major, just the same. You came here to make a deal with José, and I'm gambling that the stones are on you."

"You're wrong, old chap. I came to tell José that I had no deal to make with him. However, I don't suppose you'll believe that, so go ahead and search."

The sergeant's search was thorough, but fruitless.

"Well, I'm beaten," he confessed at length. "Suppose I'll lose my stripes for this. You've played merry hell with the Force, Major; especially when you bilked the chap who tried to trap you. Those stones you took from him belonged to the big boss of the mines. He's made the dickens of a fuss about it; and the chief has threatened to reduce us all to the ranks if the stones are not returned. He'll do it, too. I've never known old 'Daddy' Grayson go back on his word yet."

"What? Do you mean Grayson has been reappointed?"

"Yes. That new chap they imported from Scotland Yard didn't last a day after you fooled him so nicely. The Force is grateful to you for that little thing, Major."

"Good of you, I'm sure," murmured the Major. "But cheer up. The stones will turn up some day. Where are you hanging out? I'd like to know in case I happen to run across them."

"At Junvas's *kraal,* about five miles down the river. I've got a post there; border guard, you know."

The sergeant slowly mounted his horse.

"Oh, by the way," exclaimed the Major as though struck by a sudden thought, "what are you going to do with the money José left behind?"

The sergeant laughed shortly.

"That's yours, isn't it? Didn't he buy the cigar case from you?"

"Why, yes, of course. How stupid of me. Have you a pencil and a piece of paper? Ah. Thank you. I'll leave a receipt here, in case he should come back."

And the Major wrote:

> To Senhor José.
> In account with the Major.
> One Cigar case.... Five hundred pounds.
> Received with thanks,
>   THE MAJOR.

"And I think," he murmured as he pinned the note to the tent pole, "that I almost *honestly* earned that five hundred."

THE BUSH resounded with the shouts of the native hunters who were driving the game toward the place where the Major and Jim were lying in wait among a clump of Mapani.

Nearer, ever nearer, sounded the wild, shrill cries, and the beating of drums.

Already frightened animals were darting by the place of concealment. Small duikers, gracefully leaping impala, a herd of snorting zebras, wild dogs and hyenas, passed swiftly by nor gave one glance to the thicket where sudden death was concealed.

But still the Major's gun was silent. He waited the coming of the kudu, the lordliest buck of them all; the kudu, who, in order to preserve him from complete extinction, has been classed as royal game by the British Government, and so spared from the hunter's gun. Only when the buck raid the crops, as they had raided Tomasi's crops, was the ban lifted. Even then it was only permissible to kill the old bull, the leader of the herd. That was always sufficient to drive the herd to parts not frequented by man.

"Here they come, *Baas*," Jim exclaimed suddenly.

But it was long after he spoke that the Major heard the furious thudding of hoofs, and longer still before a herd of kudu, led by a magnificent old bull, came into view.

Closer and closer they came, until it seemed as though the two men would be trampled underfoot. And then the Major fired.

The old bull lurched in his stride, stumbled to his knees, recovered, and then fell headlong to the ground but a few yards from the Major. The rest of the herd divided into two streams and so, with never a thought of their departed leader, vanished into the shadows of the bush.

Solemnly the Major walked over to the fallen monarch and measured the length of his horns.

"He was a great chief, Jim," he said. "How old was he, think you?"

But Jim did not answer. He was watching, with puzzled eyes, a furtive movement in the bush nearby.

"Quick, *Baas,* to the right of you," he shouted suddenly. "Silwane charges."

The Major wheeled in time to see the massive, tawny form of a lion hurtling through the air toward him.

He fired. But no bullet could have stopped the beast's express charge. Dead or alive, his very momentum would have carried him to his objective. Nor had the Major time to leap aside before the beast was upon him, and he fell over backward, the snarling lion prone on top of him.

The Major's shot, hurried though it was, had punctured the lion's lungs. Its death was sure, ultimately, in a few short minutes perhaps. But until that time came it was still capable of rending the Major limb from limb. One blow, playfully given, would have crushed in the Major's skull like an empty egg shell.

The Major, realizing this, remained perfectly motionless; he did not flinch, even, when the lion's long whiskers swept across his face.

Then Jim, the Hottentot, whose fear of lions was only equaled by his fear of firearms, cautiously took up his heavy, old-fashioned, muzzle-loader. Slowly, so slowly that it would have been hard for human eye to detect any motion, he brought the piece to his shoulder and fired.

Jim was only a few yards from the lion, but Jim was no marksman and, though of this he was ignorant, the charge missed the lion completely.

Yet the shot had its effect.

The lion discarded the Major and leaped at the petrified Jim. The very leap, feeble attempt though it was, falling far short of its mark, was the lion's last attempt. Blood gushed from its terrible jaws and then, with a convulsive shudder, a half choked roar, it died.

THAT NIGHT the warriors of Tomasi's *kraal* shouted loudly the praises of Jim, the lion killer. And Jim, seated by the side of the old headman, received the plaudits with becoming modesty.

The Major had made him a present of a long coveted hunting knife and—this it was that pleased Jim most—had given him the mission to join the feast which celebrated the hunt.

So Jim was vastly happy. He did not know, nor had the Major seen fit to tell him that the charge from his gun, missing the lion, had entered the carcase of the kudu.

He had thought it strange, however, that the Major should have elected to skin the dead buck himself, giving orders that none, not even Jim, should venture near him during the performance of that task. He wondered vaguely that the Major should have cut off a big haunch of the buck and sent it, as a present, to the camp of the Mounted Policeman, many miles away.

But his wonder was short lived.

His *Baas* was a strange man. He did many things the reasons whereof were not plain. But, without doubt, the reasons were good reasons. And so in this case.

Jim turned to Tomasi and took the calabash the headman offered him. Putting it to his lips, he drank deeply.

"It is good beer—Tomasi," he said. "Have the women brewed aplenty? "

"A plenty, O killer of lions."

"That is good." Jim breathed contentedly. "That is dam good."

LATER THAT night the sergeant was hailed by a native of Tomasi's *kraal*. In his hands he carried a large chunk of kudu meat, This, together with a note, he gave to the policeman, and then disappeared in the shadows of the bush. The sergeant read:

> Dear Sergeant:
> I hope that you will accept this little peace offering. It should afford you a welcome relief from tinned horse; specially if you follow the instruction I now give in regard to cooking it.
> Place a large pot on the fire, half fill it with water. Add about a dozen onions, and any other vegetable you can lay hands on. Then, and this is most important, slice the meat into very small portions, and knead each piece thoroughly with the tips of your fingers. I'm serious about this, old chap. If you do as I say you may discover why kudu are very justly classed as royal game.
> The rest I leave to you. Doubtless you have a fair imagination. I only want you to remember this; you can't connect me with anything.
> So put that in your pipe and smoke it, old chap.
>   THE MAJOR.

The sergeant read this puzzling document through again and again.

"I wonder what he means," he muttered.

"Probably just one of his silly ass jokes. Still; well, I'm deuced hungry and a buck stew sounds good. Might as well follow the Major's recipe. Can't do any harm."

So, after making due preparations, the sergeant sat down to his task. He did it rather shamefacedly; as though conscious that the Major was watching him with a mocking smile on his face. He was about to give up in disgust, when he felt in the slice of meat he had just cut off something round and hard.

Excitedly he cut the slice still thinner and extracted from it something wrapped in a piece of chamois leather, and a moment later was staring in dumb amazement at the diamond which rested in the palm of his hand.

"Well, I'm damned," he shouted, and then feverishly applied himself with a new vigor to his task.

Far into the night he cut and slashed the chunk of meat, carefully prodding each piece, totally unconscious of the passing of time; unheedful of the fact that the water in his stew pot had all boiled away leaving nothing but a scorched, vilely smelling mess.

He did not stop until he had recovered six diamonds—Jim had been so close to the dead buck the charge had no chance to spread— and he knew that his task was completed.

"Well, I'm damned," he muttered again, as he gazed happily at the six little lumps of stone. "But won't the boys be glad to know that the Major's really on the square!"

That was his first thought. His second was that his stripes were safe, that perhaps a commission might be his if he could only invent a good enough yarn to explain how the diamonds came into his possession.

And so, whistling happily, he prepared for bed.

KRUGER'S GOLD

THE MAJOR was annoyed; more, he was furiously angry. For once his pose of supercilious boredom had vanished. The ubiquitous monocle was discarded, and his habitual bland expression had given place to one of intense anger.

He paced restlessly up and down, outside his bell-tent, indifferent to the scorching heat of an African sun, and muttered maledictions and threats in a harsh voice which surely boded no good for the person, or persons, responsible for the arousing of his wrath.

At the sound of a low moan he stopped his restless pacing and looked inside the tent.

A native—a Hottentot—was lying on the narrow bed. A white bandage, stained in one spot with an ugly red blotch, was about his head. His face was almost green, a gray-green; the face of a stomach-sick native.

"My belly is all fire, *Baas*," the Hottentot moaned. "And my head! Au-a! It is two heads I have, and they would go different ways."

"Serves you jolly well right, Jim," the Major growled in English.

"Golly! Yes, *Baas*," the Hottentot replied and wearily closed his eyes.

The Major's face softened and, entering the tent, he gently removed the bandage from the Hottentot's head and sponged the wound.

Jim opened his eyes again and attempted to rise from the bed. Failing in this he attempted to push the Major's hand away and expostulated.

"It is not fit, *Baas,* that you should do this."

"I am of that mind also, Jim. But it must be done. Yours was the fault, a command disobeyed, and, therefore the *Baas* becomes the servant; the servant—Jim, the Hottentot, they call him—the *Baas*.

Lie still, Worthless One!"

And Jim was still.

"I feel much better now, *Baas,*" he said after a while.

"So? Then tell me all."

"It is little I know, *Baas.* I went to the *ivinkel* (store) on the veldt—thou knowest the place—and drank *puza.* The white man sold me the drink, *Baas.* Only one little drink I had. What followed is as muddy water to me; it is as the night before the breaking of the dawn. A little I remember. There were words passed between me and the black dog who is the servant of the white man at the *ivinkel.* He demanded that I pay twice for one drink, for the one drink I had. He said I had not paid. I rose to deal with him as I would deal with liars, but my legs would not hold me—and only one little drink had I had, look you!

"I fell to the ground. He kicked me, *Baas,* and the white man laughed. He has crooked, yellow teeth, that white man, *Baas.* The servant took a knob-kerrie in his hand. I saw the blow coming but could not guard against it, neither could I escape from it. My belly was weak. I could not move. And then—I remember no more, *Baas.* I had only one little drink, *Baas,* and yet I do not know how I came back to this place."

"You were lying on the veldt, Jim, between here and the store. The hyenas were gathering around you. On my back I carried you hither."

"Au-a! Great is my shame! That I should have made of my *Baas* a beast of burden. Better that you had left me out on the veldt, food for the aasvogels and the hyenas! But truly the *puza* had the strength of many evil spirits."

The Major nodded absently. He had seen other instances of the effect on the natives of the frightful compounds sold by certain degenerate white men. It was against the law to sell any form of intoxicants to natives, but these men—not content with the enormous profits which would have accrued to them in selling pure whisky to their victims—dealt solely in a vile concoction which had a corrosive acid as its base. The manufacturing cost was small, its "knock-out" qualities, as Jim could, attest, were great.

It was not only that Jim, his servant, had fallen a victim to these men, that had aroused the Major's wrath, but the knowledge that many other natives—hundreds, thousands of them—were in danger of losing their tribal heritage. They were losing their fine manhood, their marvelous stamina, their skill in the hunt. They were becoming debased, mentally, morally and physically. They were selling their crops and their cattle for the temporary oblivion induced by the white men's *dorp*.

"What is the name of the white man who keeps the store, Jim?" the Major asked suddenly.

"I heard men call him Steve, *Baas*. He the man with the yellow, crooked teeth is the servant of the big fat man at the Palace in the *dorp.*"

"Fat George, eh? I'll go and have a talk with that bally blighter." The Major rose to his feet.

"Baas!"

"Well, Jim?"

"Where does the *Baas* go?"

"To the *dorp.*"

"Then I come, too."

"Nay. Of what worth are you? Drunkard!"

"It is true, *Baas,*" Jim replied humbly, "that I am a thing of no moment, but it is not fitting that the *Baas* should ride to the *dorp* unattended. See! My strength has returned—"

Jim got up from the bed and swayed unsteadily on his feet. He would have fallen to the ground had not the Major caught him.

"So I see," the Major said drily. "Strength you have, without doubt, but it is the strength of a babe. You will stay here. You will sleep. With the coming of sundown the sickness will have left you. As for the blow, I have heard it said that Jim the Hottentot was a warrior of sorts. The blow is no great matter."

"You speak true word, *Baas*. That is already forgotten. But," he added, "the *Baas* will be careful if he goes alone to the *dorp?*"

"Oh very! Rather!" Then in the vernacular, "But what need is there of caution, Jim?"

"The *Baas* remembers the *Nonquai,* the mounted policeman, Reaney?"

The Major nodded. He remembered Reaney very well. Reaney had several times attempted to frame up a case of Illicit Diamond Buying against the Major. That seemed the only way to ensure the conviction of the most daring and audacious of the "I.D.B.s." That the Major should have successfully frustrated Reaney's attempts goes without saying, and on the last occasion he had turned the tables on Reaney, had exposed that man's system of extortion among other I.D.B.s and illicit liquor traffickers. As a consequence Reaney had been demoted and transferred from the diamond district. And he had, of course, vowed to get even with the Major.

"The man, Reaney, was at the *ivinkel, Baas,*" Jim said. "It was he, I think, who told the black dog to hit me with the knob-kerrie. He knew I was Jim, the Major's servant, and thought to strike you through me."

The Major laughed.

"Rather flatter yourself, old dear, don't you," he drawled. Fishing his monocle out of the breast pocket of his smartly tailored tunic coat, he fixed it in his eye. "Still," he continued, "there's nothing like having a good opinion of oneself. At that, I believe that there's a great deal of truth in what you say, Jim."

"Yah, *Baas,* agreed the Hottentot complacently. He didn't know what his *Baas* was saying; he did not greatly care. But the laugh, the drawl, and the appearance of the monocle was sufficient for him. He knew that, in some part, his disobedience of orders had been forgiven.

"Yes, Jim," said the Major. "I go now to the *dorp*. You will stay here. You will not leave the tent, or get up from the bed, until I return. Is it understood?"

"Yah, *Baas*. It is understood. It is an order."

LEAVING THE tent, the Major quickly saddled his horse, a sturdy Basutu stallion, mounted, and rode swiftly over the veldt toward the *dorp*, Steyfontein, a prosperous gold-mining settlement.

It was barely a mile distant from the Major's camp and, in a very short time, he was galloping down the long, dusty main street, which led—as do all African main streets—to the principal hotel.

The sun was almost directly overhead, and the town seemed deserted; the inhabitants were taking their daily *siesta.* A Chinese laundryman seemed to be the only living thing abroad and he, enveloped in a dust cloud of his own scuffling creation, distorted by the heat rays, seemed like the grotesque figure of a mirage.

The Major pulled his horse to a walk. In good condition though the stallion was, his black, silky coat was flecked with lather. The Major had ridden fast and the day was very hot.

The Major had allowed his anger to drive him and that was an error which he now recognized. In generosity, in self-abnegation, the Major could afford to be-often was—impetuous; but not in anger.

So he rode slowly now, his head bent in thought, holding conference with himself as to "ways and means" of punishing the man, or the band of men, who had been responsible for Jim's downfall.

Because of this preoccupation he did not see a man, dressed in the sober habiliments of a clerical, run out of a nearby house. Neither did he hear the hail, "Major!"

Not the first time. But the second time he did and as he turned in his saddle and recognized the man, his face lighted up with undisguised pleasure.

"Why, 'pon my soul!" he exclaimed. "It's Father Joyce!"

He dismounted and greeted the cleric enthusiastically.

"Just the same devil-may-care imp of Satan," said the priest. But there was a look of genuine affection in his eyes as he looked up into the face of the Major. He knew that the outward pose of boredom, of irresponsibility, was only a pose. He knew that inane, vacuous almost, expression, heightened by the affectation of a gold-rimmed monocle, served as a mask to hide the quick wit of the man. And the priest knew—he was the only man who did know—the past history of the man; he knew the circumstances which had led to the Major's single-handed fight against the diamond mining monopoly and the stringent laws the interests had had passed in order to protect that monopoly.

"The same to you, and all that, Father," the Major retorted. "But what are you doing here? Thought you never left your black converts back yonder." The Major, with a wave of his hand, indicated the ridge of low lying kopjes on the distant horizon.

"It's because of them I'm here."

"The dear man talks in riddles. Elucidate, old top."

He looked whimsically at the little man of peace who was so essentially a man's man, who knew no creed, and who was almost universally admired and respected.

"Before I answer your question, Major," said Father Joyce, "I want to know why you're here. You are way off your 'beat,' you know!"

"Oh, but I can't tell you. That would make you an accessory before the crime, you know."

"I want to know, Major."

"Well, if you're goin' to talk in that tone I suppose I must tell the truth, the whole truth, and all that. I'm going to horsewhip Fatty George and a few of his friends for selling rotgut liquor to Jim. You know Jim, don't you?"

"Yes. I know Jim." Father Joy looked relieved. "Pity he has such a rogue of a master, though. But," he linked his arm in the Major's and turned toward the house, "come in. Let Fat George go for a while. We are in a desperate situation and need help. Of course I thought of you, wondered where you were, and then you rode by. Quite an act of Providence, for you are the one man, I believe, who can help us."

The Major bowed.

"You flatter me, really. But why—why all the bally mystery?"

The priest was casting furtive glances up and down the street.

"I don't want anyone to see us together."

"Rather late to think of that, old dear. You should have thought of that ten minutes ago."

Father Joyce looked crestfallen.

"I know," he admitted. "But I didn't think. Still, I don't think that anyone has seen us. Let's go in." He paused again on the steps of the porch. "Can't you make your horse disappear? Everybody knows him."

The Major whistled once, a low, soft note, and the Basutu cantered slowly down the street.

"He'll go all the way back to the camp," he said ruefully as he followed the priest into the house, "and I'll have a bally unpleasant walk back. It's inconsiderate of you, Padre Joyce. Really it is and I—"

He stopped short and looked reproachfully at the priest as he suddenly noticed that a girl was sitting in a low chair at the back of the room.

"Helen," said Father Joyce, ignoring the Major's frowns, "this is the Major. You've heard of him, of course. He is going to help us."

The girl rose gracefully from her chair.

"Yes, indeed, I've heard of the Major, and I'm sure he can help us— if he will."

Her voice was low and musical and the Major, woman-shy though he was, recognized that hers was no common beauty.

He looked at her helplessly, mouth agape. He took out his monocle, polished it, and replaced it in his eye again.

"Rippin'! I'll be charmed, really," he drawled. "Do anything in the world for you. Absolutely anything. Sew beaded aprons for the heathen or anything like that, you know. Of course—"

"Sit down, Major," Father Joyce mercifully intervened. "We're not going to ask you to sew aprons for the heathen."

The Major affected to look relieved.

"I'm glad of that. But I'd be quite willing to do so, you know. You understand that, don't you, Miss Helen? But I'd be out of my element, so to speak."

"We need your help to give Fatty George and his friends a—a licking," continued the priest.

"Ah! Then I must be on my way. I was going to do just that, you know."

"I don't mean a physical licking—though heaven knows they need that, too—but a political one."

"I begin to smell a rat."

"You'll see a rat in a little while, Major. Do you know John Sewell?"

"Isn't he the chappie who's seeking political honors, public prosecutor, an' all that?"

"That's the man. Do you know anything about his platform?"

"Must you know? It's deucedly embarrassing for me to answer. I've heard that in his speeches he's continually blasting—your pardon,

Miss Helen; word used in the sense of blowin' up, so to speak—all I.D.B.s. He has dragged my name through the slime of politics. He has called me the biggest rogue—and really I'm quoting the mildest of his terms—in Africa, and he has pledged himself to send me to the Breakwater for twenty years should he ever have the opportunity of prosecuting me. But worst of all, he defends the Draconian Laws and considers every person with an unregistered diamond in his possession as a criminal who should be sent to prison. It's monstrous! I've a bally good mind to run against him on that issue. Oh yes, I've heard of Sewell. But why do you ask?"

The Major looked very hurt.

"Then you're prejudiced against him and won't help us?"

"Well! I'm not exactly prejudiced against him, dear Miss Helen; but, on the other hand, I'm not exactly in sympathy with him."

"Oh, but you would be if you knew him!"

"But he would ruin my—er—business, Miss Helen."

"He'll ruin another business if he's elected, Major."

"And that, Padre?"

"The selling of liquor to natives."

"Ah! Now I do smell a rat," the Major breathed softly. "And what is your difficulty?"

"The election is in three days. Granted a fair deal, Sewell would win by a small majority."

"And you don't expect a fair deal? But surely, old top, they won't dare to try any illegal voting?"

"No! Perhaps not."

"Then!"

"It's like this, Major." The girl spoke breathlessly at first and somewhat as if she expected the Major to show contempt of her. "I'm the bar-maid at the Palace and this morning I overheard Fat George telling one of his friends how they plan to defeat John—Mr. Sewell. They have a picture of him in convict clothes and, on the morning of the election, they are going to put up copies of that picture with a statement that he is an ex-convict."

"I see. That rather knocks things into a cocked hat, doesn't it? And so Sewell is an ex-convict, is he? Has rather a nerve, hasn't he? What?"

"But he's not an ex-convict!" the girl exclaimed indignantly. "They trapped him; he's—"

He stopped as the priest held up a warning hand.

"I'll explain, Helen," he said. "Two or three weeks ago, Major, Reaney arrested Sewell. It was quite late, and they wouldn't let him get word to his friends; locked him up over the night. In the morning, of course they couldn't hold him. Reaney apologized; said it was a case of mistaken identity, asked Sewell not to say anything about it as it would get him—Reaney—in trouble. Sewell, who had treated it right along as a joke, agreed. I don't think he has said anything about it to anyone.

"When he was leaving the cell to go to breakfast with Reaney, a negro laborer, by accident apparently, upset a bucket of water all over him. Reaney, again very profuse in his apologies, insisted on having John's clothes dried and pressed for him and—as a joke—gave him a convict suit to wear. Sewell didn't suspect a thing, Helen heard Fat George boast, and while he was walking across the prison yard someone took his portrait."

"Well! I don't see any harm in that to the Sewell cause. Sewell can easily explain, can't he?"

"You're terribly dense, Major. He could explain, of course, if he had time. But they're not going to do anything until the morning of election and then it will be too late. That photograph, and the caption, will be the first thing the voters see when they go to the polling station. That photograph will beat him."

"And you see," further explained the girl, "John is making a final trip round the outside district and we can't get in touch with him. It's the farm vote he counts on to elect him and he's making a personal canvass of all the farmers. The town people do not come in contact with the natives. They don't care whether the natives get liquor or not. And the mine owners are secretly on Fat George's slide. They believe that the only way to get, and keep, laborers is to provide them with liquor. And if John is defeated it will mean that a man in the pay of Fat George will be re-elected and—"

"So you see, Major, we need your help."

"Ah, yes." The Major stroked his chin thoughtfully. "Bai Jove, yes. We must do something. Dear old John must be elected, positively yes. What can we do? I have it. We must steal that bally picture from Fat George."

The girl shook her head.

"That's impossible."

"How impossible, dear Miss Helen?"

"Fat George keeps it in his safe, and it's a strong safe."

"Safes have been opened, you know."

"But even if you got the snapshot, there'd still be the posters. They're all ready made up by the printer."

"Hum! Then, can't we get out some posters—little tracts, you know—exposing the whole scheme."

"We'd already thought of that, Major," said Father Joyce heavily, "but there's only one printer in town, and he's in their pay."

"Then let us pay him higher. I've just pulled off a little—er—business deal; quite profitable it was, and I'm absolutely rollin' in the root of evil, as it were."

The priest shook his head.

"The printer is Fatty George's brother, Major," he said. "You can't bribe him."

The Major looked nonplussed for a moment. Then he said cheerfully:

"It all looks very sad, doesn't it, old dear. But we must not get down-hearted. I set out to thrash Fat George and, bai Jove, I'm goin' to do it. Yes. I think that I can positively state that I can do that mucker one in the eye."

"But how?" The two voices sounded as one.

"That's my little secret."

It's time for me to go back," said the girl dispiritedly. She could not share the Major's assurance. She rose slowly to her feet. Then, "Oh, Major!" she exclaimed. "I had nearly forgotten. Be on your guard. Don't buy any diamonds. Reaney plans to trap you. I overhear a great deal, don't I? But men seem to ignore my presence, sometimes. He'll try to arrest you in the Palace Bar before all the people, if he can. Some of them don't think he's any good, and he believes that, if he can arrest you, it will set him right again with his superiors at headquarters."

The Major's eyes sparkled.

"Thanks, Miss Helen," he murmured. "Just keep up the good and well known spirits, dear and honored miss. It will be just as well if you don't appear to know me when I come into the Palace Bar tonight.

And please serve me with
stout—you won't forget? It
does not agree with me. I absolutely loathe the bally stuff.
So I never drink a whole glass.
Leave some at the bottom,
don't you know? But stout is
black and opaque and, this is
very important, be very careful
with my glass when I set it
down. It may contain a
message from me. Written on
a piece of parchment, or something of that sort, and wrapped

around a little stone. So please keep whatever you find. Do you understand?"

"Yes, I think so, Major. Good day. Good day, Father Joyce. No.
Please don't come to the door with me."

A moment later they saw her, head erect, walking with an easy,
graceful carriage up the dusty street.

"And will you tell me, Padre Joyce," the Major exclaimed when the
girl had passed out of sight, "what a girl like that is doing behind the
bar of the Palace Hotel? And what sort of a man the Sewell Johnny
is to let her?"

"She came out to keep house for her brother, and he's a waster. So
she went to the hotel. Nothing else for her to do here. She wouldn't
accept help; too proud. Besides, she had an idea she could help her
brother by so doing. And, by the powers, she's doing it. It rather hurts
a man, if he's got anything at all in him, to see his sister serving drinks
behind a bar. As for Sewell—he's blind, but he'll open his eyes pretty
soon. He doesn't know he's in love with her—but I do."

The Major nodded absently.

"There's one important thing I had forgotten," he exclaimed suddenly. "Can you see Miss Helen again this afternoon? I mean, without
those other Johnnies getting the wind up if they see you two together?"

Father Joyce inclined his head.

"I think I can manage that," he said. "What do you want me to
tell her?"

"In a minute. First tell me more about this Sewell chappy. Apart from his political beliefs, and all that, is he the sort of man you would—er—take into the bosom of your family, so to speak. You know what I mean?"

"Yes. I know what you mean, Major. He is all that. He—"

THAT SAME night the Major again left his camp on the veldt and headed for the township. He whistled gaily as he rode. He was content to let his horse pick its own pace, for it was long after sundown and the darkness was almost impenetrable. No stars were visible, but ahead the will-o-the-wisp like lights of the *dorp* glowed faintly.

As he reached the outskirts of the town a dark figure materialized out of the darker night. A hand clutched at the bridle.

"Say, mister," said a thick voice. "Do you want to buy a sparkler?"

"That depends," the Major answered cautiously, "on the size of the diamond, and the amount of money you want."

As he spoke the Major glanced sharply to the right of him. He thought he heard the halt-stifled whimper of a horse; thought he saw a mounted figure.

"Let's go on until we come to a street lamp," he continued.

"All right," the other assented, but he retained his hand on the bridle and checked the horse just at the farthest edge of the circle of light cast by the flickering oil lamp.

"There's no need to go any further," he said. "I don't want to know who you are, and you don't want to know who I am. That makes it A I at Lloyds, don't it, mister. This is light enough for you to know I'm selling you a diamond, and you can't fool me about the money. Now, what do you think of this?"

He held up between his thumb and forefinger a stone about the size of a pea.

"I must hold it in my hand, my dear chap. I can't judge it while you're holding it."

"All right, take it," the other growled. "I guess I can trust you; I got to."

"Yes. You—er—got to," chortled the Major as he took the diamond. "Will twenty pounds satisfy you?"

"Twenty! That's worth fifty."

"To you, yes, but not to me."

"It's a buy. My! But you've got a bargain, mister."

"Yes? I rather fancy so myself. Here! Mind if it's all in gold? Fine. One, two—" He counted out twenty pieces. "And now I must ask you to take your hand off the bridle. I must be on my way. Ta ta, old chap."

The Major rode off at a gallop, singing loudly. He paid no attention to a possible pursuer, though he was almost sure there was one, and a few minutes later he came to the Palace Hotel, hitched his horse to the rack and entered the bar.

It was crowded with miners, rough-looking, rough-living men, all of them, yet the Major noticed, in just that moment of hesitation before he stepped from the doorway, that they treated the girl behind the bar with courtesy; rough, to be sure, but sincere. The Major felt greatly relieved. He had rather dreaded seeing the girl in the atmosphere of the Palace barroom.

Her eyes met his as he came forward, but they showed no signs of recognition. She was prepared to play her part.

Many of the men in the room crowded around the Major. Most of them knew him and were genuinely fond of him. All of them had heard of him.

"The drinks are on you, Major," shouted one.

He smilingly indicated the bottle-lined shelves, a silent invitation to them to name their drinks. In the babel of shouted orders the fact that the Major did not name his drink, that he had not spoken at all, passed unnoticed. And when the miners turned to shout "Chin chin," "Cheerio," "Good hunting," "Here's how," and "May the pol'is, bad cess to 'em, never catch ye," he raised his glass, a glass of stout, nodded a smiling response to their toasts, and put the glass to his lips.

And then from the door a curt voice, a voice with a sneer in it, shouted:

"Get away from that dude, boys. And you, Major, get away from the bar and stand in the center of the room with your hands above your head. Sharp now!"

Wonderingly, but quickly, the miners obeyed the command. Less swiftly, the Major placed his half-emptied glass of stout on the bar and moved into the center of the room.

As he did so a short, heavily built man, a private of the police, came from the doorway, revolver in hand. A leer of triumph was on his face.

"What's it all about, Reaney?" asked Johnson, one of the mine owners.

"What would you expect, seeing this is the Major? This is the man who's boasted the police would never catch him; who's done more I.D. Buying than any other ten men in the colony. He's made a laughin' stock of the police. He showed me up afore a lot of people. Well, now I'm going to show him up."

"Up where, dear man?"

Reaney ignored the Major's remark and continued:

"You see, boys, I caught him dead to rights tonight; saw him buy a diamond from a stranger—think he was a half-cast.

"Oh!" The Major's ejaculation was one of supreme innocence. "Then why didn't you arrest me at the time, old dear?"

"Fat chance I'd have had of doing that, in the dark and you mounted."

"In the dark? But how could you see me then?"

"Aw! Stow your gab. You've got that diamond on you and I'm going to search you. Come on!"

"Come on where?"

"Into Fat George's office. Think I'm going to search you out here?"

"That's the only place you will search me, my dear chap. You have tried to—er—frame me once or twice before and failed. So you see I prefer to have witnesses of this search of yours. Otherwise you might try to frame me again. I don't suppose you'll take my word of honor that I have no diamond on me? No? Very well, our mistrust is mutual, so to speak, isn't it? Eh, what?"

"I've got no objection to searching you here," said Reaney. As a matter of fact, that was just what he wanted. "Will you go in the other room for a bit, miss," he said to the girl behind the bar.

"Now I'll attend to you, Major. Keep your hands where they are—see?"

"All right, old chap. Anything to oblige. Don't get ratty, but there's one thing I must insist on. Before you come any nearer to me take off your coat and roll up your shirt sleeves."

"Anybody'd think I was under suspicion, not you," growled Reaney. "You can't give orders to me, let me tell you that."

"You do just as the Major says," said Johnson. "And we'll all be watching you pretty close, Reaney, so don't try any frame-up tricks."

Reaney grumbled, but, seeing that the miners were in sympathy with the Major, obeyed. He removed his coat and rolled up his shirt sleeves, consoling himself with the thought that the Major, clever though he was reputed to be, clever as he undoubtedly was, could not escape the trap this time.

"Anything else you want me to do?" he growled.

"Why—er—yes. You might show your hands—like a prestidigitator, you know—to prove that you're not concealing anything, absolutely nothing. And," the Major continued as Reaney with ill-grace obeyed, "I will ask all the gentlemen in the audience to watch this trick closely. Mr. Reaney, you know, has been known to discover things in places where there was nothing. He has discovered diamonds in empty pockets."

"We'll watch him closely, Major," said one of the miners. "If he finds a diamond on you it will be because there is one there ready."

"Ah! Thanks! Then let the search begin."

And Reaney, without more ado, commenced. And his search was thorough. The parasite of a flea, had there been such a thing on the Major's body, would not have escaped scrutiny.

As he progressed with the search Reaney's spirits sank lower and lower. The premonition that he was to fail again grew stronger and stronger. Yet he did not see how he could possibly fail. The Major had bought the stone, he was sure of that; and the Major had had no cause for suspicion. Therefore he had not got rid of the diamond. Therefore it was still on his person.

But it wasn't.

Reaney was forced at last to admit defeat—an admission that the miners hailed with loud jeers.

He turned on them savagely.

"He's passed it on to one of you fellows," he charged. "You're in with him. I've a good mind to search the lot of you."

"You can start right in with me, sonny," said one grizzled miner known as Yankee Yates. "I'm willin'. An' if yuh find the diamond I'll make no fuss about it. But if yuh don't find it I'll knock yuh high'n a kite. Sure as shootin' I will."

"And that goes fer me, too, Reaney," shouted another.

"And me."

"And here's another."

There was not a miner in the room who did not issue a similar challenge.

Reaney paused a moment in indecision. Then, with a muttered curse, he pushed his way through the jeering crowd and entered a room leading off the bar.

As the door closed behind the policeman the miners showered questions upon the Major.

"One at a time, old dears," he pleaded. "You make my brain whirl, really. And, 'pon my word, I can't tell you anything. As you see, there's no diamond on me. Mr.—er—Reaney must have been mistaken. And now suppose you let me devote my time to dressing. It's a deuce of a job without Jim to help me. A perfectly priceless valet, that lad. When I'm dressed we'll ask the charming Hebe to return and serve us with drinks. We'll have a merry time drinking the health of our good and well known police force."

FAT GEORGE was well named. His eyes were almost hidden by huge rolls of fat. He seemed to have no neck or, rather, what was his neck seemed to be but a slight narrowing of his barrel-like body. The girth of his chest was enormous; but that of his waist-line was elephantine. No ordinary chair would support Fat George's bulk. Any chair he used had to be reinforced with iron struts. Otherwise it ceased to be a chair and became kindling wood.

When he went abroad it was in a specially constructed buggy drawn by two mules. He never walked. Generally he was to be found seated at his desk in this little room leading off the bar. And he always had on hand a good supply of food. He ate almost continuously.

Yet, such was the personality of the man, his hold on the people of the community was so great, so far reaching, that he was cognizant of everything which transpired in the town. To him, eventually, all people came for advice. Matters were referred to him for judgment.

In short, he was the crooked boss of the crooked political power which was then the ruling power in Steyfontein.

He rubbed his soft white hands together and smiled maliciously as Reaney entered and slumped down disconsolately on a nearby chair.

"So!" he smiled. "You failed, eh? You haven't got the brains to go up against a man like the Major. All you're good for is to arrest niggers for traveling without a pass."

His voice was strangely soft; its quality almost womanish.

"I don't know how he did it, George," Reaney complained querulously. "He had no cause to suspect a frame-up. Nobody knew about it, except you."

"You're not accusin' me of splittin', are you, Reaney? Because, if you are—"

"Of course not, George," Reaney said hurriedly. "Only, it's damned funny, ain't it?"

"Sure it is. Here. Have a piece of biltong."

He handed a strip of the dried meat to Reaney, who sliced a piece off and chewed on it.

"It's a mite too salty," George complained as he put a big chunk in his mouth. "But it creates a thirst."

He poured out a drink of whisky for himself and the policeman.

"The trouble with you, Reaney," he said after a while, "is that you're so simple that you make elaborate plans to catch the Major. What you ought to do—"

He broke off as a wild burst of cheering came from the bar.

"What's that?"

"Oh, they're drinking the rotter's health." Reaney's voice was very bitter.

Fat George laughed.

"We'll join them," he said, and poured out two more drinks.

"As I was saying," he continued, "you ought to find some simple plan. Knock the Major on the head, plant the diamond on him while he's still unconscious, handcuff and leg-iron him, and then arrest him. But you couldn't do that. He'd get away from you even if you did. You've got no brains."

"I managed to pull that Sewell affair off all right, didn't I?" Reaney protested.

"Yes," Fat George assented patronizingly. "You managed to provide a way to put Sewell out of the running when the time comes. But don't forget I planned that."

At that moment the girl entered.

"What is it, my dear?" George asked.

"It's about this, sir. The man with the monocle paid for the drinks with it."

She handed Fat George a gold coin. It was a Kruger sovereign. The head of Oom Paul adorned one side of it, but the other was blank.

George's eyes gleamed as he examined it, but he made no comment other than, "That's all right, my dear."

"But it's not legal tender, sir, is it?"

"Why not?"

"Well, it doesn't seem to be finished properly. There ought to be some inscription on the other side."

"Why—so there ought. I never thought of that." Fat George's voice expressed innocent wonder. "But that's all right," he added as the girl still waited. "You get back to the bar. Is the Major drinkin'?"

"Quite a lot sir. It's a pity, for he seems quite a gentleman."

Fat George chuckled.

"The Major always makes a hit with the ladies. Don't bother about this. Take all he'll give you."

The girl quietly left the room.

As the door closed behind her, Reaney jumped up excitedly.

"We've got him now, George!" he cried. "Passing counterfeit money!"

"Sit down and don't be a fool. I want to think."

Reaney subsided like a rebuked child.

The minutes passed by quickly. Now and again a burst of maudlin laughter and song came from the barroom. The Major's voice sounded above all the rest.

Reaney fidgeted continually, but Fat George sat motionless, gazing fixedly at the gold coin which he held in the palm of his hand.

"Where's that half-caste Hans?" he asked suddenly.

Reaney jumped at the abrupt question.

"He ought to be here any minute. I told him to report here. Probably he's spending the money the Major gave him for the diamond."

As he spoke the door opened and a thin, furtive-looking, Cape-boy entered.

"About time you came, Hans."

"I hurried, mister," Hans whined. "And look, look what that Major gave me."

From one of his pockets he emptied onto Fat George's desk thirty gold coins, all resembling the one the girl had brought in.

"It's not my fault," he said, "that the money is bad. I could not see well in the dark."

"Get out of here," George shouted wrathfully. "Get out, before I *sjambok* you."

And Hans got out.

"I see," said Reaney, his voice full of admiration. "You wanted more evidence before I arrested the Major. Well, we've got him now."

Fat George looked at him contemptuously.

"You're a fool, Reaney. I don't know why I bother with you. Still, you're useful on occasions. Just peek through the door and see what the Major's doin'."

Reaney crossed to the door, pushed back the piece of wood which covered a spy-hole, and peered through.

"He's got a skinful," he announced presently. "He's trying to balance a bottle of champagne on his forehead—ah, he dropped it!"

Fat George grunted and then, inch by inch, raised himself from his chair.

"Come on," he said. "We'll go out the back way."

"Where are you going?"

"Out to the *ivinkel*. I want to have a talk with Steve, an' I may have a talk with that Hottentot nigger of the Major's."

AN HOUR later Fat George and Reaney arrived at the *ivinkel* on the veldt and were at once ushered by Steve, the villainous looking storekeeper, into the squalid hut he used as living quarters.

"What is it, Boss," Steve asked jocularly as the fat man seated himself. "Has the policeman come to arrest me?"

Fat George scowled at the levity.

"What was that fairy story you were telling me the other day about Kruger's gold?" he asked.

"It's only a yarn, Boss. Fairy story is right. Yet you'd be surprised at the number of old-timers who believe it's true. It may be, at that."

"Tell it; you're too long-winded."

"It was a drunk Boer farmer who told me, Boss."

"Fools and drunks speak the truth," George said sententiously.

"He said that when Oom Paul saw that the British were going to lick him he collared all the gold coins he could and hid 'em. A lot of the coins, the old Boer said, were only half-minted. Oom Paul planned to melt 'em down, but he died before he could get the chance. And the other men who knew the secret hiding-place were killed in the last engagement of the war. That's all."

"I've heard that yarn," said Reaney, who was beginning to see light. "And I'll gamble there's a lot of truth in it. Oom Paul was a slim old devil."

"Oh, you've heard of it before, have you?" snapped George. "Then why in hell didn't you say so?" Then to Steve, "Is the Major's nigger here?"

"Yah! He's been trying to buy a drink for the last half hour, but I wouldn't serve the blasted ——. I don't trust him nor his damn *Baas*, either."

"Well! Bring him in here and bring a bottle of whisky with you— the real stuff, mind you."

Wondering not a little, Steve left the hut and a few minutes later returned with the bottle of whisky, followed by the squat, homely figure of Jim, the Hottentot.

"Now get to hell out of here, Steve," George commanded. "And don't hang around trying to hear what's not meant for you."

Jim looked uneasily after the departing storekeeper and started to follow.

"Wait," said Fat George. Both he and Reaney spoke the vernacular fluently. "Art thirsty?"

"Aye, *Baas*," Jim's face broke into a broad grin. "Always thirsty, *Baas*."

"Then drink. It is the drink of a white man, not the filth sold by the man at the store."

Fat George passed Jim the bottle and the Hottentot drank greedily.

"Au-a!" he exclaimed in disgust. "It is as milk compared to that other.

George grinned.

"Drink again, Warrior."

And Jim drank again, but in his greedy eagerness he spilled more than he drank.

"Sit you down and rest," said George.

Jim squatted on his haunches in a corner of the hut, taking the bottle with him.

For a time there was silence broken only by the gulping swallowing noises of a thirsty man who has the wherewithal to quench his thirst.

The corner where Jim sat was in the shadow, but the two white men saw that the bottle went frequently to his lips and that its contents were rapidly disappearing.

Jim began to softly croon the war-chants of his people.

"He's had enough," muttered Fat George. Then aloud, "Say now, Warrior, how was the *puza*? Somewhat stronger than milk?"

"Aye. Much stronger, *Baas*. It is a good drink."

"There is more to be had if you can pay the price."

"I can pay the price, *Baas*," Jim boasted. "My *Baas* is the Major. He has much gold, and I—I am his servant. I have gold, too. Much gold."

"Words of a braggart," scoffed Fat George. "Show us thy gold."

Jim rose unsteadily to his feet, staggered to the table and, with a triumphant gesture, threw down on it two pieces gold, two half-minted Kruger sovereigns.

Fat George looked at them and then passed them over to the policeman.

"I'm sorry for you, Warrior," he said.

"Sorry, *Baas*? Why is the *Baas* sorry for me?"

Jim was a little uneasy.

"This is no true money. It is money that lies. It is not worth that."

George snapped his fingers.

Reaney unhooked a pair of handcuffs from his belt.

"Hold out your hands, you," he commanded. "Any man, so says the law, carrying such money must go to *trunk* (jail)."

The handcuffs closed with a snap on Jim's wrists. He seemed stupefied, unable to realize the full portent of the policeman's act. But suddenly it dawned on Jim and, breaking away from Reaney, he threw himself down at George's feet, raising his manacled hands in supplication.

"Don't let them do this, *Baas*," he pleaded. "Jim did not know. His *Baas* gave him the money. How was poor Jim to know?"

"It would be a pity to send so fine a warrior to prison," Fat George mused. "His *Baas* is to blame. Is there no way out? Remember, his *Baas* deceived him."

"Of a truth, yes," assented Jim. "My *Baas*, whom I always have trusted, deceived me."

"Is there no way out?" Fat George repeated.

"Aye," said Reaney slowly. "His *Baas* gave him the money, he says. Then he must show us where his *Baas* keeps other money like this, that we may destroy it. So doing, we will keep the law and prevent other warriors from being deceived."

"Nay! I cannot do that," Jim protested. "I cannot betray my *Baas*."

"Come on!" Reaney jerked the Hottentot roughly to his feet.

"It is a great pity," George said. "The warrior will be kept in a house of stone. He will be made to labor hard. He will be past the age of manhood when the veldt land knows him again. His women will have been given to other men. His cattle will be divided among the people of the *kraal*. And all because he remains true to a *Baas* who has deceived him."

"Come on!" said Reaney, dragging the Hottentot toward the door.

"Wait, *Baas*. Let me think. Aye! It is true. My *Baas* has deceived me, therefore I no longer owe allegiance to him. I will show you where the gold is. But you will give me some? Then I can buy much of the *puza;* I can go back to my *kraal* richer than a headman."

Reaney winkled triumphantly at Fat George, who had heaved a ponderous sigh of relief.

"Yah!" continued Jim. He seemed feverishly excited. "I will have done with the man who beat me because I took but one little drink. I will be my own man. I will go and come as I please. This night I will show you the place. But tell me," he sobered for a moment, "this is no evil thing I do?"

"No," chuckled Reaney as he unlocked the handcuffs. "It is a good thing."

"Very good," George commented in English, "for us."

FOUR HOURS later, just before the break of day, Fat George's buggy came to a halt at the base of a gently sloping kopje.

"It is there," said Jim, pointing to a thorn-bush about half-way up. "The bush hides the entrance to the cave. Let us hasten—" he nervously looked back across the dreary veldt—"less my *Baas* come and find us."

"Small fear of that," Fat George sniggered. "He's sleeping off the effects of much drink. But the advice is good. We ought to be on our way back before the sun gets up too far. Hell! Why didn't I bring some grub with me?"

Jim jumped down from the buggy, followed slowly, and with much laborious effort and groaning, by Fat George.

Reaney had already dismounted from his mount and now, at a word from the fat man, he ran to help Jim outspan the mules and tether them to the wheels of the buggy.

"All right!" George said. "Let's go."

"Why don't you stay down here, George?" Reaney suggested. "The climb may be too much for you."

"Like hell I will! I wouldn't trust you out of my sight."

"That's no way to talk to a pal," Reaney complained.

Fat George looked at him contemptuously.

"Pal? You?" Then to Jim, "Lead the way, Warrior."

It took them nearly an hour to reach the thorn-bush, for Fat George was obliged to rest at almost every step. The veins stood out prominently on his fat neck; his face was crimson with the unusual exertion, and breath came in big, gasping sobs. But he made no complaint save to regret that he had brought no food.

Each boulder he came to, and the slope of the kopje was strewn with them, he sat down and rested. He seemed to possess an infinite patience; nor would he allow Reaney and Jim to go on ahead. When he was taking his final rest before entering the cave, in the shade of the thornbush, he would not allow Reaney to enter without him.

"We'll go together," he said, "when I am ready."

Reaney, all agog with impatience, had to be content with that. He did not dream of crossing Fat George. No one had ever done that—successfully.

In a little while the gross man rose and the three entered the cave.

As soon as their eyes became accustomed to the change from the bright daylight, they saw that the cave was a very shallow one; was but a hole, in fact, in the side of the hill.

At the far end was a small wooden chest, studded with brass nails and straightened with wrought iron bands. They went over to it and examined the massive padlock, an antique affair. They attempted to lift the chest, but it was too heavy for them.

"We'll have to break the padlock open," Reaney said. "Stand back, George, and I'll fire a few shots at it."

"I wouldn't do that if I were you, old chappy," drawled a soft voice. "I have the key."

Reaney turned round with a curse to face the Major. His hand leaped to his revolver, but the Major, he saw, had the drop on him and the revolver did not leave the holster.

Fat George collapsed on the chest.

"Oh hell!" he exclaimed. "I wonder—" then he stopped.

"Yes? You wonder what?" queried the Major. His face was as bland and innocent as a child's. His soft gray eyes—they could be hard gray eyes—held a most benign expression. "I don't think you ought to wonder, dear old George. It's perfectly obvious. You two rotters filled my servant with booze and made him show you this place. I could almost wonder what for. But isn't that it? Of course it is. Don't trouble to answer. Where is Jim, by the way? Oh, and of course you know that I'm a very good shot, very good I may say. The only trouble is that this bally revolver—it has a hair-trigger you know—goes off quite unexpectedly, quite unexpectedly. Quite! Sometimes, when people think I'm not looking, you know, they try to take advantage of me and *pop* goes the little popper."

George's hand, which had been moving infinitely slowly toward his hip pocket, shot up into the air.

"Fine! You got the point very quickly, old top. But I repeat: Where's Jim?"

"Here, *Baas*," moaned the Hottentot. He rose up from behind the chest where he had been hiding. "Au-a, *Baas*, I am a dog? You have a *sjambok;* beat me. I am your dog, *Baas*."

"Rest assured that there will be a beating," the Major said sternly. "First there is work to be done."

He took a stout rope which he carried coiled about his shoulders and tossed it to Jim.

"Bind the policeman," he said.

Jim swiftly obeyed. Reaney saw that resistance was futile. The Major was, as he had just said, a crack shot.

"Now the Fat One," commanded the Major.

This, too, was quickly done, and all in silence.

Reaney had lapsed into the sullen silence of indifference. It seemed that whenever he went up against the Major he was doomed to lose. What was the use of fighting any more?

Fat George's silence was that of a man who recognizes that his opponent holds all the trump cards and is willing to wait until the cards are dealt out again.

"It is done, *Baas*," said Jim at length.

The Major examined the knot and relieved the men of their weapons. Jim had done his task thoroughly. There was no possible chance of the men freeing themselves.

"Now it is your turn, Faithless One," said the Major, and he trussed the Hottentot up as securely as the two white men.

"You're a handsome trio, I must say," commented the Major. "Well, just have a good time together. I'm going for a little stroll. Perhaps I'll be able to decide what to do with you before I return. Ta-ta, little ones."

The glared silently at him, but made no reply.

IT WAS nearly noon when the Major returned to the little cave. He carried a large hamper.

The two white men, especially Fat George, greeted him with violent curses.

"What the devil do you think to gain by treating us like this?" he stormed. "When I get back to the *dorp* I'll make the place so hot for you that hell'll seem cool by comparison. I'll—"

Fat George choked with anger; words failed him. He was very hungry.

The Major made no reply, but, smiling sweetly, opened the hamper.

"You can't get away with this, Major," snarled Reaney. "Interfering with an officer in pursuit of his duty is a serious crime."

"Ah! And so you are on duty, my good man? And just what is that duty?"

"Getting evidence to convict a counterfeiter, blast you!"

The Major affected a start of surprise.

"You don't mean those Kruger sovereigns, do you? I assure you that they're not counterfeit. Why, bless my soul, I thought you were after them yourselves! How I have misjudged you!"

"Are you going to let us go, or not?" Fat George asked.

"I'm sure I don't know. It's quite a problem. I might keep you forever; no one would be the wiser, and I don't think anyone would care. But yes, I'll let you go on one condition."

"Name it!" Fat George snapped.

"Not so fast, old top. You must calm yourself. I'm afraid you'll get apoplexy."

The Major commenced to unpack his hamper, quite indifferent to the curses which came, in an unceasing flood, from George and Reaney. First he spread a snowy white cloth over the top of the chest, then set on it an array of silver and china. Followed food in great abundance. Roast chicken, and boiled chicken; an assortment of tinned meats and vegetables and fruits; bread and tinned butter. Lastly appeared two bottles of whisky.

Fat George's eyes opened wider and wider. His mouth gaped open, dripped with anticipation.

"There," said the Major. "That's not half bad. Not a bad spread, eh?"

"Never mind the jaw-wagging," George said eagerly. "Name your condition and let's eat."

"Well," said the Major slowly, "I'm rather interested in a chappy named John Sewell. I want to see him elected tomorrow."

"The hell you do! He's been bragging that he'll send you up for a long term!"

"Oh, as to that," the Major waved his hand airily, " 'first catch your hare', you know. That doesn't bother me. I repeat, I want to see him elected."

"And what can I do about that?"

"Quite a lot, Fatty, old dear. He surely won't be elected if certain posters are put up in the morning of the election. You know what I mean? Of course you do."

"I'd like to know how you know," Fat George growled.

"That's of small importance. The point is, will you write a letter to your worthy brother, the printer, ordering him to destroy all the posters; and another letter, addressed to the beloved populace at large, explaining how Reaney framed Sewell?"

"I'm damned if I do," Fat George exploded. "If Sewell's elected, it'll ruin me. I'd have to close up the *ivinkel;* there'd be no more booze-selling to niggers. That's where the profit is. You know that."

"Yes, I know that, Fatty. But I'd advise you not to talk about that or I might be tempted to say what I think of you, and I dislike swearing; it's a beastly bad habit. Point is, will you write those letters?"

"No—damn you!"

"Then—damn you—you don't eat! But if you will pardon me, I will. This chicken is delicious. Sorry you can't join me."

Reaney and Fat George—especially Fat George, who was ravenously hungry—watched the Major eat. He ate with tantalizing slowness, frequently expressing verbally his appreciation of the food.

"At least give us a drink, Major," Fat George said hoarsely as the Major, having eaten his fill, lighted a cigarette and puffed at it luxuriously.

"A drink," exclaimed the Major. "Why, yes, of course. I brought a bottle specially for you."

He opened one of the bottles and, crossing over, held it to Fat George's lips.

George drank and the next moment spat it out in profane anger.

"Blast you!" he screamed. "Are you trying to poison me?"

"Really! Do you think this poison? I'd always thought so myself, but I'm glad to have your expert opinion. This is the stuff you sell to the natives. Won't you have another drink? No? And you won't, Reaney? Well, I don't blame you. Perhaps neither of you is thirsty. But are you comfortable? How are you, Jim? Headache gone? Fine! Nothing like fasting for pains in—er—Little Mary."

With that the Major left the cave.

FOUR TIMES before sundown the Major returned to his prisoners and asked, "Will you write those letters, Fat George?"

Three times George answered in the negative and accompanied his "no" with many lurid curses and blasphemous oaths. But the fourth time George, his spirit quite broken, gave in.

"I'm glad you see reason, old top," the Major said as he untied the fat man. "Its getting late and tomorrow is election."

He handed George two or three sheets from his notebook. "Now write," he said.

And Fat George, at the Major's dictation, wrote the messages which assured the election of John Sewell.

"Fine!" chortled the Major. "Now you may eat. When you have eaten I'll tie you up again. Then Reaney shall eat, and I'll tie him up again."

"You're not playing fair, Major," George protested.

"Oh, quite fair, old top. You see I have to ride into the *dorp* tonight to stop those posters from being published. I could hardly release you and leave you alone here with the chest and—er—its contents. Jolly old chest, isn't it? But I'll be back again by tomorrow noon and then we'll all go our respective ways, rejoicing as it were. What? Of course I'll take Jim with me. After all, he is my servant, and I think he's been punished enough."

And with that, Fat George and the policeman had to be content. The Major still held all the cards.

THE ELECTION next day proved to be a big victory for Sewell. The unaccountable absence of Fat George resulted in many of the town people voting for law and order, and by noon Sewell's election was assured.

John Sewell, Helen, Father Joyce and the Major were quietly celebrating.

Sewell, a clean-cut, likeable young fellow, was listening to the part Helen had had in his election; hearing for the first time of Fat George's plot and of how the Major had frustrated it.

"I've been a conceited prig," he confessed. "I thought I could do it all alone. I'd have been beaten if it hadn't been for you, Helen; and you, Father Joyce; and you, Major."

"That is quite all right, old top. But I suppose you'd have no compunction in sending me to the Breakwater?"

"Not if you were proved guilty of I.D.B., Major. Personal friendship must go by the board when it conflicts with duty."

"Oh, noble youth!" exclaimed the Major. "How truly noble! Well! Good-by. I must be trottin' along.

"Just a minute, Major," the girl said. "I want to give you this."

She held out on the palm of her hand a good-sized diamond. It was uncut, unpolished.

The Major carefully affixed his monocle.

"Why—er—what is this, dear Miss Helen, old thing?"

"It is the diamond you left in the glass of stout."

"Did I? How could I have been so careless?" His tone was incredulous. Then suddenly he turned on Sewell.

"I see," his drawl was more exaggerated than ever, "that your first duty as public prosecutor will be to try Miss Helene for having an unregistered diamond in her possession—a very serious crime, what?"

Sewell was dumbfounded. The truth of the Major's assertion came to him with the force of a blow.

"And you won't, I'm sure," continued the Major, "let—er—sentiment interfere with duty. No, of course not."

Sewell squirmed.

Father Joyce's eyes twinkled merrily and he nodded reassuringly at Helen.

"But," the Major said, "as you don't assume office until tomorrow morning you have nothing to worry about. I'll take the diamond and I'll take jolly good care to be out of your jurisdiction before tomorrow. But you do see, don't you, that it is possible for a person to innocently have an unregistered diamond in his possession?"

"Yes," Sewell assented gravely. "Thank you for the lesson, Major. I promise you that I'll never seek a conviction on circumstantial evidence alone."

"That's top hole," said the Major. "Now may I drink to the future Mrs. Sewell?"

Sewell looked at Helen, a question in eyes. She nodded happily.

FAT GEORGE and Reaney were anxiously waiting the return of the Major. Waiting and cursing, yet finding some comfort in the thought that they might yet succeed in getting their hands on the chest and its valuable contents. They had not given up hope of that. Fat George had a plan which he was sure could not fail.

The sound of a man climbing the rocks outside came to their ears.

"He's coming," said Reaney with relief.

"Of course he's coming. Didn't think he'd leave us here to starve to death, did you? Now, don't forget how you're going to act, or what you're going to say. You've got to convince him that me and you are at outs. S-s-h! Here he comes."

But it was Steve, the storekeeper, who entered the cave—not the Major.

He burst into laughter when he saw how the two men were trussed up.

"This'll be a good 'un to tell the boys," he said.

"Stop that cackling and cut us loose, you—"

Steve quickly obeyed. Fat George was still his boss.

"What's it all about?" he asked.

"Never mind that. Lucky you came when you did. We'll fix the Major proper, now." Fat George had opened a tin of meat and was stuffing himself as he spoke. "But how did you happen to get here?"

"I didn't happen to come, Boss; I heard the Major's nigger bragging that his *Baas* was keeping you and Reaney prisoner, so I bribed him with a bottle of whisky to tell me about it, and here I am."

"Fine. I won't forget that, Steve. Now, you go outside and keep your eyes peeled for the Major. Reaney and me want to have a little business talk."

As soon as Steve had gone outside, Reaney got up and walked stiffly over to the chest. His greed for gold was greater than his bodily hunger.

The Major had left the policeman's revolver on the top of the trunk and, taking it up, Reaney aimed at the padlock.

"No! Not that," George said irritably. "Steve'll come running in and want a shave. Try and pry it off with the barrel of your revolver."

Reaney acted on the suggestion and, as the wood had rotted about the lock, with but little exertion he succeeded.

Triumphantly they raised the heavy chest and found—a letter lying on the top of stones; stones, nothing but stones!

"The slim devil," Fat George ejaculated and, sitting down with a tragic expression of resignation on his face, he recommenced eating.

He ignored Reaney's sneering remarks anent his clever scheme. All his faculties seemed concentrated on eating.

"Look at this, George." Reaney had opened the letter and spread it out.

> To Fat George.
> Dear and honoured Sir.
> Isn't Jim clever? I was so relieved when I saw Steve set out to rescue you. And the other night, too, I'm sure you thought he was drunk. You've no idea what a clever actor that lad would make, with proper coaching! The only weak spot in my little scheme was that Jim might really get drunk—he's very fond of whisky, you know—instead of

pouring the stuff you gave him on the floor of the hut. But he didn't. He obeyed orders—and your best whisky, too! Jim's really very fond of me, and I'm bally proud of it, but I had to punish him for getting drunk the other day. That was why I tied him up with you, and it also helped to carry out the illusion, so as to speak.

But all this doesn't interest you a bit, does it? You want to know how to get a lot of Kruger half-minted sovereigns. Well, I'll tell you. Get hold of all the Kruger sovereigns you can. There's still a lot in circulation. Then take the coins, one by one, and carefully file off the inscription on one side. And there you are. Quite simple, isn't it" Reaney's a bally awful ass, isn't he?

Cheerio, old top!

THE MAJOR.

Fat George actually laughed as he came to the end of the letter.

"I don't see anything to laugh at," Reaney said. "The laugh's on you, George." Then he added excitedly, "No, by God, the laugh is on the Major!"

"Yes?" Fat George was incredulous.

"Yes. I'll arrest him for defacing the coin of the realm."

Fat George spat in disgust.

"You're a—what did he say you were? 'Bally awful ass,' Reaney. Come on! Let's get back to the *dorp* and see if I still own the Palace Hotel."

FROM DEEP WATERS

TWO MEN, one a white man, the other a Hottentot, ran swiftly over the open, barren veldt.

The Hottentot, squat and muscular of build, ran easily with tireless, machine-like strides. But the white man was beginning to lag; his face was contorted with the strain of undue physical exertion; he breathed with difficulty. Blood was streaming from a wound on his forehead.

"I can't go on much further, Jim," he gasped. "Why go on?"

"Their hearts are black, *Baas*. It is not wise to stay. The river is close at hand. That crossed and we will find a safe hiding place."

He glanced quickly over his shoulder and then continued:

"They are getting very near, *Baas!* We may yet fool them. The ford is narrow and, perhaps, is not known to them."

The white man groaned but a smile flickered over his face and he quickened his steps, forging ahead of the Hottentot.

"It—is—best—that—we—separate—Jim," he said presently between labored breaths. "You—"

"Nay! We keep together, *Baas*," interposed Jim. "Do not talk. Breath is precious at a time like this."

Again he glanced behind him.

A man on a black Basutu stallion was close on their tracks and, behind him, came a man in a buckboard drawn by eight mules. This man drove at breakneck speed, swerving sharply to left or right to avoid large anthills, crashing over smaller ones and through clumps of scrub brush.

Jim's eyes were on the man on horseback. He was three hundred yards away, the buckboard a hundred more, and the river was barely fifty yards ahead.

"Yah! We shall make, it, *Baas,*" Jim cried joyfully.

As he spoke he dropped directly behind his *Baas.* The man on horseback had halted and was taking aim with his rifle.

The dust flew up between the Hottentot's legs. Came the report of the shot.

"You will run by my side," said the white man. "I will have no shield."

"We will run no farther, *Baas.* Here is the river."

They were indeed on the edge of the precipitous bank of a river swollen with the season's rains; yellow, almost red, with the soil of the hills.

"What folly to run and then find we can go no further. No man can cross with the river at the flood. You should have thought of that, Jim."

"Yes," the Hottentot agreed humbly, though there was no hint of reproof in the other's tones. "But at least we have run," he added with a chuckle. "Nor is our case hopeless. A trap may be built but the lion is not caught until he is in the trap."

A bullet whined over their heads; another, with the vicious buzz of a disturbed hornet, hurtled by Jim's ear and he ducked quickly; two reports sounded almost as one.

"Come *Baas,*" Jim cried. "We may not hear the next one."

But the white man had sunk exhausted to the ground.

Came another shot and another. The triumphant shouts of the pursuers were perilously near.

Jim stooped quickly and picked the white man up in his arms, then half-climbed, half-fell down the bank.

THE MAN on horseback—a tall, dark haired, lantern jawed man—came to the bank of the river a few minutes after the Hottentot and his *Baas* had disappeared from view.

Dismounting stiffly, carrying his rifle at the ready, he scrutinized the racing flood with hawk-like eyes. Nor did the arrival of the man in the buckboard distract his attention.

"Didja get 'im, Joe," shouted the newcomer as he, revolver in hand, leaped from the buckboard.

"No. Must have missed. But I made the dust fly close to 'em."

He spoke with a soft, lazy drawl.

"Fat lot of good yer fancy shootin' did 'hus. Why the 'ell didn't yer do as I said? Then we wouldn't 'ave 'ad all this ruddy trouble."

"Nothing to get riled about, Joe. If I didn't get him, the river has. Some satisfaction in that."

"Blast yer! There's no satisfaction at all hunless we're sure hof hit. He's a crafty devil, I tell yer, Babson."

"Yes. You've told me that lots of times."

"An' a fat lot hof good hit did yer. Just because 'e acts like a bleedin' fool's no sign 'e is one, is it? You'll obey orders from now hon."

Babson's face flushed crimson and he was about to retort angrily, then changed his mind and said placatingly, "Well! There's no harm done, Smithy. The Major won't trouble us again."

"Hi'm not so sure about that. You keep yer heyes peeled; maybe they 'ereabouts—'iding."

"You talk like an old woman," Babson exclaimed impatiently. "We both saw them come to this place; they went over the bank right here—here're their footprints—and we got here only a minute or so after. Where could they hide? A rabbit couldn't hide along here."

But Smith shook his head; his face was grave.

"Then where are they? They might be a 'iding in them there reeds."

Babson threw up his hands in exasperation.

"You haven't the brains of a louse, Smithy. They tried to swim across, of course, and this is what happened to them."

Stooping quickly, he picked up a piece of rock and threw it into the river. The current was so strong, so swift, that the rock was carried down stream a few feet before it sank.

"What chance would men have swimming against a current like

that, Smithy? Oh, come on. Look! Do you think this Major chap, and his nigger, are stronger swimmers than that beast?"

Babson pointed to where, midstream, a crocodile was being carried down by the turbulent waters, despite its frantic endeavors to make the shore.

"He's a crafty devil, I tell yer, Babson, is this Major chap," Smith muttered as he tugged thoughtfully at his tobacco-stained beard. "I don't like it. Look! There he is now."

Smith almost screamed in his excitement and pointed to a large, white sun-helmet which was sailing swiftly downstream. It was quite close to the bank.

Babson fired four shots in rapid succession and four black specks appeared on the helmet. It gyrated madly and then sank.

"If his head was inside that he's dead," Babson remarked complacently.

"You alus was a good shot, Joe, and you've got brains. But I don't like this business. If 'e was 'h'inside the 'elmet 'ow was hit we didn't see 'im before? And hif 'e warnt, why did the 'elmet take all that time to get where 'hit did?"

Babson laughed.

"He wasn't inside. He and the nigger are both over the falls by this time—dead. The helmet had caught on a rock, most likely. Come on. Let's go."

"No." Smith's tone was very decided; and, strangely, no suspicion of a cockney twang was now evident. "We're going to stay here a while," he continued as Babson was about to expostulate. "It's about scoff-time and we might as well eat here as anywhere else. All you have to do is to keep your eye on the river. I can't get it out of my head that those two blighters are around somewhere."

Babson shrugged his shoulders in disgust.

"Just because he's fooled the police with his I.D.B., you think he's a little God Almighty. I didn't have any trouble in capturing him, did I?"

"No, you didn't." The little man's tone was bitterly sarcastic and Babson cringed as before a blow. "You were damned clever, you were. Of course he happened to be delirious with fever at the time and his nigger, Jim, was all tuckered out with nursing him and had no reason to suspect you of dirty work. Of course little things like that helped you some, but you did the most of it yourself. But don't forget that he got away from you, and made us sweat blood trying to catch him."

"Oh, let it drop, Smithy. I'll admit I was a bit careless and—"

" 'Careless!' he says. My god!"

"We've got all we want from him," Babson continued doggedly, "and he's where he can't do us any harm. Glad it happened this way. Saves us the trouble of having to guard him."

"Something in that," agreed Smith. "Now I'll get scoff. I don't need help. You watch the river."

With the skill of an old campaigner Smith quickly lighted a fire, got some provisions and cooking utensils from the buckboard, and in a very little while had made a savory buck stew.

This they ate in silence, both keeping an alert watch on the foaming waters.

The meal finished, Smith charged and lighted an old, broken-stemmed pipe, and Babson deftly rolled a cigarette.

"Coffin nails," jeered Smith. "He doesn't roll them."

"I know; you don't have to tell me that all the time," Babson answered irritably. "There's no one here to see, is there? Besides, you're not acting your part now."

"I know my lines. I'm not sure you know yours."

With an obscene curse Babson threw away his cigarette, and, taking a well-filled silver cigarette-case from his breast pocket, tapped it leisurely on the back of his hand, lighted one and blew a series of smoke rings. From another pocket he took a gold-rimmed monocle and fixed it in his eye.

"These are not half bad, old chap," he drawled. "Coffin nails you call them? 'Pon my word, that's rather quaint, what?"

Smith slapped his thigh.

"You've got him down to a T," he said.

They smoked for a while in silence, Babson moving restlessly about, smoking innumerable cigarettes; Smith contentedly, and with a cat-like pur, puffing his clay pipe.

The horse and mules were huddled together beneath a stunted tree, their heads down-drooping. They were almost inanimate; all life, all spirit, seemed to have been burnt out of them. The terrific heat of the African noon-day sun was soporific in its effect. Occasionally an ear twitched, or a tail lashed, when an unusually active fly alighted on some tender spot. Otherwise they were motionless.

"Let's move!" Babson exclaimed at length and, walking over to his horse, he quickly saddled it.

Mounting, he viciously raked the animal with his spurs and rode off at a furious gallop.

Smith watched him for a few minutes, marvelling at the ease with which the man sat his mount. Then, realizing that at the pace they were going Babson would soon be out of sight, he rose and inspanned the mules, climbed up into the buckboard and drove off.

Yet he seemed loath to leave the river and, with a puzzled expression, constantly turned and scanned the bank.

"I don't like it," he muttered. "But hell! Babson's right. I'm acting like an old woman. No man could swim across that river. But I wish Babson wasn't so hot tempered. He'll go off half-cocked once too often. I hope it'll be after we've put through this job, that's all."

THERE WAS a rustling in the reeds that fringed the river's edge just above the place where the men Smith and Babson had camped. There the current was not so swift; the river was not so deep.

Again the rustling sound, then cautiously, slowly—so cautiously and so slowly that it was hard to discern any movement in the reeds other than their swaying to the current's urge—the reeds parted and a face peered out. It was of an ashy-gray color; it seemed to be floating on the top of the water.

It moved slowly toward the bank. As it came to shallower water, the wide shoulders, the powerful torso, the whole body of Jim the Hottentot appeared. He seemed to have shrunken in stature; it was with difficulty he restrained his teeth from clashing together like castanets.

For a moment he hesitated at the edge of the reeds, then, noiselessly and with infinite care, climbed the steep bank.

Near the top he hung suspended for a few minutes, clinging fly-like to his precarious perch, and listened. Then with a sigh of relief he crawled over the top and lay panting on the sun-baked veldt.

But not for long.

Rising, he took in with one sweeping, all comprehensive glance which interpreted as it saw, the place where the men had camped, and the dust cloud which was rapidly nearing the horizon.

With a glad shout of, "They've gone, *Baas*," he clambered down the bank.

"I'm jolly glad of it, Jim," drawled a voice from the reeds. "Standing in water—and it's deuced cold and slimy at that—up to one's neck isn't half as jolly as one would suppose."

Jim the Hottentot grinned. He didn't understand one word of what his *Baas* said; still it was his *Baas'* voice, and he seemed to be in good spirits. That was enough to make Jim smile at any time.

"Why doesn't the *Baas* come out?" he asked. "Or does the *Baas* desire to bathe?"

There was a subdued chuckle.

"Stop spoofin', Jim." Then in the vernacular, "I'm afraid to move, Jim."

"Afraid, *Baas?*" Jim's tone was incredulous. "The men have gone, I said."

"Maybe, but," and now the voice hardly rose above a whisper, "there's a crocodile, a big one, not three spears' lengths away from me. He's watching. He's been watching me for this past hour. If I move, I think, he'll get me. But perhaps not. Perhaps he's not hungry; assuredly he's not hungry, or he would have come for me long ago. Truly there is nothing to fear. I will come out."

"Nay, *Baas!*" Jim was panic-stricken. "Do not move."

"Must I, then, stay here forever?"

"Jim will find a way, *Baas.* Is the crocodile above, or below you?"

"Above, Jim. Three spears' lengths above and close to the bank."

Jim cautiously worked his way to a ledge of rock, jutting out from the bank, which he judged to be above the location of the crocodile. He clambered on to this and, lying on his stomach, he splashed the water with his hand, at the same time bleating like a goat in distress.

There was a sudden swirl in the water; something resembling a decayed and putrid log came swiftly toward him, and there was a vicious snapping of powerful jaws which just missed shearing Jim's right arm.

For a minute the crocodile eyed the Hottentot with a baleful glare and then, with a hoarse bellow, turned and silently sank out of sight, evidently bent on returning to its former position.

But the Major had taken quick advantage of the respite afforded him by Jim's strategy and was clambering up the steep bank.

Jim quickly followed and was concerned to find that the white man was quite exhausted by his efforts.

"*Baas!*" he cried.

The Major looked up with a wan smile.

"The fever left me weak, Jim. In a little while I will be all right. But now—I am cold."

The Hottentot quickly erected a rude shelter of branches and reeds; he cut and placed on the ground under the sun-shelter large armfuls of reeds. Then, over-riding his *Baas'* objections, he undressed the white man and, picking him up in his arms, carried him to the shelter and placed him on the bed of rushes.

"We were fools to run, Jim," said the Major presently. "I think they would have done us no harm."

"That may well be, *Baas,* but I did not trust them."

"Small wonder," the Major said dryly.

He was thinking of the manner in which the two men had taken advantage of his illness; of how they had taken possession of his property—his horse, mules, camp equipment, everything; even his monocle; how they had kept him closely confined until, feigning another attack of fever, he had thrown Babson off his guard. So he and Jim had escaped; they would have got clear away had it not been for Smith's unexpected return.

"I wonder why," the Major mused aloud, "I wonder why they wanted us out of the way, Jim?"

"Who know, *Baas.*"

"Maybe," drawled the Major (and he spoke in English now), "they were police Johnnies—plain-clothes men. But then I haven't been dealin' in diamonds lately. No! I don't think they were police Johnnies. I hardly think that's the explanation. Ah well! I can ask a few questions when we get to the settlement. I don't fancy the trip though; we'll have to hoof it all the way and beg our grub from the natives, Jim!"

"Yah, *Baas?*" The Hottentot turned from the Major's garments which he had spread on the ground to dry.

"Would you know the men again?"

"The tall, young one, yes, even if he did try always to hide his face away from me. But the other man I would not know unless I heard him speak in anger, and knew that he was angry."

"What mean you by that, Jim?"

"I can not explain, *Baas*. It is something I feel inside me—here!" Jim pressed his hands to his stomach.

The Major laughed and for a while they sat in silence—a silence which was broken when Jim pounced on several cigarette butts discarded by Babson.

Lighting one, he cried triumphantly, "They are some little comfort, *Baas*. But there is no meat to them."

The Major smiled.

"Are the clothes dry, Jim?" he asked.

His lips were blue; his cheeks hollow; he shivered violently despite the sweltering heat.

The Hottentot felt the clothes.

"Dry? Yes, *Baas*. But they are wrinkled and I cannot press them."

Jim spoke lightly, but his face clouded over as he noted his *Baas'* languid movements.

Presently, with one shoe half-laced, the Major fell back exhausted.

"The water seems to have taken all my strength, Jim."

"It is the fever, *Baas*. But sleep will bring the strength back to you."

"And then, Jim?"

"Then? Then mayhap the flood will have gone down and we can cross the river and so come to a *kraal* I know of. And the people of that *kraal*—because the *Baas* is the man he is—will give us food and horses that we may ride to the settlement and tell the *Nonquai* (the Mounted Police) of the evil done us."

"Nay. Not that, Jim. We are not children to run when we are beaten. We will deal with those two ourselves, and in our own way."

"That is to my liking, *Baas*. But when and how?"

"That Jim, old top," again the drawl, "is on the knees of the well-known gods. Absolutely, what?"

"Yaas, *Baas*. Absootly, what!" Jim echoed.

The Major laughed, a little wearily.

"Which of the two is the leader, think you?" he asked.

"The little man, *Baas.*"

"So? Yet he deferred to the other and—" the Major's voice trailed off in silence.

"In little things, yes. Those two are like lion and lioness. He, powerful, good to look upon, continually boasting with loud roars of his prowess, must yet stand by abashed when she goes to the kill."

Jim stopped abruptly.

The Major was fast asleep—the sleep of exhaustion. When he awoke, three hours later, it was to the delirium of fever, and Jim tended him as best he could.

Through the long hours of the night he watched by his *Baas.* A cold, heavy mist fell, and Jim, taking off all his clothes, wrapped them around the white man.

Through the night Jim watched and swore, vowing to make the men responsible for their sorry plight pay to the utmost.

AGGIE, THE fair-haired (very rusty at the roots!), blue-eyed, much bepainted barmaid of the Imperial Hotel, Drakesburg, was avidly reading a paper-backed novel.

So it was that the entrance of a man—a ragged unkempt appearing man—passed unnoticed. She only looked up at his involuntary exclamation on reading a poster which hung in a conspicuous place on the fly specked wall of the Imperial Hotel.

Springing to her feet, Aggie turned to face the intruder, scrutinizing him from head to foot.

"You look like the reward might come in handy," she said, with a jerk of her head toward the notice on the wall.

The man flushed, that much was evident in spite of the grizzly beard which covered his face, then turned once more to his study of the placard, which was a police circular to the effect that £500 reward would be paid for information leading to the arrest of the Major, alias Aubrey St. John, alias etc., etc. Followed a full length portrait, and description of the wanted man.

Aggie might have been pardoned for her remark about the money coming in handy, for the man before her was ragged and unkempt. His hair was a tangled mop—slightly gray at the temples; his eyes were dull, lusterless, bloodshot and watery; his whole bearing that of a man who has passed through great privations—sickness, lack of food, of water, great physical strain.

"Sit down and 'ave a drink on me, before you go out to earn it," Aggie urged in an outburst of generosity.

She seated him at one of the round tables which cluttered the room, brought him a stiff peg of whisky and sat down beside him.

"What's the Major done?" the man asked presently. "Something serious, judging by the reward they offer."

"Serious?" Aggie laughed loudly, not at all surprised at the man's apparent knowledge of who the Major was. Everyone knew of that celebrated character. "You'd call robbing the Gwelo stagecoach serious, wouldn't you, to say nothing of shooting one of the passengers?"

"You're joking," expostulated the other. "The Major's an illicit diamond buyer—everybody knows that, but that lets him out. He's no stage-robber, surely. They must have made a mistake."

"Not a bit of it, ducky. I wish hit was a mistake because he's a reg'lar gentleman if all I 'ears of him's true. Smith's fair cut hup about it, I can tell yer."

"Smith?"

"He's the driver of the coach. Hit was his first run, too."

"Ah, I see."

"Well, as I was sayin', they were goin' at a slow pace up the long 'ill w'en presently a man on a coal black 'orse rides hout from he'ind a clump of bushes. He's masked and 'as two revolvers—both of 'em pointing at Smithy's 'ead and Smithy don't make no bones about coming to a stop.

"Then the chap in the monocle tells the passengers—there was four of 'em—to hop out, 'olding their 'ands above their 'eads. And for all 'e speaks soft an' lazy like, they don't waste any time doing what 'e says. One of them, Yankee Yates, makes a grab for 'is gun, but the other 'ad the drop on 'im and shot 'im through the shoulder, sprinkling a few more shots over the landscape.

"There ain't no more trouble, and the Major makes Smithy tie the others up, then 'e ties Smithy up. Then 'e turns their pockets inside out and puts what they have in 'is. And while 'e's adoing of this 'e talks same as they say 'e always does—joking, smoking cigarettes, which 'e taps most refined like on a silver case, and putting 'is monocle up to 'is eye."

"But how could he wear a monocle if he were masked?" interposed the man.

"Smart you are! He wore the kind that covered the lower half of his face. Yankee Yates says that's the kind the holdup men wear over in 'is country."

"I see." The man thoughtfully scrutinized his grimy hands. "And that's all the Major got, just the little cash the men carried on them?"

"No, that ain't the half. Smithy was taking a shipment of gold dust to Gwelo. They valued it at £10,000, so I've heard say. The Major loaded some on 'is horse and packed the rest on one of the mules which 'e borrowed from Smith. Then 'e rode off, wishing 'em all good day and beggin' of their pardon for causing so much trouble. And they'd have been there yet if Yankee Yates 'adn't managed to cut himself loose."

The man whistled softly.

"But what," he said presently, "makes them think it was the Major? He always operates down in the diamond country and, the last time I heard of him, he was doing a good business."

"Well, you see, it's like this. Smith drove on to Gwelo and reported it to the police there. It seems that they had a description of the Major, and the sergeant in charge 'as just been transferred from the diamond fields. 'E knows the Major, personally, and as soon as 'e heard the story of Smith an' the others, 'That's the Major,' 'e says. And 'e showed them all the Major's picture, and all except Yankee swore it was the same man as held them up. Sergeant Hammond says 'e'll get the Major sure this time; says 'e's been trying to get him for ten years. I hopes 'e don't. I fell in love with the Major first time I saw 'is picture. I think Hammond will have to give 'im up. Here 'e's been on the hunt for the Major ten years and one month—the month being the time 'e's been on this case—and if 'e ain't done anything up to now, 'e ain't goin' to do anything now. The Major's too clever for 'em."

"I hope so," said the other fervently. "But where's everybody today? The *dorp's* quite deserted."

"Smithy came in today with a tale of how 'e had seen a man on a black horse riding toward the hills. Yankee formed a posse—I think that's what 'e called it—and rode out after 'im. They reckon that 'e's making a break for Portuguese territory and are going to try to head 'im off."

SO SAYING Aggie tossed her head, annoyed that she had given so much time to a sundowner, and picked up her novel.

The man waited a moment in indecision; then, with a "Good day, miss; thank you kindly for the drink," moved toward the door and passed out into the brilliant sunshine.

He made for a dense thicket of mapani bush which afforded, in the heart of it, a modicum of shade. Here he was free from the observation of any chance passerby and, making himself as comfortable as possible, he closed his eyes and in a few moments was fast asleep.

He was awakened a few hours later by a voice softly calling, *"Baas!"*

He opened his eyes slowly and grinned at the Hottentot who was squatting beside him.

"Is it well, Jim?" he asked.

A white toothed smile and a vigorous nodding of the head assured him that all was well.

He sat up, yawned and stretched his arms above his head.

"It would appear, Jim," he said, "that your *Baas* is a thief. The police will give much money to the man who gives me up. If you desire great wealth—"

"Baas!" the Hottentot exclaimed reproachfully.

The white man laughed.

"But I am in all things bad. Even now men are seeking to take me for evil I did a moon ago."

"Ough!" The Hottentot spat in disgust. "Why will the *Baas* jest? A moon ago you were taking the folly of fever and seeing the visions of delirium. Until this day you have been at Tomasi's *kraal*, sick—so weak that I had to carry you out of your hut every day that you might drink health from the scent of the earth. And now you speak of the evil you have accomplished. It comes to me that you left the *kraal* too soon; that the fever is still with you."

"Then read me this riddle. A man, riding on a black horse, wearing the glass eye, wearing your *Baas'* clothes, talking as he talks, acting as he acts, did an evil deed. And the men upon whom he worked evil said he was called 'the Major'."

"That is no riddle, *Baas*," answered the Hottentot. "A fool I was not to have scented your meaning in the beginning. Au-a! They are cunning. They thought us dead, but we shall see. They have set the trap, which shall ensnare them. Listen, *Baas.* Last night I visited the mine compounds and heard much talk of an old mine not two hours trek from here. Evil spirits dwell in the place, they told me. Au-a! What cowardly dogs these Mashonas are, running in terror from lights seen in the darkness. So I went to this place. In the darkness of the night I went. None saw me go; none saw me return. Well hidden, I watched and waited. Once a door of the hut opened and I saw a flickering ray of light; again, I heard the snorting of a horse.

"Yet when, with the rising of the moon, I crept up close and peered into the hut through a hole in the wall, I saw nothing.

"Read me that riddle, *Baas.*"

"It is read already, Jim. I will—but listen. A man on horseback rides this way."

The Hottentot laughed.

"The *Baas* is not altogether deaf, then. I have been wondering for some time past when he would hear the beat of a horse's hoofs."

"You're a fraud, Jim." Then in the vernacular, "Do the footfalls of a mosquito also sound loudly in your ears?"

"This man rides fast," said Jim gravely, ignoring his *Baas'* levity. "The horse he rides is a black horse; it was once your black horse."

"So? I wonder what he's doing here." The white man did not question the Hottentot's statement.

Jim parted the bushes and looked stealthily out.

"He's gone to the hotel, *Baas.* Ah! Now he halts his horse and dismounts. He is tying his horse to the hitching rail. He has entered the hotel."

The Major rose excitedly to his feet.

"I, too, will go to the hotel," he said.

"Nay, *Baas.* You are not fit. The fever has left you weak. It is the tall man. Let me to him."

Jim's *assegai* quivered in his hand.

"Nay," the white man replied with a reproving frown. "This is white man's business. Get you quickly to the mine and await me there. Let no man see you."

"I am afraid, *Baas.* It is a place of evil spirits. Let me stay. Perhaps my aid will be needed."

"Fearful of the light of day; running from things of darkness," scoffed the other. "Nay! I know your mind. But your *Baas* is a man;

no harm will come to him. First point me out the way to the mine, then go."

Jim quickly gave the desired directions and then made another plea to be allowed to stay.

"I have spoken," was the stern reply.

"It is an order, *Baas*," the Hottentot assented humbly. "But the *Baas* will be very careful?"

"Very careful, Jim."

AGGIE WAS still engrossed in her book, and so, for the second time that day, the entrance of a man passed unnoticed.

"Hands up, dear miss," drawled a low, musical voice.

She looked up with a start and saw a man, dressed in a white duck suit, a black silk handkerchief tied over the lower half of his face.

Her eyes opened wide, her mouth wider. Bewilderment gave way to recognition, to hero worship, to fear, and with a hysterical scream of, "Don't shoot a lady, Major!" she fainted in the very fashion of the ladies in her favorite fiction.

The man in the mask shrugged his shoulders, quickly gagged and bound her and then coolly unlocked the cash drawer with the key he had found hanging in a bunch at Aggie's waist. The contents of the cash box he pocketed, and then turned his attention to the safe—an old-fashioned, rickety contrivance. A few minutes' work with his long, supple fingers sufficed to open this. Most of the contents he pulled out onto the floor; but a canvas bag containing gold nuggets he slung over his shoulder, and then—just as Aggie was beginning to show signs of returning consciousness—stalked out of the barroom, whistling merrily.

His whistle ended abruptly and just as abruptly the light and vast spaciousness about him disappeared.

His head and shoulders were enveloped in an evil smelling sack. He struggled furiously, but to no avail. He was taken at a disadvantage—his opponent had muscles of steel, and in a little while he was tied hand and foot.

All this without a word from his captor.

And that was strange, for the Major was generally a most talkative man!

"That was a smart job, stranger."

The Major rose quickly and wheeled, revolver in hand, to face a gray-bearded, bandy-legged little man who, apparently, had been a witness to the whole proceeding.

"Glad you think so," the Major answered as he returned the revolver—which he had taken from his captive—to its holster. "Know any place where I can hide this chap?"

The little man spat thoughtfully.

"Right sudden, ain't you? Yes. I reckon he'll be safe enough in my hut. No one ever comes there; folks have learned by this time that when Yankee Yates wants company he'll invite 'em."

"Fine! Give me a hand."

With very little trouble—Yankee Yates seemed to be extraordinarily powerful despite his stunted build—the two men carried the hold-up man to Yates' hut.

"I s'pose you've got a good reason for all this," said Yates as they lowered the body to the ground.

The Major nodded.

"An excellent one."

"Well, I don't want to poke my nose in where it ain't wanted, but s'pose you loosen up a bit and tell me what it's all about. Who's this chap? What's he done? Who are you and—?"

"Just a minute, old chap," the Major interposed and removed the sack from his captive's head. The man glared balefully, but kept a sullen silence.

"Holy smoke!" Yates exclaimed. "That's the hold-up guy. You've done a good day's work, stranger. Big reward offered for that bird. That's the Major."

"I thought you told the police that it wasn't the Major."

"Sure I did, but this is the hold-up man all right, and I don't know any other name to call him."

"What makes you think he's not the Major?"

"Aw! That's easy. The guy who pulled a gun on me did it in real Western style—fanned it like a cowboy."

Yankee Yates turned swiftly to the prisoner.

"What's your State?" he said suddenly.

"Texas," the other replied, then flushed with annoyance at having been so easily trapped, and would not speak again despite the efforts of Yates and the Major. Once only he growled out the information—with some show of pride—that he was playing a lone hand.

"Pity they don't go in for rope stretching here," Yates said angrily. "You'd make a pretty corpse."

The Major laughed, and Yates turned on him with a show of irritation.

"What's this all about, anyway?" he asked.

"Well," began the other, "in the first place, I'm the Major."

"You're a liar," cried the man on the floor. "The Major was drowned over a month ago."

"Ah! That's where you made a mistake, old chap." The affected drawl now became very noticeable. "You should study the Scriptures, old man. Cast your bread upon the waters, you know—you see I'm returning to you after many days."

The other glared and again sought refuge in silence.

"Go on," said Yates admiringly, "I'd kinda suspected you of being the Major."

"Deuced clever of you, old man. Well, it was like this—"

And the Major told of how he had been captured and held prisoner by two men; of the manner of his escape from them and of how he had been recovering from a bad attack of fever in a neighboring *kraal;* of how the natives of that *kraal* had spoken of two men—one driving a cape cart, the other riding a black horse—had been seen heading toward the *dorp.*

"So I came here," the Major concluded, "as soon as I was able to travel, hoping to persuade them to give me my property back."

"The hell!" exclaimed Yates. "I betcha I can tell you the name of the other man. It's Smith, or I'm a liar."

"Yes. I think you're right," the Major murmured.

"Sure I am. I thought there was something fishy about him from the start. He fooled me this morning, though, when he ran in all excited, saying he'd just seen the Major riding toward the hills. And I got up a posse! After riding about the hills all morning, with Smithy acting mighty queer, I began to think about the pay-gold in the hotel safe, and how there wasn't a man in the *dorp* to guard it.

"So I announced that my horse was lame—and he was for the time being—left the posse in Smithy's hands, and beat it back here, just in time to see you nab this chap as he came out of the hotel.

"Pretty work of Smith's."

"Very," the Major agreed. "But he made one or two slips very careless."

He bent over the prisoner and rifled his pockets, putting their contents on the deal table.

"His name's Babson," he murmured as he examined some letters he had taken from one of the pockets.

"Babson?" Yates echoed. "That's the name of the chap they say has filed a claim for the old working two hours away, but I didn't know he'd left Gwelo yet. I reckon he meant to use that as an alibi for the gold he took from the stage, and the stuff he got today. He'd say he got it from his mine. Pretty slick."

"Very," agreed the Major, as with a little cry of joy he discovered his monocle and, after polishing it carefully, stuck it in his eye. "Feel quite clothed and in my right mind now," he added. "But where's my cigarette case? Ah, here it is."

He extracted a cigarette and lighted it.

"Feel positively chipper," he announced, "and for personal reasons— purely personal and purely pure, Mr. Yates—I'd like to handle Mr.— er—Smith myself."

"You've got my permission," Yates answered gloomily. "I reckon you can handle him."

"Most kind of you, most kind," beamed the Major. "But I need your assistance."

Yates' face lightened.

"I'd like you to take charge of this chap, Babson. See that he doesn't escape, and don't let anyone know anything about him—especially not Smith. Let Aggie tell her tale about being held up by the Major— that'll give the boys so much to think about that they won't stop to wonder where you are. And, somehow, I don't think that Smith will hang around very long tonight; I fancy he'll leave very early. Anyhow, in the morning you can tell the boys all about it, return this stuff," he indicated the gold Babson had taken from the hotel, "and start into Gwelo with your prisoner. I'll meet you there."

"I'll do just as you say, on one condition."

"Name it."

"That you tell me the rest of the story next time I see you."

"It's a bargain."

The two men shook hands.

"By Jove!" the Major exclaimed excitedly. "We've forgotten all about Aggie. Babson probably gagged and bound her."

"First time she had her mouth shut for a long time, then," Yates growled.

"I'll hurry and release her, just the same," the Major said. "You'd better keep under cover and, if I were you. I'd gag Babson. Ta, ta! See you in Gwelo four days hence."

With that the Major hurriedly left the hut.

"What a blamed fool you were, Babson," Yates said meditatively, "to think you could stack up against a man like that."

"Aw hell!" Babson exploded.

THAT NIGHT, before the rising of the moon, the man Smith rode along the trail leading to Gwelo. He was still smarting from the jeers and taunts of the posse. They, on discovering on their return that the hotel had been robbed by the Major—and Aggie's tale did not lose by the telling—were loud in their condemnation of Smith—and Smith had urgent business elsewhere.

The knowledge that his partner had successfully carried out the robbery he, Smith, had planned, somewhat mitigated the resentment he felt toward the miners, and he forgot the panic of fear which had almost overwhelmed him.

After an hour's riding he came to a watercourse and, turning from the trail and riding up the bed of it—the water was barely a foot deep—he shortly came to a hut. This hut was built close up against a low, long mound.

He urged his horse up the steep, rocky bank—no fear there of leaving a spoor—cursing viciously as he noticed a light streaming from the window and open door of the hut.

"The damned fool," he muttered angrily. "He might as well tell everybody he's here. He's dangerous." Smith's eyes, reflecting the light from the hut, gleamed a baleful yellow. "All is more than a half," he continued, evidently following some previous line of thought. "And if I did, I'd be safe—no one knows he's here, or anything about him, for the matter of that. What's more, I could take his body back and claim the reward. Happy thought!"

He dismounted some distance from the hut and, revolver in hand, tiptoed forward.

When he was but ten feet away he inadvertently stepped into the beam of light. A loud report broke the night's stillness, and his revolver flew from his hand as if plucked by some powerful invisible fingers. And the light went out!

Smith swore forcefully and luridly, nursing his wrenched hand.

"What the hell do you think you're doing, Babson?" he yelled. "Gone crazy?"

"Not at all, old chap," a voice drawled from the hut. "You acted so blamed suspicious, creeping along there with your revolver in your hand, that I thought you were up to some mischief. I don't quite trust you, you know. If I've made a mistake, I'm sorry."

"Well, forget it," Smith snarled, "and stop acting like a fool. When I saw the door open and the place lighted up like a Christmas tree I thought someone had tumbled to our game."

His voice was oily and as he spoke he crept closer to the hut, well convinced that his actions could not be seen in the inky darkness. Smith was in a fury of rage, a rage that was all the more deadly because he had it in complete control. He was determined now that Babson must go! His very existence was a source of continual menace.

"Very convincing, I'm sure." Smith stiffened with surprise, for the voice came from behind him. "Go into the hut and light the lamp. Then we will have a chat."

And Smith had no option but to obey. Somehow he felt that the owner of that voice had the drop on him even in the darkness.

Entering the hut he struck a match and lighted the lamp.

"Now turn your face to the wall—hands above your head. Fine—I see that my shot was a good one—apparently you lost your revolver. All right! Now we can talk. Won't you sit down?"

A blank look of amazement spread over Smith's face as he slowly turned and faced the man he thought was his partner, Babson. A thousand words sought utterance but he could only ejaculate feebly, "The Major! But I thought you were drowned!"

"Far from it, old dear, but I had a most unpleasant time, thanks to you. Sit down, man," the Major continued indulgently. "You seem on the verge of a nervous breakdown, and that would never do. I have so much to ask you."

Smith gurgled incoherently.

"Jim!"

The Hottentot silently entered the hut and scowled savagely at Smith.

"Yah, *Baas?*"

"Unsaddle the white man's horse and put him in the stable-hut. That done, keep a close guard outside."

The Hottentot vanished, shadow-like.

"Well! I'm waiting, Smith. I'd like an explanation."

"You've got no call to take that damned 'igh 'anded attitude with me," whined Smith. He had evidently determined to play his Cockney part. "I'd like to know wot you're adoin' in my partner's 'ut?"

"He's your partner, is he? And you were going to shoot him? Charming! Brotherly love, and all that."

"Naw! Nothing like that. I was only goin' to scare 'im. I ain't the sort that goes about killin' folks."

The Major laughed.

"No! You prefer to drown them, eh?"

Smith's eyes opened in innocent astonishment.

"Now, you ain't goin' to blame me fer that, are you? If it hadn't been fer me, Babson would have killed you then and there. I was a fool to go in with a chap like him. Makin' good money, I was. No call fer me to steal."

"It was Babson's idea, I suppose, that he should impersonate me?"

"Yus, guv'nor. He said that made the game safe; there wasn't no risk at all, he said. He was right at that. We'd have been all right if he hadn't been such a hog. He would have a go at the stuff in the hotel safe.

"Where is the blighter?" Smith continued fiercely. "I'll turn King's evidence, that's what I'll do."

"Babson's on his way to Gwelo, a prisoner. And he's already turned King's evidence. We know all about you."

"The hell," Smith exploded. "But you're lying!" Smith's cold, black eyes met, and held, the Major's. The Cockney twang had vanished from his speech. "You're lying. Babson's not caught, and if he is he's not turned King's evidence. He's not that sort."

The Major shrugged his shoulders.

"You're partly right. No. He didn't give you away. Said that he'd played a lone hand. But he's caught, all right."

Smith sighed with relief.

"He hadn't ought to have got me into this mess. It's all his fault; he knows I'm not to blame. He planned the whole thing. He done the whole thing. I haven't seen even the color of the stuff he took."

"I suppose, then, that you don't know where Babson keeps the stuff he took from the coach?" asked the Major.

"Not an idea!" Smith spat confidently.

"Well, now that's too bad. And this is such a wonderful hiding-place. I've found out quite a lot about it already. I know, for instance, that a large cave is hollowed out of the mound at the back of this hut, and that the only entrance to it is through here. Quite clever. The place can look quite deserted from the outside—men might even come into this hut, and the man in the cave could live quite comfortably. No one would suspect his presence unless a horse whinnied. And of course that could be prevented. Clever, very. I found all my equipment—mules and everything, except the Cape Cart—in that cave. I suppose the cart was too big to go through the doorway of the hut? Then what did you do with it?"

"Used it for firewood," Smith growled.

"Ah! Well, as I was saying, I found most of my stuff and positively reveled in a shave and the chance to get into clean clothes. And I've had lots of time to search for the gold. I've looked everywhere, and I fancy I'm quite good as a searcher. I ought to be; the police have searched me many times! But I'm hanged if I can find a trace of the stuff."

Smith grinned, but he watched the Major's every movement.

"Heigh-ho!" The Major yawned and stretched his arms above his head. "I'm beastly tired. Well, we'll turn in as soon as you've told me where the gold is."

"I don't know a blamed thing. Babson never told me where he put the stuff."

Smith leaned back in his chair, his thumbs hooked in the arm-holes of his waistcoat. His fingers played a nervous tattoo on his chest.

Again the Major stretched lazily, his long arms reaching to the grass roof of the hut. His head was tilted back, his eyes half-closed.

With a snake-like swiftness, Smith's right hand darted under his left armpit and out again. But now his hand held a small automatic—small but deadly.

"Keep your hands up, Major!" he said with a snarl.

A loud report answered him. The hut was filled with blue smoke and clouds of dust. Smith looked wonderingly at his hand; blood was streaming from it. The hut seemed to revolve dizzily. He saw things as through a thick mist. As from a distance, a great distance, he heard a voice say, "Are you all right, *Baas?*"

And another voice replied, "Yes, Jim. Stay on guard."

With an effort Smith pulled himself together. The mists cleared. The Major was seated opposite him. Apparently he was still yawning, his hands were still stretched above his head. But Smith now saw that the Major's right hand was closed on the butt of a revolver which had been hidden in the grass roof of the hut. And Smith felt that further fight was useless.

"I don't want to be vindictive," said the Major calmly, "but I rather hoped you would attempt something. That was a clever move of yours. Only trouble is—that is, trouble for you—that I had anticipated it. Rather a neat place to hide a revolver, wasn't it? Are you going to tell me where the stuff is?"

"No! I tell you I don't know."

"I'm glad of that. As I said before, I don't want to be vindictive, but I'm glad of the chance to practice a little torture on you. Every excuse in the world, too. But first I'll bind up that wounded hand for you. I'm not a bad shot, am I? Two bulls tonight."

Quickly and expertly the Major bound up Smith's hand, and then poured him out a drink of whisky.

Smith drank it avidly.

"Fine," continued the Major. "Now, will you let me tie your arms behind you. I'll have to tie your legs too, I'm afraid. Of course if you think of making trouble I'll have to get Jim in to help me. And I don't want to do that. I'm afraid he might stick you when I wasn't looking. Besides, it's deuced bad form for two white men to fight in the presence of a native."

"Aw! Get on with it, Major. I'm through."

Quickly the Major bound Smith, hand and foot, then, lifting him bodily, set him in a large barrel which stood in the corner of the hut. The barrel was full of water and came up to Smith's neck.

"There!" said the Major with a sigh of satisfaction. "Of course this

is not half so bad as having to stand up to one's neck in a river, as we did. There's no fear of your being carried away by the current; the water's comfortably warm; and there are no big crocs in that barrel. But there are some little crocs—oh, my, yes. Jim had a great time catching them. I don't think they can do you very much harm; still, a bite here and snip there will keep you from going to sleep, I'm sure. And yes, I nearly forgot, I told Jim to put some water-snakes in the barrel, too. They're not poisonous, of course. At least, I told Jim not to get poisonous ones. Still, I don't know. Jim is very vindictive, I'm sorry to say, and for some reason or other he doesn't like you. Now I'm going to search this hut again for the gold and you—oh you can shout 'hot' when I'm near it, and 'cold' when I'm going away from it. That will be great sport, won't it?"

As the Major spoke the sneer gradually left Smith's face, and his eyes dilated with fear—fear of the unknown.

Something, something slimy, brushed against his neck, and a muffled cry came from his lips. *Things* brushed against him under the water; something came to the surface, jumped out and landed back again with a splash.

Time passed. His eyes turned to the left, to the right, watching the Major's peregrinations about the hut. He peered downward, striving to see the *things* which swam about in the dark waters of the barrel. He twitched spasmodically.

"I'm going to put out the light now, old dear," the Major said presently. "I'm deuced tired. Pleasant dreams."

"No!" The voice rose to a scream. "For God's sake, Major, don't take away the light. This is getting on my nerves. There's a snake around my neck, *and perhaps it's poisonous!*"

"Then you'd better keep still; don't move, don't talk unless you're ready to tell me where the gold is. And really, you're being in a funk is inexcusable. When I was standing up to my neck in water there was a croc, twelve feet long, not three yards away from me. He was watching me all the time."

As he spoke the Major turned down the light.

"Wait," Smith cried. "I'll tell you where it is."

The Major turned up the wick again.

"Too bad!" The Major seemed disappointed. "Why, I'd only just begun. "Well! Where is it?"

"Take me out of here, first."

"Not so. It's your move."

"Dig down a foot or so beneath the table; it's there."

"Oh, come now, you're just joking." The Major was quite gay again. "The ground hasn't been dug up here for years and years and years."

"I tell you it's there. Take the top off the table and then you'll see."

Wonderingly, as if afraid he was being laughed at, the Major wrenched off the top of the deal table—an easy task, for only one small nail secured it to one of the legs. The other three legs—they were round and about seven inches in diameter—were hollow and, as he now saw, continued down below the ground.

"Clever," he muttered. "Oh, deuced clever."

Then, taking a spade from the rack on the wall, he commenced to dig. Soon he exposed to view the tops of three barrels. Removing the tops of these he saw, piled at the bottom of one of them, a quantity of gold nuggets and the gold which had been stolen from the stage.

"Aren't you satisfied yet, damn you?" Smith cried. "Take me out of here."

"Instantly," said the Major, and, lifting the man out of the barrel, cut the ropes which bound him. "You'd better get out of those wet clothes," he added. "I'd hate you to get pneumonia. Here's a towel."

Smith sullenly acted on his advice.

"And what are you going to do with me now, Major?"

"Take you in to the police at Gwelo of course, old chap. Thus I shall prove to the police that I am a law-abiding citizen."

"You'll only be wasting your time. They can't prove anything on me if Babson keeps his mouth shut, or even if he don't. Why not keep dark and let's go halves."

"I'm nearly tempted to put you back in the barrel," mused the Major. "Don't know why I don't, unless it's because I'm afraid you might poison the fish."

"Fish!"

"Yes, fish. You didn't really think there were snakes and crocs in that water, did you? What a sell!" The Major held his sides and laughed long and loudly.

"But what was that about my neck?" gasped Smith.

"How should I know? A piece of weed, most likely. Well, well. Hurry up!" His manner changed abruptly. "We start for Gwelo tonight. I rather fancy the police will like to see you, specially when I tell them how much you resemble Ripper Sam. Never heard of him? Quite an unusual murderer, so I've heard say. Always kept a gun under his left armpit. I could tell you quite a lot of blood curdling stories about Ripper Sam. Want to hear them? The only thing he's afraid of, they say, is snakes. He—"

But Smith had collapsed.

THE POLICE at Gwelo will never tire of telling the manner in which the Major brought in his prisoner. Smith, after the three days' trip, was footsore, tired and hungry. His body was one big ache. He was bent over almost to the ground under the heavy pack he was carrying. And that pack contained a goodly part of the haul taken from the coach!

"Watch him close," said the Major as he handed over his prisoner. "He's as crafty as the devil. I haven't had a wink of sleep for three nights. Not what you would call real sleep, you know. Perhaps I was rather vindictive. I made him walk all the way, and carry a pack. But I'm afraid I was mad. You see, the blighter stole my monocle!"

SOUTH AFRICAN TERMS

African—A colored native inhabitant of Africa.

Africander—This word, it is hoped, will take the place of Dutch Colonial, Boer, Hollanders, British South African, British Colonial, and means anyone born in South Africa of white parents.

Assegai—A native spear made of wood with an iron blade which is about eighteen inches long. Two kinds are used: The long, throwing spear, and the short, stabbing spear. The latter was introduced by the Zulu king, Chaka, at the end of the 18th Century. Before that the warriors used to break their throwing spears in two for work at close quarters.

Bantu—Name invented by Dr. Bleek, an eminent ethnologist, to designate the languages of the South African people.

Baobab—This is one of the largest trees of South Africa—about the only tree it would be safe to climb when charged by an elephant. It has an enormous and very soft trunk. Its fruit is a large nut containing citrate of magnesia, from which the natives make a cooling drink. From the bark of the baobab tree the natives make nets.

Blue Clay—Diamonds are found in beds of clay—yellow and soft clay near the surface, and a hard blue clay lying deeper. These clays, usually covered by a thin layer of rock, are supposed to be remains of mud pits due to volcanic action. The Wesselton mine at Kimberly is a deep hollow five or six hundred yards in diameter and over a hundred feet deep. Forty years ago the ground could have been purchased for $300.00. But now—well, over a hundred thousand dollars' worth of diamonds has been taken from it in a year, and it is still going strong. It is a common belief in South Africa that the De Beers Syndicate could flood the market with "stones" and bring down the price of a ten thousand dollar stone to fifty cents.

Biltong—Dried meat; jerky. The meat is cut into long, thin strips. Salt is rubbed into the strips which are then placed on racks in the sun over a green wood fire.

B.S.A.P.—British South African Police. The official name for the mounted police of Rhodesia. This little force of some six hundred whites has to police a district about four times the size of California. The pay is five shillings a day, with a ration allowance of two shillings. The term of enlistment is for three years, after which five months' leave is allowed on full pay. All commissions are given from the ranks. Applicants must be British subjects, able to ride and shoot, between the ages of twenty-one and thirty-five. After three or four months of severe training at Salisbury, the lot of a B.S.A.P. is a very pleasant one. Pleasant, that is, if he is fond of sports and doesn't mind his own company. His duty is almost entirely a supervision of the natives in the district to which he is sent. He patrols the district constantly—and some of the patrols are two or three week affairs in a country teeming with big game. Of course he is supposed to see that there is no infringement of the game laws by natives or white hunters—but who's going to arrest a policeman, and a man *must* eat.

Cape Cart—A cart specially designed for the rough roads of the Cape Colony. It is light, but very strong and very popular throughout South Africa. Has covered top and is not unlike the American buggy. The Major travels a great deal in a Cape Cart.

Compound—The native labor at the mines—diamond or gold—is contract labor and, in order to prevent the natives from deserting before their time is up, they are kept in quarters, compounds, adjacent to the mines and carefully guarded. The system was a severe blow to the I.D.B. traffic. The compounds at the diamond mines are covered with a wire netting to prevent the natives from throwing anything over the walls. No visitors—white or native—are allowed to enter and the laborers are practically prisoners—well-treated ones, however. Even so, and despite the almost unceasing vigilance of the guards, diamonds still find their way outside through other than the legal channels.

Dop—A Cape brandy. A favorite drink among the Africanders but, right now, I wonder how they can drink it as they do. Temperature 116 in the shade, warm dop diluted with warm, muddy water!

That's not an appetizing combination. Still, it used to taste quite good.

Hottentot—Name of a tribe inhabiting part of Western Cape Colony. Name was given to them by the early Dutch settlers in attempt to express the Hottentot's stammering speech. The race is not a pure one. Probably Zulu with an interbreeding of Bushmen. The latter element is evident in the leathery color of skin, the prominent cheek-bones and pointed chin. The tribe is a peaceful one—the men are cattle breeders and excellent hunters. The Hottentots are a kindly, hospitable people, but are in danger of extinction. The language is an exceedingly difficult one for white men to master, containing, as it does, many of the clicks used by the pigmy bushman tribes. Jim, the Major's servant, is an Hottentot.

I.D.B.—Illicit diamond buying, or illicit diamond buyer—according to the context. In the early days of the Diamond Fields the traffic in diamonds stolen from the mines by the laborers became so serious that the Syndicate caused the I.D.B. Act to be passed by the Houses of Legislature at Cape Town. The act was not wisely framed and destroyed one of the fundamental principles in British legislature—which always supposes a man to be innocent until he has been proved guilty. It practically put the whole of Cape Colony under the thumb of De Beers. On mere suspicion of I.D.B. a man could be expelled from the Colony and the large secret service force employed by the Syndicate made life miserable for many of the inhabitants. Not a few of the agents were dishonest and framed cases of I.D.B. in order to justify their existence. For a man to be found in possession of a diamond—no matter if he came by it innocently—was sufficient evidence to send him to the Breakwater for a long term of hard labor. One young man of good family, shortly after arriving at the fields, purchased a diamond from a chance acquaintance. He made no secret about the transaction, knew nothing about the I.D.B Act, but a few hours later he was arrested by the very man who had sold him the stone and sentenced to seven years' hard labor. He died shortly after, but, had he lived, I can imagine that he would have been just as bitter against the Syndicate as the Major is. Indeed, I've always had at the back of my mind that some such experience started the Major off on his crusade against the Syndicate.

Impi—A native regiment. Size varies—from fifty to two thousand. The impis were generally named according to the color of the shields they carried: Impi of the Red Shields; Impi of the White Shields.

Indunna—An under-chief; usually a member of the Paramount Chief's Council, and captain of an impi.

Inspan—To harness the animals and hitch them to the wagon: To break up camp.

Kaffir—Word comes from the Arabic, Kaffir—unbeliever. It was given by the Arabs to all native races of the east coast of Africa. It is now loosely applied to any negro inhabitant of South Africa.

Kitchen Kaffir—A weird jargon spoken by whites who have not learned the native language, to natives who have not learned English. It is a mixture of English, Dutch and Zulu; it has no syntax and very little sense, but by its aid a white man manages to instruct his native servant what to cook for him—and, by a miracle, escapes being poisoned. Here's a kitchen kaffir sentence: "Wena figa lo tea in lo hot manzi and make skoff."

Kopje—A small hill—generally very precipitous and boulder-strewn.

Kraal—A native village surrounded by palisade, mud wall or other fencing. It is generally roughly circular in shape. Word is used to express any enclosure. The fence which encircles the kraal is called a *scherm*—pronounced "scare-em."

Mashonas—The name is derived from the contemptuous term applied to them by the Matabele: Amashunas—"The people who go to the hills." That is, the cowardly people. The Mashonas are a peaceful people. They are skillful farmers and weavers of bark cloth. Good hunters and musical. Before the advent of the white man they were continually raided by the Matabele, who captured their cattle and made the men slaves.

Matabele—The "vanishing" or "hidden" people. So called from their appearance in battle when they were almost entirely hidden by their enormous ox-hide shields. The Matabele are of Zulu origin. Under the rule of their chief Mosilkatze they broke away from Chaka's rule and after a ten years' sojourn in the Transvaal—during which time they defeated every tribe with which they came in contact—they were driven over the Limpopo River by the Boers. There—in what is now known as Southern Rhodesia—they firmly established themselves until, in 1896, their power was finally broken by the white man's machine guns.

Muti—Medicine, also tree. This is interesting inasmuch as it suggests that from trees the natives get medicine.

Outspan—Literally, "to let the span (the team of oxen, or mules, or donkeys) out." That is, to unharness the animals and turn them out to graze. Hence: To make camp.

The Rand—The famous gold-reef of the Transvaal. It is sixty-one miles long and three miles broad. Developed by American engineers it can be worked to a depth of 5,000 feet. It is not a rich reef—not rich in quality that is; every ton of quartz mined yields only six dollars. But modern mining methods and the quantity of quartz mined make up for the lack of quality, and $100,000,000 worth of gold has been taken from the Rand in less than a year.

Reim—Crude reins cut from ox-hides. It is a Boer word and is used, loosely, to designate any kind of rope.

Reimpje—A little rope.

Ricksha—A mode of conveyance imported from the Orient. Now very popular in all the large centers of population. The rickshas at Durban are almost a feature of the place. The "boys" who pull the rickshas are big, fine-looking Zulus who bedeck themselves with gay headdresses and paint intricate designs upon their bodies. They seem practically tireless.

Sjambok—Pronounced shambock. A whip made from rhinocerous hide. The word is also used as a verb—to sjambok, to whip, to beat.

Slim—Cunning, sly, artful. The Major's enemies generally refer to him as that *"Verdoemte slim* dude." (Damned cunning dude.) A Boer—South African Dutch—word.

Skoff—Food. A Boer word. Used as verb or noun, e.g.: "Let's skoff," means "Let's eat." "Give me skoff," means "Give me food." Instead of saying a man is having breakfast, or lunch, or dinner, the Africander says, "He is having skoff."

Sundowner—Word borrowed from Australia. Means a hobo, a drifter; one who arrives at a homestead about sun-down, counting upon being entertained overnight.

Wachtenbitje Bush—A bush with a very appropriate name. Once get tangled up in its big, sharp, claw-shaped thorns and you have to "wait a bit" before you can free yourself.

Witchdoctors—It is impossible to give here anything but a very slim account of the most powerful influence among the natives. Briefly: A witchdoctor begins his training for his powerful office when but a boy in his teens; he knows the uses of many drugs; he is a keen student of human nature, and many of them undoubtedly have strong hypnotic powers. He cures the sick, he claims to make rain fall, he can foretell the future and read the past. He can be a power for good or evil—many of them choose to be the latter. From the witchdoctor the native buys charms which will cause the death of his enemy, will ward off evil, or will ensure good hunting. Once, when on a trip down the Shangani River, my camp was sur-rounded at night by lions—if two lions can be said to surround anything. There was no moon and it was pitch-black—not much chance of good shooting should the beasts take it into their head to attack us. I was rather scared and so were the native police boys until one of them thought of his *mouti* charm. He, Guffa, took a handful of red powder from his pouch and sprinkled it around our camp. "Silwane icona figa lapa, Inkosi," he said. It was true. The lions did not come near us—but whether it was due to the powder or not, I refuse to say.

Zulu—Tribe occupying the northeastern part of Natal. Early history is unknown save that tribal name came from that of Chief Zulu with whom they came from the north the beginning of the 17th Century. The Zulu are a superior tribe; the men are finely built and magnificent warriors. However the tribe was an unimportant one until Chaka became chief and joined forces with The Wanderer, chief of the Umtetwa tribe. Chaka—he has been called the Black Napoleon—was a clever general and under him the Zulu became the dominating tribe. Chaka used to mass his warriors in a crescent formation making it possible for him to flank the wedge-shaped formation used by his enemies. The Zulu are a cleanly people, intelligent.

CORRESPONDENCE

IN CONNECTION with his story in this issue L. Patrick Greene gives us some interesting information about crocodiles:

Cliff Island, Maine.

The following facts regarding the habits of the crocodile may prove interesting to the Camp-Fire folk and will help to prove that the manner of *Cenambo's*—and also the *Major's*—escape from the pool is not far fetched; that truth is stranger than fiction.

The croc's favorite method is to lie immersed close to a drinking pool. The moment anything is heard approaching, two eyes, barely showing above the surface, are cautiously protruded. They disappear and the croc, completely concealed, floats a little nearer. Arrived within striking distance, he waits until his victim lowers its head to drink, when, with a swift rush, he seizes the nose or leg. Having once got their hold, the jaws never relax. Then gradually the croc backs into the water until its victim's head is under water. Since the crocodile chooses his own ground the combat is always an unequal one. Probably the only two species which are immune are the hippopotamus and the elephant. One might have considered the rhinoceros large enough to escape, but Mr. Selous relates in his "African Notes" how one was pulled down and drowned by crocs.

Having drowned his victim, the crocodile selects some convenient ledge or cavity below water-level, where his food may be stowed until "ripe" enough to satisfy his taste. The banks of most African rivers are undercut by the current, thus providing convenient storehouses. Having no proper means for mastication, the crocodile bolts his food whole, and it is for this reason that it is eaten as high as possible. Pebbles are swallowed to aid digestion, and the gastric juices are unusually powerful.

The crocodile's dental arrangement is a matter for envy. Each one of the formidable pointed teeth is merely a shell, and under it, when removed, will be found a new tooth growing up to replace the old one when discarded. This replacement has, apparently, no limit.

Terrible as are the jaws of a croc, he does not use them to mangle and tear in pieces live prey, but only to hold it fast; therefore, the less resistance offered, the less is the resulting injury from the teeth. Antelopes have been found drowned under the river bank, apparently uninjured. Only a close examination brought to light the tell-tale punctures about the nose.

Major Hamilton, an authority an African "Big Game," tells of a native, who, having been seized by a crocodile and half drowned, returned to consciousness to find himself in a cavern under the bank, but just above the water-line. Immediately above his head was a hole through which daylight was visible. He sprang for this and scrambled out in safety, little the worse for his adventure.

Here's another fact that is not, perhaps, generally known. The lower jaws of crocodiles are stationary, and it is the upper ones which move up and down. This enables them to lie quite flat upon rocks or sand by the water's edge, with their mouths wide open.

As to the size to which crocodiles attain. One hears wild stories of twenty-four-foot monsters with a girth as big as an elephant. The largest I saw—and shot—was a little over nine feet. Major Hamilton bagged one a little over fourteen feet with a girth measurement of seven feet at the shoulders. They don't come much larger.—L. PATRICK GREENE.

IN CONNECTION with his story in this issue L. Patrick Greene brings up the question of whether the African elephant has lately become extinct.

South Ashburnham, Massachusetts.

For the Camp-Fire comrades the following may be of interest: The "head shot" by which the Major gets the first elephant, is taken in a straight line between the eye and the ear, and just in front of the latter. This shot kills the animal stone-dead. The "knee halter" is a crippling shot used a great deal by the old Boer hunters. The first shot was directed at the animal's knee or leg; and when an elephant's leg is broken or the bone badly injured he is able to move but very slowly. This enabled the hunters, who were mounted, to go after the rest of the herd, returning to finish the maimed animals when the chase was over.

At one time there seemed to be a danger of the African elephant being exterminated, so ruthlessly were they slaughtered. In 1908 it is estimated that no less than 15,000 were killed. In that same year twenty full-grown elephants were killed by one party in one day! The various African governments put a stop to this slaughter and elephants were protected, but it is sure that it will be many years, if ever, before they can recover from the ravages of past years. The elephant takes many years to come to maturity and the breeding rate is extremely slow. I have read somewhere that the British Government suspended the protection during the war and that, as a consequence, the African elephant is "no more." I am loath to believe this. Has Mr. Beadle any information regarding this?—L. PATRICK GREENE.

IN READING what L. Patrick Greene says below about his story in this issue it struck me as strange that we have heard so little in our magazine—stories or Camp-Fire—about diamonds. And other precious stones, for that matter. I'm not particularly interested in gems myself, but in such a magazine as ours a fellow would think we'd hear a good deal about them. I'm not counting the ruby eye of an idol and that kind of thing, nor stories about theft of jewels. Was thinking, rather, of gems in their "native lair," or even as treasure-trove or pirate treasure. Hold on, writers! I'm not hinting for stories along these lines. Just wondering. The fact that we haven't heard more about them tends to show that our general interest in them is not particularly keen. Yet jewels and adventure seem pretty close akin.

Anyhow, Mr. Greene's story stands on its own feet.

Cliff Island, Maine.

An article in *The Century Magazine* by George Frederick Kunz gave me an idea for the story. I quote from his article of the finding of the world's greatest diamond, the Cullinan diamond.

The day's work at the mine was over and Mr. F. Wells the surface manager, was making his usual rounds. Glancing along one side of the deep excavation, his eye suddenly caught the gleam of a brilliant object far up on the bank. He lost no time in climbing up to the spot where he had noted the glint of light. He had not been mistaken: it was really a brilliant crystal. He tried to pull it out with his fingers, and as this proved impossible, he sought to pry it out with the blade of his knife. To his surprise, the knife blade broke without causing the stone to yield. Confident now that the crystal must be a very large one, he dug out the earth around it, thinking for the moment that, contrary to all experience in the mine, the stone might be attached to a piece of the primitive rock. When he discovered that this was not the case he began to doubt that the object was really a diamond. He said afterward:

" 'When I took a good look at the stone stuck there in the side of the pit it suddenly flashed across me that I had gone insane—that the whole thing was imaginary. All at once another solution dawned on me. The boys often play jokes on one another. Some practical joker, thought I, has planted this huge chunk of glass here for me to find. He thinks I will make a fool of myself for bringing it into the office in a great state of excitement, and the story will be told far and wide in South Africa.'

"Determined to test the stone on the spot, before proceeding further, Wells rubbed off the dirt from one of its faces with his finger, and soon convinced himself that it was not a lump of glass, but a diamond crystal, apparently of exceptional whiteness and purity. With the aid of a larger blade of his knife, he finally succeeded in prying out the stone, and bore it away with him to the office of the mine. Here it was cleaned and, to the astonishment of all, was found to weigh more than three times that of any other diamond that has been discovered."

Sir William Crookes in a letter to Mr. Kunz, the author of the article said, in part:

"The diamond is a fragment, probably less than half, of a distorted octahedral crystal, the other portions waiting to be discovered by some fortunate miner."

This stone was sent to England, a gift from South Africa to King Edward, by mail. It was insured for the sum of $1,250,000.

King Edward said, when the diamond was shown to him—

"This is a great curiosity; but I should have kicked it aside as a lump of glass if I had seen it in the road."

"In order to divide the great crystal," again I quote from the article, "it was necessary to discover the exact situation of what are known as the lines of cleavage; for there is a grain in the diamond crystal which may be compared with the grain in a piece of wood, and although the diamond is the hardest substance known to us, a well directed blow, the force of which passes along one of these cleavage planes, will split the crystal with comparative care and ease."

There is much more that could be said, for the story of this great diamond reads like a romance, but perhaps I have already quoted enough of Mr. Kunz's article: enough at any rate to prove that there are no flagrant impossibilities in "Lines of Cleavage."—L. PATRICK GREENE.

A.H. BITTNER

Character Interest the Essential Feature of a Short-Story Series;
Why Many Try and Few Succeed in This Type of Fiction

IT **WAS** only a short story—hardly ten thousand words—yet when I finished reading it I felt a genuine regret, a touch of that sadness which comes at parting with an old friend. The character around which that story was written had won me so completely in that short space of words that I felt I had known him for years; his ambitions were mine; his hopes, his fears mine. Gladly would I have followed him through many more thousands of words—yet that was the last I ever saw of him: in all probability that was the full measure of his ephemeral existence in fiction.

What a waste! Surely a character so likeable and well-drawn that he can firmly grip a reader's interest is worth more than one short story. What a loss to fiction it would have been if Conan Doyle had written one story about Sherlock Holmes and then discarded a character destined to find worldwide popularity. What a loss if Cappy Ricks had appeared once and then passed out of fiction; if Scattergood Baines had had his one little fiction adventure and then disappeared for all time. And so with dozens of the well-known characters of fiction that have run through a series of stories.

The series is the logical future for an outstanding character, and too often fiction-writers waste in one effort material which well might be developed and improved in a dozen or more stories. Yet the writing of a series of stories is one of the most difficult problems a writer faces; many try and few succeed. Usually failure follows because the character around which the series is written hardly justifies a single short-story, much less a series. Particularly is a beginner prone to develop an ordinary character and immediately write a dozen stories around it. The dozen all come to the editorial office at once—and all go back on the same rejection slip. That is exactly not the way to attempt a series of stories.

L. PATRICK GREENE is one of the most successful present-day writers of the series story; thousands of readers have read the series written around "Zari, Witch-Doctor," which came out in *Adventure*. A million readers his publishers claim for the series of "Major" stories which has appeared in *Short Stories* and *Everybody's*. Indeed, these stories of the "Major" have been so successful that Mr. Greene has written a novel around this interesting character. *The Major—Diamond Buyer* is a very fine example of the extent to which a good character can be used. And Greene is still using him.

"The series story gives the short-story writer a chance to compete with the writer of novels and serials," Greene gives as one of his reasons for preferring this form of fiction. "In a single short story a writer is rarely able to make a sufficiently striking impression on a reader to insure recognition the next time his name appears in print. But when you write a good short story around a striking character, a likeable and human character, you do get under the reader's skin. Then, when you come along with a second story about the same character, the reader recognizes a pleasant fellow with whom he has had a previous acquaintance—and goes on from where he left off, much in the way of the serial. When story number three arrives, if its predecessors have been good, the reader greets it with decided pleasure and anticipation. And the writer has developed a 'following,' a body of readers who will look forward to more of his stories about this character."

A SERIES of stories, if written properly, is likely to improve as it progresses; the writer, like his readers, begins to know his character better and can portray it more convincingly. For real character-drawing a writer must live with his character; yet, if that character is to be used but once, the writer, of course, can afford to live with it for only a short time. Just as living with a human friend gradually brings out many of his fine and at first unsuspected points, so living with a character friend gradually brings out many little sidelights which on shorter acquaintance would have been lost. Thus, as the series goes on, it automatically develops its primary necessity—an outstanding character.

"First and foremost," Mr. Greene advises those who attempt the series story, "never write a series story unless you have a story to tell and feel like writing it. Nothing is so fatal to the success of a series as writing without a story. It is just as important that you have a real story that can stand up on its two feet, when you are writing it around a series character, as when it is to be an independent tale. More so. To try to make your character drag along a plotless story is the surest way to kill him. Often when a writer has a series character fairly well-established, it is a sore temptation at times to make the series pay the weekly household bills. You need a hundred dollars? All right, bang off another Bill Smith story; XYZ Magazine will take it to keep Bill Smith going. Don't do it! Probably the editor will turn it down anyway; if it does get by him it will be a disappointment to your readers who expect something better of a Bill Smith story. Never tackle a series story unless you have a real story to tell, feel like telling it, and are sure that you can do justice to your character. Otherwise you will kill the goose that lays the golden eggs."

MOST EDITORS demand that a series story be a complete entity in itself, that it stand up on its own feet without leaning for support on the series. Many new readers approach a magazine each issue, and nothing is more disappointing and irritating to one of these than to start reading a story only to find that he cannot understand it because of allusions and references to other stories which he has not read. New readers will come to your series with each story; they will know nothing of what has gone before, and it is your job to make them feel perfectly at home. If you have done your job properly they will in no way miss what has gone before, will not even know there has been a "before"; for them the series will begin with that particular story.

In ending as well as in introduction, the series story should be complete in itself. A series of short stories is not analogous to a movie serial in which the writer purposely plans to leave each episode up in the air. The series story must be complete so that, if your reader never buys another copy of the magazine in which the series is running, he will nevertheless have read a complete story. In short, the individual stories of a series should be related to each other only through the central character running through all of them.

The other extreme from the story that depends upon its predecessors is the story which contains a mass of repetition. Although new readers will approach your series with each story, thousands of regular readers will follow it from story to story. They do not want, each time, a tiresome resume of what has gone before. They want to begin this story just as if it were an independent story, except that they have the advantage of knowing the character. If in each story they run into four or five paragraphs of recapitulation they will be bored: the second chewing is never palatable, and it is often offensive to the reader, implying that his memory was not equal to the task of recalling what had gone before.

Likewise, if your reader meets four or five paragraphs of stock description in each story, he will soon be disgusted. Repetition does not always make for convincingness. I know of no better way to make a wooden dummy out of a series character than to describe him minutely and in the same way in each story; it soon is as if you presented stock character A-26 instead of an interesting human study.

It is this knowing how far to go, this delicate balance between too much repetition and not enough facts to make the story self-sustaining, which calls for all a writer's skill in handling the series story. To avoid repetition, introduce your character by a different method in each story. Once open with him, next have several persons speaking about him, then open with a scene which builds up to the point where he enters. Don't lard in the description in thick chunks. Work in the details here and there so that before he knows it the new reader has a complete picture of your character—and the old reader has not been offended by the repetition; in fact if you handle it well he will be pleased as he recognizes the familiar traits reappearing.

OCCASIONALLY IT is necessary and desirable to recount briefly the circumstances of a former story. Suppose the central character is Jones, a detective who convicted Red Smith in story number one. In story number three or four Jones clashes with Watkins, a crony of Smith's, who is out to avenge the convict. To give the new reader a proper perspective and a proper understanding of Watkins's attitude, it is necessary that the facts of story number one be recounted briefly. Don't write a four- or five-page condensation of story number one and insert it in the new story. This method will only confuse the new reader and will displease those who have read the first story. Instead, incorporate the necessary explanation in a paragraph or so, preferably in conversation. Perhaps Watkins can state his grievance to a crony; or two other characters, talking over Jones's conviction of Smith, can give the necessary background. Always remember to make it short and inconspicuous, to give your new reader a complete understanding of the situation without offending the old standby.

And also remember that no editor likes to feel that you are trying to run up the wordage by repeating stories for which he has already paid. If your story needs pages of explanation and rehash of other stories to put it across, there is something radically wrong with it; it cannot stand on its own feet. It will not measure up to the series-story requirements. Better not attempt it.

Anthony M. Rud is another writer who has had wide success with the series story, particularly with detective story series. Incidentally, the detective story lends itself most readily to the series treatment—and, by the same token, detective stores are best developed through this style. Generally speaking, the detective story is successful in proportion to the interest aroused in its central character; through the series this character has an opportunity to develop and become something more than an automaton, a lifeless creation of words.

Mr. Rud finds two main difficulties in handling the series story, keeping the stories different and keeping the character the same. Unless a writer is extremely careful, the series stories will soon become stereotyped, cut and dried. That is fatal. The stories of a series must be different, must be individual and distinctive just as much as the unrelated stories. As soon as the series loses this charm of originality its readers will fall away from it. Indeed, to keep the series story distinctive and at the same time endow it with an appealing sense of familiarity, of old-friendliness, demands all of a writer's skill.

"As the series goes along," Mr. Rud observes, "you find yourself becoming more and more cramped and restricted. You start out with Thompson, the series character, having a given set of characteristics which you present in the first story. In the second story you find some of these a bit inconvenient and find it necessary to introduce others. By the third and fourth stories you start wishing you had never given him this or that trait in story number one. Then along comes a perfectly fine story that you simply can't write because Thompson's character cannot be reconciled to the traits necessary in the new situation.

"And unless you are mighty careful you will have your series character contradicting himself from story to story. Not only must his physical appearance be the same throughout; but his mental conception, his reaction to situation, must be uniform."

To keep the series character consistent Mr. Rud advocates a complete sketching of the character at the beginning. With a complete list of his physical and mental traits laid out before you the chances of contradiction are greatly lessened.

NO, THE series story is not an easy way to squeeze extra checks out of an ordinary yarn. Far from it! The series story demands an extraordinarily good character to start with; it demands plots of the best, and a handling that will require the utmost of tact and skill. Yet it is well worth the effort. In many ways it is the stepping-stone to the novel.

www.ingramcontent.com/pod-product-compliance
Lightning Source LLC
Chambersburg PA
CBHW071844020726
47502CB00003B/601